# PRAISE FOR *STARS OF ALABAMA*

"Sean Dietrich has given us an absolu... ...nd soul-full, *Stars of Alabama* will grab yo... ...all its manifestations fill the narrative with ...ore than entranced; one feels immersed in the novel. Dietrich is an author who understands the hidden landscape of a soul; his voice both clear and authentic. The separate storylines are vivid and distinct, yet they also move inexorably closer to each other in a world both cruel and beautiful. Healing and hope come alive in these characters, allowing it to come alive in us. Moving, powerful, and dazzling, *Stars of Alabama* is a page-turning wonder of a story."

—Patti Callahan, *New York Times* bestselling author of *Becoming Mrs. Lewis*

"Sean Dietrich—you already love him. Prepare to love him even more for giving you this story—*Stars of Alabama*—the characters, human and canine, that will sew themselves to your very heart."

—Jill Conner Browne, #1 *New York Times* bestselling author of the Sweet Potato Queens series

"If you aren't familiar with Sean of the South, then you're not living your best life. Sean Dietrich's take on the American South is warm, tender, and above all other things—hilarious. His latest novel, *Stars of Alabama*, does not disappoint. It's the kind of book where you build relationships with the characters along the way and then find yourself utterly heartbroken when the time comes to say good-bye."

—*Due South*

"Dietrich offers a story of love, loss, and subsequent hope set in early 1930s Dust Bowl Kansas. The folksy writing style is a hallmark of Dietrich's storytelling and bears the tone of his podcasts and columns. Every character has some quirk and substance that will imbed them in readers' minds like memories of an old friend. VERDICT: Dietrich is a Southern Garrison Keillor. Fans of the latter and former will be pleased."

—*Library Journal*

"The characters are meticulously described in settings so real that they seem to be drawn from memory. The book is a testament to inner strength, and the good that can come from even the worst beginnings . . . historical fiction and mystery readers will find this to be a very satisfying book."

—*Booklist*

"Sean Dietrich has woven together a rich tapestry of characters—some charming, some heartbreaking, all of them inspiring. *Stars of Alabama* is mesmerizing, a siren's call that holds the reader in a world softly Southern, full of broken lives and the good souls who pick up the pieces and put them back together into a brilliant, wondrous new mosaic full of hope."

—Dana Chamblee Carpenter, author of the Bohemian Trilogy

"Set during the Dust Bowl, this pleasing, ambitious epic from Dietrich brings together unlikely allies all escaping dire situations . . . Though filled with preachers declaring judgment and prophecies of the end-time, Dietrich's hopeful tale illuminates the small rays of faith that shine even in dark times."

—*Publishers Weekly*

"Mysterious and dazzling."

—*Deep South*

"Sean Dietrich can spin a story."

—*Southern Living*

"A big-hearted novel."

—*Garden & Gun*

"Sean Dietrich's *Stars of Alabama* is a beautiful novel, mesmerizing with its complex characters, lush settings, and lyrical language. It is, quite simply, Southern literature at its finest."

—*Southern Literary Review*

# STARS
## *of*
# ALABAMA

# STARS

## *of*

# ALABAMA

✦ ✦ ✦

# SEAN DIETRICH

**THOMAS NELSON**
*Since 1798*

*I'd like to dedicate this book to the people of Alabama because it is about them. I hereby submit this work to the gnarled Alabama family tree, which I find myself a part of.*

*Stars of Alabama*

© 2019 by Sean Dietrich

All rights reserved. No portion of this book may be reproduced, stored in a retrieval system, or transmitted in any form or by any means—electronic, mechanical, photocopy, recording, scanning, or other—except for brief quotations in critical reviews or articles, without the prior written permission of the publisher.

Published in Nashville, Tennessee, by Thomas Nelson. Thomas Nelson is a registered trademark of HarperCollins Christian Publishing, Inc.

Published in association with The Bindery Agency, www.TheBinderyAgency.com.

Interior design by Mallory Collins

Thomas Nelson titles may be purchased in bulk for educational, business, fund-raising, or sales promotional use. For information, please email SpecialMarkets@ThomasNelson.com.

Publisher's Note: This novel is a work of fiction. Names, characters, places, and incidents are either products of the author's imagination or used fictitiously. All characters are fictional, and any similarity to people living or dead is purely coincidental.

ISBN: 978-0-7852-3132-5 (trade paper)
ISBN: 978-0-7852-2638-3 (e-book)
ISBN: 978-0-7852-2639-0 (audio download)

**Library of Congress Cataloging-in-Publication Data**

Names: Dietrich, Sean, 1982- author.
Title: Stars of Alabama / Sean Dietrich.
Description: Nashville, Tennessee : Thomas Nelson, 2019.
Identifiers: LCCN 2019001005 | ISBN 9780785226376 (hardback)
Classification: LCC PS3604.I2254 S73 2019 | DDC 813/.6--dc23 LC record available at https://lccn.loc.gov/2019001005

# BOOK I

# One

# HOLLERING

* * *

Paul Foldger listened to Louisville bark. The dog's black-and-tan fur dripped with water that had turned her hair curly. The dog had been swimming in Rabbit Creek all morning. She loved to swim. Louisville was old, lean, all ears, long jowls, with some white around her snout.

The old girl howled for all she was worth, staring straight into the woods that sat behind the creek, which forked into Mobile Bay. She was a tracking dog. The most obedient dog Paul had ever trained. If Paul would've told the dog to build a ten-foot-tall sandcastle, Louisville would've gone hunting for a shovel and bucket.

The morning air had an oyster taste to it. Not like a fresh oyster—more like a horrible canned oyster, the kind Paul's father ate. The air surrounding the bay always had that sort of taste. It was a smell that could gag a goat. A smell that only got worse when the weather got hot and the wind died. A day like today.

Louisville heard something. So did Paul. A high-pitched shriek cut the air. They listened to the screams together. Man and dog. Paul knew what Louisville was thinking. She wanted Paul to send her into the woods. But Paul was in no mood for tracking.

"Ain't nothing serious, Louise," said Paul. "Just simmer down."

They stood on a shore littered with brown seaweed where the creek began and the bay ended. The sand near the water's edge was so soft a man's boots could sink halfway into the earth. Paul was up to his ankles in it.

He looked toward the bay, across the gray water, at the yellow grass that stretched sideways next to the great Mobile Bay. The morning sun was strong enough to fry your skin. Paul's pale face was freckled and ruined from a lifetime in this sunlight. He'd been a redhead long ago, before his hair turned white and the sun made his skin look like it was covered in buckshot.

Louisville barked. Though it was really more of a baying. Louisville was like most bloodhounds, she didn't bark. It was beneath her. Instead, she used her low voice, and it carried across the water, only to be interrupted by cicadas and crickets. The morning insect sounds were coming from all directions in swells. Loud, then soft. Loud. Soft. A man could get hypnotized if he closed his eyes.

"Quit it, Louise," said Paul. "Ain't got time for your yapping."

But Paul knew Louisville was never wrong. Paul was listening with his eyes closed and letting the sounds of the world swirl around him.

Vern stood straight and called down from the roof of the millhouse in the distance. "What's Lou barking about?"

"How should I know?"

Vern was the tallest black man Paul had ever known. And from high up on the roof where he stood, he looked like a portrait of John Henry, only skinnier.

Below the millhouse, the truck door was open so Vern could listen to the radio. It was Wednesday. Vern always listened to radio preaching on Wednesdays. And he listened to it at a volume that was loud enough to affect the weather. The sounds of a hollering voice from the tinny speaker competed with the baying from Louisville's throat. Her voice was as deep as that of a full-grown baritone man.

"Would you turn that radio off? Between that stupid preacher and Lou's barking, I can't hear nothing but hot air."

"Oh, sorry, Paul. I's sorry."

"Quit your sorryin', Vern. It's a bad habit."

Vern's bare feet gripped the roof while he walked. His lanky frame crawled the edge like an acrobat. Paul watched him climb down, three rungs at a time. His sharp features made him look almost like a bronze statue. He lowered himself on the ladder and turned off the radio in the truck.

Vern stood beside Paul and cupped his ear. "What we listening for? Don't hear nothing."

"You wouldn't," said Paul. "You can't hear nothing."

"Huh?"

"Exactly. That dadgum radio's made you deaf."

There was the sound again. It cut through the humidity.

Louisville howled.

Paul tugged Louisville's collar and said, "Okay, honey, I hear you." She stopped howling.

Then he looked across the creek one more time, making his ears as big as he could, like a dog would do. When he was a boy, his father used to say Paul was part dog. In some ways, this was true. Paul felt something kindred with the canine. And he had proven this by squandering his life breeding and training tracking dogs. It started as a boyhood hobby, but soon he was trailing escaped prisoners and missing children. And squirrels, foxes, and coons.

"Keep laying 'em shingles," yelled Paul. "I'd better go see what she's making a fuss about."

"You going into the woods alone?" Vern called back. "You's too old."

"Old?"

"Huh?" said Vern.

"I was askin' who you was callin' old," Paul hollered.

Vern was already unfastening his toolbelt. "I told you I'll do it. Let me go."

"Now hold on, Vern. I ain't some old man. I was walking them woods before you were even a sniffle in your pa's nose."

"Better let me go, Paul. I's younger."

"You ain't *that* much younger."

Vern was at least twenty-five years Paul's junior.

"Something bad could happen to you out there, Paul. You could break a leg or somethin'."

"Vern, you stay where you is. Now that's an order."

"Huh?"

"I said stay *put*," Paul hollered loud enough to break his own neck.

"Foot? Whose foot? Yours or mine?"

"You're either deaf or stubborn. I can't figure out which."

Vern ignored him and marched toward the woods in a straight line. Vern was middle-aged and quiet. But if it weren't for the gray on Vern's woolly temples, he would've seemed like a teenager. A stubborn teenager.

Louisville whimpered at Vern. She started trotting through the high grass toward the trees.

"Lou!" Paul hollered. "You stay here with me. If I can't go, then you can't go. We're a team."

Louisville paused to look at Paul. She was thinking about this. Then she glanced at Vern, who was moving farther away.

"Back here, girl." Paul clapped, then pointed at the ground by his feet. "Come here to me. Now."

Louisville was old. She had spent a lifetime doing whatever Paul told her. She blinked at him. Then she turned and followed Vern.

# Two

# GOOD GIRL

\* \* \*

Louisville trotted ahead of Vern, pausing to sniff. She was a smart girl. Vern remembered when Paul had trained her as a puppy. The animal could track human scent and game—in the air or on the ground.

Louisville was getting white around her nose, and Vern could tell she wasn't as sharp as she used to be. She ran in hurried zigzags through the woods, looking, sniffing, sneezing, pawing, thinking, serious. Vern knew what she wanted. She wanted the praise that finding prizes would bring her. She wanted to come trotting out of the woods holding a dead squirrel in her mouth so Paul would pat her head and say, "Good girl, Lou." Those three little words made Lou's whole life worth the trouble.

The high-pitched screaming cut the cricket noises. Vern didn't know which direction to walk, so he followed Rabbit Creek. He pointed his good ear toward the sound. He stopped every few steps to focus. He closed his eyes. The screams stopped.

The only sound he heard was a woodpecker smacking its nose against a tree. Maybe whatever was making the noise had gotten spooked and stopped hollering. Maybe it had worked itself free and escaped from whatever snare it was in. Or maybe it had died.

Vern thought about turning around and going back. But not Louisville. The old girl stopped and sniffed the air. She tilted her nose toward the sun and held her tail straight up.

The woodpecker made a sound again.

Louisville followed the bird sound. Then she took in more wind through her nose. She darted into the woods, head up, nose to the breeze, moving fast.

The morning sun was glaring at Vern. He could hardly see in the early light. He spotted the woodpecker making all the noise on a nearby limb. The bird was dotted with black spots and was blood red at the corners of its mouth with long, straight tail feathers. It opened its mouth and let out a loud sound, then flew away. He watched it soar above the trees, catching flashes of its red in the daylight.

Louisville lurched forward in a clumsy run. She ran like a dog who was ten years younger than she was.

Vern followed, moving as fast as his big legs would let him. He lost sight of Louisville in the green. He paused every few moments to listen for her baying, but none came.

So Vern stood in one place, waiting for a sound, cursing beneath his breath at his bad sense of hearing. He waited for nearly nineteen whole choruses of "Keep on the Sunny Side," watching the creek water before him move in strange patterns. He wanted to call for Lou, but that would've confused the dog. Besides, it didn't work that way. During a hunt, the dog calls you.

Then came howling.

He followed the sound. He saw something in the distance. Something big. A white square under the limbs of fat trees. Louisville was facing the drop cloth slung over a low branch. It was a tent—the kind hobos used. Louisville howled louder when she saw Vern approaching.

He was moving slow, carrying a heavy pine branch he'd found, balancing it on his shoulder like a slugger. He didn't know what or who he was approaching. The last thing he wanted was to find unfriendly drifters who didn't care for his color.

He called out to them. "Hello!"

There was no answer.

"Anybody there?" said Vern. "We friendly."

No response.

"I'm friendly," Vern said again. "Ain't gonna hurt nobody."

When he neared the tent, Louisville was walking so close beside him she almost knocked him over. And then he saw it. The noise was coming from a little mouth.

Louisville wandered toward the child. She pressed her nose against the tiny white thing that was squirming in a bed of pine needles. The baby's mop of orange hair was thick and messy. Its hands were outstretched. The child looked just like the sweet little Jesus Boy himself.

"Good girl, Lou," said Vern. "Good girl."

*Three*

# MARIGOLD THE MAGNIFICENT

✦ ✦ ✦

She wasn't stealing. Or maybe she was. Marigold wasn't sure if this was, in fact, thievery, since this was her first time stealing. She'd never realized stealing was an actual skill until now. She had no idea it would be so difficult to behave naturally.

She grabbed two small sacks of pinto beans from the store shelf. She felt a charge travel through her body. A sickening jolt that made her hands tremble. This was definitely *not* stealing. She was hungry, and that made it different. This was borrowing.

She glanced behind her, then stuffed the borrowed beans into her blouse.

The beans weighed more than she had thought they would. After adjusting the packages in her brassiere, her chest gained five inches on the left side. The lump in her blouse drooped halfway to her waist. She adjusted her renegade bosom, but it kept heading toward the floor.

She walked through the general store with careful steps and an unnatural smile on her face. She was larger than other fifteen-year-olds, and she was embarrassed by this. Her brothers had teased her about it. Her hips were too wide, her chest was too big, and her legs were thick around the ankles. God, in all his cruelty, had seen fit to top her off with a dollop of fire-red hair and freckles that looked like someone had rolled her in confetti.

Her brothers called her "Marigold the Magnificent," and she hated them for it. They might as well have called her the Great Wall of China. Her size, her skin, her hair were her curses.

"Why don't you go suck an egg!" she'd often advise her brothers just before she made a serious attempt to fracture important bones in their bodies. Mainly their ribs. Ribs were always a good choice. She almost broke her brother Tom's foot once by stomping on it. She hadn't meant to hurt him like that. But he never called her Marigold the Magnificent again.

Marigold had gotten bigger after she gave birth to Maggie. Her hips had become too big for the cotton dresses she wore. Her whole body had changed. In fact, she felt like a stranger in her own skin ever since Father had done the terrible thing he had done to her.

The baby had changed her. She had purple stretch marks on every part of her. When her milk came in, she got even bigger, and it made her feel like she was a household appliance from the Sears and Roebuck catalog.

She patted her brassiere, adjusting the beans. This was definitely not stealing. Stealing was what bad people did. She wasn't bad. When she wasn't breaking ribs or ankles, she was a good person. Honest, polite, courteous.

Without this food, Marigold would die in the woods, and what would happen to Maggie?

She wandered down the general store aisle. She let her fingers run along the canned goods on the shelves. She stopped at the canned herring and sardines. The hunger inside her was crippling. And she had strange cravings ever since she'd had Maggie. Pickles were at the top of her list. She caught herself dreaming about pickles sometimes. If she could've taken a bath in pickle juice, she would have.

And oysters, she craved those, even though she had only had them a few times in her life. She looked at the can of Acme Oysters. She wished she could smuggle them without being noticed, but her brassiere couldn't handle any more weight.

The man behind the counter was watching her. She could feel his eyes. A cigarette was between his lips and his arms were folded. "Do you need help?" he said.

"No, sir," she said.

The man's eyes didn't leave her. He only raised an eyebrow. "What're you looking for?"

"Oh, nothing."

"You must be hunting something. You've been pacing for nearly fifteen minutes."

The beans were tugging her collar downward. Her enormous chest was sinking. She wanted to leave the beans on the floor and run for the woods, head straight for Maggie. She wanted to forget all about this borrowing. She wanted to scoop her baby in her arms and get far away from this town and never come back.

But she stood still.

The man's face got harder. He removed his glasses. "Little girl, what's underneath your—"

She started for the door. She could feel the beans falling toward her ribs. She felt them slip past her belly. She made a strained face, willing the beans to stop sliding downward. A bag of beans dropped and plopped on the floor between her feet.

She ran as fast as she could.

He sprang after her. Caught her by the waist. To her horror, the man reached down her blouse and removed the remaining sack of beans. She moved by reflex. She heard a crack and was almost certain she'd broken his rib. He fell to the floor and held his side. His face was contorted with pain.

"Why, you thief!" he said, coughing. "You're trying to rip me off!"

"No, I'm not," she said. "I just wanted to try them out!"

She sprinted down the street. And she almost got away. But she ran face-first into a big man who was walking toward her. She collided with him so hard that she knocked him over and lost her balance.

"Stop her!" the store owner yelled.

The big man pinned Marigold to the ground. She spit at him until she ran out of saliva. "Go suck an egg!" she yelled.

"Get the sheriff!" the store owner hollered. "She's stealing."

"I wasn't stealing!"

When the store owner got near, the big man looked at Marigold with kind eyes. "If you behave, honey, I'll let you go," he said. "You promise to behave?"

Marigold could feel the sweetness in him. She could tell things about people that they didn't even know about themselves. It was a talent from her birth.

She nodded her head. "I swear I'll behave."

"Okay, then." The man let his weight off her and wore a sheepish look on his face. "I'm sorry if I hurt you, honey. Are you alright?"

She hit the man hard enough to break his ribs.

And that's how Marigold landed in jail for the night.

# *Four*

# CHILD OF THE PLAINS

* * *

The Kansas prairie was wide and gold. And dry. The acres stretched for miles and miles, uninterrupted by even the smallest tree. The plains were hot and dusty. It was beautiful in some parts, but most areas were not. The scenery could be boring enough to drive a man nuts. The Kansan skies could get so blue they looked purple, and that was all a boy could see. Sky. Sky. And what's that in the distance? More sky.

Unless the dust storms were in the air. Then you couldn't see sky at all. In fact, you couldn't do anything but lock yourself in a closet with a wet rag over your face and pray. The dust could get so bad it killed young children. Child-size caskets were common in this world. Dust pneumonia was killing kids, animals, and old people.

Fourteen-year-old Coot waited behind the canvas tent while the dust swirled in little drifts. It wasn't a bad storm. Only a minor sandstorm. He thumbed through a pack of baseball cards. The last storm had been worse. It had destroyed parts of Deerfield. The wind was so hard it turned a car over on its side and ate the paint off the doors. Since then, the sky had been light blue, without clouds. But such pleasant skies never lasted for long.

The baseball cards came from Blake. It didn't matter which town they were preaching in, Blake always had a radio going or a newspaper unfolded in front of him. He was a baseball man, inside and out. He passed this weakness on to Coot.

Coot carried these cards everywhere. The grainy photos of men in wool caps wearing heroic looks on their stone faces. On the reverse sides were all sorts of numbers. Batting averages is what they were, Blake had told him.

Coot had only seen one professional baseball game. Blake had taken him to a game in Wichita to see the Monarchs play the Birmingham Black Barons in an exhibition. The players of the Negro leagues were the best players in the world,

Blake explained. They played a different variety of ball than the other leagues. It was exciting and loud. That day was the best day of Coot's entire life, hands down. Until that day, he'd only seen community leagues of local men who had other jobs. These men played baseball professionally.

When Coot was a toddler, Blake had outlined the rules of the game using a pencil and a peanut bag. It only took one explanation for Coot to grasp the game entirely.

"My goodness," Blake had said to Coot. "You got a camera for a mind, boy."

And this was true. Only his mind was more like a Victrola than it was a camera. He could remember anything as long as he *heard* it. It only worked with his ears. His memory was so good he could remember entire games he'd heard on the radio. Play by play. Word by word. Sometimes he would replay a game in his head before he went to sleep.

He liked the way the baseball announcers talked. They had special words for things that happened on the field.

*"Here she comes,"* an announcer would say over the small radio speaker. *"The Bugs Bunny ball takes a bus ride home . . . King Carl Morris swings . . . Lord have mercy, folks, the King gets caught looking!"*

That was the radio's way of saying "strike three."

Or an announcer would say, *"He's pitching from the stretch, and there's the delivery. Crack! Goodbye, Daddy, that train is leaving the station!"*

That meant a home run had been hit.

*"The King rounds the bases and waves at his fans, folks. This home run is brought to you by Dan's Hardware, folks. Don't forget to visit Dan's Hardware for all your hardware needs!"*

Coot stared at the baseball player's face on the card. He touched the card and wished he were far away, in a stadium, wearing a cotton uniform, playing ball. But that was not his lot in life.

Coot was interrupted by a hard smack on his ear. He dropped the cards and stumbled backward.

E. P. Willard stood over Coot and kicked dust over the cards until they were covered. E. P.'s wide body towered over Coot like a slab of rock.

"Put those things down," he said. "You're about to preach. Someone mighta seen you out here lollygagging."

He smacked Coot one more time for good measure. E. P.'s hand was so fat, it felt more like having a disagreement with a skillet.

E. P. peeked inside the tent flap. He was checking the size of the crowd. It wasn't a big crowd. A far cry from the multitudes Coot had preached for in Emporia.

Blake was standing on the stage, shouting into a megaphone at the crowd. He was wearing a white shirt that was drenched in sweat. He was warming up the audience for Coot.

"Saints of God," Blake hollered, "a generation base and wicked, seeking solace in times of trial, shall you be found ready when the good Lord calleth? Or shall we be caught looking when the Lord throws a final strike?"

That made Coot smile. He knew Blake had only said that for Coot's benefit.

Blake always introduced Coot before each service using the growling voice he was known for. And after a long introduction, Blake finally got to Coot's cue. The crowd went nuts.

"You're on," said E. P. Then he smacked Coot on the back of the head. "Get your head out of the stands, boy."

E. P. pushed Coot forward, and Coot stumbled through the canvas tent flaps. He looked back at E. P., who glared through a sliver of daylight between the tent flaps.

Last week Coot's collections had been small. E. P. had beaten Coot with his belt so hard it left purple marks on his shoulder blades.

Coot took center stage. There were sixty-two people in the audience. That's what Blake had told him earlier. Each looked at Coot. They were Kansans, white-haired farmers, tired housewives, miserable migrants, those infected with dust pneumonia. They all met Coot with curious faces. And he could practically hear what they were thinking. He'd been preaching since his seventh birthday when he was ordained by E. P.

He'd spent enough time on stages to know what his people were thinking. They were scared. That's what was at the core of these people. They were terrified of the dust that hovered above the world. They drank the dust, ate the dust. The dust suffocated their children and wilted their food. He was used to their dry faces. And he was used to preaching the money right out of their pockets like E. P. taught him to do.

Coot closed his eyes tight. He reached one hand into the air and made a fist. He squeezed the air so tight that his knuckles went pale. Drama was what he wanted here. The silent kind. The longer you waited, the bigger the reaction.

He held his hand high and waited. Silence fell on the room. Bubbling chatter turned to stillness. And even though Coot's eyes were closed, he knew every eye was on his fist.

He drew in a sharp breath. More waiting.

Silence fell over the crowd so that Coot could hear them breathing. A woman in the back corner was wheezing.

Then Coot said in a slow, loud voice, "Oh, God, it is thee we ask for help! We, thy people, who hath sought you in the hour of a terrible storm!"

Nobody reacted. No *amens*. Only a few people clearing their throats.

Tough crowd.

So Coot waited longer. The pause was the most powerful tool a preacher had. If you paused long enough, people would start weeping of their own volition. E. P. once told him that pure silence could do more than a whole sermon.

E. P. once said that he'd seen J. Wilbur Chaplain preach in Atlanta and say only ten words, and the place came unglued. If you kept a room silent for long enough, people would either start bawling or fainting. If they cried, it was a good service. If they fainted, it was a great one.

Coot's silence lasted for another three minutes. Not a single chair creak, dry cough, or ladybug sneeze was heard.

Coot went on in a soft voice, "Breathe fire from heaven on your people, O Lord. Shake the dust from their bones . . ."

Coot had just come up with that last line. A nice touch, he thought.

A woman in the audience stood first. Coot stared at her. Normally he would've stretched his hand toward her and shouted, "The power of the Lord!" but he was feeling more dramatic today.

He drew his hand back and formed an imaginary baseball bat in his fists. Then he swung toward her like he was swinging at a four-seam fastball. The woman fell backward just like she'd been paid to do. Only she put more emphasis into this fall than she usually did. Coot had heard she'd been given a pay increase a few days earlier, ever since her sciatica started acting up and she'd threatened to leave.

Another man stood. Eyes closed, palms toward the sky. Coot motioned his hand toward the man like a baseball player swinging at a seventh-inning pitch, full count, bottom of the inning.

"The *power* of the Holy Spirit!" Coot shouted.

*Crack! Goodbye, Daddy, that train is leaving the station.*

The man fell backward. The man's nickname was Chowder. Coot had known him for most of his life. Sometimes Chowder could fall so well, people thought he was dead.

When Chowder fell, the crowd gasped. Several folks started crying. Crying was good.

Coot was batting one hundred.

Another man rose to his feet. This man was the real thing. A stranger. A farmer. Farmers were hard to read. You could never tell how farmers would react. They were reserved people by nature, quiet, steady, and skeptical. Some wouldn't fall down even if you cut their legs off with a jackknife. Then again, others would cluck like chickens for Jesus.

Coot breathed inward, then swung his imaginary bat. "The power of *God*!"

The man just blinked for a few seconds. Finally he collapsed and wiggled on the floor.

Home run.

*"Coot rounds the bases and waves at his fans, folks! This home run moment is brought to you by Dan's Hardware, folks! Don't forget to visit Dan's for all your hardware needs!"*

The entire tent started hollering words that weren't words at all. They were syllables. Speaking in tongues, they called it. It was still a new thing to Coot's ears. But whenever this happened, Coot knew he had them where he wanted them.

Coot recited a Spanish poem that E. P. had taught him long ago. He told Coot to use this poem whenever a congregation started tongue-talking. After this, Coot recited a limerick in Russian. This was a real crowd-pleaser, because Russian has a lot of weird sounds in it. He had no idea what the poem was about, but he liked the way it felt on his tongue.

Coot preached for thirty minutes. He shouted. He quoted long, intricate passages from the gospel of Matthew, the book of Revelation, and even something from *Aesop's Fables*. Twenty-three people came down for salvation. Ten walked out of the tent in disgust. Fourteen claimed to be healed.

One woman claimed she'd regained her hearing. Another man threw his walking stick away. One young woman from Syracuse asked Coot to cast a demon out of her husband, who was a well-known jerk. Coot had never done this before, but he figured it was easy enough.

The service was a success. Still, these were poverty-stricken people, poor as dirt farmers without much in their pockets, and these were hard times. The ushers only collected six dollars and ninety-two cents from the crowd. It wasn't nearly enough money to make E. P. happy. It wasn't even enough to pay rent on the field the tent was in.

E. P. beat Coot with the buckle end of his belt until it chipped a bone in Coot's neck.

*Five*

# TWO MEN AND A BABY

**\* \* \***

Vern's big hand was twice the size of the baby's head. The baby was a newborn but already had more red hair than most babies have.

"Yours?" shouted Paul. "You big, stupid man. You can't raise a baby!"

Paul didn't have the patience or the maternal sensitivity to have this kind of conversation.

"We have a half-shingled millhouse that needs finishing and painting," said Paul. "And you wanna start feeding babies?"

"She all alone, Paul."

"That ain't my problem," said Paul. "Besides, she probably belongs to somebody who ain't gonna be too happy when they find you stole her."

"They *left* her."

"How do you know?"

"She told me." Vern rocked the baby and stared the little girl in the eyes. "She mine now."

Paul removed his hat and wiped the sweat from his head. "How're we gonna paint Mister Dreyfus's millhouse by tomorrow morning if you got a baby latched on your teat?"

"She need me. She mine."

"She *needs* her mama, and she's probably on her way back to this tent right now. Now put that baby down before her folks get here and carve us up with axes for manhandling their young'un."

"I can be her mama."

"Put her down, Vern."

"I can love her."

Paul removed his hat and fanned his face. He had heard of families leaving their children behind. These hard times made people do awful things.

"I can do all the things a mama do," Vern went on. "See? She a sweet girl."

"You've lost your mind," said Paul. "We got work to do, and here you are—"

"Sweet, sweet, sweet girl, yes, she is . . ."

"You oughta hear yourself. You sound like a blamed fool."

"Boogaboogaboooo . . ."

"You belong in a nuthouse, you know that?"

". . . Googaboogaboogaboogaboo . . ."

"Put that child down before someone catches us."

"You wanna hold her, Paul?"

Paul pushed the brim of his hat upward. He thought about this for a moment. "No, Vern, I don't wanna *hold* her. I got work to do, and so do you."

Vern extended the baby toward Paul.

Paul took the child in his arms. Her eyelids cracked open. She focused her lazy eyes on him. Violet eyes. Paul had never seen violet eyes before. They were the color of a night sky, just before the sun rises and cuts through the blackness of it all.

"See?" said Vern. "Told you, she a real sweet girl. Now give 'er back."

Paul stepped away from Vern with the child against his chest. "Go get your own dadgum baby."

20 · SIX DYPTYCH

## *Six*

# THE RUNNER

**★ ★ ★**

The sheriff released Marigold from the jailhouse at noon. In two minutes she was darting toward the woods, passing storefronts, pedestrians, and lampposts. The town was a pretty one, but she didn't pause long enough to take it in. She ran past the brick facades, shops, and clapboard homes on the side streets. Her heart hurt so bad it threatened to give out. She cussed herself. She cried. She cussed herself some more.

*How could I leave Maggie?* she thought. *I am a stupid, stupid girl.*

In her mind she could see Maggie's purple eyes and copper hair. She felt ashamed before her own conscience.

Her body was growing weak from hunger. The night before she'd refused to eat or drink in the jailhouse. It was a form of protest. She'd hoped the sheriff would feel sorry for her and let her go free, or at least be impressed by her magnificent courage. Instead, he ate her supper right in front of her and said, "Suit yourself, you ungrateful little brat."

*Stupid girl.*

She was stupid, weak, and thirsty. That's what she was. The sun was draining her body. Her mouth was getting dry. When she reached the edge of town, the thirst made her tongue swell. She stopped near a white house surrounded by oak trees. She caught her breath in the shade and held her stomach to keep from vomiting. She touched her chest and felt the ache in her bosom.

"Maggie," she said to herself. "I'm coming."

She collapsed beside an oak. Her legs refused to move. They were numb. She looked at the leaves above her that formed a crisscross design, blocking out the sunlight. She could see clouds through the little openings between the leaves.

"Please," she said to the clouds.

She didn't know who she was talking to or what she was saying. Whoever it was, up there behind the clouds, they certainly weren't concerned with her.

When she had given birth to Maggie in the middle of the woods, screaming at pine trees, squeezing a low branch with both hands, there had been no heavenly help. Not even a ray of sunlight. No flicker from the sky. Nothing. She decided in those moments of labor that she didn't believe in God—whatever he was. And even if she had, she wouldn't have liked the Old Man anyway.

But old habits die hard.

"Help," she whispered.

Behind the white clapboard house, she saw birds drinking from a white bowl beneath a tin gutter spout. Starlings stood perched on the rim. They ducked their heads into the water, then shook it from their feathers.

Then a bird jumped into the bowl, breast-deep. It ruffled its feathers like a dog drying its coat. Marigold wandered toward the birds on weak knees. Her thirst was so bad it made her lips feel sore.

The birds did not flutter away when they saw her. One unfearing starling looked at her with curious eyes. It tilted its head. Marigold's arms and legs gave out. She collapsed on her stomach. When she fell, the birds leapt into the air and spread their wings outward in the open sunlight. And they were gone.

She held the rim to her mouth and drank the water. She became dizzy. Her vision dimmed, and she saw a million sparks swimming in her eyes. She sat down and her dress was covered in dirt.

She passed out.

Then she awoke. To her surprise, she awoke on her feet—she was running again. It was almost like sleep-running. She was unaware of what she was doing. She was following some sort of motherly instinct she didn't know she had.

Marigold was a fast girl. Her large thighs might've been ridiculed by her brothers—just before she sacrificed their ribs—but her legs were strong. She could beat any boy her age in a footrace and still have the strength left to wrestle.

Marigold ran so fast it made her lungs hurt. The water had given her a surge of energy. She ran the dirt road until her heart felt like it was going to pop. Then her strength left her. All at once.

She stopped and fell in the dust again. Her leg muscles throbbed and her stomach was sour.

"I'm coming, Maggie."

She forced herself upright but only made it a few feet. She fell face-first onto the road. Dust got in her mouth. There was nothing she could do. She could not will her legs to move. The hunger had finally caught up with her. And she believed this would kill her.

She cried. But no tears came out. She was too dehydrated. Through some kind of stubbornness, she'd hoped she was wrong about God. She hoped something heavenly would watch over her baby—whether she believed in it or not.

"Please," she whispered. "You can kill me, but take care of Maggie."

And in her haze, she thought she saw someone. He was tall, lanky. His hair was red on top, white on the sides. She could see him. She'd never seen him before.

"Brave girl," he said. "Such a brave girl. Rest right here, brave girl."

She was not brave. She knew that.

"I'm stupid!" Marigold shouted through tears. "Not brave. I'm so stupid!"

"Rest, brave girl," he said. "You're such a brave girl." He stooped beside her and patted her hair.

Then he disappeared.

So this is how it will happen, she thought. She would die from exhaustion and starvation and there would be no coming back. Then a feeling overwhelmed her.

"I'm sorry, Maggie!" she forced out. "I'm so sorry. I'm sorry."

But the hateful sky didn't care how sorry she was. It only laughed at her.

The redheaded man disappeared.

She was alone.

And her world went black.

# Seven

# WONDER BOY

★ ★ ★

The caravan of vehicles rode the dark highway outside Greensburg. The flat fields were so big and long it was like riding on a light-colored sea. Coot had never seen the sea. All he'd ever known were dry fields, water shortages, hacking dust coughs, malnourished cattle, and poverty.

And storm clouds that were made entirely of dirt. Storms so black they shut out the sun and only left a lightless hell behind them.

But tonight wasn't dusty. In fact, he could see the stars in the violet sky. That was a rarity in this part of the world. Often, dust clouds blocked out the stars so that the night sky looked like muddy pond water. He'd forgotten how magnificent the stars were.

In the back of the covered trailer, Coot sat on a cot. A lantern on a hook above his bed rocked, making the shadows inside the trailer move from side to side. The wagon bounced with the curves and bumps in the road.

Coot stared at the headlights of the cars that were following them. The car directly behind the trailer was E. P.'s Hudson—a vehicle with chrome fenders and hand-painted letters on the door that read E. P. Willard's Gospel Troop.

Blake pulled the canvas flap closed.

"Gotta keep it shut," said Blake. "You'll let the dust in."

"But there ain't no dust tonight."

"Well, I don't want it open in case there is."

He pressed a slab of beef over Coot's neck. "How's that feeling?"

Coot shrugged. It hurt to shrug.

Coot stared at the baseball cards he'd retrieved from the dirt. He admired the stoic faces in the glow of the lantern light. They looked like fearless soldiers . . . almost. Coot was the exact opposite. He was not fearless. Coot didn't know how to stand up for himself. He was quiet and soft-spoken when he wasn't onstage preaching. He wanted to be like one of the men on the cards.

The baseball players all had strong nicknames. Not dumb names like Coot, a name that was short for an even dumber name: Cooter. Who names their kid Cooter? Who would ever take him seriously with a name that sounded like an inappropriate body part?

Ballplayers had real nicknames like "Big Jim" or "Little General" or "Georgia Lightning" or "Old Hoss." Coot wondered what it would feel like for someone to call him "Old Hoss." Now that was a name that didn't sound like a dangling participle on the human body.

For a moment he tried on that name for size. "Old Hoss," he said aloud. The name seemed a little big for him, he thought. But it did make him feel taller. A boy could get used to being an *Old Hoss* instead of a *Cooter*.

Coot knew that E. P. hadn't meant for the buckle to hit his neck like it did. It was an accident. But when the metal struck, it felt like someone had stabbed him. When the beating was over, Coot had touched his neck expecting blood. But there was no blood. Only a burning neck.

When Blake found Coot crying, he stormed after E. P. He removed his own belt and flung it at E. P. like a whip, screaming at him. He landed several good licks before E. P. tackled the old man. The choir stood outside E. P.'s tent watching Blake blow a gasket. Blake was wiry but tough. His thick handlebar mustache was bigger than he was, and his limbs were lanky. He'd done horse tricks and lasso tricks in a traveling Wild West show before he took up revival work. And he was fast.

After their brief fight, Blake pinned E. P. on the ground and forced the big man to offer a grand apology in front of everyone. And E. P. did just that. He even worked up tears. Coot forgave him publicly, but Coot knew it was only theatrics.

The lantern swung in the dark and made Coot dizzy.

"Feeling any better?" asked Blake.

Coot wasn't feeling better. He felt like someone had lit a campfire on his neck.

"Yeah," said Coot. "I feel much better."

"You sure?" said Blake, placing an unlit cigar in his mouth. "You ain't just telling me what I wanna hear? You always tell me what I wanna hear."

"No. I'm better."

"You are not. I can tell."

"No. I'm fine, Blake. I swear."

Blake let out a laugh. Then he chewed on his cigar so hard, it started to splinter in his mouth. "You're a liar."

"Why don't you never light them cigars?" asked Coot.

"Cost too much to light 'em, and in case you ain't noticed, we's poor."

Blake removed the meat from Coot's neck. He inspected the patch of skin and touched it gently. "Is the pain right here?" asked Blake.

"To the left a little."

"E. P. deserves to rot in a shallow grave."

"He didn't mean for the buckle to hit me."

"Well, ain't he the humanitarian of the year?"

Blake flipped the meat so the cool side rested on Coot's neck. The coolness felt good but did little to ease the burn.

Coot stared at the cards and imagined his own face beneath the ball caps the men wore. He would've made a good ballplayer. If God were real—and he wasn't sure about this—he wished he would've seen fit to make him a ballplayer instead of a Cooter.

"Blake, you think we can go to another baseball game if we are ever in Wichita again?"

Blake removed the crushed cigar from his mouth and spit out a few flakes. Then he touched Coot's cheek. "Got me another idea. When we get to Wichita, me and you's gonna part ways with old E. P."

Coot said nothing.

He could hardly believe what he'd just heard. He'd been with E. P. since birth. His mother had been E. P.'s church organist. All he'd ever known was E. P. Willard's Gospel Troop. The thought of leaving E. P. was terrifying and thrilling at the same time.

"Leave?" said Coot. "Where would we go?"

"Far away from that man."

"But he's just upset. He'll get over it and things will be back to normal."

"I heard your mother say the same thing too many times, Coot. He shoulda married her, you know . . ." Blake stopped talking.

It was as though there was something more he wanted to say but couldn't. Many times Coot wanted to ask if E. P. was his real father. He had suspicions that wouldn't go away. But Coot never could build up the courage to ask anyone flat-out because he didn't want to know. He wanted even less to be related to the big ugly man.

"Where would we go off to, Blake?"

The light from the moving lantern made dark shadows on Blake's face. Blake leaned close. "You leave that to me."

Coot let his mind wander toward the idea of never seeing E. P. again. He thought about what it would be like to be a normal fourteen-year-old who could play baseball, or go to school, or climb trees, or maybe even have a girlfriend. E. P. did not permit climbing trees. Or baseball. And girls were considered worse than whiskey.

"And we can go to baseball games?" asked Coot.

"Many as you want."

"What if he catches us?"

"I just hope that fool tries."

"He'd kill us, Blake. He'd really kill us."

Blake removed the meat from Coot's neck and touched his face. In some ways, Blake was the only friend Coot had ever known.

"Coot, you're almost a man now. That means you gotta try to be brave, for me. Don't mean you have to actually *be* brave. But being a man means you gotta try. Can you do that?"

Coot rolled this over the coals in his mind. He nodded.

"That's more like it. Now, I want you to trust old Blake the Snake, *Old Hoss*."

Old Hoss. Coot liked the way that sounded.

## Eight

# THE LOVABLE LUNATIC

★ ★ ★

Vern held the baby against him and smelled her hair. She was his favorite thing in the world. He had never seen hair so soft, so red, so thick that smelled so good. It was like somebody had rolled her in a field of daisies and let the flower smell get all over her. *How could anything smell this good?* he thought. Sometimes, though, the baby would make a grunting face, then poop on the person holding her. And *that* did not smell good.

Vern sat beside Paul on the tailgate. They both watched Mister Dreyfus inspect the white millhouse. Only a few minutes earlier, the last board had been painted. Vern had stayed up all night. When the sun poked over the trees, the white building looked orange.

It had taken a lot longer to build than Vern had thought it would. And even though Paul wouldn't admit it, Vern knew it was because they were not young anymore. Vern had little streaks of white in his hair. And Paul was a full-blown old man, with the stiff walk and all.

The millhouse was to be filled with all sorts of big machines for cutting pine. The whole world needed wood during these hard times. Paul had told Vern that Mister Dreyfus was a crook who would bleed money from anything he could get his hands on. Even trees. This millhouse, Paul said, would bring Dreyfus a lot of money.

Vern had spent four days painting the enormous structure. Yesterday he had painted while cradling the baby in one arm, which had slowed him. He would hold a brush with his left hand and the baby in his right arm. Or maybe it was the *baby* in his left arm and the brush in his *right* hand. He wasn't sure. Vern wasn't good with left and right. Most times Vern had to hold both hands in front of him, sticking his thumbs and pointy fingers out, to see which hand made the correct *L*. Though most times he forgot which way a correct *L* was supposed to be facing.

Dreyfus's antebellum home sat on a hill behind the new millhouse. His estate looked like a castle with fat columns and big porches and tall windows. It must've taken years to build, Vern thought. Maybe ten years or more, depending on how many men he had.

Mister Dreyfus was a stiff man with hair the color of a raccoon, kind of silver and brown. The man ran his finger along the edge of the wet paint on the wood.

"I wouldn't go running my hands all over it like that," said Paul. "Paint ain't dry yet."

"I thought," said Mister Dreyfus, "you were gonna bring this roofline farther over the doors, so rain wouldn't fall so close to the entrance."

"Never agreed to that," said Paul.

"I *distinctly* remember that we did."

Vern watched Dreyfus's two men go over the barn with careful eyes. They were checking every joint and surface. It made him nervous for some reason.

He held the child against his shoulder and gave her a little bounce because she liked it when he did that. She was happier when she was moving. She liked to always be moving.

Mister Dreyfus said, "I thought those doors were going to be wider. I ain't sure I'll be able to get my gang edger through that narrow opening."

"We measured," said Paul. "It'll fit."

"You're sure about that?"

"Sure as God made little green apples and beavers, sir."

Vern switched the baby to his other shoulder to give his right shoulder a rest. Or maybe it was his left.

"Well, I must say, you do *slow* work, Mister Foldger," said Dreyfus. "You've cost me a lot of time and money."

Then Mister Dreyfus pointed to Vern. "I don't reckon that *baby* helped move things any faster. Your friend crawled all over this place with that baby latched onto him."

Paul kept his voice low like he did sometimes when he was angry. He never yelled when he got mad. Not in all the years Vern had known him. He always made his voice quiet just before he lost his mind and lost every temper he ever had.

"We just built you a barn," said Paul. "*Without* a crew, *without* a crane, *without* the two men you promised us, *without* proper tools. Took us ten days to finish setting those posts, just the two of us."

"I still think a man oughta stand by his word," said Dreyfus. "You *said* you'd finish on the eighteenth; it's the thirtieth."

"And without no food, neither," Vern added. "We run outta food two nights ago."

Paul waved his hands at Vern. This meant to hush. Vern knew this from lots of experience.

Dreyfus went on. "How can a buyer expect to pay full price when the terms of his contract have been rendered *inexplicably null*?"

Paul Foldger seemed to be letting those words sit in his mind for a little while. So did Vern.

Vern wasn't sure what "rendered inexplicably null" meant, but he knew ugly when he heard it. And he could tell Paul felt it too, because his forehead went from tense to relaxed. Paul let a smile go across his face, and his ears moved backward like a dog's.

"You know what?" said Paul. "You're absolutely right. Ain't he right, Vern?"

Vern nodded slowly. "I think."

"Inexplicably right," said Paul.

Vern wasn't sure what to say. So he adjusted the baby and said, "I'm real sorry about the baby, Mister Dreyfus, but I couldn't leave her. She all alone when I found her. Couldn't leave no baby."

"Quit your sorryin', Vern," said Paul. "Besides, ain't nothing to be sorry for. Mister Dreyfus is right about us, and that's all there is to it. I know when I'm licked."

Paul searched in a toolbox, laughing to himself softly. Finally he removed a rag. He uncorked the can of thinner and poured it on the cloth.

"What're you doing?" said Dreyfus.

Paul removed his pocket lighter. He lit a cigarette first, then touched the glowing end to the rag. It turned into fire.

"Yessir," said Paul. "Let's just pretend this *whole thing* never happened. You'll just have to get someone else to build you another barn." Paul walked toward the barn.

"Hey!" shouted Dreyfus. "Are you outta your mind?"

"Say what?" said Paul, cupping a hand over his ear. "Gotta speak up—this is my good ear."

*"You've lost your mind!"*

Paul grinned, showing teeth that were a little crooked. He tossed the rag toward the wet paint beside the barn door. He put his thumbs behind the straps of his coveralls and watched the barn catch fire.

"Dreyfus," said Paul, touching the brim of his hat. "Have a nice day, sir."

Dreyfus ran to the fire. His men came running too. They filled buckets with well water and tossed them onto the side of the burning barn. They were almost too late. A large piece of the siding had been burned brown and black.

While they put the fire out, Paul was leaning against the side of his truck, watching them. He was lighting another smoke, staring at the flame coming from his lighter like it had hypnotized him. Paul said, "How about you pay us what we agreed on and let us get outta your hair?"

"You're a lunatic," said Dreyfus.

"Well," said Paul, holding the lighter just in front of his nose. "God made me crazy to make up for how handsome I am."

Dreyfus paid cash.

Paul shoved the money into his chest pocket. He and Vern leapt into the truck. Vern tucked the baby's head just beneath his chin. She was beginning to fall asleep, and he didn't want to wake her.

Paul yanked his gearshift, then nodded toward the barn.

"I ain't no expert," said Paul. "But it looks to me like your barn could use a new coat of paint. It looks like it's about to be rendered inexplicably null."

The truck bounced down the driveway. Vern waved goodbye to Mister Dreyfus. Mister Dreyfus did not wave back.

Paul patted Vern's shoulder and said, "Don't worry about that old goat, he's just having a bad day."

"But," said Vern, "do you think he likes the barn?"

"Likes it? Why, he *loves* it. Prettiest barn he ever saw."

This pleased Vern. Then he fell asleep smelling the baby's beautiful hair.

# Nine

# BRAVE GIRLS

★ ★ ★

The land around the bay looked like heaven itself. It was different from the mountain town she'd come from, a town plopped on the big ridge of Trinity Mountain, not far from the Tennessee River. But here, everything was different. Even the soil was different. It was not black and brown like it was in Trinity, but red and sandy in some places. There were no peaks and valleys, no hills. There were only shallow swells of land that fell right into the enormous bay. Gold grass flats shot out for miles into the water. Birds were everywhere. It was warm and salty-aired. It was a kind of heaven, no matter how you looked at it.

"Maggie," said Marigold. "I'm coming, Maggie!"

Marigold wandered the shoreline, staggering toward the place she remembered. Now and then, she became light-headed and had to sit. Her legs were shaky. Her stomach was empty. She was running on pure willpower.

She was reduced to a slow walk. When she reached a fence post with a green ribbon tied around it, she veered left. She climbed over deep canals, looking for her next ribbon. When she reached the red puddle of standing water, she clomped right through it instead of going around.

She walked deeper into the woods. She spotted poison ivy and steered clear. Marigold was allergic to poison ivy—her mother said it was one of the curses of being a redhead. But she had never let it scare her. It was part of growing up in the forests of Trinity.

She gasped for air. Her heart was beating slow but hard. The air was so hot she could taste it. The sun had turned the humidity surrounding the bay into steam and made her dress damp. Her hunger had become confusion. She was so thirsty, her body burned all over. Her breasts were swollen and throbbing. They'd begun leaking, and the top of her dress was soaked.

When she reached the gnarled oak with a ribbon on its branch, she was near camp. She spotted her canvas tent in the distance. And she almost started crying when she saw it.

"Maggie! Hold on, Maggie! I'm coming!"

She trotted toward the tent, moving as fast as she was able. She fell once. Her knee hit an exposed root. Her white knee started to bleed. It was thick, slow-moving, dark blood. When she got closer, she saw the firepit of ash. She entered the white canvas tent and saw the empty pine-straw bed.

Her body felt empty. She became cold all over. She was not brave like the old man in her vision had said. She was a coward. She was scared. She was terrified. She screamed Maggie's name and frightened the birds away for miles.

This place was anything but heaven.

# Ten

# WILD BLAKE HICKOK

## ★ ★ ★

The E. P. Willard Gospel Troop tumbled into Hickok on gasoline fumes and parked in a field behind a gas station. They'd spent the afternoon setting up the large circus tent in an open field. The red crucifix hanging atop the tallest post was so high it looked no bigger than a crimson dot against the dusk clouds.

At sunset, E. P. had taken the choir into a local diner to eat supper. It was the same old song and dance E. P. did in every new town they visited. E. P. would buy things on credit, sweet-talk shop owners, and tell outrageous stories. He'd start tabs at restaurants, drugstores, grocers, and department stores. Then he would leave town without paying his bills. He'd done this all over the South, back East, and now in the Midwest. He left a trail of debts behind him a hundred thousand miles long. And often he left the broken hearts of naive young women in his wake.

Once he got caught skipping town outside Pretty Prairie. He had to spend two nights in jail. But E. P. was a charmer. Before his sentence was up, E. P. had led two deputies to salvation and baptized the sheriff's sister.

That night Blake and Coot didn't join the others for supper. Instead, they sat in their wagon. For supper, Coot ate canned beans. Blake chewed half a cigar and drank a Coca-Cola.

Blake was too busy to eat. His hands were occupied with something more important.

Blake poured cough syrup from a small bottle into a peanut butter jar. He stirred it with a fork until the peanut butter became soupy. Then he crushed white pills with the blade of his pocketknife and added the powder to the mixture.

"You're not gonna *kill* him, are you?" asked Coot with a mouthful of pintos.

"Lord, no," said Blake. "Ain't feeling *that* generous."

"What is that stuff?"

"Laudanum," he said. "Granny's cough syrup. Used to give it to horses to calm 'em down in the horse shows."

"Back when you were a cowboy?"

"Back when I was whatever I was."

"Do we hafta give that stuff to him? Can't we just run away once he falls asleep?"

"Sure we can—if you don't mind getting whupped like a rented mule."

"He can't whup us if he can't catch us."

"He can catch us."

"Not if we're fast."

"I once saw that ape beat your mama to a pulp when she tried to leave him— God rest her soul. She was laid up for weeks because of it, back when she was pregnant with you. And don't forget about your busted neck, Old Hoss."

Coot remembered the beatings his mother endured from the hands of E. P. She would try to hide her bruises from Coot, but he saw them. He remembered the way her face looked when she would run from E. P.'s tent. He remembered the fear.

"You're lucky he didn't really hurt you this time, Coot. Next time you might not be so lucky."

"Why doesn't he like me, Blake?"

Blake dropped his eyes. He stopped mixing and seemed to be thinking. It was as if he had something to say but couldn't.

"Don't I always do what he says?" Coot went on. "Don't I always do it?"

"He don't like himself, Coot."

"I dunno why. Everyone else sure does."

"He don't like himself 'cause he considers himself a failure. Man like E. P. expected to be somebody one day, someone famous, but didn't never happen. He's just stuck in this godforsaken dust like everyone else."

"He hates me."

"He hates everybody. Most of all he hates folks who won't throw more than a few pennies into the offering bucket."

Blake mixed the peanut butter hard and fast. The sound of the fork against the tin made a clipping noise in rhythm. Then he stopped and touched the fork to his tongue. He tasted it with closed eyes, then spit it out. "Did you know that E. P. used to be friends with J. Wilbur Chaplain?" he said.

Coot made a face.

"I'm serious," said Blake. "Back before Chaplain was famous, they traveled together, did revivals together."

"E. P. knew J. Wilbur Chaplain?"

"You better believe it."

"How long ago?"

"Oh, long before the world fell apart and turned into dust."

"Was E. P. famous?"

"No, but neither was J. Wilbur. They were just two farm boys, screaming hellfire and brimstone for Jesus."

Blake crushed more pills with his jackknife. Then he pointed the knife at Coot. "Why, when J. Wilbur rolls into Kansas City, Little Rock, Saint Louie, or wherever he is, he don't even use tents like we do. He makes people build *wood* buildings, big tall ones, so they don't get blowed down by the wind or rain."

"Wood buildings?"

"More like wood tents, and he has his own train car, servants, and fancy food, people who iron his britches and everything. Probably uses a golden toilet and has a hired fella who sings to him while he does his business."

"Wood tents?"

"They build them things bigger than a baseball diamond."

"You seen 'em?"

"Shoot, several times. And when J. Wilbur leaves town, they just tear 'em down and reuse the wood."

Coot could hardly wrap his mind around this, but he tried. He closed his eyes and imagined a big building made of wood, with millions of people inside.

"Peons like us gotta set up our own dadgum cotton tents like everyone else," said Blake. "And instead of thousands, we get handfuls of dirt farmers."

"Do you think E. P. would really fight *you*?"

"I know he would." Blake thought about this for a moment. "We come to blows a few times before."

"Who won?"

"Sometimes he wins, on account of his size." Blake tapped his temple with his finger. "But sometimes I win, on account of experience."

"Can't we just leave?"

Blake chuckled. "Nope. I'm too old to fight, and you're too scrawny." He held the peanut butter to the light. "This is the best way."

Blake jerked his head up at the sound of a car.

Coot almost choked on his beans when he heard E. P.'s footsteps in the dirt.

Blake and Coot peeked through the canvas flaps of the wagon. They could see E. P. lighting a cigarette, walking inside his tent, and reading a newspaper all at the same time. They heard a radio next. The radio was blaring hothouse music. Tinny trumpets filled the night air.

Blake spoke in a quiet voice, outlining their plan one more time. When he was sure Coot understood what to do, he reached beneath the cot and handed something to Coot. It was a long box wrapped in newspaper and twine.

"I got something for you," said Blake.

"What's this?" asked Coot.

The box was as long as a man's leg and heavy. Coot could only stare at it, for he'd never received a gift that was any bigger than a pack of baseball cards.

"Go on," said Blake. "It'll rot in your lap if you just look at it."

Coot tore the paper. Inside was a long cylinder of white hickory—fat on one end, skinny on the other. The words *Louisville Slugger* were burned onto the fat part.

Hot tears were building in his eyes. He'd never touched a bat before. He'd only used pine branches to hit balls during community games in strange towns with kids who didn't even know how to play. Coot was overcome.

Blake put his arm around Coot. "Don't get too choked up, Old Hoss. That bat ain't for pleasure. It's for when E. P. catches me and tries to rip my face off. I expect you to rescue me."

"I love you, Blake," said Coot.

"Well, you got terrible taste in friends."

# Eleven

# COTTON MEN

★ ★ ★

Paul had never seen harder times than these. Every full-grown man in America was on the verge of begging. They were all wandering. Without aim. Roofers, masons, carpenters, sharecroppers, fieldmen, and cotton men. Anyone who had at least one mouth to feed. But nobody had just one mouth. There was always a chain of mouths in the back seat of every rusted car.

Always searching. Never finding. An honest day's work had become a myth.

For Paul and Vern, gravel highways were how they spent the waking hours. Sometimes, if they'd earned enough, Vern would go into town and buy a hog. Then they'd spend a day cleaning the carcass, building a rock pit, and gathering wood. Vern would cook the hog over the pit and sell food to migrants passing by. They earned decent money doing this—as long as local lawmen didn't run them out of town.

But lawmen usually did run them out of town.

Because the world had become less trusting than it used to be. People behaved uglier toward each other than they used to. When Paul and Vern rode into the rural car camps outside bigger towns, they felt the distrust floating in the air. Nobody knew what to think of the little Model A truck with a white man and a black man sitting shoulder to shoulder.

Paul handed Vern a wad of cash. "There, that's your cut."

Vern pretended to count the handful of money, then slid it into his chest pocket. He couldn't count and Paul knew this, but Vern pretended just the same.

"We all square?" Paul said.

"Oh, sure."

"You sure? I coulda cheated you outta a few bucks, you know."

Vern took the wad of cash back out of his pocket and weighed the money in his hand. "No, it's all here. I feel it."

"There ain't no way you can feel the difference between the right amount and the wrong one."

"Yes huh, I'm good at feelin' things."

Paul licked his thumb and unfurled a few more bills. "Well, here then," he said, handing them to Vern. "Here's a few extra to feel."

"You ain't gotta do that, Paul."

"'Course I do. You're a mother now."

Vern smiled at Paul. Then he kissed the red shock of hair atop the baby's head. "I is, ain't I?"

When they reached town, Paul paid a dime to run an ad in the newspaper. The clerk at the office became so fascinated with Paul's story, he even took the baby's photo to go along with the advertisement. The man led Paul into a dark room with a single window. He slicked Paul's hair backward, buttoned up his shirt to the top button, and positioned Paul on a stool with the baby.

"I can't breathe," said Paul. "My collar's too tight."

"You don't have to breathe. It's a photograph, sir."

The man walked behind a camera and draped a cloth over his head. Paul gave a grin to the camera, but the man instructed him not to smile because it made him appear moderately deranged.

Thus, when the newspaper came out the next morning, on the second page of the *Mobile Register* was a small column with a black-and-white photo of a frowning man holding a baby on his lap.

"Dadgum," said Paul, holding a copy of the paper. "I look like someone just kilt my dog."

The newspaper ad read:

Lost baby rescued near Rabbit Creek, Mobile, Ala.
Red hair, violet eyes. In care of Paul Foldger until
appropriate person or persons step forward.

Paul was upset about the ad. He walked into the *Register*'s office and pointed out to the newspaperman that the baby wasn't a *lost* child but a *found* one.

"What's the difference?" the newsman asked Paul.

"The difference is that this little girl didn't get lost. She ain't some puppy who wandered off. Somebody *abandoned* her, and that needs to be said."

The clerk didn't see much of a difference.

For two mornings thereafter, Paul checked to see if anyone had answered the ad, but no one did. The paper ran the advertisement for two more days, and not a single Christian soul came forward to offer help.

So Paul and Vern piled into their rusted truck and drove north, through miles of dry farmland—land ravaged by the boll weevil.

Vern held the news clipping with Paul's photograph in his hand and studied it. "You look funny in this picture," he said.

"You'd look funny too if they choked you with your own shirt collar. Lemme see that."

That frown made him look constipated.

"I wish he woulda let me smile," said Paul.

"You look like a crazy man when you smile," said Vern.

But Paul wasn't listening to Vern anymore, he was too busy staring at the photo. He felt something warm in his chest, right beneath his breastbone. The baby looked good in his arms, and it made him feel every bit as good as the picture looked.

"Have mercy," said Paul. "Ain't I one devastatingly handsome man."

# Twelve

# DIZZY REDHEAD

* * *

"Please," Marigold said aloud to the sky. She was alone in the woods next to a winding gray creek. There wasn't a soul for miles.

"Please," she said again.

Her chest felt bruised, a painful reminder that her child desperately needed her. Marigold cried so hard it made her vomit. But she had nothing in her belly to throw up since she hadn't eaten for days. Her bile was pink-colored. She was dizzy. Her mouth was acidic. Each time she retched and let go of her stomach, she felt more light-headed. The world was spinning.

Maggie was gone. Taken. Dead, maybe. Maybe an animal had gotten her. Maybe people had kidnapped her.

*Stupid!* she thought to herself. She felt embarrassed. "How could I?" she moaned. Her voice sounded pathetic, even to her own ears. All she could manage to say was her baby's name. She said it a hundred times. Then a hundred more.

She retched again.

The sun fell low. The night was closing in, making her feel more terrified. The woods began to frighten her. Tall trees towered overhead and blocked the moonlight. The bay had grown still; the birds had quit moving.

Her vomiting gave way to crying, which gave way to groaning. It was an instinct. She felt like a body part had been stolen from her. Like someone had cut off her hands. Or her feet. Or her heart. She touched her belly where she'd carried Maggie for so long. The skin was still loose. She pressed her face into the pine straw where Maggie had been. She sniffed. She could still smell her child. Or could she? The smell was already fading.

She went limp. Her muscles were tired from the sobbing. It was as though she were watching herself from a spot miles above herself. She drew herself into a ball. Never had she needed something to hold in her arms so badly. So she held a rock. A rock that was the size of a bread loaf. She held it long enough that the rock became warm in her arms.

"Please," she said. "Please bring back my Maggie."

# Thirteen

# PEANUT BUTTER

★ ★ ★

E. P. wiped a peanut butter–loaded butter knife on a piece of white bread. Blake couldn't stop looking at it.

When the troop had arrived in Liberal, they held revivals that set the region on fire. Each service was a full house. People came from as far away as Wichita to see the child preacher. And these people had more money than those in other towns. The troop brought in more in four days than they'd earned all summer.

On their final night in Liberal, Blake had snuck into E. P.'s tent and placed the jar of spiked peanut butter into his cooler.

Now he sat across from E. P. watching the big man prepare a peanut butter sandwich on two slices of Sunbeam bread. Blake bounced his knees and grinned. He swallowed once and reminded himself not to stare at the bread. There was enough laudanum in that peanut butter to disable a Clydesdale.

E. P. leaned backward in his chair. He said, "I've decided after Liberal, we're going to Oklahoma and Texas. Lotta revival work up there."

"That's more dust than I care to see. It's bad down there. I don't know if I can stand any more of this dust."

"Friend'a mine says folks is eating up tongue-talking stuff in Oklahoma. And I'll bet they ain't never seen a young'un preacher like ours. Why, I'll bet we could kill 'em up there."

"*Down* there," said Blake. "Oklahoma is below us, not above us."

"And I'll tell you one more thing," added E. P., pointing his sandwich at Blake. "Old Coot would be a cash cow in the Texas plains too." He sneered. "Just wait till they see a little *boy* on that stage. People see some kid preaching the Good Word, talking in tongues. We'd kill 'em up there."

"*Down* there."

"Say, what if we hire a minstrel band? Maybe work on Coot's routine a little, with a few more healings, few more miracles . . ."

The big man took a bite and made a face. He licked his lips a little and grimaced. He swallowed his mouthful and stared at the sandwich. "This peanut butter tastes like it turnt."

Blake sat so still he could've grown mold on his mustache.

"Got a friend in Oklahoma City," E. P. went on. "Man who goes around studying little towns before a revival comes. Gets up there months ahead, digs up local gossip. He knows which folks is having affairs, which folks need prayer."

"A clairvoyant act can be trouble," said Blake. "Had a mind reader in the sideshow tent in New Mexico—a tricky line, takes years of practice."

"If I push old Coot hard enough, he'll do whatever I say. I told him to learn the entire book of Deuteronomy word for word. That little cuss actually *did* it."

"You must be proud, E. P."

"Besides, Coot's getting older and uglier. We gotta add something to spice things up if we're ever gonna make the big time."

"You ain't never gonna compete with J. Wilbur, E. P., if that's what you're thinking."

The big man's face turned stiff. His mouth became tight and his eyes narrowed. "I didn't say anything about J. Wilbur."

"We're a small outfit, we can't afford a jaunt to Texas. Every vehicle we got is ragged, nearly shot to pieces."

"We got a window of opportunity, and it won't last. Once Coot's full-grown, he's finished. That's the way it works."

"Coot's a good preacher. I don't see the need to push him any harder."

"He ain't *that* good a preacher, he's just young. If he were a grown man, we'd starve to death. No, if we have any shot at making a name for ourselves, it's while he's young."

"He's a better preacher than his daddy is, I can tell you that much."

"You got a big mouth, Blake."

"Only telling it the way it is."

He scoffed. "That child ain't mine, and you know it."

"Everybody here knows where he come from. And everybody knows who he takes after."

"Shut up," said E. P., waving his hand in the air. "That boy's a bastard whose mother was a—"

"A beautiful human being."

Silence hung in the air. Blake held his glare on E. P. This made E. P. laugh to himself. It was a low-pitched laugh that began in the man's belly. "You're too much," said E. P. "Got too much integrity for your own good, you know that?"

Blake only smiled and prayed to the peanut butter gods to hurry up.

"Oklahoma," said E. P. "That's where we go. I'm sick'a this dumb state. I's ready for a change. We go up to Oklahoma, then up to Texas. That's what we do."

"*Down* to Oklahoma, *down* to Texas. Where'd you go to school, you hick?"

E. P. was almost finished with his sandwich, and Blake didn't want to miss the look on his face when the tranquilizer finally made the big man as useless as a steering wheel on a mule.

"Didn't you ever want anything?" E. P. said, licking his fingers. "Didn't you ever wish you could have a little spot of earth that was all your own? Didn't you ever have dreams?"

"What're you talking about?"

"I'm talking about making some *real* money, Blake. For once in our lives. The folding kind."

"I wouldn't know about money. You make more money than the rest of us."

"Chicken scratch. I'm as broke as anyone else. Don't you wanna have enough to buy *new* shoes instead of polishing the old ones so much you can't even remember what color they were? Don't you wanna retire one day?"

"When I retire I'm going back to Alabama."

Blake saw E. P.'s eyes become glassy. The man kept blinking, and he began to wobble. He shut his eyes and opened them slowly. "Gonna retire and get me a dog to sit on my front porch . . ."

Blake waited.

"Yessir," said E. P. with a thick tongue. "J. Wilbur Chaplain ain't nothing. Nothing." He rocked backward in his chair and almost fell over. He laughed to himself until a few tears came from his eyes. He started snorting a few minutes later. Laughter gave way to sleep. Soon E. P. was making the same snoring sound a buzz saw makes.

Blake stood and slapped E. P.'s cheek gently. He placed E. P.'s hat over the man's wide face. Then loosened E. P.'s tie.

Blake squatted on his heels before E. P. and looked at him square. "Coot's got your jaw and your eyes, and now he's about to have all your money too."

*Fourteen*

# BARBECUING THE MOON

\* \* \*

A mosquito landed on Vern's forehead. He smacked it so hard, it almost made him wet his pants and forget his own name. "That's the third one I kilt in a minute," said Vern. "These things about to carry me away."

Paul slapped his arm a few times. "Just kilt two my own self."

The trees looked dark purple by the light of the moon. A chorus of frogs croaked in the friendly way Alabamian frogs do. But their songs were drowned out by a radio. The truck door was slung open, the sound of a preacher coming through the small speaker, followed by applause and screaming *hallelujahs*.

Paul was feeding the baby from a glass bottle. Vern had followed Paul's instructions and boiled the glass bottles in a pot of water until the bottles were so hot they scalded his hands. They filled these bottles with what Paul called "form-luh," which was white powder mixed with water. Vern had never heard of formluh before, but the baby must've known what it was, because whenever she didn't have a bottle in her mouth, she screamed like her pants were on fire.

Paul leaned against a tree, feeding the baby in his arms, whispering to her. It was the first time Vern had allowed Paul to feed her. Vern didn't like letting go of the baby. It made him jealous. He didn't want the baby to accidentally start loving Paul more than she loved him.

"Can we turn that radio off?" said Paul. "All that hollering's keeping her awake. I want her to fall asleep when she's done eating."

"But," said Vern, "it's J. Wilbur Chaplain."

"So what?"

"So I always listen to preaching on Wednesday night."

"Well, now you got a baby, and things got to change. Babies need sleep, you know?"

"Always listen to J. Wilbur on Wednesdays."

Vern stood. He added wood to the smoldering firepit. He stabbed it with a stick until smoke drifted upward like fog, looking for a place to collect itself beneath the stars. He listened to the preacher's words and wondered how a man could talk that fast without taking any breaths. He had to think long and hard about every word he said. How could one person speak a new word every second without even stopping to wonder if it was the right word?

Paul slapped the back of his neck. "That mosquito was as big as a Ford," he said, inspecting his hand in the firelight. "Sucker almost paralyzed me."

Vern repositioned slabs of pork on the wire fence he'd stolen from a nearby farm. He gave the hog carcass a final rub, then slapped it. He always slapped a roasting hog before he cooked it—it was custom. His daddy had slapped carcasses, and so would he. Vern transferred another shovel of coals to the pit. He moved embers around until the pit was burning yellow. The wood popped, making sparks fly upward.

The bottle dropped. The baby was waving her hands in all directions, fussy in Paul's arms. Paul could hardly hold her still.

"What gives?" said Paul. "I thought babies was supposed to sleep all the time."

"Maybe she can't sleep 'cause she miss her mama," said Vern.

Paul gave her to Vern. The baby stopped crying when she looked at him. "Everybody need a mama," said Vern.

"I guess that makes you the mama, then."

"Reckon we oughta name her? I mean, a real name, something proper. I was thinking about naming her Verna. Or Vernlyn."

"Vernlyn? You're a narcissist."

"No, I'm Baptist."

Paul slapped his cheek. Then his forearm. Then his neck. "How about Paulette, or Pauline, or Paula?"

"Them ugly names."

The baby observed Vern with a serious face. She seemed to be concentrating very hard.

"Well, she ain't no *Vernlyn*," said Paul. "I can tell you that much."

The baby grunted and filled the air all at once. The smell was akin to something that had been passed through the system of a dying possum.

Vern pressed her against his chest. He kissed her red hair. He kept his nose against her smooth skin. Then he looked at the moon. So far away. He felt the heaviness of the baby against him.

"Where's your mama?" whispered Vern, looking at the moon. "Where that poor woman run off to?"

The baby looked upward at the sky. She reached her hand toward the moon. Then gave up and closed her eyes. She fell asleep in only a few seconds.

Vern sat and leaned backward against a tree. The fire was burning orange, and the smell of hog was in the air. The sound of the baby's breathing was the prettiest sound Vern had ever heard. "Sleep good, baby," he whispered. "Your mama love you." And he started to drift off to sleep too.

Then he felt a smack on his face that nearly broke his nose and made him swallow his tongue.

He opened his eyes to see Paul standing over him with a rolled-up newspaper and a smile on his face.

"That thing was as big as a Buick," said Paul.

*Fifteen*

# THE BORROWER

✶ ✶ ✶

Marigold snuck into the empty kitchen with gentle steps. She tried to move softly enough that the floorboards didn't creak. She saw the icebox across the room. She walked toward it on the fronts of her bare feet so she wouldn't make any noise.

Never before had she been so bold, but then, it took bravery to survive now. She was ready to eat real food instead of stolen grain from nearby barns.

It was Sunday night. She'd been planning her big move for days. That night, after the family left the white farmhouse wearing their Sunday best, she waltzed right onto the back porch. The kitchen door was unlocked.

She opened the icebox and saw a collection of rich food that almost made her cry when she put it in her mouth. She ate so fast she almost forgot to taste it. She ate cold chicken and potatoes, hoop cheese, and rag bologna and drank thick milk from a jug. And she felt ashamed. This was not borrowing. Once the food hit her mouth, it was thievery. Plain and simple. After her last bite, she left a note apologizing for what she'd done. It took her twenty minutes and two drafts just to get it right.

Dear Sir or Ma'am,

Thank you for letting me eat some of your food. It was really good. Specialy the potato salat. I dont like to take other folkses food, but I got to eat since I ain't eat in four days. Hope your church was good.

Love,
Marigold

Before she'd penned the last word, she heard footsteps. They were easy steps, shuffling against wood floorboards. She froze. She couldn't seem to get her legs to move. The vibrations were heavy on the stairs; the sound moved across the ceiling. She almost vomited all over the floor.

The steps were getting closer. She thought of running, but running surely would have given her away. Soon the feet were outside the door.

When the door opened, Marigold couldn't seem to make her body leave its position. At the door was an old woman staring across a dark room. In the darkness Marigold could only see a tuft of white hair atop the outline of an old woman's body.

The figure said, "Emily? That you?"

Marigold swallowed.

"Emily?" the woman said. Her voice sounded a million years old, dry and weak. "Emily, answer me."

"It's me," said Marigold. "It's Emily. Here I am."

"Oh, good. I fell asleep on the sofa. I had a bad dream."

Marigold did not know how to answer, so she didn't. She only glanced at the screen door and considered how fast she could get to it.

The old voice said, "Who's that? Standing beside you? Ben, is that you?"

Marigold glanced beside her at the icebox.

"I can see you both standing there," the woman said. "Ben? Ben? Is that you? Are you hungry, Ben? Emily, fix your grandfather a sandwich."

"There's nobody else here," Marigold said. "Maybe you should go back to bed."

The woman patted the wall and ran her hand along the surface as though she were searching for a light switch. Marigold turned to run, but her legs were paralyzed. When the woman's hand found the switch, the room lit up.

The pale-faced woman was ancient. She was hunched at the shoulders, leaning on a cane. Her white hair was thin, and her skin looked like weathered wood. She stared at Marigold until her brow furrowed. Then she looked directly to the left of Marigold.

"Emily," the woman said. Her face ruptured in tears. She was no longer looking at Marigold but staring at something that wasn't there. "Oh, Emily, I'm so confused." The woman came closer and touched Marigold. "I can't remember anything, and sometimes I forget who I am."

Marigold took a step back from the woman.

"I'm scared, Emily."

"It's gonna be okay, Granny," said Marigold, retreating. "Just go back to bed."

The woman began breathing heavily. A cold look fell on the woman's face.

She began glancing around the room. It was as though the walls were closing in. The woman's features contorted. "I don't know where I am." The woman began to sob. "Where am I?"

Marigold felt a sensation in her fingertips. It crawled slowly into her palms. It was a tingling that turned into warmth. Soon her hands were hot like fire. Her palms ached with a heat.

"Emily, is that you?" The woman came toward Marigold. "Help me, Emily!" she said. "Please don't let them get me!"

"Nobody's gonna hurt you," said Marigold.

"Ben! Ben! Where's Ben? Please come back, Ben!"

"Sshhh," said Marigold.

She wrapped her arms around the old woman. She placed her palms on the back of the woman's neck, and it felt like touching a potbelly stove. The woman's chest expanded with big breaths. Marigold's chest began to tingle with a thousand needle pricks.

The old woman squeezed Marigold so hard she felt herself creak. She could feel the woman's heart, pulsing beneath her ribs. It was almost as if they had become so entwined that they were one person instead of two.

Then Marigold felt confusion sweeping into her own brain so that she almost forgot where she was, or *who* she was. She saw flashes in her mind of a tall young man wearing suspenders, smoking a pipe. She saw the image of a young woman, small, blonde, blue-eyed, holding a baby on her hip.

These images abruptly came to an end when the old woman jerked backward. The woman wiped her tears with her sleeve. "Who are you? What are you doing in this house? You're not Emily."

The woman's eyes seemed clear. "This is my house," she said. "I'm in my own house. This is my kitchen. I'm standing in my own kitchen."

Marigold stepped toward the door.

"What did you do to me?" the woman said. "Who are you? How do you know me? What's happening to me?"

"I don't know," said Marigold.

"Wait! I demand to know who you are. Why are you here?"

Marigold darted out the screen door. And in moments she was running through a dark farmland toward the woods. The food in her belly was bouncing with each stride, making her sick. She ran until she almost lost the food inside her. She leaned forward, hands on her knees, breathless.

She stared at her hands. They still burned like they'd been lit on fire. She pressed a hand against her cold cheek. She looked upward at the moon. It was beautiful, the moon. But she couldn't touch it. And she couldn't touch Maggie either.

"Sweet dreams, Maggie. Mama loves you."

*Sixteen*

# THE FUGITIVES

★ ★ ★

"We're going to the Gulf of Mexico," said Blake, using a hacksaw. "You 'n' me."

"Really?" said Coot.

"Yessir. Gonna get me a little boat and go fishing off Point Clear, just like my daddy and me used to do."

E. P. was sleeping in his chair. He was drooling on himself, and a puddle had formed on his shirt below his chin. He snored loud enough that Coot could feel it in his spine.

"Is he gonna be okay?" Coot asked Blake.

"Sadly, yes," said Blake. "Just look at that fool. It would take ten bottles of dope to kill a man that size."

"You sure?"

"Yep, I'm sure." Then Blake laughed. "But I wouldn't wanna be him tomorrow morning. He'll feel like a duck walked all over his tongue."

Blake pulled the hacksaw against the padlock that was fixed on a cargo trunk beneath E. P.'s cot.

Coot wandered closer to E. P. and stared at the man's big face. He felt bad. Coot's mother used to tell Coot they owed their lives to E. P. She said he'd saved them. Coot didn't know what that meant, but he couldn't imagine this angry sleeping man saving anyone.

"Where's Point Clear?" Coot asked.

"Close to Mobile."

"Is that where you're from, Mobile?"

"You better know it."

"Is that where we're going?"

Blake stopped sawing and wiped his face with his sleeve. "Gonna be like seeing heaven, Coot. Land so green it'll make your eyes hurt. Water so blue it'll steal your breath."

"Blue water?"

"Gulf water."

"What's that?"

Blake only winked.

When the padlock came loose, Blake giggled. He opened the trunk and dug through all sorts of things inside. Ketchup bottles filled with brown whiskey, new boxes of leather shoes still packed in tissue paper. There was a basket of jewelry, pocket watches, snuff tins, and news clippings with Coot's name printed on them.

Blake held one clipping to the light. It bore a photo of Coot speaking before a tent of two hundred people in Chanute. That had been Coot's biggest day ever. The people had lined up outside the tent to see him. In the photo, Coot had his eyes closed tight, his arm outstretched like he was plucking an apple from the air.

Blake kept sifting through the trunk until he found a small tin box. When he did, he cracked it open using the blade of his pocket knife. The lid popped open, and Blake made a serious face. He pressed the brim of his hat upward and let out a soft whistle.

"What is it?" said Coot.

"Old fool must have a few thousand dollars in here," said Blake.

"A few *thousand*?"

Blake licked his thumbs and riffled through the cash. He concentrated and moved his lips slightly without saying anything. "Almost three grand," he finally said. Then he fell onto his haunches. "For the love of Mike, I expected maybe a few hundred, not this."

"But we can't *take* it," said Coot.

Blake laughed once. "Just watch me."

"He'll kill us, Blake."

"He shouldn't have this much to begin with." Blake closed the box. "E. P. owes more people more money than anyone in the state. This ain't his money. We ain't taking nothing. We're inheriting it."

E. P. began to stir in his chair. His eyelids opened. He made a sound like he was gurgling. He saw Coot and shot up from his seat. He wobbled on his feet, then fell forward. His lazy eyes landed on Blake, who held the money box beneath his arm.

"Why, you're robbing me," E. P. said in a weak voice. Then he landed his grip on Coot's arm. "You're robbing me blind."

Coot tried to tug himself free, but E. P. hardened his grip. "Why, I oughta whip you until your teeth fall out . . ." Then the large man started laughing. He rolled backward onto the dirt. "I can't hardly bleeve it . . ."

Blake stepped over E. P. until he was straddling the man in the dirt. He squeezed the big man's jaw until the skin bunched up around E. P.'s fleshy cheeks. Blake said, "I been chewing cheap cigars and reusing coffee grounds for ten years, and you got twenty-seven hundred hoarded away, you greedy little cuss . . ."

E. P. swung his limp arms at Blake. "My money. Gimme that box."

Blake used the box to tap E. P. on the forehead. "None of this is yours. It belongs to your son and his mama. I dare you to stop me, you big cheat."

But the big man was not able to sit upright. He only closed his eyes and laughed himself to sleep. "I'll kill you," E. P. mumbled.

It took Coot and Blake twenty minutes to pack their things and load it all into E. P.'s mammoth Hudson. Blake slid into the driver's seat, started the car after a few attempts. The engine roared to life and the tires crackled on the dust and gravel.

Coot sat on the passenger side, watching the large tent get smaller in the distance. The Hudson sailed into the dark, kicking clouds of dust behind it.

Blake lit a fresh cigar with a match. The coal on the end of the cigar glowed orange and filled the car with fragrant smoke that Coot could almost taste. Blake took one puff and exhaled at the windshield with a gentle moan.

"First new cigar I've had in four years," Blake said, removing it from his mouth to admire it. "Only wish your mama were here with us."

Coot leaned against the seat and stared into the distance. He watched prairie land fly past the windows in the night. "I miss her."

"She's watching over you right now, Coot." Blake ruffled Coot's hair. "You can bet your hind parts she is."

## Seventeen

# OLD TIRES

✱ ✱ ✱

Morning came with the sounds of birds. Vern lay on his back, eyes open, staring at the early sky. The colors were bright. It looked like someone had smudged gold and orange paint all over the clouds. He sat straight and felt the cords of his back tighten. He winced. Arthritis, bursitis, and all-around morning grumpiness were getting to him. Getting older was a pain in the—well, everything.

Vern saw Paul standing beside the truck, baby against his chest. He was feeding her from a glass bottle.

"You boil that bottle first?" asked Vern. "Lady at the store said you had to boil the bottles and teats first."

"'Course I boiled them. I've been boiling them all morning."

"You make sure the milk ain't too hot?"

"You're getting as skittish as an old woman."

Vern stretched, then squinted. In the distance he could see a tiny cloud of dust rising into the morning sky. A grinding sound came with the dust. The sound got louder the closer the cloud of dust came.

Vern limped toward the road, his bad ankle throbbing. He knew he ought to be using a cane to walk, but he hated canes. Old men used canes. Vern wasn't ready to get old. A limp was better than a cane. Besides, to potential employers, a cane was as good as a wheelchair.

Vern stood in the highway, hitching his thumbs in his overall straps. Louisville wagged her tail and sat beside him. She watched Vern with big eyes.

"You hear that grinding?" said Vern.

"I hear it," said Paul. "But I'm surprised you can hear it."

"Need new bearings in their wheels. That's what making the sound. Their bearings is shot."

When the car reached them, the grinding noise was so loud it sounded like a rusty water pump handle. It was a Model T, covered in mud. It rolled to a stop only a few feet from Vern.

Vern put on his friendly face and looked into the windshield. A woman was driving. In the passenger seat, a boy. The child was wearing a wide-brimmed cattleman's hat a few sizes too big for his head, with a little girl on his lap.

"Morning, ma'am," said Vern. "Just wanted to tell you your bearings is shot."

Paul appeared behind Vern. "Morning, miss." Paul tipped his hat and passed the baby to Vern. "What my friend's trying to say is, you need your tires worked on or you'll be in big trouble."

The woman gave no response but kept a hard face. The boy in the seat next to her didn't make much expression either. He looked young, Vern guessed maybe seven or eight. The little girl sitting on his lap was sucking her thumb. The woman glanced at the boy, then at Paul and Vern. Her eyes were serious ones.

"You don't have to be so friendly," said Paul. "Nobody likes a chatterbox."

The woman said nothing.

Vern could see right away that these weren't people who trusted others. They were scared. The woman wore an old cotton skirt. She had dirty skin. The children next to her were even dirtier.

The little girl shouted, "Look! A doggie!"

"Hush," said the boy.

"But it's a doggie! Mama, can we see the doggie?"

"Hush," said the boy in the big hat. Vern could see the kid resting one hand on the wood handle of a large handgun that was tucked between the seats in the car.

"Easy, Tex," said Paul. "I ain't the one you gotta worry about. I'm the one who's gonna fix your bearings before your car goes and catches fire."

"What do you mean?" said the woman. "What bearings?"

Vern kept his eyes on the kid's handgun. He felt afraid of what the kid might do. He held the baby against his shoulder, then gave her a kiss on the cheek to make himself feel better.

"What I mean, ma'am," said Paul, "is that you need your wheels regreased or you won't make it much farther before your car falls apart. We's only trying to help."

The woman looked at Paul and Vern with a pained face. Vern could see her thinking. Here was a woman who was all alone in this world. She had to think longer and harder than other women.

"And *you're* going to help us?" she said.

"Be glad to, just as long as this kid don't shoot me dead first."

A long silence passed between them. She was too afraid to open the door.

"Look!" said the little girl. "Doggie!"

The woman said, "How do we know we can trust you?"

"Because," said Paul, "you can trust a man who's been boiling bottles and teats all morning."

The woman stared at the baby in Vern's arms, then at Paul. She let her eyes sit on Paul a little longer than normal. "I'm Eulah, and this is Reese." She nodded to the boy. "And this is Pete."

Paul held out his hand. "Pleased to meet you, Tex."

Vern shot his hand to the kid next. "My name's Vern, and this baby here is Verna Sue."

## Eighteen

# COWBOYS AND BANDITOS

★ ★ ★

The handgun made Pete feel safe. It was all that made him feel safe. And feelings of safety were hard to come by. Every morning, before they covered miles in their old automobile, Pete would think to himself about the pitfalls that awaited them. The world was dangerous and cruel, and nobody was worth trusting during these hard times. That's what he'd learned since his father passed. Trust nobody. Fear everybody. And never set your cowboy hat on your bed because it's bad luck. He read that in a western dime novel once.

Pete thought about how he'd use the gun if he had to. How would he hold it? Double-handed, or single-handed with one hand resting on his belt buckle for poise? It was important to plan these kinds of things. You didn't want to go shooting people looking like you didn't know what you were doing.

Pete used the hours in the car imagining exactly how he'd use his gun if duty called. He thought about what he'd say when he drew his pistol. It was crucial to have something deathly clever to say. That's how all cowboys did things. They said things that were witty just before they pulled the trigger.

He considered the phrase, "You ain't gotta leg to stand on, bandito." He'd read that once, and he liked the way that foreign word rolled off the tongue. But this phrase had been said to a one-legged Mexican bandito before he got shot in the heart. Such words wouldn't make sense if they were used on regular old bloodthirsty roadside murderers.

He considered, "Eat dust, pilgrim." That was in one of his novels too. But he didn't fully know what pilgrims were and what they were doing in westerns, and it was important to use words he understood.

After much deliberation, Pete settled on the line, "Who's laughing now?" It was perfect. A variation on something he'd read, which had originally gone, "Who's got the last laugh now, Jeremiah?" But the simple twist of words made it shorter and therefore more piercing. It was firm, but with a little lightness to it. And it was appropriate for your everyday, basic heroic shooting. He'd seen enough picture show westerns to know that bad guys always laughed too much.

"Doggie!" said Pete's sister. "Can we pet the doggie?"

Pete's mother said nothing. She was just as unsure of these men. And this made Pete even more on edge. He gripped his pistol a little tighter. He waited for the gray-haired man to laugh for no good reason. Just one chuckle, that was all he needed.

But the old man made no laughs, he just kept talking.

"Y'all must be hungry," the man said.

It was a strange thing to say, Pete thought. Maybe he would feed them before he tried to chop off their heads.

"And you're in luck," the old man went on. "Vern just cooked a whole hog."

Pete glanced toward the black man who had walked away and now stood near a firepit. The big man was feeding a baby.

"No, thank you," Pete's mother answered. "We don't need anything."

She was lying. Their last meal had been two nights ago, in a car camp outside Lawrenceville. Pete had wandered through the lines of cars, digging through garbage after people had gone to bed. He'd found a leftover chicken carcass and a bag of rotted cabbage. His mother made soup out of it.

"We don't want no food," said Pete's mother.

Pete's stomach made a noise right after she said it.

The man stooped low and touched the hub of the old automobile. The old man spit on his finger, and when he touched the center of the hub, it made a hissing noise.

"See that?" the old man said. "This thing's red hot, Tex. The bearings need regreasing or they'll fall apart beneath you."

Pete's attention was diverted. His baby sister had climbed out of the car and was petting the black-and-tan dog and laughing. She was carefree, without a single fear in this world. Lucky girl.

Pete ignored the old man, got out of the car, and followed after his sister. He moved with caution, using as much authority as he could muster, keeping his legs wide. His gun was shoved in his belt, tugging his pants down below his haunches.

"Reese," Pete said in a low voice. "Get back here."

He was startled by a noise behind him. The old man was already cranking the car upward with a jack. The front tires were almost off the ground. The old man yelled out, "Vern, give old Tex a little bite. He's gonna need his energy to help get these tires fixed."

Pete's stomach ached when he thought of food. Sometimes he felt so dizzy he wasn't sure he could last another ten minutes. But somehow he just kept on living.

The old man loosened the nuts of the tire with a wrench. "Yessir, Tex," he said. "Old Vern's been looking for a genuine cowboy to give an opinion of his cooking. But we don't get many cowboys out in these parts."

The black man said, "I don't need nobody's opinion."

"He gets defensive," said the old man. "Sometimes you gotta mollycoddle him." Then the old man reached into his back pocket and removed a quarter. "Now tell me, Tex, does this seem like a fair price?" He placed the heavy coin in Pete's hand.

"Price for what?"

The old man winked. "You know, the going rate for your professional critiquing by a genuine cowboy?"

"Crit-eek-in?" said Pete.

"That's right. It's kinda like being a county fair judge at a jelly competition, picking the winner."

"I don't know."

The old man reached into his pocket and placed another coin in Pete's hand. "Here, this oughta square us up."

The black man filled a plate with meat and drowned it in red sauce. Pete's sister came running when she saw this. And Pete lost himself to the smell. He ate with his hands. And his sister ate from the same plate, using both her hands. He ate so fast it made his stomach hurt and his ears ring. He'd forgotten all about his gun and the clever line he would say. He only thought about the taste that was flooding his mouth. It was the best taste he'd ever known. When the plate was empty, Pete was breathing heavily. He wiped his face with his sleeve and still felt a burning hunger behind his ribs.

"Well?" said the old man who knelt beside the car. "How about it, Tex? Give us your official critique."

"My critique?"

"Don't hold back now. Vern can handle it. Might hurt his feelings, but he'll get over it."

Pete couldn't answer. A feeling was sweeping over him. He didn't know what to say. So he said nothing. Pete felt tears come to his eyes. He didn't even know why the tears were there. Maybe it was hunger. Maybe it was the food. "Thank you," said Pete in a quiet voice.

The old man hobbled toward Pete and sat beside him on a log next to the fire. He placed a greasy hand on Pete's shoulder. He let out a little laugh.

The old man said, "Does this mean you ain't gonna shoot me?"

*Nineteen*

# COWIKEE'S RAILCAR

★ ★ ★

The abandoned railway car sat in the woods, covered in thick straw that fell from the tall pines surrounding it. The wheels were rusted. The wood sides were weathered and dry. Marigold had never seen this monstrosity before, and she'd been living in these woods for months now. She'd been wandering the creeks and the shoreline of the sprawling bay but had never seen this old place. It was as though an unseen hand had dropped it in the woods.

She heard voices coming from inside the car. Loud, husky voices. She heard the sounds of boots on a hollow floor. She heard laughter.

Men entered and exited like ants in an anthill. Marigold stood far away, behind a pine, watching.

The gray boards on the railcar bore large faded yellow letters that spelled Cowikee Mills Cotton. Men in stained clothes, crumpled hats, and worn shoes walked into the railcar. They entered with strong steps; they left the place staggering.

Her head hurt and her eyes ached. She'd been starving for months now, couldn't remember what it felt like not to have a hollow stomach.

She dusted her dress, which had grown too big for her. Then she let down her hair. She combed the knots with her fingers and clumps came out in her hands. She could only imagine how hideous she looked. She drew in a quick breath and pinched the white out of her cheeks like her mother used to do on Sunday mornings.

Marigold had once asked her mother why she pinched her cheeks when she put on her Sunday clothes.

"'Cause," her mother had explained, "girls is supposed to have red cheeks. Makes 'em look pretty."

Once, Marigold had spent an entire afternoon pinching her cheeks in front of her mother's vanity to make them red. She'd accidentally bruised her face and cheek muscles so bad she couldn't smile for three days.

Cowikee's was a lonesome place that looked like it was nearly falling apart. But the closer she got, the more life she heard inside it. She walked toward it like a woman instead of a girl. There was a difference between the loose-limbed gait of a girl and the sure-footed stride of a woman. Men could tell the difference between the two. There was confidence in women that girls did not have.

The car was big. A large clapboard cabin had been built onto the back of it with a corroded tin roof spanning over both structures. The years had faded the wood siding into a dirty brown. Green mold and mildew covered the paned windows.

When she entered Cowikee's, the eyes of men landed on her. The mood changed in the room. She could feel their thoughts. Their laughter faded. Some men wore smirks. She was frightened. But she was less frightened than she was hungry.

A man behind the bar let his eyes travel from Marigold's feet to her face. And the silence seemed to last for a whole year.

"Honey?" the man behind the bar said. "You lost?"

"I'm thirsty," was all she could make herself say.

The weight of too many stares from too many strangers made Marigold breathe fast. Her chest started to thump. She didn't trust men. She didn't trust anyone who shaved their faces. Her father had made her this way. He'd ruined her. He had changed her.

She cleared her throat. Her mouth was so dry it tasted bad. "Could I have a drink?"

A tall, hairy man leaning on the bar said, "Well, have a seat. We got the cure for thirst right here."

Low-pitched laughs came from the room. She was getting too dizzy to care.

The hairy man walked toward her. He leaned close. She could smell his sweat—like onions and dirt. He removed his hat to reveal a mop of black fur, matted against his forehead. "Name's Robert, sweetheart."

She smelled the whiskey on his breath when he said it, and it almost made her gag. She wished she had never come into this place. She wished she would have just kept on walking after she saw it.

But they were interrupted by the sound of a woman's voice. "Get away from her, Bobby," said the voice.

Marigold saw a woman from the back of the room making a beeline for her. The woman pushed the man away before he could say anything else.

"She said she's thirsty," the woman said, grabbing Marigold by the arm. "Leave her alone."

The men in the place laughed. The hairy man waved the woman off and mumbled something. He walked away from her, but he did not remove his angry eyes from her.

The woman touched Marigold's forehead. "Honey, you're burning up." Marigold's heavy head was throbbing, and she felt like she was floating through the world. The woman pressed a cool hand on Marigold's forehead. "Oh, sweetie," said the woman. "You're on fire. Come with me."

They walked toward the back door. Marigold felt limp inside. The woman hooked arms with Marigold to keep her upright.

Then something struck Marigold on the face. So hard she lost her balance. She fell and hit the ground. She opened her eyes and saw the face of the hairy man who was standing over her.

"That'll teach you to thumb your nose at Robert Donahue!" said the man, pointing at her.

Marigold stared at his finger, inches from her face. Without thinking, she reached her hand out and gripped his forearm. She squeezed, and her palm became hot. In her grasp, the man's skin became so warm it felt like candle wax. She let her eyes bore into him. Immediately she felt things swimming in her mind, memories and images that weren't hers.

She saw the man standing on the shore, fishing. A boy stood beside him. She felt the man's happiness. A euphoria filled her head. Then she saw the man seated at the boy's bedside. She saw the child with a rag on his forehead. And she saw the man carrying a short casket. She could see the man crying, alone beside a creek. She could feel the depth of loss.

She squeezed him and felt his bones beneath her grip. His fragile bones. She could feel each of his breaths.

He tried to break free from her grasp but could not. The hairy man fell to his knees. He stared at her with wide eyes.

"What are you?" he said.

"I'm so sorry you hurt," said Marigold. "I'm so sorry."

The place fell silent. The man's eyes became wet and pink. Then he leapt to his feet and jogged for the door. He stumbled over a table and shot out of the railcar.

The woman lifted Marigold in her arms. Marigold opened her eyes and saw the woman's face was colored with beautiful makeup.

"Oh, your cheeks," said Marigold. "They're so red and pretty."

# Twenty

# RUN, BOY, RUN

* * *

The sun peeked through the second-story window of the small bedroom. Blake rose from the creaky bed, careful not to wake Coot. He looked at himself in the mirror. His eyelids were wrinkled, surrounded by lines that dug into his cheeks. He was not a young, handsome Southerner traveling with a western show, with a girl on each arm and a ten-gallon hat tilted on his head. He was an old man. His hair was thinning and his mustache was so thick it almost blended into the gray stubble on his cheeks. He was skinny, frail, stiff, and sore.

Long ago, he was the picture of showmanship. He could dangle from the saddle of a speeding horse while twirling a rope in his right hand. Now he couldn't even crawl into bed without wincing.

He saw a floor fan in the corner, blowing on him. He heard the sound of a radio playing in another room. It took a few minutes to rally the strength to stretch his long arms into the air and shake the ache from his bones.

He wandered toward the tall window. The view overlooked miles of prairie and spring wheat that seemed to stretch toward the end of the world. In the distance, two men were scalping a field with a binder pulled by two horses. The machine sliced swatches of grass, one row at a time. They moved in a slow but deliberate way. They paused now and then to drink from a ladle and bucket.

Blake was jolted from his thoughts by the sounds of voices coming from downstairs of the old farmhouse. Men's voices. The deep vibrations resonated within the wood home. At first he thought nothing of it. But the voices were getting louder, more intense.

He eased the window open and leaned out for a better look. A black-and-white car sat parked in the driveway. The painted star on the side made his chest sore.

He moved as quickly as he could. He gathered Coot's clothes, then nudged the boy. Before Coot's eyes opened, Blake pressed a hand over Coot's mouth.

"We're in a jam," whispered Blake. "A real jam."

Coot's eyes were big, looking straight at Blake. He nodded.

Then came the sounds of heavy footsteps downstairs.

"Hear that?" Blake said. "They're coming for us. We got a few seconds to do this right." Blake pointed to the window. "Get to that car and don't wait for me. Turn the key, gun it, and go whether I'm with you or not."

"But I can't drive," said Coot.

"Time to learn."

Coot sprang to his feet, and in only seconds he was crawling onto a hot roof, wearing nothing but his long nightshirt. Blake followed behind, carrying a bundle of clothes beneath one arm, his boots in the other hand. He tiptoed on the tin using gentle steps.

The hot metal burned his feet bad enough to leave blisters. The particular words he chose to mumble were not words used by revival preachers. Then he tossed the armful of clothes into the air. They fell onto the grass, scattering on the lawn like confetti.

"Go down the drain spout," Blake whispered to Coot.

Coot crawled down the metal pipe on the side of the house like he was a natural-born monkey. When he made it to the ground, the boy ran toward the Hudson parked behind the farmhouse. Blake had a bird's-eye view of Coot from where he stood.

He saw the boy jump into the car. He heard the engine roar to life. Blake watched the car zigzag in the lawn, making wide turns back and forth as though a drunk were behind the wheel.

Blake said another ugly word.

He heard footsteps behind him, then voices coming from the open window. He looked at the downspout and decided it was too flimsy to hold his weight. He sat on his haunches so that his bare feet dangled over the eave and said a quick prayer.

"Lord Jesus," he said, "please don't let me break my neck. It's all I ask."

Men crawled out the window onto the roof. They were yelling.

Blake jumped. His lanky body sailed through the air, his arms spread outward. He landed feetfirst and heard something in his knee pop. It felt like someone had stabbed a hot knife into the joint. He tumbled on the grass. His chin was in the dirt, his hind parts over his head. He leapt from the ground and hobbled toward the car like a one-legged ostrich. He ignored the scattered clothes on the lawn and flung the door open. He crawled into the car, slammed the door, and shouted, "Drive! Drive! Drive!"

The car shot forward. Coot held the wheel, aiming the vehicle at the gravel road. The engine of the Hudson sounded like it was going to explode. The car weaved left, then right, then left, then right. Back and forth. Side to side. It was enough to make Blake nauseous.

"Hold 'er steady," said Blake. "You're gonna make me puke."

"I told you I can't drive!"

"Just keep 'er straight."

"I can't hold the wheel still!"

Blake gripped the wheel and righted the vehicle. "Just push your foot on the gas, boy!"

Then Blake remembered the money. A pang of fear shot through him. He couldn't remember if he'd taken it inside the farmhouse with him or not. He fumbled through the glove box contents until he found the leather-bound Bible with the hollowed-out square in the center. He opened it and saw the folded bills.

"Glory be," said Blake. "At least they didn't get this."

"You okay, Blake?"

Blake leaned backward in the seat. His knee felt broken. His feet and ankles were sprained. His back hurt from tumbling on the unforgiving ground. His chin was bruised. He'd bitten his tongue and blood was all over his lips. His shoulders and wrists hurt from breaking his fall.

He touched his neck. It was unharmed.

"The good Lord answers prayer," said Blake.

# Twenty-One

# SUGAR AND CANDY

✦ ✦ ✦

A few customers had been forming a small line at the tailgate of Paul's truck all morning. Paul served them by packing handfuls of warm pork into a tin coffee mug, then turning the mug upside down onto a sheet of newspaper. Behind him, Eulah and her children were shredding bits of pork from the bone. Paul had to remind the children twice not to lick their greasy fingers whenever paying customers were nearby.

A man with a sweat-stained fedora asked for three pounds. Paul placed three pork cylinders in the center of the newsprint before wrapping them and handing the bundle to the man.

"That'll be thirty cents," Paul said.

The man scowled. "Thirty cents is highway robbery."

Paul didn't answer. He only took the man's money and God-blessed him.

"Hey," the man said. "Don't I get any barbecue sauce with that?"

"Sauce is extra."

"How much extra?"

"Nine cents."

"Just for *sauce*?"

"No, sir, not just for sauce. For the *best* sauce you've ever had."

"You must be crazy," said Fedora.

"The Lord looks out for children and fools."

The man dug into his pocket and slipped out two nickels, grumbling beneath his breath. He slapped the coins into Paul's hand.

Paul bit one of the nickels, just for show, then tucked the coins into his shirt. He handed the man a Coca-Cola bottle filled with red sauce and one penny in change. Paul lifted his hat. "Don't eat it all at once, now. The good Lord frowns on gluttons."

The man sneered, then crawled into a yellow car and drove away.

"How do you like that?" said Paul to Pete, who leaned against the side of the truck. "We go to the trouble of making the world's best sauce, and they got the gall to gripe about it?"

But Pete wasn't interested in barbecue. "Please take us with you," the boy said.

Paul was getting tired of talking about this. The more he talked about it, the worse he felt about himself. "We've already talked about this, Tex. Don't make me feel any uglier than I already feel."

Paul placed a handful of coins into a wood box. He tried not to look at the kid's big, sad eyes. They made him feel guilty.

"Please," said the boy. "I'm a hard worker."

Paul lit a cigarette and greeted the next man in line, who wore suspenders and a bow tie. Bow Tie said, "I'll take a pound, please."

Paul started to wrap some pork in newsprint. But the kid stepped between Paul and the stack of newspapers. "Here," said Pete. "Let me do it."

Paul took one step backward and watched the kid wrap the pork. It made him feel like a pathetic human being. He didn't want to leave this family on the side of the road, of course, but he couldn't support them either. He had a hard enough time finding work as it was.

Paul forced out a breath of smoke. "Tex, it ain't nothing personal, but folks gotta pay to breathe in this world, and I'm still holding my breath."

"We're worse off than you are," said Pete.

"That ain't the point," Paul said. "Your chances won't improve none with us."

The conversation was interrupted by a baby crying. Vern was holding her. He leaned against a tree, listening to the radio blaring from the open door of the truck. The sound of trumpets and trombones cut through the air. Vern opened a candy bar wrapper using only his teeth.

"Don't you do anything besides eat candy and listen to the radio?" hollered Paul.

"Who, me?" said Vern.

"No, your brother," said Paul. "Yes, *you.*"

"I cook it, you sell it," said Vern. "That was the deal."

A woman asked Pete for two pounds of pork. The kid fell into action and wrapped the pork in the newspaper like he had something to prove.

Paul patted Pete's shoulder. "You don't have to do it so fast, Tex. It ain't going nowhere."

Pete spoke up. "You don't know babies like my mama does. She knows everything."

"Son, you're breaking my heart. I wish you'd just accept that facts is facts, and the fact is I can't afford you or your family. My mind's made up. Now it ain't right, you makin' me feel so bad about it."

"Please."

Paul moved the kid out of his way. He began wrapping meat in newsprint without speaking. From the corner of his vision, he saw the boy throw his arms around his mother.

The next man in line ordered half a pound of pork. Paul folded newspaper over the warm meat and tried not to look at the kids and their mother.

"Be five cents," said Paul.

The man dug into his pocket and glanced toward Pete. "Is that kid gonna be okay?" the man said.

"'Course he will. It's just allergies."

Paul's heart dropped. His chest felt sore. Especially when he saw Eulah remove Pete's hat and hold him while he sobbed. Paul felt like he belonged beneath a pile of warm horse logs.

Vern, on the other hand, didn't seem to be bothered by anything. He unwrapped another candy bar and tossed the wrapper on the ground. He pressed his nose against the baby's face and made high-pitched noises.

The man in line cleared his throat and said, "Hey, what about my sauce? Don't this come with sauce?"

"Not you too," said Paul. "Sauce is extra."

"How *much* extra?" the man in the slacks asked.

"Nine cents," said Paul.

"Nine cents just for *sauce*?"

"It's a whole bottle."

"Of what, gold?"

"Keep talking and it'll go up to fifteen cents."

"You're out of your mind."

"Maybe. But if you keep pushing me, I'll take that pork outta your hand and rub it in my armpits."

The man gasped. He dug into his pocket again, slapped the coins into Paul's hand, and said a swear word.

Paul shoved a bottle into the man's hand. "Pleasure doing business with you, sir! Don't get lost on your way to Bible study."

"Women make everything easier," said Vern. "She could help with the wash. I ain't washed our clothes in a week. We smell bad. And them kids is sweet."

"That ain't the point," said Paul. "That ain't the point at all."

Paul looked at the family seated against the tree. They were pale and poor. Paul wished he'd never met this family, for there was nothing half as burdensome as women and children. They made everything complicated. Children needed too much money; women needed too much attention. They weighed a man down, stole his food, and crippled him. These were tough times. No man could afford women and children.

Paul sighed. He crushed his cigarette and walked toward the family. He squatted on his heels and said, "I can't take you with us, Pete. Now you can cry about it all you want, and you can hate me for it, but you're just gonna have to face the hard truth. Life ain't fair."

Eulah looked at Paul with sad eyes. "Mister, you don't owe us no explanation."

Pete dropped his head.

"I been trying to explain it to Pete," Eulah went on. "We'll be okay, we'll figure something out. Y'all done enough to help us already, and we're grateful. Ain't we, Pete?"

Pete glared at Paul.

"Pete," she said. "Did you hear what I said, boy?"

"Thank you," said Pete, even though his eyes said something else.

"You can cuss me, call me names," Paul said. "And you have every right to do that, because you're right. I'm a low-down, no-good man for turning his back on a good woman and her young'uns." Pete wiped his face with his forearm.

"Son, we're barely making it. We got a baby we don't need, who we ain't even named yet. We don't need no fussy children clinging to us."

His carefully chosen words hung in the air and did no good. The boy still wore a grave face.

"But," Paul added. "Now you listen to me carefully, Miss Eulah. Just 'cause I'm turning you away, and that's exactly what I'm doing, it don't mean that you and your family can't *follow* us. It's a free country, you know."

The boy's face broke, like sunlight poking through clouds.

"If you was to travel behind us," said Paul, "seeing as how there ain't no law against it, I couldn't do nothing to stop you."

Pete threw his arms around Paul and squeezed hard enough to cut off his wind. Paul could smell the boy's musty clothes and body odor.

"I'm a good worker," said Pete. "You won't regret this, sir."

Eulah covered her mouth and bowed her head.

Paul looked back at Vern, who wore a faint smile. Vern reached into his chest pocket and pulled out yet another candy bar.

"You're a glutton, you know that?" said Paul.

"No," said Vern with a mouthful of chocolate. "I'm Baptist." He wandered over to them, removed two more candy bars from his chest pocket, and gave them to the kids.

The boy looked at the candy in his hands. He stared at it long and hard. "Hey," Pete said. "I know what you can name your baby."

The boy showed the candy bar to Paul. "Baby Ruth."

## Twenty-Two

# RAILCARS OF ILL REPUTE

* * *

Marigold sat on the ragged porch behind Cowikee's railcar. The pines behind the place grew so high they almost blocked the sunlight. The sounds of birds were everywhere. A short fence ran through the woods in a crooked line, headed toward the horizon. On the fence, Marigold saw the carcass of a snake hanging from a post. There was a single nail driven through its head, its remains were bleached from the sun, and the ribs showed. Flies swarmed the snake. Marigold could hear the vibrations from them.

Helen stepped onto the porch. "Are you hungry again?" asked Helen. "I got some stew cooking. Got plenty of carrots in it. Carrots will give you strength."

"No thanks," said Marigold. "I'm still full from breakfast."

Helen had been practically force-feeding Marigold since she'd taken her in. And in that short time, Helen had managed to help Marigold gain some weight. Marigold's old dress was beginning to fit like it had before she lost her baby fat.

Helen had introduced her to the other girls who lived at Cowikee's. They were all so much like each other they were practically sisters. These women wore makeup and nice dresses, and they walked differently from other girls Marigold had known. But above all, they were kind to Marigold. They treated Marigold like she belonged to them. It was the first time since Marigold's family had expelled her from home that she'd felt the warmth of family.

At night, the girls often sat beside Marigold. And they weren't afraid to touch her or embrace her or dote on her or call her "pretty." And it had been a long time since anyone had touched Marigold or called her that.

"You sure you don't want any stew?" Helen asked. "How about I just bring you a little cup to sip on?"

"No thanks, I'm stuffed."

"You need to keep eating, sweetie. You're still skin and bones."

There were five girls at Cowikee's altogether. And from the best Marigold could tell, they all seemed to understand the world around them better than Marigold did. Helen was older than the others. Her long, lean figure and dark hair made her look like she'd walked out of a picture show.

But Rachel was Marigold's favorite. She was blonde, with gaunt features and a sharp nose. In the weeks Marigold had been there, she noticed that the male customers all fawned over Rachel because she was the youngest.

Earlier that morning, a redheaded young man had come to visit Rachel. He was more boy than man, closer to Rachel's age. Rachel behaved differently toward him than the girls behaved to the other men. She kissed him with her eyes closed. And she talked to him in a soft voice. Marigold asked Rachel about him, but Rachel refused to talk about it. There were some things women did not dare discuss for fear they would not come true if they did.

The weather was god-awful hot. The ground seemed to be softer than normal because of the heat. Marigold thought it felt like the whole world was melting, or maybe the whole world was dying.

Marigold's red-and-white cotton dress had holes in the seams. She poked her finger through one of the seams. She was falling apart, she thought. Inside and out.

She thought of Maggie every moment. She remembered the way the baby trusted her. That's what babies did. They trusted people. Maggie was the only creature who had ever trusted her. Marigold saw Maggie in her dreams every night. And in her dreams, she saw Maggie's purple eyes and round face.

A back door swung open, then slapped shut.

The redheaded young man walked out of Rachel's room. He was shirtless and barefoot, with a wad of clothes beneath his arm. His cropped hair was the color of a new penny. He pulled suspenders over his white shoulders and stomped past Marigold.

"Don't go, Lawrence," Rachel called to him. "Please don't go."

But the young man was obviously upset. He clomped off the porch, then crawled into a car with chrome fenders.

"I'm sorry," said Rachel, walking after him. "I didn't mean it! I'm sorry!"

Rachel walked barefoot on the gravel toward his car, gathering her skirt in her hands. "Please don't leave, not like this."

But the redhead paid Rachel no mind. He fired his motor and sped away, leaving a puff of brown dust in the air behind his bumper.

Rachel stood in the center of the road behind Cowikee's. She was too upset to even make tears. Or maybe women like Rachel had lost the ability to make tears. Maybe a girl can only make so many before she uses them all up.

Marigold came behind Rachel and observed her porcelain face—sad but dry. Marigold said, "Is everything okay?"

Rachel said nothing. Moments passed between them, and only the distant sound of cicadas could be heard. Marigold rested her hand on Rachel's shoulder. She sensed a weight of sadness. The weight became so heavy, Marigold could not even remove her hand from beneath it.

Rachel pulled away from her. She gave Marigold a bewildered look but said nothing.

"It's hot," Rachel finally said. "Someone needs to hang another rattlesnake on the fence." Then she walked to her room and left Marigold standing in the road.

Helen was reclining on the porch railing, smoking a cigarette, watching the whole thing. Rachel brushed past her and buried her face in her hands.

"What's it mean to hang a rattlesnake on a fence?" asked Marigold.

Helen smiled. "It's what old farmers used to do when they needed rain. They'd hang rattlesnakes on fences."

"Why?" asked Marigold.

"Don't know, sweetie. Folks always seem to be trying to make something happen that just won't."

# Twenty-Three

# WICHITA DUST

*   *   *

A black-and-brown cloud hung over the outskirts of Wichita, Kansas. It terrified Coot to even look at it. In the rear window of the speeding car, it looked like it was only a few miles behind them, and getting closer.

These dusty clouds didn't swirl like cyclones did, and they didn't have flat bottoms like rain clouds. These were dark, evil clouds that were black. Only a few days before, a cloud had settled on Kansas that turned the world into midnight. It had poisoned the air so that breathing could give a man dust pneumonia. All the kids Coot knew had suffered from it at one time or another. Coot had dust pneumonia twice before. Once, it got so bad he couldn't get out of bed for three weeks and had to breathe through a wet rag.

The dust in the rear window stretched for miles and had covered the sun, making it look like a reddish ball, dimming the light above Wichita. It made the town look like something from the book of Revelation. Wind kicked against the Hudson, knocking the car from side to side. The sounds of sand and dust whizzed against the window and covered the highway.

Blake gripped the wheel and made the car go faster. "I can't see the road," he said.

"You think we can outrun it?" Coot said.

Blake didn't answer.

They drove on the bumpy highway through the outskirts of Wichita and into the town. Dozens of cars were pulled onto the sides of the roads, abandoned, already half covered in sand. Coot saw people running into barns, sheds, and homes with boarded windows.

The cloud moved closer. The wind took the roof off a tin building in the distance. Coot saw the roof spin in the air and land in a hayfield, then tumble end over end.

"We're not gonna make it!" hollered Coot.

Blake hit the gas. The dust was getting so close, Coot couldn't see the horizon anymore. He only saw blackness. It seemed as though the buildings, houses, and highways had been swallowed by the Devil.

Blake swerved into a filling station and slammed the car into park. The car jumped the curb and rocked in the violent wind. They leapt out of the vehicle and jogged toward the front door. The wind gust knocked Coot from his feet. His shoes slid on the sand beneath him and he fell face forward. Dust and grit stung his cheeks and eyes. He covered his face. Blake lifted him and shoved him through the door of the service station.

Inside were people, lots of them, seated on the floor in clumps. They were listening to a radio on the counter. It was the unmistakable sound of preaching. Coot could hear the familiar cadence of words, a singsong-like delivery. He was drawn to the sound. He found a place near the radio so he could hear it better. Through the static and crackles, he heard the voice breaking through the dust.

The people welcomed Coot and Blake inside and gave them wet rags to hold over their faces. A boy who was Coot's age held a polka-dot rag over his nose and mouth. He coughed now and then. "This is a bad one," said the boy.

Coot pressed the cloth over his face. His cheeks stung from the sand, and his eyes were dry and scratched with debris.

The voice on the radio was delivering words in a way that Coot had never heard before. The man wasn't just yelling, he was firing his words like a sharpshooting rifle. He never paused to think of what he would say next. He never broke the rhythm of his words. His sentences flowed from his mouth like a steady current that could not be stopped.

The people in the room *hallelujahed* and *yes-Lorded* in quiet voices.

"Amen, J. Wilbur," said one man. "Say it."

"Amen," said a woman's muffled voice from behind a rag.

The voice on the radio belonged to J. Wilbur Chaplain. The words, the delivery, the fury made Coot forget all about the storm and feel nothing but wonder. He was mesmerized by the evangelist. He hadn't expected this. It was like nothing he'd ever heard. And when he looked at the people's faces, he could tell they were listening just as closely as he was.

When the preaching ended, an organ played, and a few people hummed along.

*"Lose all their guilty stains . . . ,"* sang one woman. *"Lose all their guilty stains."*

"They keep getting worse," said one old man, clicking off the radio. "You heard what the preacher just said. It's the Judgment."

"Worst storm this year," said another. "Ain't had no rain since October."

"God's wrath," said another old man.

"Wrath poured out without mixture upon the wicket," said another.

"All that's missing is the brimstone," said Blake.

## Twenty-Four

# SUMMER SHOWERS

✷ ✷ ✷

The two vehicles crept forward on a dirt highway in the middle of the night. The stars were so bright they cut through the thin clouds. Pete looked out the car window at the stars and felt lost in them while Vern drove the Model T coupe behind Paul's truck.

In the car were Pete, his sister, Reese, Vern, and the bloodhound named Louisville—who sat between Pete and Vern, snoring and making smells that even hardened war criminals couldn't endure without begging for mercy.

Pete petted the dog while he stared at the night sky. Vern had the dashboard radio playing. The preacherman on the radio hollered. Vern paid close attention while he drove.

"Why do you like this preacher so much?" asked Pete.

"J. Wilbur? Just do, I guess. I like to hear him get all riled up. He can sure get mad at the Devil."

Pete continued to pet Louisville. The fur between her eyes was soft as silk. She had white around her snout and beneath her eyes.

"Is Louise an old dog?" Pete asked Vern.

"Yep," said Vern. "She an old woman."

For most of the ride, Pete had met his equal with Vern. The two talked so little that they didn't make enough words to fill up a teacup. Pete was miles above the car, caught in the blue night and the stars. Ahead of them, he could see the silhouette of his mother in the truck cab.

The highway seemed to go on for hours. They hadn't passed a single car all night, and none of the rural houses had lights on. It was cool outside, and Pete thanked the stars for that. The unforgiving heat of day, coupled with the drought, made the world feel merciless.

"You been on the road with your mama a long time?" asked Vern.

"Yeah," said Pete. "A long time."

"Us too."

More silence.

"Where you sleep?" asked Vern.

"Oh, anywhere. Most times we sleep in the car."

"Us too."

Silence again.

"Do it make you tired? All this traveling 'round?"

"Yeah, my mama's tired. I can tell. She's tired all the time."

"Us too."

Pete let out a big sigh, then leaned back into his seat. He let his hand rest on the dog.

"You ever get scared?" said Vern.

"Yeah."

"Is you scared now?"

Pete had to think about this for a moment. "A little."

"Me too. But you know what J. Wilbur say? Blessed are the meek who shall inherit the whole earth."

"Meek? What's that mean?"

"Don't know, but I prays God makes me good and meek-like so maybe I can get all sorta land I can call my own one day."

"Me too."

Silence passed between them.

"Where're we going?" Pete asked.

"Butler County, Paul said."

"What's in Butler County?"

"Work."

"What kind?"

Vern shrugged. "Don't really know. I just goes where Paul goes."

Pete cranked the window down before he became dizzy from the fumes.

Vern grinned at Pete. It was the first time the big man's friendly eyes had really inspected Pete. "That's a real nice hat you wear."

Pete removed the big hat and observed it. It was buckskin, with a leather strip of rawhide tied around the crown. The hatband had been stuffed with newspaper so that it would fit his boyish head. "It was my daddy's."

"Where's your daddy?"

Pete looked at the night sky. "Way up there somewhere."

Vern looked at the stars through the windshield. "Mine too."

## Twenty-Five

# JUDGMENT DAYS

\* ☆ \*

Paul glanced into the rearview mirror. Vern and Pete were close behind. He checked his speedometer, careful to keep the needle three ticks above the number twenty. Twenty-three was his lucky number when it came to gas mileage. Whenever the truck went too far over that speed, the old thing started burning oil and making strange noises that sounded like someone was hiding beneath the hood with a short-barrel shotgun.

Paul reached for a cigarette and found that the pack in his shirt pocket was empty. He almost swore, but the woman was in the passenger seat next to him. He tossed the carton out the window and looked at Baby Ruth, bouncing in the woman's arms. He forced a smile.

Baby Ruth wasn't crying anymore, but she wasn't calm either. She was fidgety but lethargic. Much like he was feeling.

"You know," said the woman. "I realized I don't even know your full name."

But Paul didn't answer. He wasn't trying to be rude, he simply was too busy patting his pockets for a cigarette. He was certain he had one lying around somewhere. He looked on the dashboard and between the seats. He searched the floorboards and found nothing. He finally gave up searching. He pulled in a breath of air and mumbled an ugly word through gritted teeth in a whisper.

"Where'd you find this little girl?" Eulah asked.

"Who, Baby Ruth?"

"You don't have to call her that, you know. Pete just gets excited about things sometimes. He daydreams and comes up with these ridiculous ideas."

Paul smiled. "It's a good name, Ruth. My grandmother's name was Ruth."

"Really?"

"No, I just made that up. Her name was Josephine, and she was the devil."

Paul dug into his shirt pocket and showed her the folded newspaper clipping.

Eulah scanned it and said, "Good heavens. A mother leaves her baby, and in these hard times. This world is in big trouble, ain't it?"

"Worst trouble I ever seen."

"People don't act civil no more."

"No, they don't, and nobody trusts nobody."

"You reckon these is the Judgment Days?"

Paul shrugged. "Maybe."

Lots of people claimed these were the Judgment Days. It wasn't just the droughts and the absence of jobs that made them say it. It was the boll weevil eating through all the cotton. It was the food shortages in Atlanta, the scarlet fever and tuberculosis, the dust in Kansas and Oklahoma, the bread lines in New York and New Jersey, and the price of living. It was enough tragedy that it made weaker-minded men kill themselves. And suicide was becoming an epidemic in some places.

"You reckon God's gonna wipe us all off the planet?"

"I don't know," said Paul. "But it don't make no difference either way to me. God does his thing, I do mine. I don't bother him, and I ask him to give me the same treatment."

A long silence passed between them. Eulah rocked the baby in her arms until the child fell asleep. And so did Eulah. Her eyes were shut tight. She coughed now and then. It was a productive cough that sounded like her lungs were rattling. Paul watched her and felt sorry for her and for all she'd been through. He felt sorry for her children, and for the baby, and even sorrier for himself—for he was out of cigarettes.

Then . . .

The sky was lit with red-and-purple light, only for a moment. Paul could hardly believe it. The sound of thunder shook the highway. It happened again. And for a flash, the tree line became visible before an electric sky.

"Well, I'll be," said Paul in a whisper. He didn't want to say it too loud. He didn't want to wake the tired woman beside him.

Paul pulled the car over. Vern pulled over behind him, crackling on the gravel shoulder. Paul stepped out of the truck, removed his hat, and looked upward. The sky was putting on a light show for the world to see.

It hadn't rained since three weeks before they started construction on the Dreyfus barn. In fact, their dry world had gone so long without rain, Paul couldn't even remember what the stuff smelled like. And the smell of rain was his favorite smell. It awakened the farmer inside him, which was a piece of himself he thought had been eaten up by boll weevils and greedy banks.

"You think she's gonna go?" said Vern, walking toward him, looking upward.

"Dunno," said Paul.

They waited several minutes until it finally started. One drop at a time. The rain began beating the roofs of the two vehicles. Slow at first. Then harder. Soon it sounded like a freight train crashing into the world. Loud. Heavy. Warm. Water.

Paul laughed with an open mouth. He let the hot rain hit his old face and felt the weight of the heavy drops on his cheeks.

"Reckon someone must've hung a rattlesnake on a fence," said Vern.

Paul squatted onto the ground and bowed his head. He let the rainwater run over his greasy hair and down his back. He felt his shirt, saturated, stick to his back.

"God," he said in a soft voice meant only for the heavens. "If you're up there, please, I beg of you, dear Lord, please let me find a cigarette."

## Twenty-Six

# LIGHTNING STRIKES

✦ ✦ ✦

"Get up," were the only words Marigold heard.

And when Marigold opened her eyes, she was looking at Helen, who was lying beside her.

"What is it?" asked Marigold.

Lightning. Thunder. Rumbling.

"That," said Helen. "Hear it?"

The surface of the walls inside the room became white and blue for an instant. Then the light disappeared and the place went black. Then blue again. And black.

"I think it's gonna rain," said Helen.

Helen jumped out of bed and walked toward the window. She was obviously excited. "C'mon. It's a storm."

A low rumble vibrated the cabin and railcar. Then a loud clap of thunder that made Helen smile. Then another clap. The world lit up flickering white.

Helen counted, "One Chattahoochee, two Chattahoochee, three . . ." The whole earth shook like it would fall apart. Another lightning flash.

Helen counted again. "One Chattahoochee . . ."

Rumbles shook the place.

"It's getting closer," said Helen.

Outside on Cowikee's front porch, Rachel was already standing with the other girls, watching the sky. They were quiet, wearing nightgowns, smoking cigarettes, arms crossed.

It was an eerie atmosphere. The dark world was calm between episodes of thunder and flashes of light. Laughing Girl stood beside Rachel. She was a tall, slender woman with long black hair and cocoa skin. She'd told Marigold she was

Cherokee, and she must have been. Her cheekbones were so high they made her eyes look pinched.

"Don't *hear* no rain," said Rachel. "Could be it's only heat lightning."

"No, it is coming," said Laughing Girl.

"How do you know?" Marigold asked.

"My hair," Laughing Girl replied. "My hair knows when it will rain."

"That's ridiculous," said Helen.

Marigold could not remember the last time it rained. Months. Lots of months. Too many months.

Helen stepped off the porch and looked at the sky. "C'mon, Lord," she said. "Do it up big tonight."

They all watched the sky. Nobody said anything. They only waited.

The first few drops hit the tin roof of the porch and made a marvelous sound.

"There it is!" said Helen. "Don't just stand there, come on."

Helen led Marigold and the others across the dusty road, through the pines, to the peanut field down the road from Cowikee's railcar. A single oak sat in the field, surrounded by a tin shed, dead peanut plants, and a few cattle.

The girls walked through the field in the darkness, stepping between the rows of dead foliage toward the tin building. It was a leaning structure with a rusted roof. Helen unlatched the door and muscled it open. Inside were wooden barrels with rusty rings and dry-rotted tops. Helen rolled one outside, spinning it on its rim. She popped the top and positioned the barrel beneath the gutter spout of the shed.

"Don't just stand there," said Helen. "Help me. These things ain't exactly light."

"What're we doing?" asked Marigold.

But Helen wasn't listening to her. She was already rolling another barrel with Laughing Girl. They placed it beneath the eave of the tin roof.

When three barrels were positioned around the shed, the sky opened itself. The smacking raindrops got louder and sounded like a mighty waterfall. The shower cooled Marigold's red hair, and it made her wonder about Maggie. She wondered where she was and if she was safe. She hoped Maggie could see the rain.

The rain fell harder. It pelted the tin roof and made noises so loud it sounded like a train. Water ran across the tin roof and trickled into the barrels.

"Four months and six days," said Helen again. "That's almost half a year without water. Four months and six long days."

The girls stood inside the shed, watching a downpour saturate the field around them. But not Helen. She was out in it, letting it mat her hair against her head and her clothes to her body. To Marigold, the rain was the smell she liked best. It smelled and tasted like some kind of miracle. And it sounded even better.

Rachel broke the silence by saying to Marigold, "Lawrence said he's gonna take me with him when he leaves for Birmingham."

Marigold only looked at her with a warm smile. Water dripped from Rachel's brow and from her strands of light hair.

Rachel went on. "He said we's gonna buy a house, said we's gonna settle down and, you know, make a family."

Marigold touched Rachel on the shoulder. She felt a tingling beneath her hand that ran up her arm, through her head, then down her legs. It was such a strong sensation of loneliness that it almost made her stomach turn upside down. The tingling became stronger and stronger. She released Rachel's shoulder and steadied her breathing. But to Marigold's surprise, Rachel didn't seem to notice anything out of the ordinary. She was smiling and watching the rain.

"He said he loved me," Rachel added. "He loves me."

"Love," Laughing Girl said. "May lightning strike him dead if he is lying to you."

The sky flashed again.

# Twenty-Seven

# MOTOR INNS

\* \* \*

All Wichita was covered in a film of dust and sand. Cars were stripped of their paint, and streetlamps were broken. The Hudson had piles of grit on the hood and on the roof. Once, the vehicle had been a plain black; now it was bare metal in many places.

They left the windswept city and drove through the dry landscape. They passed mounds of red and tan dust piled on the sides of the dust-covered highway like miniature mountains. At least, they thought this was the highway. There was no way to be sure since they could see nothing but dust before them, behind them, and around them.

Blake pulled into a motor inn just outside the sandy city of Eureka. The wind was still blowing dust along the streets, making swirls and tiny cyclones. It was hard to see where the sidewalks stopped and the curbs began.

The motor inn was a low building with a flat roof, boarded windows, and a dirt-covered parking lot filled with dilapidated cars that were almost all paint-stripped and dented. Blake went inside and returned to the Hudson with a key ring.

"We're living high cotton tonight, Coot," Blake said.

The room was nice. It had a bathtub with a shower and a frilly curtain around a claw-foot tub. There were two single beds, and a big wooden radio sat on the dresser.

"Look at the size of that radio," said Coot.

Blake whistled.

Coot turned on the radio, and the sound of horns and banjos filled the little room. "They got jazz here," Coot said, turning up the radio.

"Sounds like it."

"Do they have jazz in Alabama?"

"Have it? Why, we invented it."

Blake lit a cigar and tapped the ember against an ashtray. He tipped his boot upside down and a stream of sand fell out of it. Coot listened to the music with great curiosity and happiness. For it was curious and happy music. A vocalist sang cheery melodies, wiggling her voice in a way that revival singers did not.

"How much longer until Alabama?" said Coot.

"Never you mind. You just listen to the Dixie music, we'll be there soon enough." Blake sat straight in his bed and knocked the heels of his boots together. "Mobile makes this place look like a burn pile."

"It does?"

"Oh yeah, Alabama's like Eden, only without all the snakes."

Coot flipped past the stations on the radio until he landed on one that played the sound of a baseball game. The cheering crowd did something to him, made him feel excited inside. A feeling he did not have often. But his excitement began to sour in him when he remembered the men in the police car chasing them.

"What if they catch us, Blake?"

Blake didn't speak. He only blew a cloudy breath at the ceiling and watched it gather around the ceiling fan. Then he leaned forward and turned off the radio. His face went from lighthearted to serious. He touched his mustache and took in a few labored breaths like he was thinking.

Blake reached into a brown leather bag and retrieved the metal box he'd stolen from E. P. It was a red tin box with a wire handle on it. He placed it in Coot's lap and said, "This money, it belongs to you, Coot. You and your mama. And if anything ever happens to me . . ."

"Blake, don't talk like that."

"I mean it. There's a lot in there, and it ain't mine."

"Blake . . ."

"There's enough in that there box to put me away for a long time. And if anything ever happens to me, you go find a bus station and go as far away as you can. Doesn't matter where."

Coot didn't like hearing him talk like this. It filled him with fear and made his lungs cold.

"Blake, I couldn't make it on my own."

"Now, you listen to me." Blake replaced the money box in the bag and zipped it shut. He plopped the entire bag in Coot's lap. "Don't never let that money outta sight."

"But—"

"Hush and let me finish. Now, you're a lot more courageous than you think you are, and I want you to remember that." He patted Coot's hair. "If I was you, I'd quit thinking about all these bad things and get cleaned up."

"Get cleaned up for what?"

"I'd put on my nice duds too. Wouldn't wanna be late, you know."

"Late for what?"

Blake leaned back on the bed, resting his head on the pillow. He let out a chestful of blue smoke and coughed. The coughing lasted a few minutes. The dust had done a number on them both.

"Where're we going, Blake?"

"I'd grease up my shoes real good and fix my hair—" Blake coughed again.

"Why, Blake? Where're we going?"

"'Course, that's just how I'd do it. You can do what you want, you're practically a grown man anyway. Besides, what a fella wears to his first baseball game ain't nobody's business but his own."

"Baseball! Are you putting me on?"

Blake coughed again. "Why, Coot, I'm offended. Would old Blake lie to you?"

# Twenty-Eight

# STEALING HOME

★ ★ ★

The baseball bat made a cracking sound that could probably be heard all the way to China. Coot had only heard this particular noise a few times in his life. He'd heard a bat hit a ball before, certainly, but never with this kind of sincerity.

The sound did something to him. So did the smacking sound the ball made when it hit the catcher's mitt. They sat in the nosebleeds, high above the small diamond. Coot watched the men on the field run from bag to bag. These men didn't just trot like the farmers in the rural leagues. These men were running full-speed, earning their paychecks when they slid into home plate.

And Coot could even hear their voices. The players would scream at each other. The umpire would shout back at them. Cuss words were abundant. Coot found himself shouting at the top of his lungs too during important plays. When the Joplin Miners took the lead against the Wichita Aviators, he became so excited he forgot all about his peanuts in the red-and-white bag. And when the game ended, Coot was sorry it was over.

Afterward, Blake and Coot walked through the corridors of the small ballpark, making their way to the exit.

"You know I used to play a little," said Blake.

"You did?"

"Little. Wasn't bad. Had me a chance to play with the Pine Bluff Judges, outta Arkansas, but I didn't do it."

"Why not?"

Blake sighed. "A woman, Coot."

"You mean *you* were in love with a girl?"

"No, Coot, a woman. That's different from a girl. A woman makes you do things you never thought you'd do. I was in love up to my eyeballs with her."

"What'd she make you do?"

"She made me as stupid as room-temperature mud is what she done. There I was, in a traveling show, and she was a high-society lady. The two don't match up no matter how you spin it."

"Is that where you learned to twirl rope, in the traveling show?"

"Where I learned a lotta worthless things."

"What happened with her?"

"She hurt me, that's what happened. I thought I'd never get over her. Last I heard, she married a banker in Greensburg. Broke my heart. You never get over someone choosing a banker instead of you."

When they neared the door, Blake stopped walking. Coot could feel Blake's body tense. He gripped Coot's shoulder and held him back. It all happened so fast that it took a moment for Coot to even realize that something was wrong. His mind was too much on double plays, home runs, and infield flies.

But Blake's eyes were fixed on men in the distance. Men with badges. Coot could see them. Four men in khaki uniforms, lingering by the exit sign. One man wore a leather jacket, with a hat tilted sideways on his head.

Blake coughed a few times into his fist. He closed his eyes. He stroked his thick mustache.

"Are those cops?" Coot said.

"They sure ain't the welcome committee, I can tell you that much."

"What'll we do?"

"Hush and follow me's what you do."

They wandered through the ballpark, weaving through rows of seats, up the aisles, pausing every few moments to look behind them. Coot carried the bulky leather bag with both hands. Blake moved fast, and Coot moved quick behind him. Soon they were on the field, jogging across the cropped grass toward a tall outfield wall. A large advertisement for B&R Headache Powder was over the left field. Blake found a door within the giant "&" on the wall. The door led into the dirt parking lot with a few tractors and chalk spreaders and baskets of baseballs.

They crept toward their Hudson, pausing to take cover behind vehicles. Blake told Coot to get on all fours and peek beneath the cars to see if the coast was clear. When they neared the area where they'd left the Hudson, they could see the vehicle surrounded by more men in official-looking uniforms. The door of the vehicle, though it had been battered by dust, revealed the faintest remnants of text on the side advertising the gospel troop.

Blake swore.

"What now?" asked Coot.

"I'm thinking, Coot."

They backtracked through the stadium and found the nosebleed seats again, then they crouched low. They stayed there for a few hours, until the park emptied and the sun went down. Neither of them spoke a word. Finally Coot fell asleep, using the brown leather bag for a pillow.

When the sky was black, they climbed the fence on the east edge of the park. They walked back toward the motel room through the darkness until Coot had developed blisters on his feet. When they reached the motor inn parking lot, Blake stopped walking and squatted beneath a delivery truck tire. He swore again.

"What is it?" Coot said. But no sooner had he said it than he saw what Blake was cussing at. It was a man in the distance, wearing a badge, standing beside their motel door.

"Those rabbit-chasing grunts ain't got nothing better to do than go after an old man."

"Are we done for?" said Coot.

But Blake was in no mood to answer. He remained quiet, letting his mind work overtime. After several moments, Blake finally flashed a flimsy smile and said, "We ain't licked yet."

And Coot knew that even though Blake had promised he never would, he was lying.

# Twenty-Nine

# THE LONG GREEN

★ ★ ★

"No thanks, I got all the tobacco pickers I can stand," said Mister Harrison. "If it's work you're looking for, go ask my competitor for a job. They probably pay worse than I do, though."

"I know you already got you plenty of pickers," said Paul. "But you ain't got *five* pickers for the price of two."

Mister Harrison leaned against the dry barn and removed his hat. He used a handkerchief to dab his black hair. He was a short man, broad shouldered and stout. He let out a colossal sigh, then studied Pete, Vern, Eulah, Reese, and Baby Ruth with hard eyes.

"Can them two young'uns work?" Mister Harrison asked.

Paul scoffed. "Why, those two can pull their own weight better 'n any two young'uns you ever saw."

"How about the bull?" said Mister Harrison, nodding toward Vern.

"He's got him a name," said Paul.

Mister Harrison let out a demeaning chuckle. Then Harrison looked into the distance at the long green fields of tobacco leaves. Harrison's workers labored in the sunlight, wearing straw hats and canvas sacks slung around their shoulders. They picked weeds from between the wide, leafy rows, placing the field daisies and the jimsonweed into bags a handful at a time. Harrison whistled at two workers who were close by.

Two men came running. They were wiry, with long necks and leathery skin. They stood before Mister Harrison with bent backs and humble faces.

Mister Harrison rubbed his chin, staring at them. He seemed to be thinking. Finally he announced, "One of you's fired."

His words didn't resonate right away. It took a few moments before they settled on the men. The faces of the young men became long and serious. They looked at Harrison, waiting for more words, but there were none. Mister Harrison was only wearing a strange smirk.

One man answered, "Boss? You're firing us?"

"No," said Mister Harrison. "Just *one* of you."

The men wore confused faces.

"Which one of us?" said the other man.

Mister Harrison crossed his arms. "Whichever one of you beats the other."

The men looked at each other in what was obviously disbelief. They removed their hats and let out nervous laughs. "But, Boss, Clarence is my friend. We's been friends since we's kids."

"Don't make me repeat myself, you two," said Mister Harrison. "I got a man to fire, and one of you better get to kicking the other one's tail, or you'll *both* be out of a job."

The men grew uncomfortable on their feet. One man threw down his weed sack and his hat.

But Paul had already had enough. He grabbed the hands of Pete and Eulah and said, "We don't need jobs that bad. Good day to you, sir—"

"No!" shouted Mister Harrison, keeping his attention on the two field-men. "Now I just gave you boys an order . . ." His voice was low and threatening. "You gonna sit there and defy me? Or is you gonna listen to your boss man?"

The men pleaded. They begged. Mister Harrison swore in a voice that rang throughout the county, then removed his hat. He shot forward and threw his heel into the back of one man's knee. The man fell face-first onto the dirt.

"I give you an order, son!" shouted Mister Harrison through clenched teeth. "An order, you hear me?"

The other man rushed toward Mister Harrison and tackled him. The three men rolled in the dust together until Mister Harrison was on top of one of the men. But before he could take a swing, Vern handed Baby Ruth to Paul and strode toward the men with a calm gait. Vern picked up Harrison with both hands. He lifted the man's body high above his head.

Onlookers who had started to gather wore big eyes at the giant who held Mister Harrison in the air. Vern walked slowly toward a barn, holding Harrison with massive arms. Paul had never seen such a display of strength.

Vern set the man on the ground easily. He straightened the man's collar. Then he glared at Harrison and said, "Blessed are the meek, for they shall inherit the earth."

Paul and Vern took the children and Eulah and left.

*Thirty*

# HEARTBREAK

* ✦ *

It was a magnificent Saturday. The crickets were making such a loud noise it seemed as though they were singing. The tavern at Cowikee's was empty, and so were the rooms. The girls reclined on the porch, listening to the tranquilizing sounds of the piney forest.

Then came the sound of tires on gravel.

A chrome-fendered car rushed into the drive, and the doors flew open. A woman, a sophisticated woman with pearls on and matching earrings, jumped out. Her hair was done. Her shoes matched her green dress. The woman walked onto Cowikee's back porch uninvited and unannounced. Her shoes made loud noises on the floorboards, like a log drum.

And she had children with her. One child was balanced on her hip. The other, a toddler, was standing beside her, holding the woman's hand. The woman looked out of place on a porch like this. The girls, barefoot, wearing silk robes, became uncomfortable.

Helen approached the woman first. The woman, however, did not move or give Helen a smile. She only cut Helen off before she could ask anything.

"I'm looking for Rachel," the woman said.

The girls stiffened. They stabbed cigarettes into the coffee tin filled with sand and looked at each other. One by one they stood and wandered into their rooms.

"Okay," said Helen. "Just calm down. What's this about?"

The woman's face was not getting calmer, but red. She adjusted the child on her hip and said, "I *am* calm. I want to see *Rachel*. Please."

Helen didn't move her body. She only nodded toward Marigold. "Go inside and get Rachel."

In a few minutes, Rachel stood on the porch before the woman in green.

Marigold noted how the two couldn't have looked more different. Rachel looked younger than the woman and less sophisticated. The woman set her child on the porch. She smoothed her dress and stepped toward Rachel with slow steps. She placed inches between their noses and made her eyes small.

"So you're the one?" the woman said.

Marigold could see the faces of the others looking through the windowpanes.

"It's you?" the woman went on. "You're the one Lawrence keeps coming to see?"

Rachel looked embarrassed.

The woman took another stride forward. Then she reared back and slapped Rachel. The loud sound made Marigold cringe.

But Rachel only looked at the woman. Silence passed between them. Then Rachel touched her own face and started to cry.

The woman pointed to the children who stood behind her. "You see those children?" she said. "They *belong* to Lawrence. And me. I want you to have a good look at them."

The children stood motionless, wide-eyed.

"Look at them," the woman said. "Do you see them?"

Rachel nodded.

"Now you listen to me," the woman said. "You're *nothing* to him. *Nothing*. And that ain't even the saddest part. The sad part is Lawrence don't even have the *guts* to tell you what a *nothing* you are to him, and he sent me to do it for him."

The woman held her gaze, almost as if she were daring Rachel to do something. Finally she lifted a child onto her hip and gripped the other by the hand. And then she was gone.

Marigold stepped toward her. She let Rachel collapse into her arms. Rachel began to sob with groans that were too deep for words. Marigold felt the heat build in her palms, like it had before when she'd laid her hand on the hairy man in the bar. This time her hand was so hot it stung. It frightened Marigold, but with an unexplained urge, she touched Rachel's face. When she did, she felt a sharp pain in her chest, just below her breastbone. The sensation was so piercing, it made her moan. Rachel touched Marigold's hand and pressed it harder into her own cheek.

"Oh, Marigold," said Rachel. "I feel like my heart is bleeding inside me."

"I know," said Marigold. "I feel it too."

And the crickets sang all night long.

*Thirty-One*

# BEST FRIENDS

★ ★ ★

The morning light spread across the uneven cobblestones. Coot stood before a
bus holding a brown leather bag containing the money box, a few sets of clothes,
and the collection of trinkets he held dear.

The bus engine before him spit gray exhaust into the morning air. There were
men in suits carrying duffel bags, and women in skirts with handbags. They all
boarded the bus in a horde. They seemed busy, hurried, and they behaved like
their lives were more important than they truly were.

The sign on the front of the large silver vehicle read Birmingham, Ala.

Coot waited on the sidewalk, observing his own reflection in a shop window.
Behind his reflection were mannequin torsos wearing suits. In the reflection he
looked awkward. His long, skinny neck. His puny shoulders. He thought himself
to be an ugly kid. Maybe the ugliest who ever lived.

Blake was several yards away, speaking to the bus driver. Their voices were
drowned out by the sound of the heavy engine. But Coot could see the driver
nodding and listening to whatever Blake was saying.

Coot looked at his own reflection again. Why couldn't God have made his
ears a little bit smaller? Or at least God could've made his neck shorter.

"We're all set," said Blake, appearing in the shop window reflection behind
Coot. "Nice-lookin' men, ain't we?"

Coot shrugged.

Blake tousled Coot's hair. "You'll grow into your paws. Give it time."

Then Blake squatted on his heels before Coot and fixed his collar. "Gosh,
Coot. I'm sorry I couldn't get your baseball bat. Too many cops around the car."

"It's okay."

Blake shook his head. "No, it ain't okay. That was your bat."

Coot was indeed sorry he didn't have the bat. It was the most impressive thing he had ever owned. But the truth was, he'd forgotten about it ever since they'd been running from dust and hiding from deputies in dark corners of a foreign city.

Blake placed his hand on Coot's head. The hand weighed more than Coot thought. "One day you're gonna forget all about me, you know that?"

"No, I won't."

"Yes, you will, and you *should* forget. You know I ain't brought you nothing but trouble. I shoulda taken you away from E. P. a long time ago. I hold myself personally responsible for all you went through."

"Stop it, Blake."

"I'm bad luck, buddy." Blake cleared his throat and flashed a big smile. "But hey, we're gonna start a new life, you 'n' me, right? We'll have big fun together. This bus is gonna take us straight to the promised land, and maybe, once you finally see Alabama, you'll forgive me."

"Blake, you ain't done nothing wrong."

Blake brought himself eye level with Coot and looked both ways. Coot noticed the old man's eyes were pink and wet. Blake said in a whisper, "I'm putting you in charge of our money, hear me?"

Coot nodded.

Blake made his voice soft. "Now, the first rule of carrying money is always be touching your money. Always. Understand?"

"Why do you want *me* to carry it?"

"Repeat the first rule back to me, Coot."

"Always be touching your money."

Blake cupped his ear. "How often should you be touching it?"

"Always."

Blake grinned. "Second rule is don't let *nobody* else touch it, never. *Especially* not a friend. Lotta friends in this life will do you wrong, Coot. It's just human nature. They don't mean nothing by it. People is just people, and people can be so cruel."

Then Blake smacked Coot's shoulders. He gave Coot a big look, with the weight of pride behind it. "I love you, Coot. And you deserved that blamed bat. I'm only sorry I couldn't get it for you."

"Blake, shouldn't you be the one to carry the money? I don't think I'm—"

"You're a brave kid, brother. Bravest I ever knowed . . ."

Something was very wrong, Coot could feel it in the air.

The bus driver stepped off the bus and hollered. People fit in last goodbyes. Men kissed women, children hugged mothers. People hurried onto the bus.

The driver exchanged a look with Blake. Blake only nodded at the man.

"C'mon," said Blake. "We gotta bus to catch."

When they reached the door, Blake stopped walking. He tousled Coot's hair and said, "Coot, you go ahead and get us a good seat. I gotta use the john."

The engine fired. The bus brakes creaked.

"Hurry, Blake."

Blake winked at Coot. "I'm right behind you."

Coot boarded the bus. He walked the narrow aisle toward a seat in the rear. He placed the brown bag beside himself. An old man walked by and tried to sit next to Coot, but Coot waved him off. The old man mumbled something when he walked away. Another passenger tried to sit beside Coot. A woman with a toddler.

"Sorry," said Coot. "Seat's taken."

The woman said, "You can't reserve seats on a bus, kid. Ain't the way it works."

"My friend's in the bathroom."

The woman stormed off and took her toddler to the back of the bus.

After a few moments, the bus driver threw the vehicle into gear.

"Wait," Coot shouted. "My friend is still in the bathroom!"

Coot could see the driver's face in the large rearview mirror. The bus driver's eyes were solemn. "I'm really sorry, kid," he said. "Really sorry." He pulled the doors shut and gunned the engine.

Coot shot forward, toting the leather bag in both hands, stomping down the center aisle. He fumbled past the passengers, knocking the bag against them on his way to the front. "Stop! My friend's still out there!"

But the mammoth vehicle was already rolling forward. Coot froze in his tracks and realized what was happening. He looked out the narrow glass doors. He could see Blake standing on the pavement in the rear window.

"Please!" shouted Coot. "Look! He's right there. Back up and let him on the bus!"

The bus did not stop.

Blake's figure was getting smaller in the distance. The tall, wiry man with the mustache stood on the curb.

"Blake!" Coot said through tears. "Don't do this!"

Coot could feel the bus engine beneath his feet. The driver changed gears and picked up speed. Soon they were on the highway. Blake's figure was a pinpoint on the far-off landscape.

The driver gave Coot a look. "He told me it was for your own good, son," he said. "But he told me to give you this." The bus driver removed something from behind his own seat.

A hickory baseball bat, brand-new, wrapped in ribbon.

# BOOK II

# Thirty-Two

# BABIES INTO GIRLS

*★ ★ ★*

Paul watched the sun rise over the tobacco field. Whenever sun spread itself on the leaves, it looked like the backyard of heaven, dotted with the first colors of a coming autumn. The fading green color of the world was overwhelming, the scent clean smelling. The aroma of wet dirt and earth was strong enough to taste.

The sound of a radio nearby cut through the rural morning. It was blasting an official voice into the air, one that talked about a war and the invasion at Pearl Harbor. The voices on the radio had changed since the war began. Men talked a little louder and more staccato. They had anxiety in their words, and fear.

Paul's family had worked on four tobacco farms in three years before they finally found work with Mister Pettigrew. And in those years of uncertainty, Paul had never found a man who was as kind as Pettigrew. Most men in tobacco farming were bitter, looking for fast money, and treated their mostly black field workers with cruelty. The hateful things Paul had heard and seen done had changed the way he viewed the human race.

But Mister Pettigrew was not like this. He hired Paul, Vern, Eulah, and Pete and had paid them the wages of three workers. Even though they did the work of eight workers, it was steady money. Pettigrew treated them like his own family. During holidays he invited workers to his own home to celebrate. He gave gifts to the children of the field workers. He served mountains of food. Long tables were filled with casseroles, pies, and dishes of all kinds. And his men worked hard for Mister Pettigrew because of it.

In the early sun, Paul watched the morning's first workers move through the crops before the midday heat got too strong.

Paul had not cared for tobacco work when he first arrived. This work wasn't at all like cotton picking, peanut picking, plowing, timber framing, roofing, or dog training. Tobacco work was careful work, slow moving and downright boring. But somehow he'd changed the way he felt about it. He'd come to love the easy rhythms.

Maybe it was because he was getting older and tired. Maybe it was because he was slowing down. After six years of tobacco, he'd grown used to the light pace of work.

The best part of the job was the housing—if you could call it that. It was a crude cabin made of rotting clapboards, a dirt floor, a leaky tin roof, a fireplace made of mud and rock. There were dozens just like it. Crooked structures with cockeyed gables and chickens roaming dirt yards. Eulah and the girls slept inside. Paul, Vern, and Pete slept in a lean-to where the chickens often gathered and left little gifts on their pillows if they forgot to cover them with tarps.

But mornings brought simple blessings. Coffee over a campfire. A sunrise. Paul's homemade biscuits from a sack of flour. And children. The children had gotten older since they'd first come to the Pettigrew farm. They were taller, leaner, and just when Paul thought they couldn't get any more beautiful, they proved him wrong.

Eulah's children had become the best part of Paul's life. So had Ruth. Eulah kept to herself and could go full days without saying much. With each year, the children grew into miniature adults. They acted like it too. Ruth had found her favorite phrase: "I know." She said it all the time, and it made Paul smile every time the self-assured six-year-old reminded him that she "knew" something.

Paul could practically write her future. She would grow into a confident girl who didn't need anything from anybody. And this made him proud of her, even as he hoped he'd live to see that version of her.

But he might not. People died every day from little things. It was never the big things that got you. It was always the little things that swept you from this planet. But it didn't concern him, for his purpose in life was clear. These children had become his purpose. And until he'd met them, he only wandered through life with Louisville and Vern. There was never a reason for doing anything. Now he had more reason than he could stand.

He heard Ruth's energetic footsteps on the porch. Ruth was often the first to wake in the mornings. Though sometimes Reese would beat her to it. Most mornings, young Ruth would wander onto the porch, half-awake, and sit on Paul's lap and watch the sun lift itself above the ground and wake up the world. And he would touch her shock of red hair—which was Paul's favorite thing in the world.

Ruth galloped down the steps of the ugly house. She was all hair. Paul greeted her, but she was too sleepy to answer.

"What're you doing up so early?" he said.

Ruth rubbed her eyes. She crawled into Paul's lap and rested her head against his chest. If there was a better feeling in the world, Paul didn't care to know what it was.

She watched the world get brighter with him. The sun was becoming warmer every second.

"Louisville was fussing in her sleep," said Ruth. "Can't sleep with all that noise. I wish she'd sleep outside with you."

"She's old and deaf, baby. Her bones are sore. She can't help all that whimpering."

"I know, but it's hard to sleep."

"Oh, you be sweet to my old girl."

"How old is Louisville?"

"Pushing nineteen."

"That's old in dog years, right?"

"That's ancient."

"Yeah. I know."

"You sure know a lot."

"Yeah."

"In a dog's world, nineteen's a record."

"Are you older than nineteen?"

"Not by much."

"What will Louisville be like when she's *your* age?"

"I expect Lou will be sitting next to the Lord by then, the lucky girl."

Paul ran his fingers through her red curls. Her hair was thick and fell over her shoulders. She was the prettiest child he'd ever seen.

"Are we really at war?" said Ruth.

"You and me ain't, but the rest of the world is."

They watched the sun climb. He rubbed her head—more for his satisfaction than for hers. This know-it-all girl was the most important thing he ever did with himself. Sometimes he looked at the stars at night and wondered if this was the reason he was created. For her.

He said in a whisper, "Almost time to eat. You want me to show you how to stamp biscuits with an upside-down glass? It's sorta fun."

But there was no answer. Her eyes were shut. She slept with her cheek against his chest.

Their lives weren't beautiful. In fact, their lives were hard. And whenever they settled into a routine, along came something that changed it. They always seemed to be a few meals away from starvation, and they seemed to have less each month than they had the month before. *But life doesn't have to be beautiful to be pretty,* Paul thought. *All it needs is red hair.*

"I love you, sweetie," said Paul.

"I know," she whispered.

## Thirty-Three

# GIRLS INTO LADIES

* * *

Marigold admired her image in the mirror. She had never admired herself before. But she was admiring herself now, and it was a rare moment of happiness that she did not usually afford herself. But today she was in a good mood. There was something happy in her.

Helen sat in bed, reading a newspaper. She was sipping coffee from a tin mug and paying no attention to Marigold.

Marigold smoothed her dress against her tummy. Somewhere along the way, she'd outgrown her girlish frame and childish clothes. She'd become a tall, slender woman. It had all happened right before her eyes so that she never really noticed it. But today she did. And was grateful for it. Most often, when Marigold looked into a mirror, she saw ugly. She saw a big-boned, copper-topped fifteen-year-old.

"You believe this?" said Helen. "They're calling up all the men."

"What do you mean?"

"The government, they're gonna steal all our men, ages eighteen to forty-one. Says it right here in the paper."

"Take the men? You mean they're sending them to war?"

"Well, they sure ain't gonna teach them to play patty-cake." Helen turned the page and shook her head. "This war's gonna put us outta business."

Earlier that week, Marigold had gone into town and stood in line at the post office. There she'd met an old lady in a blue dress with a matching hat. Most women avoided Marigold, but not this woman. They had talked. The woman was a pleasant woman who was better at conversation than most people. Before they'd parted ways, Marigold felt a familiar heat in her palms. It started in her palms and moved upward to her elbows, then her shoulders. She was no longer afraid when it happened. She knew what it meant, and she knew what she had to do when her hands became hot.

She did not ask the woman before she laid her hand on her neck. No sooner had Marigold touched her than she developed a headache that was so splitting it made her vision blur and her teeth hurt. The woman had only closed her eyes and started to cry. Marigold embraced her outside the post office.

"Sometimes," the woman told Marigold, "my migraines get so bad that I go two, three days without sleeping."

But Marigold already knew this before the woman said it. She had seen the woman's pain when she touched her.

"Are you a healer?" the woman had asked Marigold.

"No," said Marigold.

"What are you?" the woman asked.

Marigold shrugged. "A redhead."

Marigold was interrupted from inspecting herself in the mirror by a horrible sound. Helen had dropped her newspaper and leaned over the edge of her bed. She wrenched forward. She moaned. The sound of splattering came next.

Marigold ran to Helen, who was doubled over, vomiting onto the floor. She hurled again and again, until nothing more came up. She wiped her mouth with her forearm, caught her breath.

"I can't believe this," Helen finally said. But she was interrupted by more heaving.

Marigold touched her. She wanted to help Helen, but there was no heat in her hands, only her normal, clammy skin.

"Can't believe what?" Marigold said.

"I'm too old for this," Helen moaned. "This must be some kinda joke."

"What's a joke?"

"I thought I was all dried up inside. I thought . . . I thought . . . I thought I was all used up."

Helen leaned over her bedpan. She missed. The floor was painted with bile. The smell made Marigold ill.

"This is my punishment," said Helen. "This is judgment, judgment for what I am."

She heaved several times until she was kneeling on the floor, leaning over the bedpan, crying.

Marigold rubbed her hands together. She willed them to become warm.

She wanted nothing more than to rid Helen of nausea. She concentrated on her palms, but nothing happened. She tried patting them against her thighs. She closed her eyes. She even said a short prayer. But nothing happened. So she rested her hand on Helen's neck, which was covered in a thin film of sweat.

"What am I gonna do with a *baby*?" said Helen.

The words made Marigold think of Maggie. She thought of the day she lost her. She remembered everything about the day. And in this moment, she became a dumb fifteen-year-old all over again. She felt as lost in this world as she'd ever been. And her hands became as hot as fire.

She touched Helen on the shoulder. She felt a current pass between them. It was like electricity, only gentler. The heat grew so hot, Marigold's hand became slippery. When the heat dissipated, Helen stopped vomiting and wiped the corners of her mouth and turned to face Marigold.

"What in the devil did you just do to me?" Helen backed up against the wall. "What did you do to me?"

"I don't think the Devil had anything to do with it," said Marigold.

# Thirty-Four

# LABORERS

★ ★ ★

"Coot's in love," said Aaron in a singsong-like voice. "Coot's in love. And he's got it bad too."

"Yeah," said Billy. "He's in love, alright. Look at him, the big dummy."

The night sky over the Oswalt sawmill was peppered with a million stars that seemed to get brighter with each passing minute. Teems of young men twirled their young ladies on the pinewood dance floor. Lanterns dangled above and candles adorned tables, but Coot thought these were poor substitutes for stars.

The sounds of shoes on the dance floor were almost louder than the fiddle band that serenaded them. Clomping sounds of waltzing people filled the night with happiness and the kind of imagined adventures that youth offers.

Coot was watching from a distance with the other mill workers near the barn. Coot was watching her. He always watched her. She was the loveliest thing on two feet. He could feel his face wearing a grin, even though she was so far away. Judy Bronson spun like a fairy out on the dance floor. Her blonde hair caught the light from the lanterns. It was illuminated and made her look like a heavenly being.

Coot had never been in love before. Not even close to it. But he believed he was in it now. With Judy Bronson. Of course, she hardly knew he existed, but this was only a minor technicality.

"Hey, Coot," said Aaron, snapping his fingers in front of Coot's eyes. "Are you even with us?"

"Think he's had too much moonshine," said Billy.

"No way," said Aaron. "Not the preacher. He don't never touch liquor."

"He's a regular J. Wilbur Chaplain, ain't he?"

One boy slapped Coot's shoulder. "Tell me, Mister Chaplain, are you for or against the Eighteenth Amendment? Inquiring minds wanna know, Reverend!"

The boys laughed so hard Coot thought they were going to empty their bladders in their britches.

But Coot didn't care. He was busy watching Judy. Judy knew how to dance, and Coot had never known this until tonight. She was nothing but graceful. No, *poised* was a better word for it. She was long and poised. *Fair.* That was also a good word for what she was. She was very fair. She had white-blonde hair, and a charm that made even the grossest mill workers behave like Sunday school teachers when they were near her.

Coot knew he didn't have a chance with her, but he was in love nonetheless. And you can't control who you love. Even if it's bad for you. You can control what you know and what you think and what you do. But not who you love.

"Hey, Preacher," said Aaron. "You're creeping me out with that face you're wearing."

More laughter.

Judy was in the arms of Baby Joe, the boy with dimples. Girls loved Joe's dimples. Coot had once tried to give himself dimples by exercising his smiling muscles until they were sore, but it didn't work. What he would've given for a pair of dimples like Baby Joe's. Those things were top-shelf.

Joe spun Judy in a circle, her hair lifting from momentum. Coot wanted to die a slow death when she passed him. He knew she would never see anything in him.

After all, girls were only interested in men who wore army uniforms. Ever since he'd started working at the mill, Coot had noticed he'd gotten even uglier than before. His ears seemed to get bigger every time he looked at them. And his pants were falling off him from all the hard work and small suppers. He'd become a telephone pole with floppy ears and donkey teeth.

And tonight he looked even worse than usual. Tonight Coot wore an uncomfortable necktie he'd bought in town. He'd chosen green because he once heard Judy say that green was her favorite color. *What a waste of money,* Coot thought to himself. *She doesn't even know I'm alive. She'll never even notice this stupid green tie.*

Judy spun past Coot. She flashed a smile when she saw him staring. "Why, Coot," she said in passing. "I ain't never seen you in a necktie before."

Coot kicked himself for not buying seventeen hundred green neckties.

Baby Joe stuck his tongue out at Coot. The other men who stood nearby were all dressed in green uniforms and side caps. They laughed at Coot.

"With friends like Joe, who needs enemies?" said Aaron.

"Joe's a cocky little twerp," said Billy. "The Germans will cut him down to size, just wait."

"Twerp?" said Aaron. "Why, he's taller than *you* are."

"No he ain't," said Billy. "We're practically the same height. Ain't we the same height, Coot?"

But Coot could not be jolted out of his own thoughts. He was already plotting his trip into town the next day to spend every dime he had at a men's clothing store, where he would make the biggest necktie purchase ever recorded in county history.

"Coot," said Billy again. "Am I as tall as Baby Joe?"

"Close," Coot said.

Coot himself was one of the tallest workers at the Oswalt Mill. In the group photograph taken that year, the photographer put him in the back row. The only man taller than Coot was Dieter Schlaff, the German man who could hardly speak English without spitting on himself.

But even though Coot was tall and broad, he would never wear a uniform. The doctor at the military office had heard something irregular when he'd listened to Coot's heartbeat. Coot would never forget the way the man frowned and said, "Afraid to tell you this, son, but you're 4-F." Ineligible for service all because of a strange sound within his heart.

When the music ended, everyone clapped. The dancers on the floor dispersed. The music became fast and lively. A few couples took the floor and started stomping their feet, kicking, and making hollering noises. Buck dancing was something the country people did, and it was almost humorous to see.

Judy Bronson came near the clot of young men where Coot was standing. Her presence made Coot nearly urinate on himself and forget how to say his name.

"Ain't got music like this in Columbus," said Judy, who stood close enough to Coot that he could smell her perfume. "This here's a real string band."

Coot nodded. He'd meant to say, "How are you doing tonight, Judy?" or "Isn't it stunning weather on this fine summer's eve?" But what came out of his mouth was a collection of sounds with no intelligible meaning.

Judy looked at him with furrowed brows. She studied his face and said, "You're a funny one, ain't you?"

He couldn't get any words out. Behold the Great Preacher of the Plains. Big ears. Long legs. Classification: 4-F. And completely tongue-tied.

William Oswalt suddenly appeared before Judy. The young man wore an officer's uniform with a gold emblem on his cap. He asked if she wanted to dance. William was built like a spruce, with broad shoulders and a square jaw. The uniform made him look like a hero even though his feet hadn't touched foreign soil yet.

Judy handed her drink to Coot. And she was gone.

"How do you like that?" said Aaron. "Stupid Will can have anyone he wants here tonight, and he took Judy."

Coot didn't answer. He only stood watching.

"Am I as tall as William?" asked Billy. "He's not *that* much taller than me, is he?"

Aaron laughed. "Would you quit worrying about how tall you are?"

"I think I'm as tall as he is," said Billy.

"He's a whole foot taller than you, shrimp."

Will was the son of the wealthiest mill owner in south Alabama. The Oswalt Mill had been the largest mill for too many decades to count. Will's father also raised beef and dairy cows on twenty-five hundred acres. He owned more land than anyone in the state almost. The newspapers called the Oswalts the Kings of Alabama. Kings. With a capital *K*. And no necktie, no matter how green, could compete with that.

Coot loosened his necktie and left the clot of young men.

"Hey, Preacher," said Aaron. "Where're you going?"

"Don't know," said Coot. "Anywhere else."

"He's probably going to listen to J. Wilbur Chaplain," said another boy.

"Shut up," said Aaron.

"Hey, Preacher," said one man in a uniform. "Don't forget to say your prayers."

Coot wandered into the darkness and hitched his thumbs in his pockets. He had gone from feeling low, to high, to low again. That's how love worked, he guessed.

He thought about the old man who twirled a lasso beneath prairie stars. He wondered where the old man was in the years they'd been apart. He missed Blake, but he half hated him too for sending him away. Still, on nights like this, Coot wondered what sort of advice the old man would've given him. Blake always had good advice.

Maybe he would've told Coot, "You don't want nothing to do with girls who got white hair." Or maybe he would've said, "You don't wanna go fight a dumb old war nohow."

Coot stared upward. He thought how different the stars looked over this country than they did over the prairie. Memories came back to him by the boatload. He remembered what it was like, speaking to audiences in big tents, with real energy to his voice. He remembered feeling like he could do no wrong, waving a Bible in the air. He remembered what if felt like to be beautiful.

The music in the distance had stopped. People were leaving the party. Young men had girls hooked on their arms. William Oswalt had Judy Bronson on his. His service cap sat uneven on his head, like a movie star might have worn it. He was only toying with Judy, just like he did with all the girls. A wealthy young officer like him would not be seen in broad daylight with a mill worker's daughter like Judy. But she didn't seem to know this.

"Hey, Coot," said Baby Joe, with a brunette around his arm. "Come go swimming with us."

"Swimming?" one young man shouted. "The water wouldn't even come up to Coot's knees."

Everyone laughed.

Coot pressed his hands farther into his pockets and said, "No thanks. Got an early day tomorrow at the mill."

"We *all* got early days tomorrow, Coot," said another young man. "We're going to Europe to show old Hitler who's boss!" He screamed it at the top of his lungs.

Other boys joined in and howled at the sky like a pack of coyotes.

They piled into an automobile that was brand-new. The engine roared to life. Will sat behind the wheel, revving the motor for the enjoyment of those nearby. The car sped off. Coot watched its taillights bounce away in the night.

Before they were all out of sight, he reached his right hand into the sky. Then he closed his eyes and made a tight fist, just like he used to do for tents filled with farmers and grain elevator workers. He held it high, to create the drama that tent preaching required. Then, in a quick motion, he waved his hand, like he'd once done, at the taillights. Long ago, when he was somebody, one wave of the hand would make people fall over and start mumbling gibberish. But this time, nothing happened.

# Thirty-Five

# LOUISVILLE

**★ ★ ★**

Vern brought a load of leaves into the barn and laid them in neat piles. The women came behind him, carrying leaves in their carts. They sang while they worked. It reminded Paul of his mother, who used to sing made-up songs when she worked cotton fields.

An elderly, dark-skinned woman came with a wheelbarrow. On her way, she was cut off by a screaming toddler with no pants on. The toddler's name was Baker.

*"Aaaaaahhhh!"* said Baker, which represented every word he knew.

It had been a monumental day when Baker took his first steps. The whole farm knew about it.

"Careful," said Paul to the screaming child.

*"Baah aahh aahhhh,"* said Baker.

"Watch out for people. You gonna run into someone."

*"Aaaah."* Then Baker paused and made a face. It was a serious face, accompanied by a few grunts.

"I got better things to do than be watching a young'un mess in his pants," Paul said. He stabbed the fire from where he sat. "Go find your mama, Baker."

*"Aaaah baah aaaah."*

"Make sure you tell her you have a present for her."

Baker ran out of the barn, a child on a mission.

Above Paul, the tobacco strings hung from the rafters like vampire bats. The smoke from Paul's smoldering fire rose through the leaves, then out through the tin-metal chimney gap in the roof. Rows upon rows of leaves dried above the fire Paul was tending.

Paul's job was one of the most important on the whole farm. If one spark escaped his curing fire, it would cost an entire harvest.

Only months earlier, a drying barn on the Harrison farm had burned to the ground. And after the fire, the Harrison tobacco had no place to be stored. Nearby farm owners bought Mister Harrison's leaves below market price. It was highway robbery, but Paul couldn't think of a man who deserved robbery more than wicked Mister Harrison.

Paul was older than the other workers—though there was one woman who was older than he was. Her name was Chula. Chula strung the wide leaves onto long poles, singing a rhythmic song. Her skin looked like rawhide. She only had three teeth in her smile.

The women sewed leaves onto long pine sticks. Then quick, lean young black men climbed the rafters and hung the pole skewers of leaves in the drying racks above the small fire. It was a glorified dance. Stringing. Singing. Climbing. Stringing. Singing. Climbing.

"Hey, Paul," said Vern from a distance. His baritone voice interrupted Paul from a daze.

"Water, Paul," said Vern. "Lou needs water, quick." His voice was laced with anxiety, and Vern was never anxious.

"What?" said Paul.

"Lou needs water."

Paul exited the barn. He saw Vern carrying the furry black-and-tan body in his arms. Vern walked through long rows of green, keeping the dog close to his chest.

"Get out the way," said Vern to the others. "Out the way." The dog's body lay limp in Vern's arms, lanky limbs swaying with each step.

Paul felt his chest tighten. He'd known a moment like this was coming—for a long time, he'd known. But the old girl just kept on living and defying the odds of her species.

He pushed back tears. He touched Louisville's face. The old girl was panting. Her tongue was out of her mouth. Her chest moved in rapid rhythm.

"What happened?" asked Paul.

"Found her behind the tractor, panting. She didn't look right. Reckon she needs water."

This was beyond the remedy of water. Paul touched the soft fur between Louisville's eyes. Her old, almond-colored eyes were tired. He could see weariness in them.

Vern laid the animal down before the old man who had bred and raised her. Who remembered the September morning when her mother had deposited her into this world. Who remembered when she first learned to use her throaty voice.

She'd been born during the height of happiness. Long before the hard times ever hit the world. And she had lived longer than any dog Paul had ever known.

She opened her eyes to look at Paul. He stroked her snout and said, "Oh, honey."

He closed his eyes and remembered the day he held the black-and-tan puppy in his arms. He remembered how this animal used to sleep on the pillow beside his head at night when she was still growing into herself. He remembered the moments when she peed on him. The times he would bury his face into the soft skin of her neck. He remembered how he used to hold her in his lap, even when she was a full-grown animal who believed she was a puppy.

Louisville rested her head against Paul. Paul sat beside her and lifted her body into his lap. Louisville curled her long, lanky body into a ball and breathed like a freighter.

A man wandered in from the field and said, "Could be tobacco poisoning? I seen a dog eat tobacco before."

"No," said Paul. "She's too smart to eat that stuff."

"She's a dog," the man said with a chuckle. "Dogs do all sortsa stupid things."

"Not her," Paul said.

Pete came running toward Paul with his hat in his hands. "What's happening, Paul?"

"She's sick," Paul said in a half whisper.

Vern said, "She's a tough old girl. She be alright."

Louisville coughed, then panted again. She leaned her head into Paul and labored for air.

"Take her into the woods," said another man. "That's what I'd do with an old dog like her. Fast and easy."

"No, sir," said Paul with a smile. "This is my girlfriend. I'd never do something like that to my best girl."

"Just how we did things on the farm," said the man.

"Congratulations," Paul said. "You must be proud."

The onlookers went back to work. Vern sat on the ground beside Paul. Pete did the same. They all touched Louisville and spoke in a whisper so quiet that nobody could hear what they said. Paul kissed Louisville on the face and held her long, floppy ears. There were few things he loved more in this life than her ears.

He held the animal until the sun dipped low behind the trees and all the children had gone to bed. He held her until Pete and Vern had fallen asleep. He held her until she exhaled a loud, whimpering breath and her body became soft. He held her until he felt the pulse inside her stop.

Paul looked at the night sky and cried. His crying turned into a deep moan. He could hear the strained sounds of his own throat. In some ways, his voice sounded like baying. He cried until the sun came up. And then some.

She was a good girl.

## Thirty-Six

# THE LAME

★ ★ ★

Marigold washed bedsheets in the large washtub. She scrubbed them until her knuckles were red. Laundry was how she spent her life at Cowikee's. She cooked, she cleaned, and she washed things. Hers was the only occupation at Cowikee's that didn't involve what the other girls referred to as "doing business."

Marigold scrubbed the white fabric against the metal ribs of the washboard, then wrung it out. She draped it on a string between two tall pines along with a collection of delicates, nylons, and silky clothing.

Helen sat on the porch, watching her. "Pregnant," said Helen. She pushed a chestful of blue cigarette smoke into the air. "Don't even know what to expect. I don't know many mothers."

"Sickness," said Marigold. "*That's* what you can expect. Lots of it. But it goes away, sorta."

Helen chuckled. "How would you know?"

"I know."

"You ain't that old. How could you know?"

"I'm older than I look."

"You had a baby?"

"I have a baby."

Helen said nothing, she only took another drag from her cigarette and held it in. "I'm a lot older than you," she finally said.

"You're young enough to be pregnant."

"Pregnant. I hate this baby already."

Her words didn't fall well on Marigold's ears. Marigold remembered when her mother took her to the preacher in the woods, once she learned Marigold was with child. The man in black had touched Marigold's belly, squeezed her skin, and uttered odd prayers about sinful babies.

Her mother wanted the pregnancy to be over. She wanted the child to disappear, wanted to pretend it had never happened. But Marigold did not. She loved her Maggie, even before she could feel her.

The preacher rebuked the "sinful child" inside her and prayed against it. He sent Marigold away with the words, "Go and sin no more, child." They were words that never left her, because they were all wrong somehow.

"I hate it," Helen went on. "I wish it would just go away."

"Don't say things like that. It ain't good for the baby."

Helen laughed. "Well, I don't care. I don't want this child, and I ain't gonna keep it."

"You're not serious."

"'Course I am. I never asked for a child."

"You don't mean you're going to go and . . ."

"Ladies in my line of work don't raise young'uns, sweetie. Ain't the place for 'em. I don't know what other choice there is."

"You could change your line of work."

"Change? I'm too late for changes."

"You can do something else."

"Are you out of your mind? Men can't find enough work to feed their families, and they actually got trades they can claim. My only trade is sin, sweetie."

"You could start a new life. We could do it together. Two people is better than one. We could do something new, go somewhere else."

"I am what I am, honey. That's how it works. People are what they are. You don't get second chances."

"But maybe you *are* something else, and you just don't know it. Maybe this ain't you."

"You've lost your mind."

"Maybe you were meant to be something more. Maybe I am too, and we just don't know it. Maybe somewhere down inside us there's more."

"I wish you could hear yourself. This is crazy talk."

Marigold suddenly felt foolish for saying such things to deaf ears. She twisted the water from a pillowcase and watched the foam make swirling designs in the water. Even so, she knew there truly was something inside her that was waiting to get out. She couldn't put her finger on it, but she felt it.

Helen lit another cigarette. "How about we talk about what's for supper tonight? I could eat a horse."

But Marigold was too lost looking at suds in the washtub. The white foam made pretty shapes in the tin basin of gray water.

Helen called from the porch, "Hey! You hear me?"

But Marigold wasn't listening. She was thinking of Maggie. Always Maggie. She was wondering about the way Maggie talked. Could she talk? Could she walk? Was she alive?

Marigold was interrupted from her thoughts by a vehicle engine. A red car with chrome fenders and white tires pulled beside the porch. The car rolled toward the railcar slowly in the dusty driveway. The door opened. A man crawled out and stepped onto the porch. He was short, gray-haired. He stopped and paid a glance toward Marigold, then tipped his hat. He leaned forward and walked with an uneven gait. His limp was pronounced, his posture crooked.

"Evening, ladies," he said.

Helen stamped out her cigarette. "Evening," she said.

The man removed his hat and twisted it in his hands. He couldn't seem to get words out. Marigold had seen this same look on most of the men who visited Cowikee's railcar. Some were too timid to say what needed to be said.

"Y-y-you see," he began. "I-I-I'm here because . . ."

Helen laughed. "Yeah, I know *why* you're here. But we're closed for business. Come back later."

He replaced his hat and spun on his heel. He tipped his brim to Marigold again and started to walk away. He opened his door and crawled inside his car with great effort. Marigold watched him struggle to swing his legs into the vehicle. She heard him moan.

Marigold said, "Wait."

He stopped, rested his head against his seat, panted.

"What's wrong with your legs?" she asked.

"Ain't my legs," he said. "It's my back."

"What's the matter with it?"

"Bifida. Only looks worse than it is. Just takes me a little while to get going."

"Does it hurt?"

"It never *quits* hurting."

"What's bifida?"

"A fancy word that doctors say."

"How did you get it?"

"My daddy gave it to me as a gift." He pinched the bridge of his nose and chuckled. "I was born with it."

Marigold felt something building in her chest, a buzzing inside her that made her head feel light. She almost felt as though she could see through this man somehow. Not inside him, but just beyond him. And the world changed around her. The sounds of the earth faded into nothing, and it was only her and this man, standing in a large, open place. No trees, no grass, no sky, no birds, no railcar.

She could see that he was a sad man. A man without a wife and alone, living in a large green house with white shutters. She knew he struggled to put on his clothes. She knew he ate his supper in loneliness each night. She didn't know how she knew these things, but she knew them just the same.

"I wanna help you."

The man wore a strange look. "I appreciate that, darling."

"I mean it. I wanna help."

"Help me do what?"

"I wanna make your back better."

He furrowed his brow.

"Let her," said Helen, who was standing on the porch, leaning on the railing. "Let her try."

The man removed a handkerchief from his pocket and wiped his face. He started to laugh. "Just what in the heavens is all this?"

"I just want to touch it," Marigold said. "I won't hurt you."

"Now just wait a minute, darling," he said.

"I promise." She inched closer to him. "I just wanna touch it."

The buzzing in her head and chest became so strong she could not feel anything but the vibration of it. Her hands became so hot she could hardly bear the pain of it. She touched him and could feel the muscles in his back popping beneath the skin. He let out a grunt, then a sigh. And it happened. He tensed his muscles and forced himself straight. His spine became erect. His shoulders aligned. His neck was no longer hunched forward.

She stepped back from him. The buzzing in her had stopped. Her hands were cold again. She fell to her knees. An exhaustion overwhelmed her, and she found it hard to breathe.

"Go," said Marigold. "And sin no more."

# Thirty-Seven

# HIGHWAYMAN

★ ★ ★

Pete drove on a dusty highway, following behind Paul's truck. They were moving again. That last time they'd been on the move, he'd been a boy. But now he was a fourteen-year-old, and that was practically the same as being an adult. His mother slept in the passenger seat. The vehicles loped along short hills, weaving through the countryside like a wagon train.

Thus far, autumn had stolen too much from them. One dog and one steady job. The tobacco farm had all but dried up since the war began. And now it was working its devilry on his mother, who didn't seem capable of doing anything but coughing and sleeping. Eulah had developed a cough that had been with her for six months and only grown worse.

He draped his arm out the window. The whole world was dried and faded. The grass was gold; the trees were changing colors. Pete's mother rested her head against the window. Her eyes were shut. She breathed softly. He could hear her wheezing. Sometimes during her sleep she coughed so hard she couldn't breathe. She was getting too lean for her frame. Her skin was paler. Her body was weaker.

Pete squinted through the windshield. The pollen on the glass was so bad he could hardly see. So much yellow dust filled the air, it was obscene. The large sheets of yellow fell from the sky like an eerie rain. Some people were allergic to the dust. Others could breathe it in with no problems. But it didn't seem to bother Pete, Reese, or Ruth. It crippled his mother.

Eulah coughed again but did not wake up.

Pete held one hand steady on the wheel, the other on his mother. He didn't know where Paul was driving—Paul hadn't discussed it with anyone. But ever since Louisville died, Paul had become a different man. He didn't do much discussing.

Pete hit a bump in the highway that lifted him off his seat. Eulah shifted. She rested her hand on Pete's hand.

The bumps on the highway were many. The old vehicles seemed as though they would rattle apart.

When the tobacco harvest ended, Mister Pettigrew had announced that he would be selling his farm and moving to Georgia. These difficult times were getting worse with each coming year. Money was a myth, Pete sometimes thought. He hardly ever saw any, but the world seemed to run on the stuff. The newspapers only talked about war and about Germany and Hitler. Not the hard times. But the hard times hadn't gone anywhere, no matter what the papers said. Farms were collapsing. Families were falling apart. Children were going to bed hungry.

They left early in the morning. They drove all day, all night, and all day again.

Reese leaned forward and whispered, "Is Mama okay?"

Pete touched his mother. She was cold to the touch. She slept with two blankets draped over her. She coughed, and every muscle in her neck showed through the skin. The coughing woke her.

"Go back to sleep," said Pete.

"Pete," she said with a faint grin. "Pete, you okay?"

"I'm good, Mama."

"You are a good boy, Pete. A very good boy." Then she fell back into a deep sleep.

*Thirty-Eight*

# MIDDLE OF NOWHERE

✦ ✦ ✦

It was late. Even the crickets had gone to bed. There were no sounds in the cold woods that night. Marigold and Helen stepped out of the car and heard their feet crunch on the gravel beneath them. The barn stood in the distance, tall, weathered, sheltered by pines. You could hardly see the place until you got close enough to touch it.

"Are you sure this is it?" said Marigold.

Helen pulled her coat tighter. "This is it."

They walked toward the ugly barn and knocked on the door. It made a booming sound. There was no answer. Helen pounded her fist against the door again.

"Do you think he's here?" said Marigold.

"Oh, he's here."

Then it started to rain. First small drops, then fat drops. In only a few moments, the rain was coming down hard, landing on their shoulders and wetting the fabric of their clothes.

A muffled voice came from inside the barn, shouting over the sound of the rain. "State your business."

Helen removed a folded piece of paper from her pocket and read it aloud: "'Tis I, be not afraid, though dark the day, duty laid . . .'" She stopped reading and stared at the door.

There was a long pause. Finally the voice answered, "You have to finish the whole thing."

Helen rolled her eyes and read through the words quickly. "'Duty laid, drives fear away, safe by the Lord I stand. Amen.'"

The big door opened with a creaking sound and shot spears of orange light into the woods. Behind the door was a short man with thick eyeglasses.

The man observed Marigold with squinty eyes. Then he smiled his few teeth at her. "You're the lady healer."

Marigold didn't answer him. She only directed her gaze to the floor.

"Heard what you did, straightening Bill Lorman's back. I went to school with Bill. He's been crooked his whole life. No doctors could help him."

Ever since claims of the healing had spread, people had been visiting the railcar for Marigold's touch. She obliged them, though she wasn't sure why. Sometimes her hands got hot and people got what they were looking for. Other times nothing happened.

"My cousin came to see you about his daughter's skin problem," the man said. "Said it went away in two days flat." Then he looked both directions and reduced his voice to a whisper. "What in tarnation are you doing *here*?"

"What do you think we're doing here, Dale?" said Helen, stepping forward.

He pointed toward Marigold's belly. "You . . . you mean you're . . ."

"No," said Helen. "Not her. Me. And I'm getting cold waiting out here. Now c'mon, let's hurry this thing up."

They followed him into a plain wooden room with sawdust on the floor. It was a terrible room, where terrible things happened. Marigold could feel this.

On the other side of the room was a man. He had slicked hair and sat in an easy chair, reading a newspaper. A table lamp sat beside him. He didn't lower his paper but only said in a clear voice, "Get their money up front, Dale."

The small man held out his hand. "You can pay me, ladies."

Helen dug into her jacket and removed a wad of bills the size of a baseball. The small man counted it and whispered, "My cousin says her skin problem just up and disappeared. She's had it ever since she was a toddler. Now it's gone."

"Well, hallelujah, brother," said Helen. "Can we hurry this up?"

The small man showed the women to a private room. He handed Helen a white nightgown that was open in the back.

"What am I supposed to do with this?" she asked the man.

"Put it on." Then he left the room.

"Helen," said Marigold. "I don't like this place."

"Oh, pipe down," said Helen.

"I'm serious, Helen."

"Aw, hush. Doc Maler does all the uppity girls in town. You wouldn't even believe how many girls visit this place if I told you."

"I don't care. We shouldn't be here."

Marigold was getting sick inside. She remembered how it felt to have Maggie in her belly. A weighty sensation beneath the heart and ribs.

"We've got to go," said Marigold. "I have a bad feeling here."

Helen looked at her. "What's wrong with you?"

"I feel something . . . something . . . in my belly."

"What?"

"We should go, Helen, now."

"Would you hush? You're starting to give me the willies."

Marigold drew in a breath and closed her eyes. She tried to steady her nerves and forget about the sharp sting in her belly, but instead she felt like she was about to lose her insides. Her head started aching. Her ears started ringing.

"Helen," said Marigold. "This is a mistake. If you don't leave this place, Helen, you'll . . . you'll . . ."

"I'll what?"

Marigold couldn't bring herself to say more.

"You can't be serious," said Helen.

"Please, let's just go, right now, and go far away from here."

"Don't be silly, not after we drove all this way."

The small man knocked on the door. He said, "Doc will see you now."

Helen removed her jacket and handed it to Marigold. "Now quit being ridiculous and help me change."

But Marigold lurched forward. A burning in her gut became so hot she didn't know if she would survive it. The pain brought Marigold to her knees.

"What's happening to me!" screamed Marigold. She hollered loud enough to rattle the roof.

"What on earth is wrong with you?" Helen shouted.

The small man rushed into the room. "What's wrong with this girl?" he said.

"I don't know."

Helen shouted again, "What's the matter with you?"

Marigold closed her eyes tight and clenched her jaw. She could feel a quick pulse in her head. "It's a boy," she said in a forced whisper. "A pretty boy."

"What on earth are you talking about?" said Helen.

"You should see him, Helen. I wish you could see him. He's beautiful."

The room fell silent. The small man approached. He knelt beside Marigold and rested his hand on her back and stroked her shoulders. "You're burning up, sweetheart. Tell us what you see."

Marigold smiled. Eyes still closed. "I see him."

# Thirty-Nine

# BAD DECISION

\* ⭐ \*

Coot lay in bed, staring at the ceiling. It was early morning, and the sun wasn't up yet. The world was still lit by the moon. He crawled out of bed, threw on his clothes, wandered down to the kitchen, and placed a pot of coffee on the stove. He rubbed his eyes. He stretched and looked out the window. It was dark. And bitter cold. It would be a long day at work.

When he looked out his window, he saw a shape sitting on a bench. He knew who it was even though her hair was over her face and her face was in her hands. He had to rub his eyes to make sure he wasn't seeing things.

He opened the screen door on the back porch, careful not to let it slap shut. "Judy," he whispered. "Judy, is that you?"

The quiet sobbing coming from the silhouette stopped.

"Judy, what's wrong?" He could see his own breath when he said it.

No answer.

He walked near her, barefoot in the ice-hardened grass.

"Go away," she said.

"Are you outta your mind? It's freezing out here."

"Go away, I said."

It crushed him. He almost turned around and left, but he thought better of it. He sat beside her on the bench. He could sense that she wished he hadn't. This made him hurt. She was good at hurting him. He loved this girl, even though she usually made him feel like a bumbling fool.

She was freezing, shivering from the cold. He scooted close to her and held her near him to warm her.

"What's the matter?" he asked.

She sighed at him. "You wouldn't understand, Coot."

There was vinegar in her voice. He felt like a child beside her, even though she was three years younger than he was. She sat staring into the coldness. Her posture told him she wanted him gone, but she was too cold to do anything about it. So they listened to the sounds of the earth.

"Maybe I would understand," Coot said.

"You ever been in love?" she asked.

Coot was so grateful for a sincere question from her, he almost sang a hymn. "Sure I have."

"Really?"

"Yeah. Lotsa times," he lied.

And in that moment, Judy seemed to take Coot a little more seriously. She scooted away from him and turned to face him. "You have?"

"Oh sure."

"With who?"

Coot thought to himself about what his next words would be. He rubbed his hands together and thought very hard. It was important not to look like a complete toadstool before a girl like Judy Bronson. He wanted to appear to be a man of the world, a man who knew things.

"Her name was Evelyn," he said.

"Evelyn. That's a pretty name."

"Oh yeah," he said, mustering up the most casual-sounding voice he could. "Old Evelyn, she was a heartbreaker."

"Really?"

"Yep," said Coot. "She was a . . . a . . ." And Coot's mind went blank for a moment. He was caught between his own words without a safety net. He was sinking fast. "A schoolteacher," Coot blurted out. "She was a schoolteacher, and I was in a traveling western show."

Judy frowned. "A *western show*? You?"

He was laying it on pretty thick.

"What'd you do in the show?"

"Twirled a rope, did a few horse tricks." Coot cleared his throat and made his voice a few notes lower. "Sharpshooting."

"Really? You're not just putting me on?"

"Oh no. Would I lie to you?"

Judy sighed, and Coot saw the steam exit her mouth and rise upward. She seemed amused by what he'd told her. They sat in silence, watching the icy sky go from dark blue to purple.

"What happened with the girl?" Judy finally said.

"Who?"

"Evelyn. What happened?"

"Oh, her?" Coot said. "She didn't think I was good enough for her. She came from money, and I was just a lowly calf-roping stranger. We were from two different worlds."

*Lowly calf-roping stranger.* That was a nice touch, he thought.

She was beginning to cry again. Her profile was so lovely she looked like a sculpture in the early daylight. "I know how you musta felt."

Coot kept shoveling. "Yeah, she ended up getting married to a banker out in Greensburg. Broke my heart's what she did. Broke my heart in two."

Judy wiped her face with her hands. Coot felt bad about lying to her, but then, he would've jumped off a shallow bridge headfirst just to get a small shred of her attention.

The weather started to change. Tiny bits of ice began falling from the sky and covering the world. Slivers of it fell in Judy's hair and on her eyelashes.

"He makes me feel like I'm worthless," she said. "Will makes me feel like I'm a—"

But her words were cut off. Judy turned her head away from Coot. She covered her mouth with her hand. She leaned forward and retched, losing the contents of her stomach all over the grass.

And all at once, Coot knew why she had been crying.

She pressed her hand on her stomach. "I love him. I love Will, and he doesn't want me." She rubbed her belly with both hands and closed her eyes. "And now he's messed up my whole life, Coot. My *whole* life."

Coot touched her blonde hair. It was soft. She pressed her face into his shoulder and cried. She ruined his shirt with cold tears and saliva, and he was glad to sacrifice the shirt to her cause.

"He'll never love me back," she said in a voice that was muffled. "He'll never love me back."

Coot knew exactly how she felt.

*Forty*

# COLD, COLD HEARTS

★ ★ ★

It was dark. The service station off the dirt highway was empty. The windows were covered in sleet. The ice was coming from the sky in large sheets. Pete was worried about his mother. She slept so hard that she wasn't moving.

"I love you, Mama," said Pete. He'd been saying this to her as often as he could so that she wouldn't forget it. "I love you, Mama," he said again. But she made no indication she'd heard.

He glanced out the window. The sight of ice had mystified Pete. He'd never seen anything like this before. It fell like shards of crystal, then melted on the windowpanes as though it were only an illusion.

The inside of the filling station was lined with racks of canned goods, boxes, and jars. A cooler in the corner contained sliced meats and hog head souse. There were coolers full of Coca-Cola and Nehi.

Ruth and Reese were bundled in blankets, wearing turbans over their heads. They sat huddled together, their teeth chattering.

"I'm scared, Pete," Ruth said. "What if they find us? We ain't supposed to be in here."

"Aw, don't worry," he said. "Who's gonna find us?"

"*They* could find us."

"Who's *they*?"

"I don't know, but *they* might not be very nice."

"Try not to worry," Pete said.

But the truth was, Pete was worried. They had pulled over at this vacant station late that night. And while Pete was making water on trees behind the garage, he'd heard the sound of glass breaking. Pete had gone running toward the noise only to discover that Paul had broken a window. Then Paul lifted a sleeping Eulah in his arms and announced they would be making camp for the night.

"I'm so cold, Pete," said Ruth, tucking her hands beneath her arms.

"Come here," he said. Pete held Ruth close and felt the coldness of her little body, even through the blanket.

Ruth said, "What if *they* find us?"

"Don't worry. Paul's smarter than all us put together. He won't let nothing happen."

She squeezed him. She was shaking, from either cold or fear.

"Ruth. It'll be alright."

"How do you know?"

"I just know."

"What if it's not alright?"

"Then I'll eat my hat."

"What?"

"You heard me, I'll eat it all up."

She gave a nervous laugh.

Paul whispered to Pete from across the room, "Get over here, all three of you. We gotta put our heat together for your mama. She's freezing."

Everyone came together and made a huddle with blankets and bodies, keeping Eulah in the center. Reese's shoulders were bobbing back and forth. Ruth's teeth were clicking. The only person who didn't seem to be affected by the cold was Vern. He was wearing a T-shirt under his coveralls, nothing more.

"Mama?" said Pete. "How're you doing?"

She only coughed.

"I love you, Mama."

Another cough.

"Your mama's one tough bird," Paul said. "She'll be fine. Don't worry."

Pete could see white flurries catching the moonlight through the window. Reese and Ruth watched too. It was like they were in a fairy tale. Pete had never seen it except in magazines. He'd always thought the illustrations of snow looked beautiful, but on this night the snow wasn't. It seemed terrible somehow.

"Can't we start a fire in the furnace?" said Reese. "For Mama?"

"No," said Ruth. "Because someone might find us."

"Don't need a fire," Paul said. "Your mama's getting warmer with us beside her, just gotta give it time."

"So what if we do get found out?" said Reese. "I'd rather be found than be froze to death."

Eulah coughed. Her coughing gave way to hacking, then choking. It terrified Pete to hear his mother make that sound. Pete wrapped his scarf around Eulah's neck and face. Her eyes began to close, and she seemed as though she were a hundred years old.

"Hey, know what?" Ruth said, breaking the silence. "If Lou were here, she'd be keeping us all warm."

Silence followed this remark.

"No, she wouldn't," said Paul. "Old Lou'd be right in the middle, taking all *our* heat. Selfish thing thought the world circled around her."

Ruth scooted until she was seated in Eulah's lap. Eulah wrapped her arms around her. And everyone became quiet. The only sound heard was sleepy breathing beneath the blankets.

Vern whispered to Paul, "If someone find us, we gonna be in it, deep in it."

"Will they kill us?" added Ruth.

"Hush," said Paul. "Now quit that talk, Vern. You're scaring the young'uns."

"But what if we get caught?" said Vern. "Breaking in like this. You know what they do to black folk out here close to Jay."

"Vern, hush," said Paul. "Quit your worrying and let's try to get some sleep. No use borrowing trouble."

"Good night, Mama," said Reese.

"Night, Miss Eulah," said Vern.

"Good night, Miss Eulah," said Ruth.

Paul kissed Eulah's cheek and whispered, "Rest, sweetie. Just rest."

"I love you, Mama," said Pete.

★

When Paul awoke to the sound of a radio in the service station, it startled him. It was the sound of a preacher hollering, interrupted by crowds cheering. The volume was low but audible. He turned to see Vern in the dark with his ear pressed against a wooden desktop radio.

"What in the world?" Paul said. "Turn that thing off."

Vern looked at the radio and said, "It's J. Wilbur."

"I don't care if it's the king of Siam, turn that thing off. Someone might hear."

Vern clicked off the small radio.

Paul was still holding Eulah's sleeping body. His arms were frozen around her. The rest of the family was still huddled around her too. Paul had been drifting in and out of sleep but fought it for as long as he could.

"Vern," Paul said, "I wish you'd go to sleep. You're worrying me half to death, moving around like you is."

Vern said, "They'll kill me if they find me. Be just like J. Wilbur say, be like judgment come down."

"Nobody's judging nobody, Vern."

"They kill black folks here in Jay. Everybody know that. All dressed in white robes and stuff. They kill them just for coming through town. Hang 'em from a limb."

"Would you hush?"

"If they catch me, I's done."

Eulah coughed so hard it sounded like she ruptured a lung. She shivered beneath the blankets. Paul squeezed her tighter, but she still shook.

"Listen to me, Vern, if we hear so much as a possum fart, just head for that door and get outta dodge. Simple as that."

"Where I go? We's practically in Jay right now. They probably hang me right here. Maybe from that tree."

Vern looked toward the window again and let out a sigh. His eyes looked heavy.

Paul was busy thinking of the next thing he would say but fell asleep by accident. It felt so good to nod off. He was low on sleep. During his short sleep, he managed to forget all about sadness, cold, and starvation. But it was short-lived.

A sound woke him.

It was the noise of Vern adjusting the knob on the radio and the static sound of preaching at a low volume. He could see Vern staring at the glowing radio dial. Paul almost told him to turn it off again.

But then, it *was* J. Wilbur.

★

Paul was startled awake. When he opened his eyes, he heard a sound. A loud sound. A banging. He could see lantern lights outside the front window. He heard the sounds of dogs.

"They gon' kill me," said Vern. His eyes were wide open, his nostrils flared. "They gon' flat kill me."

Paul whispered, "Vern, get outta here."

Paul could see sweat forming on Vern's forehead. The big black man touched his family. He touched sleeping Pete's face and did the same with Ruth and the others.

"Git," said Paul.

"Tell everyone I love 'em, Paul. Tell 'em for me."

"Shut up."

"Please tell 'em."

"Okay, fine, fine, I'll tell 'em. Now go."

Vern walked to the door and wedged his big body into the cold. In only seconds, he was gone. Dogs barked. Men shouted. A gunshot rang out. Then another. Then the place filled with icy air and the sounds of hollering men. Another gunshot echoed.

It sounded like a scattergun. The noises woke the children.

Paul leaned forward and talked straight into Pete's ear. "Anything happens to me, I want you to do something for me."

"What?"

"Go find Vern."

"Huh?"

"That's right. Don't stop looking until you find him. He can't be on his own, not in these parts. They'll kill him if they find him."

"What?"

"Promise me."

"I promise."

The voices got nearer and louder.

"Take everyone to the front of the store," said Paul. "Go wait behind that counter. Keep everyone outta sight, and keep 'em quiet."

Pete did as he was told. Reese, Ruth, and Pete gathered behind the store counter beneath the cigarette and cigar display.

The door smashed in. Boots stomped on floorboards. Guns. Dogs. Shouting. Swearing men. Howling. The dark figures were aiming rifles at Paul, who was covering Eulah. They were screaming for him to move away from the woman.

Hounds made baying noises. One man kicked Paul in the ribs. Then he kicked him in the thigh and jammed a rifle between his shoulder blades.

Paul hollered over the sound of the dogs. "The woman, she's sick."

The man shouted something again, pressing a rifle deeper into Paul's cheek.

"We're friendly!" yelled Paul. "Don't hurt the woman! She's sick!"

But these men were not interested in reasoning. One man crawled atop Paul and tore into him with both fists. Paul could feel the bones in his face being tested.

Then a shot rang out.

Then silence.

The men stood against the wall.

Paul checked his body and felt no wounds. He ran his hands along his shoulders and chest. He looked at Eulah and inspected her body. She was untouched too. Another gun pop.

And another.

"That kid shot me!" shouted one dark figure. "Shot me in the elbow!"

Paul glanced toward the front of the store.

Pete stood strong, pistol pressed against the head of a man with brown curly hair. Pete held the man in a choke hold, gun touching his temple. The man wore big eyes and a terrified face. The other men saw this, dropped their weapons, and raised their hands.

"Who's laughing now?" Pete said.

# Forty-One

# MOTHERS AND DAUGHTERS

★ ★ ★

Marigold touched Helen's belly. The other girls marveled at Helen's round stomach. Over the winter months, Helen had gradually quit participating in the day-to-day activities with men that took place at Cowikee's.

Motherhood, even in its early stages, was changing her. Often she wore happy looks that made her seem twenty years younger than she was. And the lines on her face seemed to disappear too. Her hair had more curl to it. Her skin had a healthy hue. She was new.

Laughing Girl let her Indian eyes rest on Helen. "I have never seen Helen in such good spirits." Laughing Girl's long dark hair was braided behind her in a ponytail that stretched to her knees. She knelt beside Marigold and placed her hands beside Marigold's.

"I'm trying to feel," said Marigold.

"Feel what?" said Laughing Girl.

"I don't know. It's sorta like saying hi."

Laughing Girl concentrated on her own hands. Her long braid coiled itself on the floor beside her. "What happens to your hands?"

A hush fell over the other girls. Marigold guessed they had all wanted to ask this same question but were too afraid.

"I don't know," said Marigold. "I can't control it." She stood and wandered to the furnace. She positioned the wood in the potbelly stove using a stick. The log caught the rising flame and started to pop. It shot sparks outward like fireworks. She shut the iron door and sniffed the scent of fire. The smell of wood was one she liked. The strong odor of pine was one of her favorites.

Laughing Girl didn't press the matter. She only kept her hands on Helen's tummy and closed her eyes. "I cannot feel anything with my hands."

"What's Helen gonna do with a *baby*?" said Rachel.

"Well, she won't stay here," said another girl. "Babies don't belong in places like this."

"She's gonna be happy," said Marigold. "*That's* what she's gonna do with a baby. The rest will just work itself out."

"Well," said one girl, "girls like us weren't meant for birthing babies. I don't think motherhood will suit her."

"Motherhood is not supposed to suit people," said Laughing Girl. "It is a natural thing, like going to the bathroom. Everyone knows how to go to the bathroom."

"That's ridiculous," said Rachel. "How would you know?"

"I just know."

Marigold stood beside the window, watching the snow fall. White tufts drifted toward the ground. All the girls were excited by the snow. It was such a rare and beautiful thing in this part of the world. It had been snowing all winter long, off and on, and it had become a minor obsession among them all.

"You ever seen snow before this winter?" Rachel asked Laughing Girl.

"No," Laughing Girl said. "I have only heard people talk about it."

Another girl said, "I didn't know it was *really* this white."

Helen kept her eyes closed but opened her mouth to speak in a low voice. "This is nothing. In Chattanooga, I seen a blizzard once."

"Chattanooga? You've been to Chattanooga?" Rachel said.

"It is where she came from," said Laughing Girl.

Helen went on. "One Christmas I remember I had to parade around town right through the snow. I was wearing a tasseled dress. We were keeping company with rich men who needed a trophy on their arm."

"Tassels?" Rachel said. "Oh, aren't you lucky."

"Shiny too," said Helen. "With glitter on the chest."

"Never seen a dress made of glitter," Rachel said.

"Neither have I," said Laughing Girl.

"The blizzard kept everyone inside for days. We were miserable."

"I wonder what glitter dresses cost," said Rachel.

"I think I would look good in glitter and tassels," said another.

"I was so young," said Helen.

The girls got quiet.

Marigold touched Helen's stomach again. She closed her eyes. She concentrated on the feelings that moved through her hand, up her arm, and into her heart. And she felt something. She felt the little boy. Smiling.

"There you are," said Marigold.

"You can see him?" said Helen.

"Yep, he's smiling at me."

"Tell him I love him."

"He knows," said Marigold.

# Forty-Two

# THE ROOT OF ALL

* * *

It was midnight. Coot stepped on the shovel. It sank into the soft earth behind the outhouse. Judy stood guard beside the wooden latrine, holding her distended belly.

Over the winter months, Judy had gone from being flat-stomached to fully pregnant. When the spring came, Judy's dresses had become too small on her body and her face had gotten puffy. People began to talk. They called her terrible things, and she'd become a mockery.

A breathtakingly beautiful mockery.

"Couldn't you have picked somewhere *less* disgusting to bury it?" whispered Judy. "I think I'm gonna vomit."

"Disgusting was the whole idea," said Coot.

"Well, hurry up. I can hardly stand the smell. It's making me sick."

"Just tell me if you hear anyone coming."

"I'm nauseous."

"Keep your voice down and keep watching."

Coot didn't remember burying the box so deep, but he was at least three feet into the earth and still saw no sign of it. This worried him. Someone might have stolen the money. He tried not to entertain this idea. He had worked up a sweat from digging. Spring mornings were warm and humid. He removed his shirt so that he was wearing only his undershirt. He dug two more feet downward.

"Geez, how deep did you bury it?" said Judy. "All the way to China?"

He wondered to himself about what he would do once he found the money. Where would they go? What would they do? It was a mixture of excitement and sadness for him. Judy had agreed to let Coot take care of her, but it was only because she had nowhere else to turn. Nobody wanted a woman who carried a bastard. She knew this. He knew this. And it didn't make her love him. He knew that too.

"Wait," she said.

Coot stopped digging.

She held her hand up. "I think someone's coming."

"What?"

She shushed him.

A slamming screen door. Footsteps in the grass. Coot wiped sweat from his dripping forehead and squinted in the dark. It was Danny Terrance, stumbling out the back door, unbuttoning his overalls.

Judy hid behind the outhouse, standing next to Coot, plugging her nose. She kept close to him, pressing her body against his. He held her tight. It was the closest she'd ever been to him.

They heard the sound of Danny fertilizing the grass. He coughed a few times, sniffed, then cleared his nose. Coot noted how very well hydrated Danny Terrance seemed to be. It sounded like he was letting go of the Chattahoochee River.

The stream of water stopped. Then silence.

"Hey, who's out there?" said Danny.

Judy's eyes became big. Coot could see the whites of her eyes in the dark. She pressed a hand over Coot's mouth. "Sshhh," she whispered.

"Hey," said Danny. "I can *hear* you. Who's out here?"

Coot tried to think of something to do, but nothing was coming to mind. He was too preoccupied with the smell of the outhouse.

"Hey," said Danny. "I can see you two out there. Who is that?"

Judy grabbed Coot's hand and led him from behind the outhouse in one swift movement. When they were in Danny's full view, she pulled Coot into her and kissed him right on the mouth. She kissed Coot so hard it felt like his head was going to pop off his neck and drift right into the pearly gates.

It was the first time a woman had ever kissed him.

Coot kept his eyes open. Her eyes were open too. Their noses were smashed together. Behind Judy, he could see Danny in the dark, watching.

Danny let out a single laugh. It was a demeaning laugh. "Don't you have any pride, Coot? That girl's nothing but trouble."

Coot tried to open his mouth to speak, but he was too busy trying to remember whether his name was actually Coot.

Judy answered, "If you keep standing there, watching us like that, I'm gonna charge you admission."

Danny waved them off and walked away, saying, "You could do a lot better, Coot. A lot better."

In a matter of seconds, Coot was holding a shovel and digging again. The blood had rushed into his head and was making his face feel hot. He imagined Judy walking a church aisle, wearing white. He imagined living with her in a cabin on a hill with a family of children running around his feet while he read a Sears and Roebuck catalog, smoking a pipe.

His shovel hit something unforgiving.

"I found it," he said.

He dug the tin box out of the earth with his bare hands. The box was rusted orange and brown. He wedged the lid off using the blade of the shovel. There it was. A roll of cash, tucked inside a rubber hot water bottle, unaffected by the years.

Judy looked at the money with an open mouth. "How much is it?"

"Enough."

"How long have you been hiding this?"

"A long time."

She grabbed the wad of cash and held it in her hands. Her eyes sparkled. Her face was glowing. "Coot, I didn't think you had *this* much. We're rich. Rich."

Coot started filling the hole with dirt. Judy pressed the cash against her chest, even though it soiled her clothes. She held a solemn look. "Sorry if I shocked you earlier," she said. "I mean, kissing you like that . . ."

Coot kept shoveling. His mouth was still numb from the throes of unbridled passion. He was working on a marriage proposal that was eloquent but succinct.

"I just didn't know what else to do, you know?" she went on. "I improvised. That was all."

"It's okay, Judy."

"I mean, it's not like you and I are . . ."

Coot stopped with the shovel and looked at her.

"Coot," she said with sympathy in her voice. "I just don't want you to get the wrong idea. I ain't your girl or nothing."

The quiet passed between them. Coot wanted to crawl into the tiny hole behind the foul-smelling outhouse and live the rest of his days there until he died from the stink.

"'Course I know that," he said.

"Good," she said. "Just as long as you understand."

She turned to walk inside.

She took the box with her.

# Forty-Three

# LOST AND FOUND

✳ ✳ ✳

Paul stood over a mound of dirt holding his hat. He wanted to cry, but he couldn't bring himself to do it. It would've made the girls cry even harder. He wanted them to feel strength, not tears.

Pete was staring at the grave marker. Two sticks of pine, tied together to form a cross. Vern rested his hand on Pete's shoulder. "We all with you, boy. We all with you."

But Pete said nothing. He only stared.

He had become a man in only a few days. It happened to every boy sooner or later. Sooner for some. But never had Paul seen a child do it with such bravery. Pete had defended his family, pistol in his hand. Some men wouldn't be that courageous. Pete had wounded a man, threatened a slew of others, then shot at their car when it sped away. He was a man now.

Vern lowered his head. "We all with you, boy. Say what you got to say."

Pete didn't say a word. So Paul tried to speak for him, but he couldn't find any words either. The tears were building up behind his eyelids, waiting to be freed. He decided to keep his mouth closed so that he didn't fall apart completely. He closed his eyes as tight as he could. Ruth was sobbing. So was Reese. The girls had placed spring bouquets on the mound of soil. Pink, yellow, and white wildflowers, lying in the dirt. The girls had faces that seemed every bit as pure and lovely as the flowers were, too innocent to be burdened with death.

Paul shook his head. "I'm just so mad . . ." But his words got broken in two. His voice was lost. His tears came by the gallon. And soon everyone was coming apart.

Except Pete.

Pete stepped forward. He removed his hat and unfolded a piece of paper from his pocket. He stared at the wooden cross poking up from the ground. Paul had watched the boy spend two hours carving his mother's name into the crossbeam of the grave marker.

Pete cleared his throat. His demonstration of courage was enough to make Paul's chest sore.

> "Can I see another's woe,
> And not be in sorrow too?
> Can I see another's grief,
> And not seek for kind relief?
> Can I see a falling tear,
> And not feel my sorrow's share?
> Can a father see his child
> Weep, nor be with sorrow fill'd?
> Can a mother sit and hear
> An infant groan, an infant fear?
> No, no! never can it be!
> Never, never can it be!
> And can He who smiles on all
> Hear the wren with sorrows small,
> Hear the small bird's grief and care,
> Hear the woes that infants bear,
> And not sit beside the next,
> Pouring pity in their breast,
> And not sit the cradle near,
> Weeping tear on infant's tear,
> And not sit both night and day,
> Wiping all our tears away?
> Oh no! never can it be!
> Never, never can it be!
> He doth give His joy to all;
> He becomes an infant small;
> He becomes a man of woe;
> He doth feel the sorrow too.
> Think not thou canst sigh a sigh,
> And thy Maker is not by;
> Think not thou canst weep a tear,

And thy Maker is not near.
Oh! He gives to us His joy
That our grief He may destroy;
Till our grief is fled and gone
He doth sit by us and moan."

Nobody spoke for several minutes, sniffles and throats clearing the only sounds in the desolate woods.

"She liked that poem," said Pete. Then he folded the paper and placed it at the foot of the grave.

Vern's black cheeks were shiny and wet. His big shoulders bobbed up and down. His crying sounded large and low-pitched. His lower lip trembled.

"She held on long as she could, Pete," said Vern. "Always remember that. She held on long as she could."

Pete wore a numb face. "Yeah."

Vern touched Pete's shoulder. "We all with you, boy."

Reese buried her face in Paul's stomach. Ruth knelt beside the dirt. Pete stood still.

"Hey, Pete," said Vern. "You okay?"

Pete turned to face Vern. The boy's eyes were beginning to fill with water. Pete fell into the big man's arms, and his body became limp. Vern lifted Pete into himself like he was a small child instead of a teenager. Pete's feet dangled high above the ground. His shirttail had risen up to his shoulder blades so that his bare back showed. And Pete screamed into the chest of the great man like a child who was all alone in this world.

"We all with you, boy," said Vern in a soft voice. "We all with you."

*Forty-Four*

# SPRING WILDFLOWERS

\* \* \*

The spring sun was enough to make a person dizzy. The air was crisp, and the sun was hot. The whole world was beginning to bloom, and it made Marigold feel pure excitement.

Marigold gathered flowers near the river. The kingcups were her favorite kind of flower. It was the yellow she liked. Yellow was her color. She didn't know if everyone with the name Marigold chose yellow as their favorite color, but from a young age, she'd felt as though she really had no choice in the matter. If your name was a yellow name, you had to like yellow. She couldn't imagine someone with the name Rose picking green as her favorite color. Or someone with the name Violet preferring beige.

Yellow was easy to like. It reminded her of happy things. And springtime was nothing but yellow. Yellow sun, yellow flowers, and yellow cotton dresses. She liked to pick Cahaba lilies, daisies, and black-eyed Susans.

She'd found a place near the river where a big patch of kingcups grew by the dozen. And she became so excited when she found so many that she stayed for a few hours, just sitting in the tall grass, breathing them in.

People stopped by the railcar at all hours of the day and night to get her to touch them. Men, women, children, and even one man with a hunting dog with a broken back leg. She would touch them all, without discrimination. She would give each of them her complete sincerity. Some people walked away claiming they'd been healed. Others cussed her when it didn't work and called her names. It all left her feeling drained.

Of course, she'd heard the names people called her. People called her the "magic lady" or the "seer." Some people called her a "prophetess," but this was ridiculous. The most often used name was the "harlot healer." It was a cruel name.

Especially since Marigold was only a handmaid to the girls behind Cowikee's and had never entertained a single man in her life.

She walked through the woods, looking at the sky, trying to keep the smell of the flowers in her mind by holding them to her nose now and then. It was going to be a spring like no other. She could feel it. She could feel things stronger than she ever felt them before. It was almost as if something had heightened her senses. She couldn't explain it. She could feel people's moods before they hit. Sometimes she had this strange feeling she knew what people were thinking.

Then a feeling hit her.

The feeling hit her in the chest. It was a throbbing. Then a pulsing. Then a pounding in her face and temples. Her ears started to ring. Her head was swimming with excitement. She dropped the flowers and closed her eyes, touching her forehead. Sweat gathered on her neck, her stomach felt tight, and her legs ached. She was out of breath for no reason.

She bent to gather her flowers, but the ringing in her ears got stronger so that she couldn't bear it.

She knew what was happening.

"Helen," she said.

Joy swept over her. She leapt to her feet and jogged through the brush and the straight pines. She left her flowers behind and made her way through undergrowth, fallen logs, and hanging vines. She ran so hard it felt like her heart was going to split.

When she neared the railcar, there were customers on the porch, standing in a clot. The group of gawkers had gathered near Helen's door. Rachel cut through the men, making her way toward the water pump with a bucket in her hand.

When Rachel saw Marigold, she started crying. "It's Helen," Rachel said. "Something's wrong."

"Let me through," said Marigold.

She muscled her way through the men. She saw Helen lying on her bed, a puddle of blood beneath her.

"Marigold," said Helen, who was panting. "Help me."

# Forty-Five

# O LITTLE CHILD

**✷ ✷ ✷**

"Call a doctor," Marigold told Rachel.

"Doctor won't do nothing for us," Helen shouted.

"'Course he will. I'll just send Rachel into town and call him. Rachel, don't forget to tell him about all the blood."

"Can't," said Helen. "He won't come."

"What?"

"He's a Baptist deacon. We tried calling him for Chelsea's broken ankle and he wouldn't come."

"What do you mean he wouldn't come?"

"He just told us to leave him alone."

"We need a doctor," said Marigold.

"We don't need no *stupid* doctor," cried Helen.

"Yes, we do."

"It's too late for doctors," said Rachel. "You're gonna have to do it, Marigold."

"Why me?"

"Because you are the only one who has ever had a baby," said Laughing Girl.

"Fine, then get more towels!"

"Okay."

"And another pillow!"

"Right."

"And blankets."

"Should she be drunk for this?" said Laughing Girl. "My mother was very drunk when she had me. She told me it was her first time being drunk, and my first time too."

Helen let out a high-pitched scream. More blood was gathering beneath her.

"I can't do this!" said Marigold. "I need a doctor or somebody."

"Look, he's coming!" Rachel hollered, pointing.

Marigold started to fall apart. She almost passed out when she saw the top of the little head.

Laughing Girl covered her mouth. "He's never gonna fit."

Marigold pushed Laughing Girl out of the way. "Get me some more towels."

Then Helen touched Marigold's hand. "What's happening to me, Marigold?" she said.

"I don't know. Just hang on, you're gonna be okay," Marigold said.

"I'm scared, Marigold."

"Don't be, but I need you to push or that baby's not going anywhere."

"I can't," said Helen. "I don't have the strength."

"I see the head," said Laughing Girl. "Should I be doing something?"

"Is she supposed to bleed this much?" said Rachel.

Helen moaned. Her moaning was replaced with screaming. Her face became red, and the veins in her forehead were showing. Marigold saw more of the head make its appearance.

"More towels, I said!"

"That's a whole lot of blood," said Rachel.

Helen grunted. "Marigold, what's happening to me?"

"You're having a baby, now push." Marigold pressed her hand on Helen's shoulder and said, "Push, Helen!"

Helen locked her jaw and grunted. She sat forward and squeezed Marigold's hand so hard it made her bones hurt.

"That's too much blood," said Rachel.

Marigold hollered, "Keep pushing!"

"Push, Helen," said Rachel.

"Push," said Laughing Girl.

"Push!" screamed Helen.

Marigold saw men customers peeking in through the windows. Five or six heads piled together. "Get away from there," she hollered. "Rachel, go close the curtains."

Helen touched Marigold on the forearm and said, "I can't do it, Marigold. I can't." She began to cry. "I think he's stuck."

Marigold steadied her breathing. Her eyelids fell gently, and she let all sound fade into nothingness. She rested her hands on Helen's belly. She concentrated on her palms. She concentrated on the baby. She concentrated on her own breath.

She felt herself float high above the room and drift above the rooftops, above the forest, and above the bay. And in a few moments, she saw herself in an open field. There were no trees to interrupt the flatness of it, just miles of gold grass. And she saw in the distance a small girl with red hair, staring at her. The girl wore a yellow dress. She raised her hand in greeting when she saw Marigold. She wanted to run closer to the girl and get a better look at her. But she was pulled from this place by the loud sound of Rachel's voice.

"Marigold!" said Rachel. "Your hands! What's happening to your hands?"

Marigold opened her eyes. The skin on the backs of her hands had become so white it was translucent. Blue veins showed through, and so did muscle and bone. Her hands were numb with heat. The skin of Helen's tight stomach also became translucent. A collection of tiny pink blood vessels began to show through the surface, along with marbled muscles.

"What's happening?" shouted Rachel.

Laughing Girl yelled, "You are doing good, Helen!"

"Push!" said another.

"Here he comes, Helen."

Helen howled. Her cheeks and forehead turned purple.

"Keep going, Helen!"

"You're doing good, Helen!"

"That's it, Helen!"

Helen let out low bellows.

"Almost there!"

"One more good push, Helen."

"You can do it, Helen."

Helen gave it all she had. And after one final scream, her body went limp. Next came the sound of tiny lungs crying. It was a boy, lanky and long.

The girls clapped. A man's muffled voice came through the window. "What is it? What'd she have?"

"It's a boy!" shouted Rachel. "She had a boy!"

"Hallelujah!" shouted another male voice. Whooping and hollering were heard on the porch.

Marigold whispered in Helen's ear, "You did it, Helen."

Helen's eyes were lazy, and she was slick with sweat. "Let me see him. I wanna see him."

Marigold handed the baby to her.

Helen's face was covered with exhaustion and pride. "I want you to touch him, Marigold," she said in a weak voice. "I want you to bless him with your . . . your hands."

Marigold took the child from Helen. She held the child against her and remembered the way she'd once held Maggie. She placed her hand around his little head and felt the softness of his skin. And in a moment, Marigold's entire body was ignited with the feeling of infant joy. It was as though she were drawing her first human breaths right along with the baby.

Then she handed Helen the child again, wrapped in a blanket.

"See?" said Helen. "Piece of cake. I told you we didn't need no stupid doctor."

## Forty-Six

# JUDY BRONSON

★ ★ ★

It was late. The train depot was empty. There were no families waiting on the large wooden platform, only one old woman with a shawl and a large suitcase. The frogs were out. So were the stars.

Judy held Coot's arm tight. This confused Coot. He wasn't sure why she was being so affectionate, but he didn't question it. He didn't want to. She was too easy to love.

Coot sat on a bench with Judy beside him. He wore his only pair of trousers and a linen shirt. Beside him was his leather bag. And it reminded him of the bus trip that had brought him to Alabama long ago. Just thinking about it made him feel both anger and warmth toward Blake.

Also beside him was Judy's suitcase. It was a heavy case. She had stuffed so many clothes inside it that she had to sit on it just so Coot could latch it shut.

Coot had bought two tickets to Atlanta. He paid six dollars per ticket. Atlanta seemed like a good place to go. There was supposed to be good work in Atlanta, he had heard.

Coot leaned against the wall. He waited in silence, watching the cotton field in the distance.

Judy kept glancing at a large clock overhead. Coot noticed her eyes darting to it, then to him. The clock. Then him. The clock. Then him.

"Why are you so nervous?" he asked her.

She patted his hand. "I just don't like trains."

"You ever been to Atlanta?" said Coot. "I heard it's huge."

She didn't answer. She only checked the clock again.

"Heard they got jobs everywhere," he went on.

Coot let his eyes drift to the cotton field across the railroad tracks again. The field was almost pure white in the moonlight. He thought about what it would be like to grow old with a woman who didn't love him. He wondered if he would ever be able to make her feel something for him.

"What about Will?" Coot asked. "Did you tell him you were leaving?" No sooner had the words exited his mouth than he was sorry he said them.

"Yeah, I told him. But far as I'm concerned, he's dead to me." Judy cut her eyes to the clock again. "I ain't gonna grovel for no man."

The sound of frogs broke the stillness in the air. There must've been a billion of them singing together. It was a wonderful sound, Coot thought. He looked at the old woman on the platform. He smiled. She did not smile at him.

Finally Judy stood abruptly. She said, "You know, I don't feel so good, Coot."

"Huh?"

"I'm sick."

"Sick? You were fine two seconds ago, honey."

She made a face. "Please don't call me that. I don't feel good. Come with me to the restroom, Coot."

He hooked her arm around his. She guided him across the empty platform. The old woman in the shawl watched them pass.

They reached the side of the building. The entire side of the depot was dark where lantern light didn't reach. Coot could see the silhouettes of the outhouses in the distance. But Judy wasn't walking toward them. She was standing still, glancing in all directions. Uneasy.

"Why're you stopping?" Coot asked. "The outhouses are over there."

Judy didn't answer.

A train whistle squealed in the distance. A small white light was miles away, getting bigger. Coot felt the vibration that went with the whistle. "C'mon, Judy, we gotta hurry. You can use the bathroom on the train—"

Something smashed against Coot's head. He heard something in his face break. He fell backward on the dirt. Something hit him again.

Judy screamed, "You idiot, don't kill him!"

Warm blood came out of Coot's nose and ran all over his face. He squinted his eyes and saw the figure of a man in the moonlight. He saw dimples. Coot moaned, "Baby Joe?"

"Sorry, Coot," said Baby Joe, tossing a baseball bat onto the ground. "But if you try anything, I'll have to kill ya, buddy."

"Baby Joe, what are you—"

"Just shut up, Coot. This'll be a lot easier if you shut up."

Then Baby Joe opened Coot's bag and fumbled through the clothes. He took the tin box in his hands and weighed it. He smiled and said, "Pleasure doing business with you, Preacher."

Judy said, "We gotta hurry, Joe. Train's almost here."

"Baby Joe, what are you doing?"

"Nothing personal, Coot. This is just business." Then he took Judy's hand and started to leave.

Judy stopped him. "Joe, he's got more money in his sock."

"He does, does he?"

Baby Joe removed Coot's shoes and socks and said, "Jeez, Preacher, wash your feet once in a while, would ya?" Then cackled.

The approaching train was shaking the earth beneath Coot's back.

"C'mon," Judy hollered over the vibration.

Baby Joe nudged Coot's limp body with his boot. He whispered to Judy, "Should I break his legs or something?"

"No, don't be crazy."

"But what if he chases us? He's a lot bigger than me."

"He ain't gonna chase us," said Judy. "Just look at him."

"But what if he does?"

"He wouldn't hurt a flea," said Judy. "Just leave him."

Baby Joe squatted low and whispered in Coot's ear, "You come after me and I'll cut you up good, you hear me? I mean it."

Coot was too dazed to answer.

The loud train hisses filled the air. They were so loud they drowned out all thoughts in Coot's wounded mind. For a moment it seemed as though the end of the world was happening. Armageddon. That's what this was. He'd preached about it when he was a boy, but he'd never actually believed in it. Now he did. He looked through blurry eyes at the figures of Baby Joe and Judy standing over him.

Baby Joe slapped Coot's face. "Answer me, Coot. Don't make me break your legs. Tell me you understand."

Coot couldn't answer.

Baby Joe slapped Coot's cheeks again. "C'mon, Coot, answer. I don't wanna hurt you, Preacher. Gimme your word you won't come after me."

"Baby Joe," said Coot, using all the strength he had. "Take good care of her."

*Forty-Seven*

# SAD FACES

\* \* \*

The truck was traveling slow down a long dirt road, leaving swirls of dust behind them. Ruth scooted closer beside Pete. She watched the trees shoot into the distance behind the truck. She rested her head on Pete's shoulder. She didn't know what it was like to lose your mother, but she knew what it was like not to have one.

"Wonder why they call farmworkers farm*hands*," Ruth said to Pete, who was sitting beside her in the bed of the moving truck.

Pete didn't answer.

"You know," Ruth went on. "Why not legs, or feet, or backs?"

Vern answered, "Just what they called."

"Hands?" she said again. "I think it should be farm *legs*. Seems to me men use their legs more on the farm than their hands."

Pete wore his cowboy hat low on his head so that his eyes were pretty much covered. He wasn't responding to anything she said. Reese sat on his other side, wearing the same face. Ruth felt alone without their personalities to keep her company.

She'd wondered about her own mother. Sometimes she would lie in her bed and think so hard about her mother she would dream about her. They were always short dreams. Ruth would be standing in a large hayfield or a meadow of flowers, and she would see a woman in the distance, backlit by the sun so that she could only see the woman's dark shape. But she always knew who the woman was, and when the dream ended, she always woke with the same sadness Pete and Reese were feeling.

They were so sad it was making the whole world sad. Ruth didn't like to see them like this. Especially Pete. She loved him more than anything in the entire world. Even though he was much older than she was, she'd never seen a handsomer or more wonderful boy than him. Not in all her life.

And he was hurting so badly she could practically taste it. She didn't like to see things hurt. Especially not boys like Pete who had perfect little noses and sweetheart eyes. She touched his hand and he let her. It sent a surge through her. His was a heavy pain that she could feel.

Ruth felt things more strongly than most people. She knew this about herself. Once, she'd found a dead turtle in the highway, and she almost collapsed from anguish. The shell was crushed and its insides were showing. It bothered her so badly she figured she'd take it off the highway and give it a good funeral. She scooped up the turtle with a shovel and buried it beneath a pine tree. She visited the turtle's grave often and left flowers for it. She must've been the only girl in the world who adopted a pet turtle after he was already dead.

Paul finally pulled the truck over. He turned off the engine. Ruth stood in the truck bed to see where they were. She'd been looking so hard at Pete, and his wonderful little nose, she hadn't even seen where Paul was taking them.

It was a farm, deep in the country. Trees were everywhere. A creek ran in front of an old farmhouse. There were barns, sheds, pens of goats, chickens, hogs, and even a few horses.

Paul said, "C'mon, young'uns," like he was calling dogs.

"What're we doing here?" asked Reese.

Paul lifted Reese from the truck and said, "We're begging for work, sweetie."

"Are we gonna be *hands*?" said Ruth.

"God willing," he said.

Pete and Ruth jumped off the tailgate. They walked toward the farmhouse in the distance. Vern followed behind. They stepped onto the porch of a clapboard house that looked like it had seen better days. The paint was flaking from the sideboards, which were rotting in some places. The porch was crooked and leaning sideways.

Ruth got lost in the view from the porch. It was so wide and open that she couldn't even keep her face sad like Paul had reminded the kids to do. She was too excited to see so much prairie and so much sky all in one place.

"Pete," Paul said, tapping the boy's shoulder. "Take off your hat, son."

Pete removed his tall hat and held it in his hands against his belly. Vern and Paul did the same. They stood in a group before the faded front door like they were posing for a picture. Paul moved the three children in front; he and Vern stood behind them.

"Remember," Paul whispered to the kids, "sad faces, *really* sad."

"Like this, Paul?" said Reese.

"Not that sad, darling, we don't want her to think we're dying from the flu. Just starving." Then he snapped his fingers at Ruth. "Ruth, honey, you even paying attention?"

Ruth was too busy taking in the view to make her face droop.

"Ruth," said Paul. "Make your face sad."

So Ruth frowned as hard as she could until her cheeks hurt and the muscles in her neck tensed and her lower teeth were showing. This was what she often referred to as her "pooping face."

"Cut that out," said Paul. "You look like you need wheat bran, for crying out loud."

Ruth grinned so big that her whole mouth showed and her eyes squinted.

"Would you knock it off?" said Paul. "This is serious. We need this job. Now think of something sad or go back to the truck."

Ruth let her face relax. She held Pete's hand. His sadness hit her hard, and she wished she could take it away from him.

"Alright," said Paul. "Everybody ready?"

Paul stepped forward and knocked on the door. Then he took his place behind the kids again. "Remember," Paul said, "you're hungry and sad."

A woman answered the door. She was tall, gray-haired, and sophisticated. Her hair was pulled back in a tight bun, and her glasses were low on her nose. She wore a floral cotton dress, and it struck Ruth as curious because she herself had never worn anything but overalls. The woman did not wear a very friendly face. She looked skeptical and confused.

"Can I help you?" the woman said.

"Yes, ma'am," said Paul. "Heard in town that you're looking to hire a few hands."

## *Forty-Eight*

# SAINT HELEN

✦ ✦ ✦

The child rested on Helen's chest. Helen did not sleep. She only stared at the baby.

*The face of a baby*, Marigold thought, *is saintly*. The baby's tiny eyes were closed, his mouth slung open. His baby fingers and toes were so small. The first time she held Maggie against her shoulder she felt the same things she was feeling right now.

Helen whispered, "What should I name him?"

"Don't know," said Marigold. "But it's gotta be something good."

"What'd you name your baby, Marigold?"

"Maggie."

"Maggie, that's a good name. How'd you pick it?"

Marigold smiled. "Oh, it's silly."

"What do you mean?"

"I heard a song playing on a radio when I was a kid."

"Really?"

"On my grandfather's radio."

It was a radio no bigger than a bread box. It sat on a ledge beside her grandfather's bed. Marigold remembered the exact day she heard the song coming from the speaker through the open window. She remembered the way the tune of this mournful ballad stuck with her. The melody was simple and beautiful. Today, however, the thought of it only made her heart sore. Sometimes she felt so distant from Maggie. Other times an unexplainable feeling within her told her she could reach through the fabric of the universe and touch the child if she tried hard enough.

"Will you sing it for me?" said Helen.

"Oh, you don't wanna hear me sing. I can't carry a tune in a bucket."

"Please? We both wanna hear it."

Her voice was not smooth, but shaky and unsure of itself. And she didn't remember much more than the second verse. But she sang it. Helen closed her eyes and smiled when she did. *"The green grove is gone from the hill, Maggie, where first the daisies sprung. The creakin' old mill is still, Maggie, since you and I were young."*

When she finished, the room was filled with silence for a few minutes. And Marigold had a single tear rolling down her cheek.

"Maggie," said Helen. "I love that name."

"Yeah," said Marigold.

"What was your grandfather's name?"

"Abraham Obadiah Butterfield, but everyone called him Abe."

"Did you love him?"

"Yes."

Helen pressed her nose against the baby's forehead. "Then that's what I'll name him."

# Forty-Nine

# TRACKS TO NOWHERE

★ ★ ★

Coot followed train tracks in the dark. He stumbled forward, one foot before the other. He was singing. He didn't know why. It was delirium, he knew that. But he had a memory that contained every song he'd ever heard. And tonight he was taking requests.

When he was a boy, he would sing for the revival workers until the sun came up. They would name a song to try to stump Coot. But they rarely ever did. He had a particular knack for song lyrics, even as a child.

The aching located in the center of his face had gotten worse. His nose felt broken, and his head throbbed so bad it felt like he was going to pass out. He wandered on railroad ties, wondering where he was and where he was going.

Nothing looked familiar. He felt unclear in his thoughts. Confused. Disoriented. Dazed. This place looked like the middle of nowhere.

He stopped walking and looked in all directions. He wasn't even sure how he'd gotten here. It was as though he'd awoken, standing on his feet, on these secluded tracks.

He had vague memories of opening his eyes and seeing stars hanging in the night. He remembered seeing the roofline of the empty train depot. But after that, he didn't remember anything.

The night sky over the black trees was bright from the full moon. It gave enough light to see the blood that covered his clothes. And he felt the sticky warmth soaking through his shirt and on the back of his head. This scared him. He hated the sight of blood.

He kept walking. He stumbled forward, unseeing on his feet. He felt sleepy with confusion. But he forced himself awake by singing. His words came out more like drunk mumbles.

*"Come to the church by the wildwood, oh, come to the church in the vale. No spot is so dear to my childhood as the little brown church in the vale."*

This made him laugh. There was nothing "dear" in his childhood. Nothing. In fact, his childhood had been one big, ugly mistake. There were no little brown churches, no wildwoods. There had only been dry prairies, dusty tents, hateful people. He felt bitterness come to the surface. Bitterness turned to hate.

He hated E. P. for hitting him. He hated Blake for leaving him. He hated Judy for ruining him. He hated his mother for abandoning him. He hated God for sitting on his thumbs and letting it all happen.

No. Actually, he hated the *idea* of God. He didn't believe in the Old Man enough to hate him personally. He hated the lies people told about a big, phony creature in the sky. That's what he hated. He thought of other songs to sing to keep himself awake.

*"Frankie and Johnny were sweethearts, O Lordy, how they did love. Swore to be true to each other, true as the stars above. He was her man, he was doing her wrong."*

He laughed at this song. The laughter was not a natural kind, for there was nothing funny about the song. He remembered when his mother had taught it to him when he was a little boy. She marveled that he could remember every single word to it. All the verses. She taught him several songs. She taught him the song about the *Titanic*, about floating river trains, about building the railroad. He sang a few of these melodies to himself.

Coot finally reached a train yard. The large stock cars were lined up in the night like big wagons in a circle. He could hear the sounds of cattle coming from them. He wandered toward a light in the middle distance, glowing yellow and red. A flickering.

When he neared it, he saw four men sitting on overturned buckets. They were dressed in rags, unshaven and red-faced. They saw Coot, and they all leapt to their feet with the jerky movements of old men. One man stomped on a cigarette. Another pointed a handgun at Coot. The men said something to him, but Coot was in too much of a daze to understand them.

His only response was, *"How sweet on a clear Sabbath morning, to listen to the clear ringing bells; its tones so sweetly are calling, oh, come to the church in the vale."*

The men moved closer to him.

"He's bleeding," one said. "Like a stuck hog."

Coot fell to his knees. His mind was beginning to shut down. He fell forward onto his chest. His chin hit the ground. He tasted dirt and gravel and saw the ratty shoes and boots gather around him. They carried him toward the fire and placed him on a pallet of blankets. One old man touched Coot's face and said, "What happened, son?"

"Get him some water," hollered another man.

A man pressed a cool bottle against Coot's lips. Coot took a pull from the bottle and nearly choked. Whatever he was sipping wasn't water. It burned his tongue and lips and throat. He gasped for air and coughed.

Coot pushed the mug away. "No, I don't drink," he said.

"You do now," said the man.

"Best medicine there is," said another.

He felt his body go soft. In a few moments he felt delirious. He wasn't sure where he was. He wasn't sure who he was. He wasn't sure why he was.

He mumbled, rallying his energy to speak, but couldn't find sentences to say. All that came out were songs.

*"They built the ship* Titanic *to sail the ocean blue, and they thought they had a ship that the water would never go through."*

The hobo touched the back of Coot's head, made a whistle, and said, "This kid needs a doc in a bad way."

*"But the good Lord raised his hand and said, 'That ship will never land.' It was sad when the great ship went down."*

The old man doused a rag with the bottle's contents. He pressed the damp rag against Coot's wounded head. It made Coot's head sting like his head had been lit on fire. Coot moaned.

"This will help," the man said. "Believe me, I don't like wasting hooch any more than you do."

The man wiped tiny bits of gravel from his wound, and Coot let out a howl.

"Sshhh," said the old man. "Gotta get this cut clean, don't want it to get infected, now." He used his finger to wipe the sand and grit from Coot's open gash. "Sing us some more songs."

He opened his mouth and sang through the pain. *"Would you be free from the burden of sin? There's power in the blood, power in the blood. Would you o'er evil a victory win? There's wonderful power in the blood."*

When the wound was clean, the man wrapped Coot's head in a rag. He gave Coot the bottle again and said, "Take one more swig. It'll help the swelling go down."

Coot did as he was told. The alcohol made his mouth burn so that he could hardly breathe. There was no discernible taste to it. Coot imagined this was what drinking kerosene was like.

The old man touched Coot's shoulder. "Name's Joseph," said the old man. "But you can call me Joseph."

The others laughed.

"I'm Coot," he said.

Joseph gently rested a hand on his head. "Coot, I don't mean to sound presumptuous, son. But you don't happen to take requests, do you?"

Coot began to chuckle. It made his head hurt. "Try me," he said.

"How about 'Billy Boy'?" said one man.

Coot sang it.

"Do you know 'Buffalo Gals'?" another man asked.

Coot knew every word.

The man named Joseph said, "Do you know 'When We Were Young, Maggie'?"

Coot let out a laugh. He sang, *"I wandered today to the hills, Maggie, to watch the scene below, the creek and the creakin' old mill, Maggie, as we used to long ago."*

# BOOK III

*Fifty*

# MAN IN THE MIRROR

\* ★ \*

Paul looked at his own face in the hand mirror that was hanging in the barn. He ran the razor across his cheeks and felt it nick him. Bright red blood ran along his chin.

Vern was listening to the radio in the other room. It was blasting. The noise had changed from music to preaching. The sound of a man's self-righteous voice hollered to the masses.

"Turn that off, Vern," said Paul. "It's killing my good mood."

"But it's J. Wilbur Chaplain," said Vern.

"Do I look like I care?"

Vern turned it down to a low volume. Paul could still hear it, but he pretended he couldn't. Vern had been listening to J. Wilbur Chaplain since the invention of the short wave.

He wiped his blood and stared at his own reflection again. Paul had once been a beautiful man, but not anymore. Now he was hideous and old. This was no beautiful man in the mirror, only a haggard thing.

Beautiful men did not have lines at the corners of their eyes that reached clear down to their knees. Beautiful men did not have old-man ears that were fleshier than a young man's ears. Beautiful men did not have joints that creaked in the mornings. The man in the mirror was not merely "older," this man was ancient. Elderly, even. How did this happen? Life had killed the beautiful man and replaced him with an old man. Life did this to everyone, sooner or later.

He had once heard a preacher say that life was like a mountain railroad. The twists, the turns. It beat you up. You picked up different passengers along the way and dropped others off. And this was certainly true enough.

In the years he'd spent running from boll weevils, from dead cotton fields,

from bill collectors, building roofs, building barns, working tobacco plantations, he'd picked up several passengers on life's train.

He'd never wanted passengers. But that's just how the trains worked. You
didn't get to choose who rode in the seats next to you. You were near them for
better or worse, and if you were smart, you learned to like it. If you were really
smart, you learned to love it.

Over the years he'd watched the children grow longer, leaner, and stronger.
Pete was a man, almost as tall as Vern, skinny as a stick and shy. It seemed like
just yesterday Pete had started shaving and his voice had dropped. All traces of
youth had left Pete's person. He was a square-jawed, big-shouldered, quiet man.

And Ruth. A woman. A young woman. But a woman nonetheless. She was
stubborn, not easily broken, and her violet eyes had almost as much spirit in
them as her wild hair. She was seventeen but did girlish things like splashing
in nearby creeks, traipsing through mud, capturing frogs, and raising squirrels
in shoe boxes. She worshipped Pete. Paul saw it in the way she looked at him.

Maturity had landed on all of them. Age was working on each person
whether he wanted it or not. It made beautiful men turn ugly. And baby girls
become striking. But none of the children had matured more than Reese. The
baby fat in her face had left her, and she became a lady almost overnight. She
cared more for her appearance than anyone else on the Warner farm. She was
not vain, but she was closer to it than Ruth was.

Miss Warner had done well with Ruth and Reese. The girls had learned
all sorts of feminine things. How to behave at supper tables, how to cross
their ankles when seated, how to wear their hair for preaching. How to read,
write, and work with numbers. How to set the table. How to behave around
young men.

Miss Warner had taught them how to be pretty. There was a skill to being
pretty. It didn't just happen, not even to pretty girls. It had to be coaxed. There
was more to being pretty than having good looks. Long ago, Paul had always
believed girls were born either beautiful or not. But that's not how it was, Miss
Warner had told him.

"A woman's beauty is of her own engineering," she'd once said.

Reese had always wanted to please Miss Warner—she was a natural pleaser.
And Reese seemed to fill the space Miss Warner's late daughter might have
filled had she been alive. Reese and Miss Warner loved one another.

The same could not be said of Ruth and Miss Warner. Ruth was her own woman. And sometimes she went clomping through the woods in overalls and boots, even though Miss Warner forbid such clothing, and such activity. She was just like Paul, is what she was. She was not owned by anyone, or any convention. This made Paul proud.

Paul finished shaving and wiped his face. He tore small pieces of newspaper and wet them with spit, then stuck them to the cuts on his face.

"You ugly dope," he said aloud.

Pete appeared in the barn doorway. His silhouette was strong. He was dressed in a full suit, with a yellow wildflower in his lapel, and wore a brown hat. He was just as wiry as he was tall.

Paul could only stare at him.

"You ready, Paul?" said Pete in a deep voice.

Paul neared Pete and took him in with his eyes. "Where'd you get that monkey suit?" Paul said, touching the fabric of Pete's jacket.

"It used to belong to Miss Warner's husband, before he died. Why, do I look stupid?"

Paul felt a throbbing in his throat. "No," he said.

"I wanted to wear regular clothes," said Pete. "But Miss Warner said she'd murder me if I wore overalls to a wedding."

Paul reached a hand upward and touched Pete's rough cheek. Stubble and bone. He was a child in an adult body.

"You're a beautiful man, son. Beautiful."

★

When they'd boarded the train, Miss Warner told Paul, "I think I'm going to be sick. I have vertigo."

"Just breathe," said Paul.

"I'm trying," she said. "But I'm sick to death."

"Well, don't die on me, not here. That would be rude, and I've never known you to be rude."

The train was filled with people. Men in business suits with briefcases. Families with children. Throughout the train ride, Paul would rest his hand on Miss Warner's shoulder. Paul knew what she was suffering wasn't vertigo. It was the same thing he was suffering. Loss.

Together, Miss Warner, Paul, Vern, Pete, Reese, and Ruth sat in their bucket seats, watching the world go by through the glass. Trees flew past them at lightning speed. An entire countryside passed them in only a few blinks.

"You alright?" Paul asked Miss Warner.

"I'll be better once we get off this behemoth," she said.

He tugged at his collar. He wore a suit and tie that Miss Warner had bought for him in town. It was the cheapest one the store had, and it made him itch all over. Ruth wore a frilly dress, trimmed with a blue sash. Vern wore what he always wore—his overalls—with a scuffed jacket.

To see the world go by at eye level like this was quite a feeling. It made Paul's stomach swim to climb tall hills, then roll down them. It was like one of the rides at the fair—only this ride had velvet seats and cost approximately the same price as dental surgery.

But this was not just scenery zipping past him, he thought. This was life going by right before his eyes. And all he could do was stay in his seat. That was all anyone could do. Before he knew it, he would soon be looking behind himself and seeing a whole world. Faraway. Like it belonged to other people. People he did not belong to.

"What're you thinking about?" said Reese, who sat across from Paul.

"Nothing, baby."

"You don't look like you're thinking about nothing."

"What do you think I'm thinking about?"

"I don't know."

"Neither do I."

He was thinking about how it had only taken a few years for Reese to become a magnificent female, with all the class of a set of fine china. Paul was thinking about how beautiful she was, and how much she looked like her mother. He was thinking about how just yesterday she was a child who looked to him for safety, food, and shelter. And now she would look to another. He thought of how empty life would be after he walked her down the aisle and gave her away. That's what he was thinking.

"Are you sad?" Reese asked.

"Sad? No, baby. I'm happy as a lark."

"Really?"

"I couldn't be happier if I were four people instead of one."

"I'm so nervous."

"That's normal," he said. "When I got married, I puked outside the chapel. I almost didn't go through with it."

"I didn't know you were married," said Reese.

"Once."

"To a woman? You?"

"That's generally how it works."

"What happened to her?"

"Tuberculosis."

Reese rose from her seat and sat in Paul's lap the way she did when she was a girl. It cut the circulation off to his thighs and made his back ache something fierce. But he made no faces of pain. He only remembered the young girl who had once picked a bouquet for her late mother. He remembered a lot.

"What if I throw up from nervousness?" said Reese. "Like you did."

"You won't."

"Are you gonna give me away, Paul?"

"You better know it."

Reese kissed his cheek. "I'm sorry I'm leaving you."

"Quit your sorryin'," he said. "Besides, I ain't sorry about anything, except that your mother ain't here."

★

Reese wore a veil of white. Her groom came from a Birmingham family with more money than Father Abraham. It was a well-attended wedding. The church in the heart of the town was alive with cars and people. And onlookers too.

When Paul walked into the vestibule where she stood, he felt his eyes start to leak. Reese looked like something from a storybook. Tall, slender, majestic. She was perfect. And he never felt so ancient in his life. Ruth straightened the train of Reese's dress, flinging it with both hands.

The music played.

He walked Reese down an ornate aisle covered in wine-colored carpet. And when the preacher said, "Who gives this woman away?" Paul answered, "Me, Your Honor."

The young groom lifted Reese's veil and kissed her. And bells rang. And people clapped. And the sounds of happiness abounded. And when the ceremony was over, Ruth approached Paul with her head down. Her red hair was tied in blue ribbons. Her eyes were wet with tears. She was a wreck.

Paul squeezed her so hard he heard her shoulder pop.

"Ain't your sister beautiful?" said Paul.

But she only looked at Paul and cried. "I'll miss her so much." And the violet eyes that used to look back at him with infantile trust still held the same sincerity they always had.

"You know, you look so handsome today, Paul. You know that?"

He kissed her forehead.

"What can I say?" he said with a wink. "When you're good-looking, you're good-looking."

# Fifty-One

# MEN OF FORTUNE

\* \* \*

Coot was awoken by a foul smell. The smell of manure. And when he opened his eyes, he saw the source of it. The stare of a black cow, standing only a few feet from him, greeted him. He smiled back at her. She seemed to be curious about him.

The bright morning sun poked through the slats of the fast-moving stock car. The car was jerking back and forth on the tracks, rattling over the landscape. He peeked through the gaps in the wood and saw the rolling hills, the small ponds, and the hamlets dotted with trees.

The cattle in the stalls behind him were making low groans. The cattle in front of him were too. And the cattle beside him. They were looking at him like he was one of their own.

He wiped morning dew from his face and stretched his stiff muscles. His back was sore, and his neck hurt. And the smell of cow pies was strong.

"Was wondering when you'd get up," said Joseph, who sat in the corner. "Thought you'd sleep all the way to Mobile."

Joseph was already eating peanut butter from a can for breakfast, fingerful by fingerful.

"How long have you been up?" Coot asked.

"Long enough to watch you have an ugly dream," said the old man.

"Me?"

"You was moaning and groaning at something. Maybe it's 'cause you stink so bad."

Coot sniffed his own jacket. He smelled like manure. "You don't smell too good yourself, you know," said Coot.

"Maybe, but I didn't sleep all curled up with that black mama cow like you did."

Joseph licked the peanut butter from his finger like it was an ice cream cone. Joseph loved peanut butter because it didn't interfere with his whiskey habit. Bread, for instance, interfered with whiskey—it soaked up all the contents in the stomach, he'd often tell Coot.

Joseph extended the can toward Coot. "Want some peanut butter?"

"No thanks," said Coot. "It's all yours."

"You sure? A boy needs breakfast."

"I'm sure."

Coot rubbed his face and felt the beard growing on his jaw. He wondered what he looked like. He hadn't seen his own reflection in weeks. He knew his general appearance had probably gone downhill. He probably looked as ragged as the old man did.

Joseph was a good man with questionable morals. But a good man nonetheless. He took Coot under his wing the moment he met him the night in the train yard. They became inseparable almost immediately. And the more Joseph's health declined, the more Coot began to find himself responsible for the crippled old man, until it almost seemed as though Coot was Joseph's babysitter.

Soon Coot alone was responsible for Joseph's survival. He did his best to ensure Joseph had at least two meals per day and a place to sleep. They were glorified hobos, but if Joseph had been on his own, he would've surely died in a train yard somewhere, unnoticed.

But the old man's personality was as vibrant as any Coot had ever known. He perceived life in a different way than Coot did. He was a brilliant man dressed in rags. Coot had never met a man so smart. There was a lot Coot didn't know about the man. But in the years they'd been together, Coot had come to almost idolize him.

Coot stood and patted his clothes. Clouds of dust came from him, lit by the sunlight streaming through the slats of the cattle car. Then he sniffed his clothes. He almost gagged.

Joseph laughed. "Aw, what's the matter, Coot? Can't stand the smell of a little cow pie?"

"I'd really like to take a bath."

"Baths are overrated."

Joseph replaced the lid on the peanut butter jar and wiped his hands on his coat, leaving peanut-colored streaks. Then he wiped the oily residue in his white hair to give it volume and body. He removed a flask from his vest pocket and took a snort.

"Want some?" he said, offering the bottle to Coot.

Coot refused.

"Suit yourself," said Joseph. "I'll have to drink your half for you." He took one final sip, then replaced the cap. "We're close to Mobile. I can taste salt in the air."

"Salt?" said Coot.

"The Gulf. Makes the air salty. Makes everything salty. It makes metal rust and turn into pure nothing too. You ever seen the Gulf?"

"Nope."

"I envy you, seeing it for the first time." The old man smiled. "It's bewitching. It changes a man."

"How?"

"Well, it's big and blue, for one. That much blue all at once is a sight to see. It can break your heart."

Coot looked out the wood slats. He could see a city in the distance, approaching. "Do you think we'll find work in Mobile?" said Coot.

"Don't know," said Joseph. "We always seem to find work somehow. Maybe."

"Yeah, but not since the war ended. Nobody's hiring."

"Barges come in and outta Mobile Bay by the hundreds. They need plenty of strong backs, and you got one."

"Yeah, well, there are more men than there are jobs. Nobody wants to hire a bum when they can hire a war hero."

"You worry too much, son."

"You don't worry enough."

They had moved from place to place, working thankless jobs and long hours, since they'd met each other. They had worked turpentine plantations, and they'd picked cotton in Demopolis, peanuts and corn in Senoia. They had manned gang edgers, mill saws, and splitters in Georgia. And Coot had used every bit of elasticity his young lower back ever had. Sometimes he couldn't sleep through the night because the muscles along his spine would seize up. He'd have to stand upright just to ease the pain.

"You know," said Joseph. "There are always *other* ways of making a living."

"Other ways? Other ways than what?"

"What I mean is, honest work ain't the only kinda work there is. Not if you're smart."

Coot didn't know how to respond.

Joseph went on. "You might not know this about me, but I'm sorta famous in Charleston."

"You mean, where you used to play cards with politicians?"

The old man laughed. "*Infamous* is probably a better word, come to think of it. People still talk about me up there for the things I did. And I did a lot more than take money out of politicians' pockets—though I'm very proud of that."

"What sorts of things?"

Joseph wore a far-off look. "Well, money was good back then. People had more than they could stand, everybody had work, economy was good. If you played your cards right, you could talk a man right out of his own cash."

"What are you talking about?"

"Games, gimmicks, stuff like that."

"You mean card games?"

Joseph started to chuckle. "Card games are for men with no creativity."

"You stole from people? Is that what you're telling me?"

"I prefer to call it 'winning.' And I won more times than I lost. I once won a man right out of a twelve-hundred-dollar cashier's check."

"By games?"

"Yep."

"What kinda games?"

"They don't have names, but they all go the same way. You meet a man, you size him up, you set him up, then you knock him down. You either win or lose. Simple as that."

"You are a con. You know that?"

"Nope, a con goes to jail. I never did no time. I'm a legend to some people."

Coot thought about the prospect of earning easy money by cheating people. And it made him sick to his stomach. He'd cheated enough people in his time. "I don't wanna steal from folks."

"Who said anything about stealing? We play them a game is all we do. And we make sure we win."

"And how exactly would you do that?"

"Oh, there're lots of ways. You got your fiddle game, pig in a poke, hot checks. Once I almost sold a man a piece of land he thought was owned by the U.S. government for three thousand bucks. And I woulda got away with it if he hadn't been a congressman."

"You were a thief."

"I was a legend."

"If you were such a legend, what made you quit?"

"I was young. I thought I was invincible. That's when you start getting sloppy, and I almost got caught."

"Well, I ain't no thief," said Coot. "I'd rather work for a living." Coot lit a cigarette and pulled in a breath of morning to erase the smell of cattle. "I'd rather have honest money."

"Yeah," said Joseph. "'Course you would. Forget I mentioned it."

"It's forgotten." Coot tugged the door handle of the massive rolling door and slid it with a broad sweep of his arm. It made a loud, booming noise.

Joseph squinted his eyes at the sunlight and brilliant scenery. Green hills, wildflowers of every color, ponds, live oak trees, and virgin farmland passed by. The scenery was almost as breathtaking as the smell.

"You jumping first this time," asked Coot, "or am I?"

"Better let me go first this time," said Joseph. "Or else I might chicken out again."

"You want me to push you out like last time?"

"No, I can do it. Just gimme a second. My old body don't wanna move this morning."

Coot helped the old man onto his feet. The man lifted the large suitcase, which was almost as big as Joseph. A case so full it was wrapped with two large belts just to keep it shut.

Joseph held on to Coot with scrawny arms. He grunted. "I'm all stoved up," said Joseph. "Let me breathe, let me breathe."

It took several minutes to get the old man steady. Coot could tell he was trying to hide his agony, but the old man hurt from years of hard living. Joseph straightened his back and let out several more moans of discomfort. "Lord, I can hardly move anymore, Coot," said Joseph. "What would I do without you?"

"Without me?" said Coot. "A con like you? You'd probably be rich."

The old man gripped Coot's shoulders, and for once, his eyes were serious instead of witty. "No, I mean it, boy. You're the angel God sent to me. An old man like me don't deserve you."

"Oh, you're just buttering me up, Joseph."

Joseph patted Coot's cheek. "Can't blame an old con for trying." He pinched Coot on the chin. "I do love you, boy. But you smell like a horse log."

The old man kicked his suitcase from the speeding railcar and jumped.

## Fifty-Two

# BLACK AND TAN

* * *

The sunshine blared onto the porch. It hit Ruth's thighs, her chest, and her face, and made her feel warm all over. The house had become a tomb ever since Reese had left them. There was nobody left to talk to. Pete, Paul, and Vern worked all day. Miss Warner was above girlish chitchat. Ruth had lost the only sister she'd ever known.

She missed the nights they'd spent talking, carrying on about anything and everything in soft voices. Mainly they talked about boys and the day-to-day. And boys. And the things they wanted in life. And boys.

She missed braiding Reese's hair, playing checkers, and picking out dresses for Sunday service. She missed everything. Now that Reese had moved to Birmingham, it was like she'd lost half of herself.

Ruth held Leon the lizard on her hand. It had taken her three weeks to get this particular lizard to trust her enough to let her hold him. Before that, he'd been living on the trim of her bedroom window. Now that she'd won his trust, she figured she'd better name him. So she chose the name Leon. It seemed to fit. He was lime green, with a bright red money bag that unfolded from his neck. She'd tried several names before landing on this one.

She petted Leon with her finger and spoke softly to him. He was a quiet creature. He wasn't a very good substitute for a sister, but he was a good listener.

She thought about Pete. She always thought about Pete. Sometimes she could think about him for three or four days without even thinking of other things. Sometimes she noticed him staring at her, and it would send her heart soaring. She looked at him the same way and hoped it made his heart feel the same way. But then he wouldn't even talk to her. She couldn't understand him. Long ago they had been best friends. Now they were people leading separate lives on the same farm.

Pete had changed. He'd become so painfully quiet around her that some-times he'd blush when she spoke to him. She was seventeen, and that was practically old enough to vote. But sometimes he treated her like a child.

She wondered if Pete ever thought about her. She sighed. She wished for things. And she wished against things too. She wished against the possibility that he would one day find some beautiful girl and leave the Warner farm, just like Reese did. If that were to happen, she would never recover from such heartbreak. It would surely kill her. But every day she feared it. She worried that he didn't care for her.

At the sound of a vehicle, she opened her eyes and saw a truck in the distance, loping up Miss Warner's long dirt driveway. A trail of dust followed behind. It was Paul's truck. It circled the long driveway and parked before the porch.

Ruth wandered toward the porch edge.

Vern stepped out of the passenger side first. His face was lit up like a flame. "You gonna wanna see this, Ruthie," he said, big teeth showing.

Ruth placed Leon on the ground and leapt off the porch.

"See what?"

"Just come here, right over here."

"What . . . what?"

"Just come on."

She ran toward Vern, barefoot in the dust. Vern reached into the flatbed of the truck, beneath a tarp. With both hands, he lifted something that yelped. He brought out a puppy in his arms. He balanced the animal against his chest. "We got us some new friends," he said.

She shouted, *"Ohboypuppiespuppiespuppies! Ohboypuppies!"*

This made Paul and Vern erupt with laughter. After only a few moments, she'd touched each and every puppy they'd brought home. Ruth bathed herself in puppies. She let them crawl on her and nibble her ears. She pressed her nose into their puppy fur and smelled their silky coats. She let them lick her face until they'd made her skin raw.

Pete ran his hand along the smooth fur of a black-and-tan puppy Ruth held against her shoulder. Pete was close enough that she could smell the sweat on his hair. He touched the puppy with such gentleness it made her heart hurt.

"This one's Stringbean," Pete told her.

"Oh," Ruth said. "You've already named them?"

"No," said Paul. "Just the one you're holding. We *tried* to name the rest, but Pete here wouldn't let us name 'em."

"He wouldn't?" said Ruth. "Why didn't you let anyone else name them?"

Vern smiled big at Ruth. "Pete wanted you to name them."

*Fifty-Three*

# GIRLS OF THE DAY

\* \* \*

There was a small gathering near the porch of Cowikee's. Seven people waited.
A woman with her elderly husband. A middle-aged man holding a toddler. Two
teenage blonde girls wearing rag dresses. And a man in a black overcoat and a
white collar. They were waiting for Marigold to touch them.

And she obliged them. Over time, Marigold had learned how to make her
hands become hot whenever she concentrated. And she had learned how to
understand the feelings and signals she felt within the people who visited her.
To her, those who visited had entire stories within them. Myriads of images,
memories, and scenes from a life lived.

Sometimes she could see these stories in her mind. Sometimes people didn't
want her to see them, and then she couldn't see anything. Some people wanted
to be touched. Others were skeptics with hard faces. Marigold touched them all.

People came to her daily. Some came from as far away as Birmingham or
Huntsville. One man came all the way from Atlanta to see her about a cancer in
his stomach.

A woman came from Virginia whose husband was dying of consumption.
Marigold touched her, and the woman went home. Weeks later, a letter came in
the mail. The man's health was improving, the letter read.

Hardly a day went by without at least one person coming to visit Marigold
the Magnificent in the woods. Some tried to pay her. Others brought gifts in the
form of food, jams, or baskets filled with dry goods.

Sometimes the girls at Cowikee's would sit on the edge of the porch and
watch with mouths open as Marigold touched the ones who visited. Often Helen
would stand near the porch, watching Abe chase the cats through the nearby
woods, while Marigold pressed her hands on any who stood before her.

She disappointed some, satisfied others. She offered no wisdom because she had none. And she always tried to make them smile, if at all possible. Marigold knew next to nothing of God, or the Bible, or his immense universe. But she knew that smiling was holy.

Claims had been surrounding Cowikee's ever since Marigold began receiving guests. The rumors circulated around town, so that when they got back to Marigold, they were more grandiose than the truth.

Like the man who claimed he'd regained vision in his right eye that had been injured by an accident. By the time the rumor had circulated around the county, people were saying Marigold had healed a man born blind from birth.

And the woman who begged Marigold to touch the large scar on her calf muscle. The scar vanished within three days, but someone claimed Marigold had made a lame woman walk.

And the child with the stutter. Marigold only touched his throat, and the boy spoke with less trouble than he had before. People claimed she'd made a mute person speak.

But nobody could forget the man who came to them with a bloody leg and crushed body. He'd been the victim of a cattle trampling in Milton. He was a sight. The man's friends laid his limp body on the porch. He looked like a man who was about to die. Marigold kept her hands on the man for ten minutes. His wounds finally stopped bleeding. And the man stood upright and limped home. People in town said she'd raised a man from the dead.

And the people kept coming. Like they were on this beautiful day. They had started arriving early.

The man with the toddler stepped onto the porch. He asked if Marigold could heal the child's rash. Marigold told him what she told everyone: "I don't do anything."

Marigold touched the child. The rash did not change, but the man began crying happy tears and thanked her. When he left, the two girls in the ratty dresses stepped toward Marigold. They had their heads down. They didn't want to speak, Marigold could tell. She had to drag the words out of them.

"Hello, girls," she said.

They mumbled.

"How are you today?"

"Good," they said in unison.

The forest was quiet except for the sounds of crickets and frogs in the distance. And the sound of Abe dragging a cat by its tail across the yard.

One girl said, "Can you take away sins?"

Marigold sat on the porch step before them. "No," she said. "I can't *do* anything."

The girls didn't answer, only stared at their own shoes.

"Why don't you sit and tell me what's wrong?" said Marigold.

The oldest girl looked at her. Her blue eyes were watering, and her jaw was quivering. "I done something, ma'am. And they gonna kill me for it."

"Who's gonna kill you?"

"My daddy."

"Why?"

"'Cause it's not good."

"Tell me why it's not good."

The girl only looked at the ground.

Marigold warmed her hands. She touched the girl on the cheek. She closed her eyes. She let sensations travel across her hands and into her own heart. Then she smiled.

"What's your name?" Marigold asked.

"My name's Mary. And this is my sister, Lee."

"Mary. That's such a nice name."

"Thank you."

"Girls, I want you to listen to me. Will you do that? Will you listen to me if I give you some free advice?"

"Yes, ma'am," they both answered.

Marigold moved her hand to Mary's heart. She could feel an ache in the girl that was a familiar one.

"Mary, what you carry inside you is not the product of sin. It is a gift."

"What?"

"The gift is life, Mary. You are about to know something you never knew before. You're about to understand life a little bit better."

Mary looked at Marigold and said, "What's that mean?"

"It means you are about to become who you were always meant to be, Mary. You are about to feel the love you were always meant to feel. And when you finally meet this child in your belly, you'll know what I'm saying is true."

The girl began sobbing lightly. Then her face busted wide open. The girl's sister hugged her. Marigold hugged them both.

"I once knew a girl," said Marigold. "A girl a lot like you. She never thought she would find a place in this world, and she was as sad as you are now, sadder maybe."

"And what happened to her?"

"She grew up and turned into me." Marigold kissed the girl on the forehead. She felt a spark in her lips. "Oh my," said Marigold, withdrawing herself from the girl's forehead.

"What happened?" the girl said.

"You're having a girl."

# Fifty-Four

# THE GAME

* * *

Joseph wore a white linen suit, a necktie, and a tweed vest. He stood a full foot shorter than Coot. They leaned against the wall of the alley watching the men exit the tavern. Joseph knew what he was looking for, it seemed. And he waited until he found it.

Coot saw a man exiting the tavern across the street. A big man with overalls and a straw hat.

"That's our man," said Joseph. "Probably got a pocketful of cotton money and a headful of whiskey."

Coot observed Joseph in his suit. He'd never seen the man wear this sort of thing before. "You look like you're going to church, you know that?"

"Hush and pay attention, boy. I'm telling you, *that's* our man."

"I don't feel right about this, Joe. It just don't feel right."

"You wanna eat tonight, or don't you?"

Coot hung his head. He'd stood in work lines all week in Mobile and had been turned away from every job he'd applied for.

Joseph tugged Coot's collar and brought him closer. "Here," he said, filling a leather wallet with several phony hundred-dollar bills. He pressed the wallet against Coot's chest. "Go get 'em."

"I don't know if I remember it all."

"You do."

"But . . . you're sure he's our guy? What if something goes wrong?"

"That man's ripe for the picking."

★

Coot watched the big man stroll past the wallet on the ground. It was splayed open with phony bills poking out, just like Coot had positioned it. The man stopped. He let his weary eyes rest on the thing. Then he bent to pick it up.

No sooner had he reached for it than Coot kicked the wallet from the man's hand. "I saw it first!" shouted Coot, who had already clutched the wallet and made a run for it.

But the big man was faster, and stronger. He pulled Coot by the collar. "You didn't see *nothing*," he said. Then he plucked the wallet from Coot's grip and shoved him. "Now beat it."

Coot kicked the man's shin. The man returned the favor by smacking Coot on the back of the head. When Coot got to his feet, he jumped onto the man's back and held on for dear life. He swatted the man and shouted, "Mine! Mine!"

The man spun in circles, wearing Coot for a backpack. He rammed Coot against a brick wall. It knocked the wind out of Coot's lungs and made his eyes bulge. He released his grip and fell to the ground.

The man opened the wallet and was about to count the money when he was interrupted by Joseph.

"Excuse me, gentlemen," said Joseph in a genteel accent. "But if you keep making all this noise, you're going to attract the police."

"Take a hike, old man," said the giant. "This don't concern you."

Coot couldn't gather enough oxygen to speak his line, so he only nodded.

"But if the police come," Joseph went on, "then none of us will enjoy the spoils of that purse."

"Us?" said the big man. "This ain't got nothing to do with you."

"Yeah," Coot wheezed. "Scram."

"We *all* saw the wallet," said Joseph. "Any of us could report it, maybe even collect a reward." Joseph leaned forward and whispered, "Now, may I suggest we can work this out as gentlemen."

Coot stood to his feet. It felt like his ribs were broken, and his head was throbbing. "Nobody asked you, mister!" said Coot.

"Shut up," said the giant. "It's too late now, he's already seen it. I don't need no more trouble with the law."

They gathered behind a brick building. Joseph counted the money beneath the watchful eye of the big man who reeked of whiskey and sweat. "Sixty-four dollars cash," Joseph finally announced. "And a check for twenty-two hundred dollars, which is worthless. So that comes to twenty-one dollars cash per man, and some change."

Joseph distributed the bills, tucked the check into his coat pocket, then tipped his hat and wished them good day.

"Just wait a blamin' minute, old man," said the giant. "Where do you think you're going?"

Joseph ignored him and kept walking.

"Hey!" the big man shouted. "I said get back here! What about that check you're runnin' off with?"

Joseph stopped. He faced the man. "What about it?"

"That's a lotta dough," said the giant. "You must think you're pretty slick, makin' a getaway with all that money."

Joseph removed the slip of paper. "Why, this is nothing but paper. It's made out to someone named George. We might as well tear it up."

"If it's worthless," said Coot, "then why're you so quick to run off with it?"

"Hand that check over," said the giant.

"Why should I give it to you?" said Joseph.

"Because I'll smash your head in with a brick if you don't."

"Sounds reasonable to me," said Joseph. "But do you truly think a bank will cash this to either of *you*?" He laughed. "You look like you fell off a hay wagon."

Coot and the giant exchanged a look.

"They might," said Coot.

Joseph laughed even harder. "Well, good luck, lads." He placed the check in the big man's hand, touched the brim of his hat, and began to walk away.

"Wait!" said the giant. "You sayin' the bank might cash it to you?"

Joseph shrugged. "Oh, I don't know. I am a stranger in this town. They don't know me. Maybe."

The giant held the check to the light. Coot and Joseph waited for him to say something, but he remained silent. Coot could almost see his pickled brain working overtime.

"Okay, you go cash it," the giant said. "And I want half."

"Half?" Coot shouted. "You get a *third*!"

Joseph stroked his chin. "Now hold on. That's a pretty big chance I'd be taking, just so you both can collect." He shook his head. "Sorry, gentlemen, no deal." He turned to walk away again.

"Wait!" the man said, reaching beneath his coveralls. He removed a money belt and unfurled a few bills from a large roll of cash. "Fifty bucks, and another fifty when you get back."

Joseph removed his hat and fanned himself with it. "Fifty dollars? I'm sorry, fifty bucks isn't worth spending the night with the sheriff."

"Seventy-five," said the giant.

"Two hundred and fifty dollars," said Joseph.

The giant shook his head. "Eighty bucks, take it or leave it."

"Leave it," said Joseph. "Have a nice day."

"Wait!" said Coot, jogging after Joseph. "I'll pay it. I'll pay the two fifty if you split the check with me." Coot removed a wad of one-dollar bills from his shirt pocket and started to count them aloud to Joseph with his back facing the big man.

"Who do you think you are?" said the giant. "You don't get half, you greedy little cuss. You get a *third*, like we agreed on." The big man shoved Coot out of the way and stood before Joseph. He towered over the old man by at least two feet. He glared at him without saying anything.

"Well?" said Joseph. "You got something on your mind, then say it."

The big man licked his thumb, then counted out two hundred and fifty dollars. He placed the money into Joseph's hand and said, "You'd better be quick, old man, or I'll use that brick I was telling you about."

Joseph tucked the money into his breast pocket. "Pleasure doing business with you."

# Fifty-Five

# LEAVES OF GRASS

✷ ✷ ✷

Vern listened to the radio blaring in the truck. The preacher's voice came through the speaker, saying, *"There is a fountain filled with blood, flowing from Emmanuel's veins, and sinners plunged beneath . . ."*

Ruth watched Pete hide from the dogs behind the tall grass. It was late at night, and the moon was throwing a blue glow on the world. Vern sat with his hands folded behind his head.

"Vern, turn that stupid thing off," said Paul. "It's distracting."

"But it's Wednesday night," said Vern.

"So what?"

"It's J. Wilbur."

Paul reached over Ruth and snapped off the radio. "I've been listening to that dummy's sermons every Wednesday night for a hundred years, whether I want to or not. We're working right now. Go listen somewhere else."

Vern crawled out of the truck and wandered toward the barn. Paul explained to Pete and Ruth that it was better to train the puppies at night than in the morning. It forced them to use their noses instead of their eyes.

Ruth thought it was magnificent to watch the animals in the glow of the headlights. The animals were only three months old but getting long and lanky. And they seemed to know exactly what to do when it came to using their noses.

Training the dogs to track short distances was done with an exercise. She and Paul held the dogs by the collars until they were yelping with excitement. Then Pete would walk far away, duck beneath the tall grass, and let out a single whistle.

Then Paul and Ruth would turn the pups loose. The clumsy animals would follow the trail Pete had left in the grass, tripping on oversized paws, long ears, and each other. And Pete would praise the dogs with such sincerity that Ruth could feel his gentle spirit from where she sat, even though she could only see his tall shape in the moonlight. She could hear him sweet-talking the puppies like they were his best friends. She loved him with all her heart.

Paul placed his arm around Ruth. He said nothing, only held her.

"What's on your mind, young lady?" he said to her.

"What?"

"Oh, nothing. You just look like you're thinking about heavy things."

She leaned against him. "I wish I could've met my mother."

"Me too."

"I just wanna know what she looked like, that's all."

"Well, I can tell you what she looked like."

"You can? How? You never met her."

Paul held her a few feet out from him. He observed her, then touched her cheek. "She was pale skinned, just like you." He rested a flat hand atop Ruth's head. "Probably about yay tall, with your eyes." He kissed her on the hair. "And sweet."

"You don't know that."

"I do."

"How can a mother abandon her baby? How can a mother just leave her child to . . ." She began to cry. Ruth slumped against Paul. "Oh, Paul, sometimes I just feel like I wasn't wanted."

"No, no, honey. That ain't the way it was. That ain't how it was at all. See, the truth is, you was wanted by *so many* people at once that God had to sorta pick the best man for the job. And since I begged so hard, I wore him down, you could say, and he finally gave you to me, just to shut me up."

"Oh, stop it. That's silly."

"It's the truth."

"You didn't ask God for me."

He was silent for a few minutes, watching the dogs circle around Pete. Paul finally said, "When I was a young man, newly married, happy as I thought I'd ever be, I wanted a baby. *We* wanted a baby. We wanted one so bad we could taste it."

"How old were you?"

"Twenty. We had a pretty little farm, a nice place, fresh eggs from the chickens in the mornings, a swing on the front porch. Was everything a man could want."

"What happened?"

"We were so happy. Not just happy. We were the luckiest people on the planet. That's how you feel when you're in love. All our friends started having young'uns. Most my buddies wanted boys, but not me. I wanted me a girl, always wanted me a girl I could spoil. But things don't always work out how you want."

He stopped talking, and Ruth could hear him sniff his nose.

"What was her name, your wife?"

"Her name was Delpha Ann," he said, leaning his head backward to take in the sky.

"Do you think my mother's out there somewhere?"

"I don't know, sweetie. But if she is, I know one thing's for certain, she's thinking about you right now."

"How do you know that?"

"Because we never stop thinking about the people who leave us."

# Fifty-Six

# WHERE WILDFLOWERS ARE

\* \* \*

The woods were filled with flowers. Little yellow flowers. Millions of them peppered the landscape beneath the tall trees near the bay. Bright, golden flashes of color, scattered among the green, stretching as far as Marigold could see.

Abe ran ahead of Helen and Marigold, shouting. But they paid him no attention. Helen and Marigold hooked arms and walked easily. They listened to the bay water brush upon the gritty shore. Marigold got lost in the flowers surrounding them. Helen was happier than Marigold had ever seen her. They had gone for miles without speaking, just watching. Watching the world, watching the sky, watching Abe.

"You ever think about her?" asked Helen. "Your Maggie?"

"Always. I think about her always."

"What do you remember?"

"Oh, I remember the way she felt inside me, and the way I could tell she was just like me even before I met her. And when I first held her. I think about that a lot."

"Do you ever wonder about where she is?"

"Most of the time I wonder if she's even alive. And I wonder what she thinks of me if she is."

"But you were so young, Marigold."

Marigold forced a smile. "Maybe, but I'll never forgive that stupid young girl. I don't think I ever could."

Helen said nothing, only stooped to pick flowers. She placed them in a basket with an armful of others. Marigold almost didn't recognize this serene woman beside her.

"I don't forgive myself for a lotta things," said Helen. "But that doesn't mean

I have to beat myself up for them either. I've done things worse than you. A lot worse."

"Nothing could be worse than losing your own baby."

"Losing yourself is almost as bad as losing a child."

"I just wonder how I could've ever been so stupid. That's what I always think of when I think of Maggie."

"Everybody's foolish sometimes, sweetie. Especially when they're young. You've got to be merciful to yourself."

Helen was right, of course. Marigold had been holding her own personal sins against herself since she was a child. She'd been her own judge, jury, and executioner since the beginning. But it was hard to exercise mercy upon yourself.

They stopped beside the water's edge and looked at the grass flats in the distance. A pelican dropped from the sky and plunged into the water. He emerged with a fish in his mouth.

"What's it feel like?" Helen said.

"What's what feel like?"

"When you touch someone. What happens?"

Marigold shrugged. "I don't know. It's a thick feeling."

"Thick?"

"Like being stuck in mud kinda."

"Being stuck in mud?"

"You know how when you hug Abe and you feel sort of overcome? It all just swoops down on you and buries you? And you feel like you might just drown beneath it all?"

Helen nodded.

"It's kinda like that. Only the feelings aren't all happiness and love. People don't have happiness and love in them when they're hurting."

"So you feel stuck in their mud?"

"I feel their sadness and their hurt and whatever else they're full of."

Helen was quiet.

"Why do you keep doing it if it's so sad?"

"I dunno. It's kinda like how I imagine drowning would feel. It sorta feels like you can't get your breath, and if you did take a big breath, it would kill you. But it's so peaceful in the water, so serene in those seconds before you pass."

"I've never drowned before."

"Well, now you don't have to."

They weaved through the woods and toward the railcar. They stopped by the creek that meandered through the grove of live oaks with wide trunks and twisting limbs. Momentarily they thought they'd lost Abe, until they heard the unmistakable sound of a ten-year-old boy making water on a flat rock.

When they neared the railcar, they saw a single-file line of people waiting on the steps. Men were holding their hats in their hands, and women stood with their children beside them.

Helen and Marigold stopped walking. Helen touched Marigold's arm. "I never thanked you, you know."

"For what?"

Helen touched Abe's head. "For the best thing in my life."

"I didn't do anything."

"You say that, but it's not true," said Helen. "You do something to people, and you don't understand it, and I don't understand. We might never understand. But it's something."

Helen pinched the bloom from a yellow flower and tucked it behind Marigold's ear, then straightened Marigold's messy hair. "Go and make them feel what I feel."

"What do you feel?"

"Glad."

*Fifty-Seven*

# GO-GETTERS

\* \* \*

"Now *that* little girl's got heart," said Paul, pointing to the bloodhound with the black body. "She's gonna make a go-getter, that one."

Pete stood beside Paul watching the lanky animals chase each other through the shallow creek, splashing water in all directions. They were chasing a coon, and howling while they did it.

"She don't like to lose," Paul added. "She's a natural leader, that one."

"Hard to believe she was the runt," said Pete.

"Only in size, not in heart," said Paul. "That one has heart."

"How do you know?"

"Look at her. She's wild and uncontrollable, and she's one in a million. You can just tell."

He was right. The old man was always right when it came to the animals. It was a gift, as though he had canine in his blood. Pete had the gift too. He had become a good dog trainer, and that was a quality that couldn't be taught. It was something a man was either born with or he wasn't. Paul was a natural dog man. And now Pete was taking up the family business. He'd gone the first part of his life not knowing what or who he was. Now he knew. He was a dog trainer.

"That old girl's the pick of the litter," said Paul. "She'll take the highest price."

Pete rubbed the back of his neck. "I don't know if I can sell her. She's one of my favorites."

"They're all your favorites, Pete. Just look at her. That dog was made to hunt. If you keep her, she won't get to hunt a lick. No sir, that dog's got *heart*. She was made to use it."

"Yeah, I guess so."

"All part of raising pups. You give 'em all you got, do everything you can to make them into the best, then you let 'em run."

The sound of a screen door slapping interrupted them. The sound echoed across the wide-open field. In the distance, Pete could see Ruth running toward them. She was long and lean, and her red hair whipped behind her like ribbons.

Pete held his eyes on her, watching her high-step through the tall grass. She was hollering, playing with Pete's own dog, Stringbean, the only dog of the bunch he hadn't trained to hunt because she was too gentle.

Paul placed a thick hand on Pete's shoulder. "Hey, I wanna ask you something, Pete."

"What is it?"

"I want you to promise me something."

"Huh?"

"Promise me something, son. I want you to do me a favor."

"What do you mean?"

Paul's eyes were sharp, but the face around them was old. His hair was white, his skin crumpled. "Take care of my Ruth, will you?"

"What's that supposed to mean?"

"It means what I just said. Just promise me you'll take care of her, Pete."

Pete shook Paul's hand. Paul squeezed a little harder than he normally did.

Paul nodded toward Ruth. "That little girl's got a lotta heart."

# Fifty-Eight

# HOMECOMING

✶ ✶ ✶

Joseph coughed until he couldn't. His cough sounded like an engine in need of fuel. His chest sputtered and rattled. He leapt out of the Model A and leaned against it, hacking until he was out of breath.

"You okay?" asked Coot.

"Fine, I'm fine."

"You sound worse than the car does."

Joseph laughed. "And this car's a lot younger than I am."

"It's nicer looking than you are too."

"Now, is that any way to talk to your meal ticket?"

"I don't know about this."

"We spent every dime we had on this here car. This is just to buy us supper is all. Think of it like picking apples off a tree that ain't yours. No big crime, right?"

"This is *not* like picking apples. This is taking advantage of innocent people."

"Church people, Coot. These people give their money for the cause of charity. And that's how we plan on using it, don't we?"

"You shoulda been a lawyer, you know that? Or a preacher."

Coot wandered toward a shop window and saw his reflection in it. The six-dollar seersucker suit fit him just right. He rotated in all directions so he could get a better look. He was nothing but a stick.

A poster hanging in the window caught his attention. In big, bold letters it read Revival Comes to Alabama.

On the poster was the illustration of a man with a square jaw, steel-rimmed glasses, and oiled hair. The poster was decorated with crosses and drawings of angels.

Sponsored by three hundred churches, a service for
all faiths, divine healing and salvation, J. Wilbur
Chaplain brings the Holy Ghost to Alabama.

There he was. J. Wilbur Chaplain, in all his glory. Coot had only ever heard his voice, never seen his face. This man was older than Coot imagined him, and he looked like a dime-novel hero in the poster.

Joseph leaned on his cane, gasping for wind. He stood beside Coot in front of the shop window.

"I don't know, Joseph," he said. "I'd prefer not to hurt anyone."

"Well, that makes two of us, Coot."

"We coulda bought a year's worth of suppers with that money instead of buying that ugly, run-down car."

"That car ain't just a car, boy. It's also a house on wheels, and it prevents us from having to ride trains with a bunch of cutthroats and godless thieves. That car is gonna save our life."

They walked to the edge of town. Coot held Joseph's arm for balance, but more for effect. They kept a slow pace, pausing every so often for Joseph to cough.

They arrived at a small clapboard church. The front door was open, the orange light spilling into the darkness from the open door and windows. The place was packed. Men were huddled in the rear of the room and gathered on the church steps. Children were seated on the floors and ladies in the pews.

Coot and Joseph walked into the building and stood behind the last row of seats. Coot whispered to Joseph, "I don't like it here. I've changed my mind. I wanna go."

Joseph patted Coot's shoulder. "You got money for food I don't know about?"

"No."

"Then you stay right here and trust your old buddy."

The man at the pulpit tapped a mallet on the wood. It was a business meeting of sorts. The man held a clipboard and a pencil in his hand. People were murmuring among themselves, and the sound of their voices overpowered the man with the mallet.

"Folks! Folks!" the man behind the pulpit yelled, beating his hammer. "Folks, can I have your attention, please? We've got a lot to discuss. We need to hurry this meeting along!"

People quieted themselves.

"Thank you," the man said to the audience. "Now, I need volunteers to help disk John Malcolm's peanut field for the tent. The field's far too rough and covered with weeds, and John Malcolm's too sick to run his tractor. Who'll volunteer to drive?"

A man in the front shot up his hand; so did a few in back.

The man with the clipboard smiled and said, "Thank you, Tyler," then wrote something down. "Thank you, Charlie."

People started to murmur among themselves again.

"Folks!" the man shouted, swatting the mallet. "Folks! We're not even close to being finished. Now, if I could just have everybody's attention so we can all go home."

The people grew quiet again. One little boy in the very back used this golden opportunity to press his palms against his mouth and make a farting noise.

Trickling laughs turned into one giant roar among God's chosen people.

"Folks!" said the man on the stage. "Folks, please! Please!" The man was almost pleading now. "There are *fourteen* area revivals and *thirty-two* prayer meetings all happening in preparation for Reverend Chaplain's revival in Saraland. Now, please. Let us carry on with the work of the Lord in all fervency. We want our town revival to be every bit as good as Mount Vernon's or Perdue Hill's, don't we?"

"Let's make it better!" shouted one man.

A hushed murmur swept across the crowd at the mention of Chaplain's name. Even Coot felt a sense of awe when he heard it.

Coot saw the little boy press his palms to his face again, but before the child could provide an encore performance, a frail old woman grabbed him by the earlobe and smacked the child's thigh with her pocketbook. Screaming ensued.

The man with the mallet announced, "And that brings us to the tent itself! We need ten volunteers to erect it tomorrow morning at six! We need men with strong backs, please."

Joseph elbowed Coot, who raised his hand.

The man with the clipboard pointed his pencil at people in the audience.

"Your name, sir?" Clipboard said to a man in front.

"Rusty Miller," the man answered.

Clipboard scribbled, then pointed to a man in back. "And you, sir?"

"Philip Whittle," said another.

While the man with the clipboard was still scribbling, Joseph stepped forward and said in a loud voice, "Carl and Robert Allen, sir." He coughed a few times. "We hereby volunteer to help the reverend erect his good tent."

The man looked up from his clipboard. He glanced at Joseph and grinned. Joseph pulled Coot forward for the man to see. "I'm Carl, and this is my boy, Robert. We're volunteering for the committee."

"Thank you, Mister Allen, your help is a blessing to us all," Clipboard said, then wrote on his board again.

Finally the meeting was adjourned and the man ended with, "Tomorrow at six sharp, men, the truck will be here. Don't forget that lunch will be provided by the lunch committee . . ."

Joseph whispered, "I suwannee, they got committees for everything here. Probably got a committee to help a fella take a squat in the woods."

"Men! Men! Please, everyone's attention, please!" The man on the stage went on, "Men, please wear clothes you don't mind getting dirty this time. The church will not be held responsible for ripped trousers or torn britches like last year."

People laughed. And the boy in the back row made another loud fart noise.

The man tapped his wood hammer again. The meeting was adjourned, and people stood to their feet and faced the pulpit. A woman walked onto the stage. She wore a yellow skirt and had black hair that was down to her hips.

The woman sang "To God Be the Glory," and people sang along with her. Joseph, too, sang in a loud, off-key voice until it made him hack.

While they sang, Coot loosened his tie and walked out of the church. Joseph hobbled after Coot, leaning on his cane.

"Hey," Joseph said to Coot. "Slow down. Old man like me can't move very fast."

Coot didn't bother slowing. He'd had enough church for one night. He didn't even look back at Joseph.

"Robert," Joseph called out. "Where're you heading to, son? Robert, hold on!"

"Don't call me that," said Coot.

Joseph moved as fast as he could with his bad legs. "Wait! Wait up for your old man, Robert!"

Coot stopped and turned to him. "Don't call me that, Joseph."

"Just hold on a hot minute, son."

Coot flung his hand away. "Quit calling me 'son.' I'm not your son, you old cheat."

"What's wrong with you?"

"Me? Nothing's wrong with me. What's wrong with you? Those people are innocent people just looking to hold a revival. They don't deserve to be stolen from."

Coot turned and started walking away. Joseph followed, wheezing and making swallowing sounds. "Please, Coot! Wait!"

Coot stopped walking. He looked at the night sky and suddenly felt ridiculous in his seersucker. He removed his necktie and tossed it into a public mailbox. "I don't want to swindle those people, Joseph. They can have their stupid revival and shout at each other and wiggle like worms on the floor, for all I care. But I'm not taking their money."

Joseph touched Coot's arm. He was gagging on his own wind. "Easy, boy. Easy." He started coughing. He coughed until he doubled over. "You win, we ain't gotta swindle nobody. We'll play it your way."

The old man removed a bottle from his coat pocket and took a sip.

# Fifty-Nine
# LOUD NOISES
**★ ★ ★**

Pete fired a scattergun into the air. He was training the dogs not to react to gunfire. Watching this gave Paul pride. A lot of pride.

The bloodhounds sat in a cluster, watching the trees, when Pete fired the gun. They rested only on their haunches, except one dog, Judith, who bolted for parts unknown after the first shot. Paul grabbed her before she got away. He held the frightened dog close to his chest and said, "There, there, sweetie, ain't nothing to be afraid of."

But it did no good. Some dogs were like Judith. In Paul's experience, no amount of training could purge fear from some animals. Judith bolted from him, running so hard she kicked grass behind her.

Pete turned to see the dog running.

"Let 'er go," Paul said. "Maybe she'll make a good squirrel dog, or at least a coon tracker."

Paul had turned the training duties over to Pete little by little, until Pete was doing all the training. And Paul marveled to see the boy instruct a pack of bloods the way he used to do, long ago when he was a young man. Pete had sensitivity with animals that Paul himself did not have. It was a kind of talent that was almost holy.

The swells of parental pride grew bigger within Paul. They grew beyond simple emotions, until he felt an actual pain in his chest. The pain became sharper. It was a physical agony that made his breathing labored. And his arm hurt. His neck got tight. His vision dimmed. Now he was getting worried.

He rose and wandered from Pete, loosening his arm, pumping his fist. The pain was getting worse. And worse.

The sound of a scattergun filled the world.

Dogs baying.

Whimpering.

More gun noise.

More howling.

Paul stumbled toward the barn. He collapsed in the dirt behind the barn, where nobody could see him. He panted. He moaned. The pain became so great he almost lost consciousness. His stomach felt weak, and his mouth salivated. He leaned against the barn, staring at the sky. He expected to see the clouds open. But he did not.

Another shot.

Dogs wailing.

The pain was worsening. He gritted his teeth. He had all sorts of things he wanted to say to the Old Man Upstairs, but the only words he could get out were, "Take care of my babies, Lord."

He said it over and over. He said it so many times it became less about the words and more about keeping his mouth moving, to prove to himself he was still alive.

*"TakecareofthemLordtakecareofthemLordtakecareofthemLord . . ."*

Then he saw Ruth standing before him. She appeared so quickly, he almost missed her altogether. He stared at her tall shape against the sky. He could see the sun's brightness poking through strands of her red hair.

She was his angel. She'd always been his angel.

"What's wrong, Paul?" she said. "What's happening?"

The sight of her did something to him. It gave him strength. His breathing slowed, and the pain started to disappear. He blinked his eyes and felt his heart begin a normal rhythm again.

He didn't mean to, but he started crying. And it was the only time he could remember crying in front of her. He'd gone so many years keeping his own emotions from the rest of his dependents. She held him. And it was as though they had traded roles. No longer did she belong to him, but he belonged to her.

Another gunshot.

Dogs yelping.

A hound ran toward Paul. It was Judith. The old girl buried her head into his chest. Her whole body was shaking from the sounds of the gunshots.

"There, there," Paul said. "Ain't nothing to be afraid of, sweetie. Don't be afraid. Don't ever be afraid."

He wasn't sure if he was talking to Judith or himself.

# Sixty

# FAMILY REUNIONS

\* \* \*

It was hot. Very hot. Coot swung a large hammer that weighed as much as a Chevy. He glanced back at Joseph, who was sitting on the flatbed truck, shading himself from the powerful sun with a tarp over his neck and shoulders. He was watching the men work from a distance, stealing sips from his bottle now and then.

Coot worked alongside these men in the bone-melting heat of the day. All the men could talk about was J. Wilbur Chaplain. The men were more impressed with the man than they were with what he said, it seemed. They knew little about his uncanny gift with the spoken word, like Coot did. They only knew of his popularity.

But Coot was glad to be doing honest work for a change instead of cheating people with phony wallets and checks. The sounds of hammers driving the giant wooden stakes into the ground made Coot feel good. He didn't want to be here, but the free lunch was motivation enough for any man. He'd only eaten three meals in the last four days.

The church ladies had prepared a grand lunch for the men, putting out a spread like Coot had never seen before. One young man who was wearing sweat-laden overalls said, "I can't wait to shake J. Wilbur's hand tomorrow night. I'll probably faint. Been listening to him on the radio near 'bout every week. Even when we's over in Europe, they played his sermons on base."

"You big dumb-dumb," said another man. "J. Wilbur ain't coming here tomorrow. This tent's for a small-potatoes revival that raises money for J. Wilbur."

"Small potatoes?" said Overalls.

"This revival's only a warm-up. All the towns are having little revivals to get the saints and sinners fired up for when Chaplain comes. And he ain't coming *here*, anyhow. He's gonna be in Saraland."

"Then who's coming here?" asked Overalls.

"How should I know? Some preacher who's supposed to get us whipped up and used to shouting."

"Revival's fixing to hit Alabama," said Army.

"Glory," said another man.

Coot had remained silent all day. This was familiar work. Coot had seen more tents erected than any man in the field. He tugged ropes, drove stakes into the ground, cinched canvases tight, and wrapped lines around large wood poles. By the time the sun was beginning to settle above the trees, the monstrous tent stood like a religious monument. And something about this sight warmed Coot from the inside. The familiarity of it—no matter how much he might have hated it—was still familiar. And familiar things carried warmth.

The men passed water jugs among themselves in the sweltering sun. Their torsos were sunburned, and their faces were soiled.

Then cars arrived in the peanut field. Large Fords came rolling through the dirt field like a wagon train. The lead car was bright red with white text painted on the driver's door. The familiarity of it was almost too much for Coot to bear.

Coot inspected the door of one car, which read Reverend E. P. Willard.

Coot almost lost his balance. He felt his stomach churn.

The cars rolled to a stop. The men who stepped out of the vehicles wore suits and boater hats. One of them was a big man wearing a white fedora. He had a red complexion, silver hair, and a familiar face. Coot felt his blood freeze solid.

The big man introduced himself and pumped hands with the workmen. He offered a "God bless you, son" to each one of them. His sincerity was overwhelming.

The men all thanked the big man and removed their hats when he came to them. When he got to Coot, the man shot his hand out and glanced at Coot with hard eyes. Coot ducked his head. The years had been unkind to the old man. And this made Coot feel glad somehow.

"Name's Reverend Willard," said the man. "But you can call me E. P."

Coot almost lost himself in the moment. He couldn't find his voice. He could only look at the man's shoes. They were brown leather with white spats and black buttons. Coot remembered polishing E. P.'s shoes for hours on end, sometimes staying up until the wee hours because E. P. wanted them done right.

He could remember the way the big man used to hit his mother when he'd had too much to drink. He could remember the long nights when Coot would lie beside his battered mother in bed and she would insist to Coot that E. P. wasn't a bad man but that he'd saved them. Bitterness rose in him.

"Robert," said Coot. "Name's Robert Allen, sir."

The big man held his eyes on Coot for a few moments.

Coot let his eyes meet the big man's. The anger behind his face started to make his teeth hurt.

"Bless you, Robert," said E. P.

"You too," Coot lied.

The men guided E. P. into the tent. Coot did not follow. He stood in the sunlight and felt sick. He wandered toward the flatbed where Joseph sat. The old man was lying on his back, his legs dangling off the back of the truck. His torso and face were covered with the tarp, draped over himself to shield him from the sun, and he was singing quietly.

Coot lifted the tarp and whispered, "Joseph,"

Joseph kept singing, *"Believe me, if all those endearing young charms . . ."* He was waving his hands like a bandstand leader.

"Joseph, get up."

*"And around the dear ruin, each wish of my heart would entwine itself verdantly still . . ."*

"Joseph, you drunk goat, get up."

He laughed at Coot and coughed a few times. He kept singing. *"As the sunflower turns on her god, when he sets, the same look which she turn'd when he rose . . ."*

"Joseph." Coot pinched the man's side as hard as he could.

"Ouch!" said Joseph. "Don't be violent with your elders."

"Joseph, would you listen to me? I've changed my mind."

"You did? Well, it's too late, I already drank it all."

"No, not about that. I've changed my mind about the other thing."

"What other thing? What do you mean? You mean you're finally gonna let me teach you to play the accordion?"

"Will you straighten up?" said Coot. "I mean I'll do it."

"Do *what*?"

"I'll run whatever game you wanna run on these people."

Joseph leaned forward to get a better look at Coot. "I thought you were a man of convictions."

"Not anymore."

"Why the change of heart?"

"It's personal."

Joseph showed a big smile, shielded himself with his hat, and turned his empty bottle upside down. He tossed the bottle to Coot. "J. Wilbur Chaplain's gonna be awful disappointed in you, son."

# Sixty-One

# CARRY ME

\* ⭐ \*

The field stretched toward the end of the world. It was dark and looked soft against the moonlit, violet sky. Pin-pricked stars shined above the dark shapes of the trees and lent their light to those below. Pete and Ruth high-stepped through the tall grass, making a scent for the dogs to follow.

Pete carried a scattergun beneath his arm. Ruth followed closely. Pete paused now and then to consider where it was they were heading. Pete had left many scent trails before, but never one this long. This trail was two miles long, and Ruth could tell he was nervous that the dogs wouldn't be able to follow it. His pride hinged on their success.

When Pete had asked Ruth to come with him, she agreed immediately, but she hadn't worn the right shoes for a hike through the mud.

When they came to the creek, they stopped. Pete suggested she turn back home so she didn't get her feet dirty. She refused.

"It's too dark to see back home," she said.

"Home's just that way," he said. "I can see the light on the porch from here."

"I'm not going back."

So Pete leaned his shotgun against a tree, removed his hat, and lifted Ruth in his arms. He carried her across the creek. She felt her heart start to do strange things inside her, like it was backfiring.

When Pete placed her feet on the ground, she did not release her arm from his neck. His eyes met hers. The whites of his eyes were blue in the moon's light. She could see something come over him. He pulled her toward himself. She leaned her head forward. It was only a light kiss, but it erased pain. It thrilled her. It felt like the world was opening up for her.

All her life she'd been a girl whose mother didn't want her. A child who'd grown up in a pair of coveralls, without a true place she could call home. A child among a bunch of coarse men who spit tobacco and struck matches on the soles of their shoes. But right here, right now, she was a woman. And someone loved her.

Pete pulled his head back.

"I'm sorry," he said.

"Quit your sorryin'," she said.

She kissed him again.

Pete retrieved his hat and gun from the other side of the creek, then rejoined Ruth. They held hands and walked until they reached the highway. There, Pete pointed his gun into the air and fired twice.

"You think Vern heard that?" said Pete. "Two miles is an awful long way."

"I think he heard it."

"Yeah, but Vern can't hear squat. I never thought of that until just now."

She kissed him again. This time it was not a light kiss. She held him so tight she could feel his pulse. And she felt Pete give in to it. His hands held her waist, and she was against him. It made her start to weep. She hadn't meant to ruin the moment by crying, but she had felt so alone for so long, she couldn't help herself.

"Why're you crying?" he said.

She embraced him. She rested her head on his shoulder and soaked his shirt with salt water. She knew she didn't have to tell him why. She knew Pete was among the only people in the world who understood her. So she said nothing, and he only patted her back.

Finally she released him and wiped her eyes, sniffing her nose. She felt embarrassed, sobbing like she had.

"I'm fine," she said. "I'm sorry."

"Quit your sorryin'."

# Sixty-Two

# LITTLE MIRACLES

*★ ★ ★*

Abe walked beside Marigold through the maze of straight pines. The sunlight filtered through the thick branches overhead. He was whistling, but unsuccessfully. She'd been trying to teach Abe how to whistle all day. She regretted this because the shrill sound of wind passing through his fat lips was about to drive her to an early death.

Whenever he landed on what sounded like actual whistling, he'd get so excited he'd say, "Did you hear *that*, Aunt Marigold? I'm whistling, ain't I?"

"Yep, I was listening," she'd say. "You're getting better."

"I am?"

"You are."

"Really? Wanna hear me whistle some more?"

"Maybe we should take a break from wh—"

More ear-piercing whistling.

She considered strapping the child to a tree using his suspenders and coming back for him after three days.

"Am I getting good?" Abe asked.

"You're getting so good I can hardly stand it."

And this was all Abe needed in the way of encouragement. He just needed to know his aunt was listening. That's what Marigold was to him. An aunt. A second mother.

Abe carried the basket of wild blackberries, his face stained with purple smears. Between bites of berries, he whistled tunes that were not melodies at all but sounded more like a bird getting eaten alive by a house cat.

She stopped walking. She saw an old man waiting on the porch of Cowikee's. She remained still and looked at the man who was sweating through his white shirt. She knew he was waiting for her. She could tell it by the serious look on his face.

Abe whistled. "That's enough whistling for today," said Marigold.

As Marigold neared the railcar, she saw Rachel sitting on the edge of the porch with a shirtless young man. They held cigarettes between their fingers.

"Got someone here to see you," said Rachel.

The old man on the porch stood when he saw Marigold.

He seemed uneasy. He approached her with his hand outward. He was dressed nicely. His weathered skin gave away his age.

"Afternoon, miss," he said. "Name's Marion. I come from Montgomery, originally I's from Raleigh, but I come to Alabama when I was . . ."

She nodded and listened to his every word. People seemed to want to tell her about themselves before she touched them. And she always listened. Some people recited an entire dictionary to her before they told her why they were there.

Still, something in her felt that listening to people was more important than touching them. People, she thought, wandered through life feeling alone, lost, and terrified. Sometimes they just wanted to be heard.

"Pleased to meet you," she said, pumping the man's hand. "What can I help you with, Mr. . . ."

"Marion," he said. "Call me Marion."

"Okay, Marion. What can I do for you?"

Abe whistled. "I can do it, Aunt Marigold!" said Abe. "Did you hear that? I can do it."

"I hear you, Abe," said Marigold.

"I hear you too, Abe," said Rachel, taking the boy inside. "Let's go inside to see Mama. Aunt Marigold's got company."

The shirtless young man leapt off the porch and stomped out his cigarette. He wandered toward the woods to give Marigold and the man privacy. He lingered by the fence, perhaps in hopes of seeing Marigold the Magnificent at work.

The old man looked at his feet. "Well, ma'am, see, it's my wife. She's been gone a few years . . ."

"I'm sorry," said Marigold.

"Was TB that took her. She fought hard."

"I'll bet she did."

"Anyhow, I heard in town that you . . . Well, I just wondered if you could . . . I was hoping maybe you could tell her something for me."

"Mister Marion, I'm very sorry. I don't do that."

"Oh, I know, miss. I know you don't, but you see, I reckon you got a better chance of getting a message through than I got. Just thought maybe you'd try for me. I can pay you whatever you want."

"It's not that I don't want to, but it doesn't work that way."

"Yes, ma'am, I understand."

"But why don't you tell me about her? She sounds lovely."

"Oh, she was, ma'am. She was exceptional."

She sat beside him and listened. He told her about his wife. She listened to his stories about young love, early marriage, and family living. About when the doctors told his wife she couldn't have children, but she did anyway. About the years they went for long walks together after supper. About everything. Marigold listened and felt a yearning inside her. She'd never known simple love from another. Not like this.

When the man came to a stopping point, Marigold said, "Marion, she hears you."

His eyes became wet. "How do you know?"

"It doesn't matter. Now I want you to do something for me. Can you do something for me?"

He wiped his eyes, then nodded.

She said, "I want you to close your eyes and think about her. Think about her real hard. Can you do that?"

He closed his eyes.

She watched his old, dry cheeks become shiny with his own tears.

She took a few breaths. She had no idea what she was doing, but she was trying nonetheless. She touched his chest with both hands. She placed them on his breastbone until she could feel him sturdy himself against her.

Marigold felt the young man watching her. She saw him light another cigarette and move closer. She saw Rachel and Abe watching from behind the screen door. She saw Helen's face through the window.

Marigold closed her eyes and concentrated.

She could feel the old man breathing. She worked past his breathing and into feeling the rhythm of his heart. She felt the pulse of the man. She felt his eyes flutter. She heard a light sobbing sound he made, but she knew this sound was not coming from his mouth, only inside him.

"I miss her," he said. But it was not his voice that said it.

"Sshhh," she said aloud.

She felt a gentle warmth radiate from her palms. It was different from the heat she normally felt. His sadness seemed to scab over, and the feelings of loneliness began to die down inside him. She felt color and elasticity come back into his face.

It made her smile. When she opened her eyes, she saw him smiling too.

"She got your message," said Marigold.

"She did?"

She removed her hands from his chest. They sat in silence for a few minutes.

"How do you know?" he said.

"Because I can see it on your face."

The old man was still smiling. "I feel better knowing she sees me."

"Me too."

Then the sound of whistling came from behind the screen door. It was not a steady melody, but a sound that could crack glass.

"Hey, that's pretty good, boy," said the old man, replacing his hat. "You keep that up and you'll be a professional whistler one day." He stood, bid them good evening, climbed into his car, and drove away.

The shirtless young man asked, "What'd you do to that fella?"

"Nothing," she said. "I just listened."

"Looked like you did a lot more than that," he said.

"I think we all just want someone to listen to us."

"Yeah?" the man said. "So who listens to you?"

# Sixty-Three

# TAKERS

* * *

Coot listened to E. P. preach. Once he got past the eerie feeling it gave him, it felt like being at home again. After all these years. Home. A very disturbing and blood-chilling home. But you can't choose home. It chooses you.

Tents like this had been home for an entire childhood. White tents filled with sinners who wanted to get rid of their money in exchange for a miracle.

Excitement, that's what revival preachers sold. Temporary excitement. And even though it was a big farce, Coot had never realized how much he'd missed this excitement.

When E. P. preached it made him feel like he was right back in the warm place he'd always been. Only his own warm memories were a lie, and he knew that. Time had a way of softening harsh things.

E. P. shouted his guts out to a full tent of sinners. There must've been three hundred people seated in wooden folding chairs. They watched the big man pace the stage with wide eyes. E. P. was hollering like a fool, waving his hands in the air, shouting scripture. People hollered back. This was an animated crowd, bordering on rowdy. They whooped. They shouted.

He had never noticed how good E. P. was until that moment. The man was a master at reading his audience—that's all good revival preaching was, discovering what made an audience tick. Coot had been good at it during his teenage years. But not like E. P. This man was beautiful.

The big preacher walked across the stage like he was pacing his own living room.

Coot stood in the rear of the tent, mesmerized. He had wanted to see E. P. make a fool of himself on this stage. He had wanted to see his greatest adversary strike out. Instead, E. P. was batting one hundred.

Coot was an usher. He wore his seersucker suit with a red ribbon pinned to his lapel. Joseph stood beside him wearing the same red ribbon on his lapel. Joseph whispered, "That fella's a preacher and a half."

"Yeah," said Coot. "He's good."

"Look at these people. Looks like they's about to start throwin' money at the stage."

"Yeah."

"You okay?" said Joseph. "You ain't said two words all night."

"I'm fine."

"You ain't having second thoughts, are you?"

"No."

"You want a drink to steady your nerves?"

"No."

The head usher was a man named William. He was tall and balding with a small mustache. He spoke with a nasal Midwestern accent, and he obviously liked the sound of his own voice because he used it a lot. He passed empty tin buckets to the volunteer ushers.

The troop had been collecting money the same way since before Coot was born. Coot had seen it happen enough times to know how it would work. The ushers would collect money in tin buckets, flash smiles at the parishioners, then place the full buckets into E. P.'s automobile trunk. *Some things never change*, Coot thought to himself.

"Remember to smile, gentlemen," said William in a forced whisper. "Let them see Jesus in your countenance."

"Yeah," said Joseph, elbowing Coot. "Smile, Coot. Let 'em see the love of Jesus all over you."

There was enough liquor on Joseph's breath to knock a hog off a stink wagon.

"You remember what to do, right?" whispered Joseph.

"Yep."

"You got everything ready?"

"Yeah, it's all ready."

"Good," said Joseph with a satisfied look. "Now relax or you're gonna get us shot."

"Huh?"

"I said relax. You look like you're gonna catch fire any second."

"I *am* relaxed."

"If you're relaxed, I'm sober." Joseph slapped Coot's shoulder. "C'mon, loosen up, boy. People can spot a stiff a mile away."

E. P. finished preaching, and a young woman guitarist took the stage. She was blonde and wearing a white dress with a ribbon for a guitar strap. Coot already knew which hymn the young woman would sing before she even opened her mouth. The same hymn his mother had played so many times her fingers could play it without the help of her brain. "Softly and Tenderly."

Coot thought about his mother. His jaw tightened and his eyes tensed. Wearing a phony smile, he passed a bucket along the first row of people. They placed handfuls of cash into it.

The usher on the end of Coot's row received the bucket, then passed it to the next row. The bucket returned to Coot even heavier than he'd thought it would be.

Row after row, people in overalls, plaid shirts, and cotton dresses dug into their pocketbooks and gave.

When the collection was over, there were eight buckets altogether. Coot, William, and two other ushers carried the buckets outside, behind the tent.

William unlocked the trunk of E. P.'s car and flung it open. The man lit a cigarette and checked his pocket watch. The ushers lined up, then set their buckets inside the trunk of the vehicle. Coot placed his bucket with the others.

"Where's Brother Carl?" asked William.

"Who?" said Coot.

"Your father. Where is he?"

"Oh, him. I don't know, he was right behind me."

On cue, Joseph hobbled from the tent carrying two heavy buckets in his arms. The old man was wobbling like he was about to lose his balance.

William pointed his cigarette at the old man and said, "Quick, someone go help him. He looks like he's about to drop dead."

Joseph tripped. He fell face-forward. Never before had Coot seen a more beautiful, more dramatic fall. The buckets flew into the air. Coins and dollars spilled like confetti into the night.

William gasped. "You *stupid* man!" he shouted, tossing a cigarette on the ground. "You *stupid, stupid* man!"

William and the other ushers congregated around Joseph and began gathering the money.

Joseph writhed on the ground, moaning in pain. "I think I broke my wrist," Joseph hollered. "I think it's broken."

Coot moved fast.

He went to the trunk of the vehicle and removed the six buckets two at a time. He shoved the buckets of cash beneath the car, just behind the rear passenger tire. Then he placed six heavy buckets full of washers, bolts, screws, and paper money into the trunk.

"Robert?" He heard William's voice call to him.

Coot had almost forgotten his own false name.

"I'm over here," Coot called from the other side of the vehicle.

"Your father's hurt. Get over here."

"Be right there," said Coot. "Nature called, I had to answer."

When Coot marched from around the car, he was pretending to button his trousers.

"I think I broke my wrist," said Joseph. "I can feel it."

"Daddy," said Coot as he rushed to Joseph. "I told you not to carry more than one bucket."

"You know me, son. I always try to do too much for the glory of the Lord."

Joseph was laying it on a little too thick.

When the ushers finished collecting the scattered money from the ground, refilling the buckets, they placed the two buckets into the trunk of the big car. William slammed the trunk closed and locked it. He said to Coot, "Take your father home, Robert. We can all smell the liquor on his breath."

Then William looked at Joseph with an aggravated look on his face. "You *stupid* old man."

"At least I'm drunk," said Joseph. "What's your excuse?"

William straightened his collar and walked toward the tent with the other ushers. When they were out of sight, Coot let out a sigh and almost fainted.

"Better hurry," said Joseph. "That jack mule might get a hankering to come back out here and pray for us."

Coot stooped beneath the car and emptied the full buckets into a large burlap sack as quietly as he could. One by one, until the sack weighed more than a ten-gallon bucket of mud. When he lifted the heavy sack, he paused. The gravity of what he was doing was finally sinking in. This was not just a huckster game with a decoy wallet. This was theft. Heartless, merciless thievery. He leaned against the car and took a few breaths to think it over.

"Hey," said Joseph. "What're you doing?"

"That man on the stage," said Coot. "I know him."

Joseph hobbled toward Coot. "The man preaching?"

"Yeah."

"How?"

"It's a long story."

"The old days, huh?"

"Something like that."

All of a sudden Coot's entire life seemed pathetic. He felt ridiculous, stealing pennies and quarters from a bunch of people who were only hoping for miracles. He felt like a child trying to get revenge.

"You gonna be okay?" said Joseph.

"Yeah," said Coot, slinging the bag over his shoulder. "I just wanna go home."

"Don't we all, son."

# Sixty-Four

# THE MIGHTY

✶ ✶ ✶

Paul carried a mop and a wooden bucket filled with tar. After putting it off for eight months, he was finally going to patch the barn roof. The roof of Miss Warner's barn had taken on rain. The problem had gotten so bad that leaks had formed in the cow stalls, making puddles in every nook of the barn. Water had saturated the dry feed and turned the entire barn floor into a soupy brown sludge.

"Would you look at this slop?" said Paul, standing in the barn doorway. He stomped his foot on the ground. His boot almost got stuck in the mud.

"Look at Murgatroyd," said Vern, pointing to a cow. "She ain't happy."

The cow looked miserable beneath the falling water. Paul walked to the stall and stroked the old girl's head. He spoke softly into her ear. "We'll fix that roof, sweetheart. Don't you worry."

Paul climbed onto the tin roof carrying the bucket of tar. The metal roof was slick from last night's rain. He walked toward the weak spot over the cattle stalls. He could see water pooled in a small crater on the tin. There were rusted holes around the puddle. He swore to himself. This was a bigger job than he thought it would be, and it would require twice the tar he had.

He walked toward the soft spot, keeping his steps careful and light. All his adult life, Paul had been light on his feet. All his life he'd been a mighty man. And he was an expert on roofing crews. He'd laid nearly a thousand of them in his day.

But age catches up with everyone.

Without warning, he dropped his bucket. It rolled off the roof and sailed to the ground. And in this moment, he realized why he'd dropped it. He felt a stabbing in his right arm, like dull knives cutting through his muscle. He dropped to his knees on the slanted roof. He gripped his shoulder. He tried to lay himself flat on the roof so he wouldn't fall, but he slid sideways. He could feel himself slipping from the edge of the roof. And he felt the exhilaration of falling from it. In a way, it almost felt like flying.

He hit the ground so hard, he heard his own chest make a cracking sound. He landed on his bucket of tar.

"Paul!" he heard Vern yell. "Paul!"

Paul couldn't speak. He only closed his eyes.

# Sixty-Five

# BEARING WITNESS

\* \* \*

The sun was setting. The world was lit orange and yellow from the colors of dusk. The forest was alive with frogs and insects. The gnats were making their cause known to all who lingered outside. The mosquitoes were inflicting God's wrath upon mankind.

And the railcar was alive with voices. Men's voices. The tavern was overrun with men who drank whiskey, played cards, stomped their feet, and laughed a little too loud. There was even music. A blind boy named Josiah played guitar along with an old man on a fiddle from Saraland every weekend.

Friday night was big business. A good Friday could earn a working girl enough money to last a few weeks.

The girls of Cowikee's were inside, making themselves ready. They applied makeup to their faces and sprayed perfume, primping themselves for a big night. Marigold watched them from the porch. She saw them through the windows. They were prettier than she was. They were more alive than she was. Sometimes she wished she were one of them. Their lives were so exciting, so free. But she was not like them. She was forever bound to her purpose in life. She was charged, somehow, with the task of being something altogether different.

She knelt before a washtub, scrubbing dishes with Helen. Abe sat beside them, whistling. He'd gotten good at making music with his mouth. He could whistle "Oh My Darling Clementine" and "Oh! Susanna," and Marigold could even make out his melody.

"That's good, Abe," Helen said. "But how 'bout we try another song before we all go try to drown ourselves?"

"Like what, Mama?"

"Anything different will do," said Marigold. "Try singing 'The Crawdad Song.'"

"I don't know that one."

They sang it for him, and their weak voices made them laugh. They sounded like two Labradors with chest colds.

They were interrupted by the sounds of footsteps. Two men came walking the dirt path in the darkness. She could hear them before she could see them. Their feet crunched on the ground. She expected them to wander toward the front of Cowikee's like all men did on Friday nights, but instead they approached the porch.

They were young men, with trim hair, wearing slacks, pressed shirts, and loosened neckties. These were not Cowikee's customers.

"All business is up front," said Marigold. "We don't take customers unless they go through the front."

The men exchanged uncomfortable glances. They walked toward her and placed a paper flyer on the porch. "We're not here for that kind of *business*, ma'am."

The paper had a drawing of a large circus tent on it. The words *Holy Ghost Revival* were printed in large letters, surrounded by crucifixes and angels. There was an illustration of a man with a square jaw and steel-rimmed glasses.

"Who's this man?" she said.

"Why, you've never heard of Reverend J. Wilbur Chaplain?" one man said, glancing at his friend with big eyes. "He's God's man for our time."

"Revival is coming to Alabama, miss," said the short man. "It's happening all around you. All the towns are getting ready for an outpouring that's gonna set all paths straight and make the rocks cry out and the trees bow down, and stuff."

"Outpouring?" she said.

"Yes, ma'am. There's a Holy Spirit revival just south of town tomorrow night." The tall man handed her another flyer.

"'Holy Ghost Revival,'" she read aloud. "'E. P. Willard and His Full Gospel Troop,' tomorrow night."

"Yes, ma'am," the tall man said. "And after that, J. Wilbur Chaplain is gonna be in Saraland. Revival is hitting Alabama."

The short man said, "Glory."

"The Lord sayeth," the tall man went on, "that the wicked shall perish, ma'am, and perish they shall if they reject the goodness of the Lord and all his power."

"Revival's hitting Alabama," said the short man.

"Glory," said the tall man.

"What is a revival?" she said. "Ain't never heard of one."

"Preaching of the full gospel," said the tall man. "And singing and praying."

"And miracles," added the shorter man.

"Miracles?"

"Yessum, from the Lord Almighty himself."

"Glory," said the other man.

"What kinda miracles?" Marigold asked.

"Why, divine healings and salvation of the sinner. The restoration of God's people on the earth. The union of the Holy Ghost with his people. Revival is coming to Alabama."

"Mmm-hmm, sure is. Glory."

The tall man said, "'For the Lord saith unto thou—'"

"No, not *thou*," interrupted the other man. "It's *thee*, not *thou*."

"Ah, yes. My brother appears to be correct. 'Draweth nearer unto *thee*' . . . Uh . . . I mean 'thine' . . . No, that's not it."

"Aw, you muffed it, Danny," said the shorter man. "Let me say it." The man cleared his throat. "'Draweth nearer unto *thine* and he shall'—that is—'thee, and ye shall' . . . I mean, 'he shall' . . . Uh . . . 'Thy will be done' . . . No. Aw, hellfire, that's not it either."

"See, Phillip?" said the tall man. "You don't know it no better than I knows it, you big fathead."

"Don't call me a fathead," said the shorter man in a whisper. "We're bearing witness."

The tall man pulled a small book from his pocket and began riffling through the pages. After a few minutes, he finally said, "Pardon the confusion. Here it is, ma'am: 'Draw nigh unto God, and he shall draweth nigh unto thee. Cleanseth your hands, ye sinners . . .'" The man stopped reading and looked at Marigold's pruny hands. "'Ye wicket, wicket sinners, and purify your hearts.'"

"What's *nigh* mean?" asked Marigold.

This clearly confused the men. "Well," said the short man. "It means sorta like *tither* or *hither*."

"Really?" said the tall man. "I never knew that. What's the difference?"

The short man gave a sour look to his friend. "There's lots of *tithers* in the Bible, ma'am, and a few *hithers*. You know, it's just the way God wanted it."

"Glory," said the tall man.

"Anyway, ma'am," said the short man. "We come to tell you that we have a van that'll come pick you up tomorrow and take you to service if the Lord doth press it upon your heart. And if you have a mind to go see J. Wilbur Chaplain next weekend, we're picking up saints and sinners from as far away as Coffeeville."

Marigold inspected the flyer again. The drawing of the tent showed a large crowd gathered inside. "That looks like a lot of people."

"Oh sure," said the short man. "This state is just ripe and ready for Jesus."

"Jeeee-zuss," said the tall man in a whisper.

The short man said, "Folks is coming from all over to see the New Work."

"Will I get to see healings?" she asked. "Real healings?"

The men looked at each other. "If the Lord wills. You'll see everythin' there ever was to see."

"Revival is fixin' to hit Alabama."

"Glory," said the short man.

# Sixty-Six

# CHANGE OF HEART

**✶ ✶ ✶**

Joseph and Coot slept in hammocks near the giant bay. The sound of water lapping against the sand was enough to make Coot remember an entire lifetime. It was a beautiful night. It was humid and chilly, even though it was summer. The air was so damp, it made Coot's cold clothes stick to him, and he could see his breath in the night air. He could see why Blake had missed this place so much. It was a kind of heaven.

Joseph was awake in the hammock beside him, smoking a cigar.

"Can I try one of those fancy smokes?" Coot asked.

Joseph lobbed a paper box of cigars at him. Coot removed one and smelled it. He didn't care for the aroma. He lit one end and puffed on the other, but nothing happened.

"I must be doing something wrong," said Coot.

Joseph laughed but did not rise from his hammock. "You dummy, you gotta bite off one end first."

Coot bit one end, then spit it on the ground. It made him remember Blake and the stubs he used to chew. Coot lit the cigar until the tip radiated orange in the darkness. He took one puff and almost gagged. "This thing tastes awful," he said.

Joseph nearly passed a kidney stone from laughter. "An acquired taste, son."

"I don't wanna acquire it."

"Well, don't waste it. Give it to me. I'll smoke two."

Coot handed him the lit cigar. Joseph placed it in the other side of his mouth and grinned. "You are a different boy," said Joseph, removing both cigars at once, blowing smoke. "First time I met you, I said to myself, 'This fella's special.' I can read people, you know. But I'm not as good inside as you."

"I ain't good."

"You're too good for your own good." Joseph coughed. "I wish I were half as pure as you."

"That cough doesn't sound so good, Joe," said Coot. "Don't you think we oughta get it looked at?"

"We sure gave them holy rollers what-for tonight, didn't we, boy? Made me feel fifty years younger."

Coot looked at the burlap sack full of money. It was full of four hundred and ninety-eight dollars. Silver dollars, quarters, nickels, and pennies. He didn't want it. None of it. He knew that now. Now that he had it, he wished he could throw it into the bay and forget all about it.

Joseph said, "Ain't you gonna tell me why you wanted to rip that preacher off so bad?"

"I don't wanna talk about it," said Coot.

"You ain't even gonna give me a hint?"

"I don't wanna keep that money," said Coot.

Joseph sat forward. "How's that?"

"I don't want it."

"Are you nuts? Don't want it? You're the joker who made me go through with it."

Coot was embarrassed. "I know, but I've changed my mind."

"You change your mind more times than a woman. Now, are you gonna tell me what's goin' on here, or do I have to beat it outta you?"

"It's a long story. I don't wanna talk about it."

"Well, it's not your decision to make. I come close to breaking my wrist for those dollars and all I have to show for it are a few cigars I can't smoke without choking."

"I'm sorry, I just can't keep it."

Joseph leaned back onto the hammock. He flicked one cigar into the bay water. "Fine. Suit yourself. I'll keep your cut for you. Problem solved."

"No, Joseph, I wanna give it back."

"*Give it back?* You outta your gourd? They'll hang us, or send us to a road crew, busting up little rocks with hammers."

"I don't feel right having it."

"Why, I'm sure they'll applaud us when we waltz right inside that dadgum tent and lay five hundred bucks at the altar, saying, 'Sorry, folks, we had a change of heart! God bless.'"

Joseph swung his legs over the hammock. "Now you look here, young'un. I helped *git* that money, and that means I have a say in what *happens* to half of it. And unless you start telling me what's going on, I got half a mind to whup you."

Coot stood and lifted the burlap sack. "My mind's made up, Joe." He tossed it into the front seat of the truck. "I know those people, and they steal for a living. They always have, because they ain't nothing but liars and thieves. I can't be like them. I just can't. Not anymore."

"Hey!" said Joseph, leaping from his hammock. He limped after Coot. "This ain't the way you 'n' me work! Don't my opinion count for something?"

"Sorry, Joe. This was a mistake."

"You ungrateful little spit, get back here."

Coot hopped into the driver's seat and slammed the door. He fired the engine. He pressed his foot on the gas a few times for effect. He'd always wanted to do that. But he drove nowhere. He only waited.

The old man stood in the headlights, staring at him, cigar hanging from his mouth.

"Now let's talk about this," said Joseph.

"Are you with me or not?"

The swindler studied the eyes of his best friend. He hobbled toward the car. He threw open the door and said, "For the love of Christmas, son, at least have the decency to let me drive. You can't drive worth a cuss."

★

Coot snuck toward the row of tents that looked like illuminated paper lanterns in the night. In the distance, the large canvas structures looked like a miniature city situated in a peanut field. The five small tents sat behind the big tent.

The sound of a radio came from one tent. A tinny radio voice, the sound of music, audience laughter.

He stepped through the high grass toward the open flap, then peeked in. A young woman was reclining in her bed. It was the woman who played the guitar. She wore a white nightgown, her hair wrapped in rags. She was reading a magazine.

Coot glanced behind him to get his bearings. He could see Joseph's truck at the edge of the scalped field. It was idling, and he could hear it beneath the song the frogs were singing.

The next tent was filled with several cots pressed together, with men lying on them. A few men were playing checkers by lantern light; another man was ironing clothes with a flat iron, humming to a song in his own head.

But it was the tent at the end of the row that Coot was looking for. E. P. was in a heated discussion with a tall, skinny man. E.P was shirtless, suspenders slung over his bare, hairy shoulders. He was standing before a washbasin and mirror washing his face. He dipped his hands into the basin, then wiped the rag on his face. He swore at the skinny man.

The unmistakable sound of the big man's voice carried Coot to another time and place. A terrible place. It was a time when Coot was on the receiving end of such swearing. Long ago, E. P. would cuss and holler just before laying his hand aside Coot's young face. The memory made Coot swell with anger.

But he was not here for revenge, he reminded himself. The reason he was here was not totally clear to him, but he was not here to get even. He wondered what it might feel like to make eye contact with his tormentor. The idea worked on Coot until he'd entertained it. The more he watched E. P. swear at the skinny man, the more Coot wanted to confront the man who'd made a serious attempt to ruin his life.

Coot decided he would make it quick. As soon as Skinny left, Coot would rush into the tent, say a few dramatic words—preferably with his chest poked out—fling the sack of money at the big man, then leave in righteous fury. It was perfect. Short and sweet. It was a little self-righteous, but not enough to feel bad about.

He heard the skinny man say, "Don't blame me, E. P. I didn't do nothin'." And he saw E. P. draw back and slap the skinny man with his heavy hand. The man stumbled backward and held his face.

E. P. said, "Who on earth *should* I blame, then? Cary Grant?"

The skinny man stormed out of the tent holding his face. Coot saw the man duck into another tent and heard him kick a few things. This was followed by the sound of clanging metal.

Coot seized his opportunity.

He darted into the tent. It was almost too much to bear. A few moments ago, he was Coot, the man who wandered the world in freight trains. But here, he was the Child Preacher of the Plains, standing before the Devil himself.

The big man's eyes moved to Coot's hands. He eyed the burlap sack. Both men were silent for a few moments.

"I was wondering when you'd come back," said E. P.

Coot wanted to say something very clever, and in fact, he'd been thinking about it all night. But before he could get a word out, he felt something stiff jam against his shoulder blades. He turned to look behind him but couldn't get a good look.

"Evening, son," said a deep voice behind him. "I don't think I'd move if I were you."

Coot took one step sideways. He felt the stabbing in his shoulder blades get harder. "I mean it," said the voice behind him. "You try anything and you'll wake up carrying a harp."

*So this was the big plan,* Coot thought. *Rush into a tent and get suckered by a man with a gun. Some plan.*

Coot said nothing. He dropped the sack and raised his hands.

E. P. walked toward Coot. He gripped Coot's jaw, pressing his cheeks together. He glared at Coot with reddened eyes. "You ain't changed a bit. You look just like your mama."

Coot felt a pang in his gut when E. P. searched through the contents of the burlap bag. Finally he closed the sack and frowned. He flung it against the wall. He stepped toward Coot and let his face contort with hatred. He flicked Coot's nose and said, "I'm pretty disappointed in you, Coot. I raised you better 'n this."

"You didn't raise me," said Coot.

"You're right. You're absolutely right. I did more than just raise you. I gave you life, you wretched boy."

Coot felt his heart beating in his ears. "You're a liar."

"Well, now, you have a point," said E. P. with a smirk. "But I'm also your *pa.*"

"You're nothing."

"Your mama told me you was mine the night she had you. Told me you were my responsibility. I didn't believe her, and I never believed her. Until now."

The man walked toward the small mirror hanging above the washbasin. He unlatched it from the hinges and brought it to Coot.

"See that?" said E. P. "Same hair, bones, eyes. You're more mine than you were hers."

"You're a liar."

"Believe me, I ain't any happier about it than you are." He laughed. "But don't think just 'cause you're kin means you get special privileges, *son.* You're still a little thief."

Coot felt a blow behind his head. He hit the ground. He felt his eyes get heavy beneath the weight of unconsciousness.

The large man squatted to get a better look at Coot. He brought his eyes even with Coot's. "You're a thief, just like your old man is."

He felt another blow to his head, then Coot's world went black.

# Sixty-Seven

# IN CARE OF PAUL FOLDGER

\* \* \*

He was in Miss Warner's bed. That's where he was. He knew by the wallpaper on the walls. The flowers with little ivy around them. But it took a few moments to realize who he was. His brain was moving slow. Very. Slow. One thought would come to him, but before he understood that thought, another one took its place. And the two thoughts were unrelated. He was confused and in pain. He felt like his head was going to explode.

Ruth and Miss Warner fed him broth. He saw them do it but could not understand what he was seeing and was unaware that he was eating at all until he felt hot liquid run down his chin. And it made him laugh. When he did, he spit broth all over himself.

He opened his mouth to speak and felt his diaphragm tense. He meant to say, "I'm a good-for-nothing slob, ain't I?" to break the tension in the room. But all he could get out were unintelligible moans.

So he closed his mouth. He was a prisoner in his own body.

When they finished feeding him broth, they changed his stained clothes by leaning him forward in bed. He was vaguely aware of what they were doing. But most of the time he was years in the past, with her. He could see her, standing beside a clothesline, smiling at him.

He felt jostled from his own memories.

It was Pete who rushed to him and embraced him. "I love you, Paul. I love you."

Paul struggled with more words. He really worked at it this time because Pete had never showed this kind of concern before. He wanted nothing more than to set Pete's mind at ease. To tell him it would all be okay. To reassure his family that he would pull through this and everything would work itself out. That life would go on, and nothing was ever as bad as it seemed.

But he couldn't get any words to come out. He struggled to get his jaw open. His neck muscles trembled, and he leaned his head against the headboard. He became so frustrated with himself that he tried to writhe right out of bed. He was going to will himself to stand up by nothing but hardheadedness. That's how he'd made it through life, after all. Stubbornness. But he couldn't move anything in his body. Not a single muscle did what he wanted it to do.

"No, Paul," said Vern. "Stay where you is, stay right where you is. We all right here. We love you, Paul."

Ruth held his hand. "We love you so much, Paul."

Miss Warner stood in the back of the room with her hands folded against herself, head down.

It was beginning to settle on Paul's weary brain what was happening. He'd always known it would happen, of course. It happened to everyone. Paul had been thinking about it since his teens, when his father died. But he'd never thought about how it would feel. It felt ominous, and big, and kind. Whatever it was, it felt like it was washing over him like a spring rain. Then like a waterfall. Then like a landslide. Like acres of mud, grit, and earth falling upon him and enveloping him.

He tried to draw in a sharp breath but felt nothing in his lungs. He only felt hot. He decided to give it one last shot. He opened his jaw. "I-I-I," he moaned.

*One word down, fifty more to go,* he thought.

"What do you need?" Ruth asked. "Do you need to use the bathroom?"

"Are you hungry?" said Pete.

Then he laughed. His laugh sounded awkward to his own ears, and all wrong. He couldn't say what he needed to say. And there was no way it was going to happen. Not with the world falling upon him like it was.

So he stared at Ruth. It took all the energy he had to keep his eyes on her without getting drawn away by the woman by the clothesline. He could feel her calling to him. He could see her standing beside a doorway to another place, another time, and another world. Her hair was bright in the sunlight, and she was waiting.

Ruth touched Paul's face. She was crying. Her tears fell upon him. They saturated his clothes and gathered in the wrinkles on the skin of his aged neck.

And he was whisked away from his own mind for a brief moment.

The woman from the clothesline had carried him away into a memory. She took him through an entire storybook of his own life. A life he never knew he was so proud of until this very moment. He saw the farm where he was born. He saw the swing his father hung from the old tree by the well. He saw the chicken coops. He saw the woman he married. He saw the day of her funeral. He saw Vern as a young man. He saw a lot.

Then his journey was stopped. He saw an old newspaper photograph. It was old. Dry-rotted at the corners with age. In the photo was a man, a younger version of himself, looking at the camera, with a baby in his lap. The child on his knee. It was his child. Even though it was not his blood, she was his life's ambition. She'd given him something he never knew he needed. Something without a name.

He forced himself back into the land of the living. But he didn't have the energy to speak.

Ruth kissed him. Over and over again, she kissed him.

Pete had crawled into the bed beside him and kept his body close to the old man.

Vern knelt at the bedpost and held Paul's limp hand.

He had his family with him. He had them. He'd always had them. They were more than a family. They were the guide for a meandering life, giving him what a man like him was not worthy to have, but somehow received anyway by an act of divine mercy.

He was pulled from the world again. The woman from the clothesline led him to a cotton field, then a tobacco field, then a firepit.

Then he was in the newspaper office. He was holding the redheaded baby. He was looking at a newspaper clipping that read:

LOST BABY RESCUED NEAR RABBIT CREEK, MOBILE, ALA.
RED HAIR, VIOLET EYES. IN CARE OF PAUL FOLDGER UNTIL
APPROPRIATE PERSON OR PERSONS STEP FORWARD.

Ruth's kisses on his forehead brought him back.

With all the effort he had, he gained control over his right arm. He gripped her wrist. He brought his gaze to her violet eyes. He labored beneath a broken jaw. He felt a longing inside himself that could not be satisfied. Not this time. A longing to live. Not for himself, but for the young man beside him, for the girl who kissed his forehead, for the young married woman a whole state away, and for the black man who held his hand. And he felt like he'd failed them all, somehow.

"I-I-I'm sorry, Ruth," he said.

She smiled and wiped her tears away. "You can go, Paul. You can go if you have to. You can go."

No sooner had she said it than he felt warmth surrounding him. The heavenly forces holding the landslide released their barricades and allowed the inner dome of the world to fall upon him. A light filled the room momentarily, and he began to let out a short chuckle. It was beautiful. It was all so beautiful. He'd never known it to be this beautiful, even though it was around him all the time.

He could feel a laugh start inside him. It was only inside him. And it felt so good. It felt better than anything he'd ever felt.

"Oh, Delpha," he said.

And Paul Foldger died.

# Sixty-Eight

# GOING TO MEETING

✶ ✶ ✶

"I ain't going to no stupid revival," said Rachel, plopping herself in the chair beside the fan. "I'd break out in a nervous sweat if a preacher so much as looked at me." The fan blew Rachel's blonde hair backward. She held her arms up to catch the breeze beneath them.

"I don't think it's like that," said Marigold. "They say there's *healings* there, and miracles."

"We got enough healings going on right here," said Laughing Girl. "People come from all over just to see you, Marigold, not some holy roller."

"I don't trust church people," said Helen, who was making the bed on the other side of the room. "Those people are liars."

"So what if they are?" said Marigold. "It doesn't mean I have to tattoo their name on my forehead or anything. They say they have healings and miracles."

"They're full of it," said Helen. "You already know what you're doing. Who needs them?"

Marigold sighed. "There must be somebody out there like me. Somebody who feels like I do."

"Those people would humiliate us," said Helen. "They know who we are, and they know what we do. They probably have posters with our mug shots in all their holy little church lobbies."

Rachel laughed at this.

"Helen's right," Rachel said. "I don't think whores oughta be going to no revival. Ain't good for business."

"Well, I don't wanna go by myself," said Marigold.

"Why go at all?" said Laughing Girl. "Those people are not like us. They will look at us with religious eyes and make us sorry."

"That's not the point," Marigold said. "I wanna see what the healings are like. I wanna see who does them."

Rachel placed her bare feet on the windowsill and let the fan blow against her silk robe. "I ain't going. Besides, I ain't got nothing to wear to a church service."

Laughing Girl added, "Me neither. I have nothing to wear."

"What do you mean?" said Marigold. "You both have more clothes than anybody."

"But nothing decent," said Rachel. "Nothing a preacherman wants to see."

The girls laughed again.

Helen placed both hands on Marigold's shoulders and said, "People like us don't belong there, Marigold. Just the way the world works."

Marigold walked outside to the porch. She leaned against the railing and looked at the sunset above her. Helen followed and let the screen door slap behind her.

"I feel alone," said Marigold. "I feel like a freak sometimes."

"Honey, you're not a freak," said Helen.

"I'm someone mystic people come to see in the woods, and that's all. They don't wanna know me, they don't wanna meet me, they don't wanna have me over for supper or invite me to church to sit beside them. They just want me to do something for them. And when I do it, they're gone."

Helen said nothing.

"I do our laundry, I cook the food, I watch Abe, and I watch the men come in and out of Cowikee's by the droves to escape their pitiful lives. And at night we're alone. I'm alone. Nobody comes calling on me. Nobody even cares." Marigold began to cry. "I just wanna know if there's anyone else like me out there. Anyone."

Helen wrapped her arms around Marigold. She kissed her cheek. "Okay," she said. "Okay, we'll do it."

"You will?"

"I said we'll do it, and we will."

"Well, I won't," Rachel hollered through the open window. "Not unless you want us all to get struck by lightning before we even find a seat."

"She'll go with us," said Helen. "She will go. So will Laughing Girl. And so will Abe. We'll all be there. Front row, if you want us to be."

# Sixty-Nine

# I SHALL NOT WANT

✳ ✳ ✳

Vern felt strange in his suit. He knew he must look as strange as he felt. He had never worn a suit before, let alone a necktie. Not ever. Miss Warner had bought it for him in town and persuaded him to wear it. "Wear it out of respect," she had said. Vern didn't see how a necktie was respectful, not when Paul himself had hated them. But it wasn't worth arguing about. Miss Warner could keep a small argument burning for several decades. He'd never exchanged a cross word with her, and he didn't want to start now. Besides, he wanted Paul to be respected, so he wore the ugly thing.

It was impossible not to tug at the tie every few seconds. Pete tugged at his tie too. Their neckties were nooses, reminding them of what today was all about.

Over the past days, Vern had cried so hard his neck muscles hurt. He had never cried that hard. Not even when his own father went on to glory. Vern had sat in his bunk behind the barn, sobbing into a pillow so nobody would hear him. It was the end of the world, he thought. The real end. The earth felt hollow and dead. Nothing was the way it had been when Paul was alive. Nothing. There was no sunshine and no sounds of birds. It was like living in a graveyard.

Pete and Vern had pooled money together for a pauper's funeral. Miss Warner gave them a burial plot that had been in her family at the Methodist church. Still, Pete and Vern were eleven dollars short when they paid the undertaker.

The funeral consisted of nothing more than a pine box, a linen sheet, and a Methodist preacher. Pete and Vern dug the grave themselves.

The long walk to the cemetery, with Paul in his narrow box, felt odd to Vern. It was as though these events were happening to some other family, not his. It was like a different Vern was grieving for a different Paul, not the real Vern and the real Paul. It was as though somewhere in the world, the real Vern and Paul were still out there living and doing what they'd always done, replacing roofs, cooking hogs, picking tobacco, and raising young'uns.

Pete, Vern, and two other men lowered Paul's pinewood box into the deep hole using ropes. It was more difficult than Vern had thought it would be. The rope slid out of his grip and burned his hands. Another man lost control of the casket too. Paul's box slammed into the pit. The lid popped loose, and his white hand could be seen flung outside the box. Those who'd gathered to pay their respects pretended not to notice what had happened.

The preacher went ahead with the service, even though Paul's hand was showing. All Vern could think about while the preacherman read his words was that hand. He thought of all the things that hand had done in its years. The hand had made things from wood, held babies, and paid their way through the world.

Pete's dog, Stringbean, sat among the small group of people, watching the service. Ruth stood beside the dog with a blank face. Pete stood beside her, looking like a ghost.

When the preacher finished, Vern stepped forward and cleared his throat. He knew it was improper for a man of his color to speak at a white-people church, but Paul was his best friend, his brother, and sort of a father too. He was speaking not just to Paul but for him. He wanted Pete, Ruth, Reese, and Miss Warner to be comforted. It was a job Paul had assumed all his life. To comfort those who were afraid. And now it was Vern's occupation.

"The Lord, he is nigh to the brokenhearted," said Vern. "And he saveth those who is crushed in spirit. The righteous man might have a good many troubles, but the Lord shall deliver him outta all of 'em, so that not even a single bone in his body shall be broken."

"Amen," said the preacher.

"Amen," said the rest of those gathered.

Vern took one step backward and rejoined Ruth, Reese, and Pete.

"That was lovely," whispered Reese, squeezing his arm.

"Thanks," said Vern. "Ain't my words. J. Wilbur Chaplain wrote them, I think."

Then it was time. Vern tossed the first shovelful into the hole. He choked back tears that started. So did Pete, who wiped his eyes with his palm.

Miss Warner did not cry. She only stooped low and sprinkled a handful of dirt on the pine box. Then she took Ruth by the shoulder and said, "Let's get back to the house before the others. I have a sponge cake in the oven."

But Ruth did not leave. She knelt beside the mound of dirt beside Paul's grave. She held her face in her own hands until Pete came to her. She gripped his white shirt and squeezed. Ruth plunged her hands into the mound of dirt and threw the soil into the grave. Then she wiped her face with a filthy hand, leaving a streak of brown across her nose and cheek.

She bent low to scoop more dirt. She used two hands. Then she started kicking the dirt into the hole and making loud grunts. Vern quit digging. He only watched her. Some people needed to get mad. Some people needed to get their hands dirty.

She finally collapsed onto the grass and cried into the earth. Vern lifted her in his arms and carried her home. When they arrived on the porch of the house, he set her onto her feet.

"Ruth, honey," said Vern. "Is there anything I can do? I'm worried about you."

"Just take off that stupid tie," she said. "You look ridiculous."

*Seventy*

# DREAMS

**✷ ✷ ✷**

Coot was having a dream. A wonderful dream. In the dream, he was a fourteen-year-old, standing on a platform positioned in a wide tent. He stood before hundreds—no, thousands—in Greensburg, Kansas, on a dry summer day. He could see his mother playing a pump organ. She was wearing a white dress, and she had flowers in her hair. Her face was as youthful as a teenager's, younger than he'd ever seen it.

The child preacher was speaking in a wild voice, with hand gestures and dramatic movements. He was wearing a white linen suit and brown shoes. He felt good. He felt alive. He felt like he was doing something real. But it was only a dream.

He paced the stage and spoke to half of the congregation. Then he spoke to the other half. He shouted. They shouted. People hollered, screamed, threw their hands upward. Then he touched them. Folks fell backward under the power. People giggled, squirmed like worms. One man gobbled like a holy turkey. They cheered him. And he felt as though he was reborn.

Then the tent became bright. So bright it nearly blinded him. Through the back of the tent flaps, he saw her. It was just her shape, backlit by a white light. Her hair moved in a steady breeze, and the hem of her dress was flapping sideways.

Her violent red hair was like fire. She was wearing powder blue. And she stood in the center aisle, looking at him. She held one hand in the air. Her skin was milk-white, peppered with freckles. He wanted to speak to her. He wanted to know more about her. He tried to approach her, but a crowd of people stood between them. The more he tried to work his way through them, the more people appeared, until they were separated by a multitude of bodies. He saw her standing in the far-off distance. People surrounded her, closing in from every direction.

Coot clawed his way through them, one person at a time. He climbed over a sea of people. When he finally reached her, he was so taken by her beauty he could hardly speak. He opened his mouth to ask her something but was interrupted.

*Tap, tap, tap.*

He was startled awake. It was a high-pitched tapping noise. He opened his eyes and felt disoriented in a spinning world. He closed his eyes again. A sharp ache boomed behind his temples, and the back of his head throbbed something awful. He tried to make himself fall asleep.

There was the tapping again.

So he forced himself straight. He discovered he was inside a car with tan leather upholstery. He saw an embroidered cross dangling from the rearview mirror. It took a few moments to remember what had happened the night before.

He tried to move his hands but realized he couldn't. Neither could he move his feet. He was hog-tied and gagged. His feet were bound with twine, and his hands were snug behind his back with bailing wire, a handkerchief in his mouth.

More tapping.

He let his lazy eyes focus on the shape in the window. A face. A familiar face. It was Joseph, smiling at him with big eyes. Joseph tapped on the window and pointed toward the lock on the inside of the door.

Coot could see Joseph's mouth moving, but he couldn't hear him from behind the glass.

Coot squeezed his eyelids together to bring the blood back into his head. He was dizzy. He felt a couple miles above his body, floating in a world of nausea. He couldn't tell what time it was. It looked like the sun was starting to go down.

*Tap, tap, tap.*

Joseph pointed to the locking mechanism again. "Hurry," Coot heard him say in a muffled voice. "Unlock the door."

His body moved in an uncoordinated way, but he lumbered into action. The lock on the door was a chrome post, poking from the door panel. It had been pushed down, so that only the top of the post showed. Coot adjusted himself and tried to lift the post with his feet, but his boots were too big and bulky. He pinched both soles against the post and tried to lift it upward, but it didn't work.

Joseph tapped again, then made a chomping gesture, pointing to his teeth. "Use your teeth, Coot," he said. "Your teeth."

So Coot leaned forward and bit down on the handkerchief so his teeth were exposed. He worked his overbite around the small post, then pulled upward with a jerk from his head. It took several tries, but he finally heard the mechanism click.

Joseph tugged the door open. Coot spilled out of the car.

"Sshhh," said Joseph, unlatching a jackknife. He started slicing through Coot's ropes.

"I had to wait all dang day for you to wake up," whispered Joseph. "It's late afternoon. I thought you was dead."

"How long have I been out?"

"Long enough for me to think you were playing a harp. Now, we'd better hurry before all those tongue talkers start showing up. That is, unless you want these nuts to show us what hell looks like personally."

When Coot's hands were free, he rubbed his wrists. The events from the previous night came back to him.

"Guess there ain't any love lost between you and that preacherman," said Joseph. "I don't know *what* they was fixing to do with you or *where* they was fixing to take you, but I don't think you would've liked it."

"Joseph," said Coot, but he couldn't say anything else.

"What is it, son?"

Coot stood to his feet but felt off-balance. "Where's the truck?" he said.

"We're on foot," said Joseph. "I parked a mile back that way."

Coot looked at the old man who was catching his breath, doubled over. "Can you make it a mile?"

"I made it this far, didn't I? I'm a big boy. I can do it."

"This was one big mistake, Joseph. I never shoulda . . ."

"Guilt won't do you no good now. Right now we walk or we get the ax."

Joseph coughed. His cough turned into hacking. Coot pressed a hand over Joseph's mouth. But there was no stopping the cough. It lasted for a few minutes until Joseph wore a red face and was out of breath.

"C'mon," said Coot. "Now let's hurry before anyone—"

Coot heard a clicking noise behind his ear.

He heard E. P.'s voice. "You going somewhere, son?"

# Seventy-One

# PUPPIES FOR SALE

✳ ✳ ✳

The painted sunset was made of many colors that hung above the world, indifferent to it all. The colors never changed, and neither did anything else. Life kept going, even after death. And it seemed so cruel, somehow, that things should continue as if it were business as usual.

Ruth watched Pete load the bloodhounds into the chicken wire crate at the rear of the truck. They were quiet animals, easy to handle and tranquil. They didn't fuss; they only looked at Pete with heavy eyes that seemed to sag clear to the ground. She sat on the truck bumper, watching him with a sadness hanging over her.

"I don't know how you can sell them," said Ruth, on the verge of more tears. "I just don't think you should do it."

Pete wiped his forehead with a hankie and sat against the bumper beside her. Stringbean sat beside his feet.

"Paul's the one who arranged this buyer, Ruth, and for a lotta money too. It's what he woulda wanted."

"But can't you just wait a few days? I'm not ready to say goodbye."

"Can't. It's been planned for weeks. Fella wants them now, and he's gonna pay top dollar if I can get them to Mobile on time."

"Can't you just give it a few days?"

Pete hung his head. "I would if I could."

Ruth started to lose composure. She'd hoped she was finished with all her crying. She'd put in enough hours of sobbing to last a lifetime. "Oh, what're we gonna do without Paul?"

She had spent the entire morning staring at the newspaper clipping she'd found in Paul's cigar box. The faded clipping had turned brown with age. In the photograph, he was not a young man, but he looked younger than she had ever known him. He looked happy.

"Paul woulda wanted me to hold up my end of the bargain," said Pete.

It hurt to talk about Paul in the past tense. It didn't feel real. It felt like a bad dream that was happening to someone else, and Ruth herself was only an observer.

"Oh, Pete," she said. "Don't leave me."

Pete scooted closer to her. "I'll be coming back in a few days."

She threw her arms around him and moaned into his chest. She missed Paul. She missed everything about him.

She drew back.

"Your shirt," she said. "Is that Paul's old shirt?"

It was. It was the shirt he'd always worn. Green plaid with red in it. She breathed Paul in. It was Paul's scent Pete wore. And it brought it all back to her. The way Paul used to hold her in the early mornings, overlooking the tobacco fields of her youth. The way he talked to her—like she was every bit as adult as he was. Paul had always talked to her differently than he talked to anyone else.

"Don't go, Pete."

"I'm just dropping the dogs off in Mobile and coming right back. Don't worry."

"But what if something happens and you never come back?"

"Ruth, don't be silly. Nothing's going to happen to me."

He held her. She held him.

"Come with me," he said. "Then we can do it together. And you can say goodbye to the dogs yourself."

He brushed a strand of hair from her face. He kissed her. It was a light kiss on her cheek.

In that moment, she noticed how much older he looked. He was no boy beside her; he was a man. A whole lifetime showed on his face. He was a million years older than she was.

"Come with me," he said.

"I can't leave Vern. Not now."

"Vern? He'll be fine."

"He hasn't even left his room in three days. He doesn't eat anything I leave outside his door. Someone's gotta watch over him and make sure he takes care of himself."

"Let Miss Warner do that."

Ruth let out a scoffing laugh. "She's not exactly Miss Warm and Fuzzy, you know."

Pete held her. She could feel the strength in his arms. She worried if he left her that something bad would happen and she would never see him again. It was irrational and ridiculous, but she felt it just the same.

"I'll be back soon," he said.

She held him tight. "Call me when you get there, when you've sold the dogs. Just to let me know you're safe."

"I will."

"Promise me."

"I promise."

"Swear it."

"I swear."

# Seventy-Two

# SWINGING AND HOLLERING

* * *

Joseph was the first to throw a punch. He landed his fist alongside E. P.'s nose. The big man fell backward and dropped the gun. Then the old man tore into E. P. like a windmill in a thunderstorm. Hands flailing, legs kicking. He fought dirty.

"Joe!" shouted Coot. "What're you doing?"

"Run, Coot!" shouted Joseph. "I got him right where I want him!"

Coot had never seen an old man fight before. It looked like the funny papers had come to life. He marveled to see a man his age fight without morals. Joseph kicked, scratched, bit, head-butted, spit, and tore, and no region of E. P.'s body was off-limits to the old man.

"Run, Coot! Run, boy!" Joseph yelled just before landing a swift kick to the big man's vulnerable regions.

But Coot did not run. He knew E. P. would kill the old man if he did. Coot injected himself into the fight and shoved E. P. backward.

Joseph leapt atop the big man's chest and polished his cheeks with both hands, saying, "Take that, you big, dumb, holy butthead!"

Coot tugged Joseph off E. P., and as soon as he had done it, he knew it was a mistake.

A gunshot rang out, scaring the birds from the treetops.

Joseph curled on the ground. He rolled in circles. The moans were unlike any sound Coot had ever heard the old man make. Joseph held his gut and lay on his side. Purple blood formed a puddle beneath the old man.

"I told you to run, Coot," said Joseph. "You hardheaded boy."

E. P. stumbled to his feet, holding a gun in his hand. The preacher's suit was soiled, and his white spats were covered with mud. He fixed the gun barrel on Coot.

"I got no problem pulling triggers, boy," said E. P. His face was bloodied. A trickle of red came from his lower lip. "Just try me."

"He needs a doctor," said Coot.

E. P. wiped his lip with his shirtsleeve. "He ain't gonna get one."

"Please." Coot bent low to touch the old man. "He's hurt."

Another gunshot. Coot heard the slug hit the ground beside his foot. Dirt scattered where the bullet struck the earth. Coot leapt backward. "Are you *crazy*?"

The mammoth man trained the gun barrel on Coot. "Leave him alone."

People were already running from the tent to see what was happening. A group of people hurried to the scene. The crowd formed around Coot and E. P. They made a ring around them, murmuring, gasping.

"Everyone stay back!" shouted E. P., firing a shot in the air. "This man was trying to rob the children of God blind. Nobody robs the chosen!"

"You're *done*, E. P.," said Coot. "You're done."

"Coot!" Joseph shouted. "I can't see. Can't see nothing."

"You hear me, E. P.? You're done!" said Coot.

A man from the crowd shouted, "Somebody call a doctor."

E. P. fired a round at the man and missed. "Stand back, Kirkland. This don't concern you, and it don't concern no doctors neither."

"You can't do this," said Coot. "E. P., this man is dying. Somebody call the sheriff! Anybody!"

"E. P.!" screamed one woman in the crowd. "You've lost your mind!"

E. P. kept the gun steady. Coot watched the big man rock from foot to foot like he did when he was preaching the Good Word. He knew E. P.'s stamina was wearing thin. He knew the man had taken too many hits to be fresh. E. P. was no prizefighter.

It was an impulse, and Coot knew it. He had one chance to get it right. Coot drew in a sharp breath, crouched low, closed his eyes, and ran forward. He did it so fast it took a moment for E. P. to realize what he was doing. He rammed his shoulder into the big man's waist. Coot felt his shoulder pop on impact. His momentum lifted E. P. from his feet. The deep thump of E. P.'s massive rib cage when he hit the ground was loud.

People in the crowd circled around them.

Coot yanked the gun from E. P.'s hand. He felt a stabbing pain in his collarbone. He remembered being slapped with the big man's belt when he was a boy. He remembered the bone in his neck that E. P. chipped long ago. For most of Coot's adult life he had fantasized about this moment, when he would overpower E. P. But he didn't feel like he'd imagined. It was not triumphant. It felt pathetic and sad.

Coot felt a hand on his shoulder. "Look, your friend is . . . ," said a man behind him.

A woman in the crowd was leaning over Joseph, listening to his chest.

He ran to Joseph and fell to his knees. He dropped the gun. "Oh, Joe, hold on for a little while longer."

Joseph opened his mouth and said, "I told you to run, boy. Why don't you never do what I tell you?"

He coughed a few times. Then he let out one large breath. And Joseph was gone.

# Seventy-Three

# ON THE BUS

\* \* \*

The two holy rollers arrived at Cowikee's in the late afternoon driving a white van with chrome bumpers and white tires. They were dressed in full suits, wearing crimson ties and linen shirts. They had sweated through their shirts so that their neckties were bleeding onto their shirts. They stood before the vehicle's open doors waiting for the girls, who were busy fanning themselves.

When the girls stepped off the porch, the eyes of the young men became as big as washtubs. Rachel wore a low-cut blouse. Laughing Girl wore a lace and floral dress that might as well have been painted on her body. They walked with short steps, careful not to stumble in their tall heels.

The young men swallowed so many times they looked like choking victims.

"What's the matter?" Helen asked. "Ain't you never seen a *girl* before?"

The man nodded. "The Lord be with you, ma'am," he said.

Marigold trailed behind them dressed in a powder-blue dress she'd bought for four dollars in town. It was the most expensive thing she'd ever worn, and it had a matching hat. The young men led the women to the van and helped them step up into the back seat.

When Rachel stepped into the back, one of the young men said, "How are you ladies on this fine evening?" in a tone reminiscent of the first stage of puberty.

"We're hot," said Rachel. "It's hot outside." Rachel dug a cigarette from her handbag and said, "Anyone got a light?"

The young men almost came to a fistfight over who could get to their lighter first. The short man held his lighter toward Rachel with a shaky hand. Rachel grabbed his wrist to steady him.

"Thanks, doll," said Rachel. Then she winked.

Marigold sat beside a teenage boy whose face turned red when she squeezed next to him. Helen sat beside a black woman who carried a baby on her lap.

Rachel and Laughing Girl sat in the very back with a group of teenage boys in sport coats who all wore the looks of the recently deceased on their faces.

The ride was a long one, wrought with bumps and twists on one-lane dirt highways through the forest. Marigold had only ridden in vehicles a few times in her life. Just feeling the vibration of the motor beneath her was thrilling.

The sun was lowering behind the trees. The rural world was slowing down for the evening. They passed creek bridges, desolate farms, and places so far from town they had to mail-order sunshine. They drove past places Marigold had never seen before. And it occurred to her how little of the world she had experienced and how small her life was in such a big universe.

The van turned off the main road onto a dirt pathway. The vehicle followed two tracks through a scalped field toward a giant tent that stood atop a hill on the horizon. It was a bigger tent than Marigold thought it would be. It was already lit orange in the dim early evening.

When they neared the tent, she could see vehicles parked in haphazard clumps.

"What in the world?" said the young man who was driving. "What's going on?"

"Beats me," said the other holy roller. "Something's not right."

Marigold could see a crowd of people gathered outside the large tent, surrounding black-and-white squad cars. Lights were flashing, and people were huddled together.

"What in the name of . . . ?" the young driver said.

"What's the sheriff doing here?" said the other.

The van rolled toward the crowd but was stopped by a man wearing a badge. Marigold craned her neck out the window to see. The man in the uniform rapped on the van's window.

The driver rolled down the window and asked what was happening.

"Get these people outta here," answered the man with the badge. "Ain't gonna be no revival tonight. Sorry, folks, everybody needs to go home."

"But what's wrong?" said a woman in the back seat.

"Sheriff's business, ma'am. Now, everyone just go on home." The badge smacked the van door and said, "Take these people home, boys."

"Is someone hurt, Sheriff?" Helen shouted.

The officer looked inside and said, "Helen Burlington? What in the world are you doing *here*?"

"What happened?" said one of the teenage boys.

"There's been an accident, folks. A man was shot. We need this area cleared so we can get back to work. Now don't make me tell you twice."

Without warning, Marigold's hands became hot. She looked at them; they were bright red, almost like she'd been burned. She glanced out the window but couldn't see through the crowd of people.

"Sheriff," said Helen. "I think we can help."

The sheriff seemed annoyed by this. He leaned into the window. "You?"

"That's right, us."

The sheriff smirked. "Thank you, Helen, but these men don't need that kind of help. Right now I just need this place emptied." His voice was getting louder.

"Hey," said Rachel. "She was only trying to help."

Marigold stared out her window and saw a break in the crowd of onlookers. She saw a young man kneeling on the ground. Someone was hurt. She could tell that much. She looked at her hands. The skin had become so white that she could see the veins and arteries showing through. She flung open the door beside her. She kicked off her shoes and stomped through the field toward the group of people.

The sheriff turned to see her leave. "Miss!" he shouted. "Get back here!"

"Wait!" said Rachel, who had already leapt from the vehicle. "Wait, Marigold!"

Marigold turned to see Rachel, Laughing Girl, and Helen leaping from the van. They trotted through the mud in their heels.

"Marigold!" said Helen. "Wait!"

"Helen!" said the sheriff. "Get back here, I said!"

"The sheriff looks mad," said Laughing Girl.

"Let him be mad," said Helen. "He was never mad until his wife found out about us."

"Helen!" the sheriff shouted again. "I said get back here!"

"You and the sheriff?" said Laughing Girl. "Really?"

"I was young. He was stupid. Besides, he's gained a lotta weight since then."

The girls laughed.

Marigold ran toward the scene of the accident. She shoved her way through the huddled masses.

Helen ran behind her, holding Abe by the hand. Laughing Girl ran as well, pausing to spin on her heel and stick her tongue out at the sheriff.

Rachel turned and yelled, "Helen thinks you're fat!"

# Seventy-Four

# MOBILE

**\* \* \***

Pete was nearing Mobile. He followed the highway until it led him through the large underground tunnel, plunging beneath the mighty Mobile River. It was the strangest structure he'd ever seen, this hole in the ground. It made him nervous to be beneath the water rushing above him. It seemed unnatural. He glanced behind him. In the rear window, he could see his dogs staring at the cars behind him, tails tucked.

He missed her. He'd never thought about how much he would miss her until this moment. He replayed his entire childhood while rolling beneath this tunnel. They had spent nearly every day of their lives together. Ruth was always there, in every memory and every scene in his life.

The city of Mobile was paved with cobbled streets and lined with majestic and colorful homes that looked like royal places. Iron balconies, hanging ferns, ornate trim work, and tall streetlights. It was more beautiful than anything he'd ever seen. He felt a thrill at being so far from home. But he couldn't enjoy it. Not without her.

He drove through the city, taking it all in, trying to forget the heaviness that gnawed at him. Paul had been the only father he'd ever known. He had guided the family through an uncertain world and ushered them through hell. Who would guide Pete now? Who would teach him about life, and people, and dogs, and how to be a good man?

Stringbean snored in the seat beside him. He rested a hand on her. She moaned when he did.

Once he made it through the city, he followed a new stretch of highway the prisoners were still working on. Men wearing blue denim and swinging hammers and pickaxes stood in the ditches. They were guarded by men on horses bearing shotguns. One prisoner waved at Pete when he crawled past them. Pete waved back to him. The man had red hair and no teeth.

Pete pulled over to glance at the map in his lap. His route was outlined with red pencil. He turned the paper sideways. Stringbean made water beneath a large oak tree in a cotton field. Pete walked into the field and observed the acres of white. He breathed in the smell of it. It was the smell of dirt and foliage and summer air.

He drove again. He rolled down empty dirt paths and passed more men in denim swinging pickaxes. He passed more stretches of new highway. He passed hayfields lit orange in the dusk, a county work camp lined with fences of barbed wire, and bunkhouses with bars on the windows.

He almost missed his turn. It was a nondescript dirt road in the middle of the forest.

He rolled into the driveway and was greeted by a team of Labradors who followed his old vehicle down a long path. Then he saw it.

It was a home that nearly took his breath. The estate was bigger than anything he'd ever seen. It had stately columns, fat and white, towering over a brick patio. The house was surrounded by live oaks and azaleas. There were so many pink azaleas. It was beautiful.

Pete drove beneath the canopy of manicured trees and whistled to himself. Stringbean sensed their journey was coming to an end, and she sat straight in the seat.

"You seeing all this, Bean?" said Pete. "This fella must be awful important." Stringbean saw it.

Pete parked in front of the home. He leapt out and leaned back to get a view of the tall house. It was like nothing he'd ever seen before. Tall as a mountain and wide as a county.

He saw a man wearing a pale yellow suit with a cigar poking from beneath his thick brown mustache. The man was rocking in a chair, legs crossed, surveying the countryside that was behind the house.

Stringbean stepped out of the truck and followed closely.

"Evening," said Pete.

"Evening," said the man, rising onto long legs.

All of a sudden Pete felt very underdressed. His crumpled shirt and stained coveralls were rags compared to the man's clothes. Pete removed his hat, though he wasn't sure why. It was something he'd seen Paul do in the presence of important people and ladies.

"Evening," said Pete again. "I'm looking for Mister Ryals."

The man smiled. "Call me Ferris. The only folks who call me Ryals are men who owe a debt to society."

"You mean like those men by the road?"

"The very ones."

"You mean you're their . . . their . . ."

"Their warden. The prison belongs to me."

Ferris met Pete at the rear of his truck. He eyed the dogs and grinned at them, then stuck his finger through the chicken wire to touch their faces. He spoke to them in a high-pitched voice.

"These're handsome dogs, son."

"Yessir, I hate to see them go."

"I know you do."

"They's sorta like my family, you know."

"I know."

Pete ran the dogs hard. He showed the man how the dogs could work in tall grass after laying trails. He demonstrated how unafraid the dogs were of gunfire by firing a scattergun beside them. He showed the man how the biggest blood-hound, Leroy, could track through standing water.

When the demonstrations were over, Ferris patted Pete's back and said, "Your daddy was right about you, you know that?"

"Sir?" Pete said.

"When we made the deal, your daddy told me you were a good trainer, but I didn't think you'd be this good. I didn't think anyone could be this good."

"He wasn't my daddy. He was just a friend."

"Really? Because he called you his son when I met him."

"He did?"

"He sure did. He bragged on you so much it irritated me. But now I see he wasn't bragging. He was only telling the truth."

Ferris removed a roll of bills from his breast pocket and paid Pete a hundred dollars more than Paul had agreed upon. Pete counted the money twice to be sure, just the way Paul had taught him.

"I think you overpaid me," Pete said, handing the man a hundred-dollar bill.

"No," said Ferris. "That's for your daddy. Folks around here know he was the greatest gun-dog man in the state."

"Really?"

"When I was a boy, my daddy took me hunting with the governor. He had these dogs that did whatever he said. They were the best gun dogs I ever seen. I asked the governor where he got them dogs, and he told me they come from your daddy. I never forgot it. Best dogs in the state."

"He wasn't my daddy. He sorta adopted me and my sister, but we ain't blood kin."

Ferris lit a cigar and said. "Well, blood is just a liquid. He was a good man, your pa."

"He was that," said Pete.

"And there aren't many of those left."

"No, sir."

Pete loaded Stringbean into his truck. He watched the dogs run in the country-side behind the sprawling estate, and he whispered goodbye to them. He fired the engine. He waved to Ferris and left with an empty truck bed.

He cried. Not just for Paul, but for life. It was so short. Too short. And it made him feel an urgency inside. He drove past the prisoners again and the new stretches of highway, and when he reached the tunnel, he knew he would ask Ruth a very important question when he returned home.

# Seventy-Five

# ANGELS

## ★ ★ ★

The deputies tried to hold the red-haired woman back, but she could not be held. She broke through them and walked toward Coot. He was startled to see her. He felt he knew her, almost. It was the way her face was shaped. It was familiar. It was almost as though he'd met her before.

The chatter of the crowd died into a hushed whisper when she approached Joseph's cold body. She knelt beside the man. She pinned up her bright hair behind her head and looked at Coot. She asked, "How is he?"

Coot said, "He's not . . . He's gone."

The woman said nothing. She only bit her lip and touched Joseph's face. She let her eyes sit on him, like she was searching for something.

"I just took his pulse," said Coot. "He's no longer . . ."

"He's not dead," she said. "He's only sleeping." A faint smile ran across her fair face. "What's his name?"

"Joseph," said Coot. "His name was Joseph."

Her eyes were closed. Her nostrils widened slightly with each breath.

The crowd of onlookers had fallen completely silent. Even the noise from the crickets and frogs had faded.

"Joseph," she said. "Now that's a nice name."

The woman pressed her hands on Joseph's belly. She laid them so gently, Coot wondered if she was even touching Joseph at all. She breathed in a slow rhythm. The sounds of the world had ended.

"Hello, Joseph," said the woman.

A stillness overtook Coot. And the world seemed brighter. Even though the sun had almost set, it seemed as though it were midday somehow. He closed his eyes because the sincerity of the moment seemed to demand it.

All he could hear was the sound of breathing.

Coot opened his eyes and saw Joseph's chest rise, then fall. The old man lurched forward and coughed like he'd inhaled a fist of flour.

There were gasps from the crowd and several *hallelujahs*, along with a few screams. One baby started to cry.

The deputies had removed their hats. Even the sheriff stood with his hat pressed against his chest. Then applause. Then the light clapping turned into the roaring sound of voices, chattering in what sounded like another language. People pressed in to get a better look and began to lose their minds.

The deputies did their best to hold them back, but failed. The crowd was pressing in and about to suffocate them. People started clawing at the redheaded woman. Someone pulled her hair. Someone tugged on the woman's powder-blue dress so hard the sleeve tore.

But the woman didn't seem to be affected. She only moved her hands to Joseph's chest.

She held them there until his cough died into a gentle wheeze. Joseph's eyes opened. He wore a look of confusion. "Myrna, Myrna," said the old man. "Is it you, darling?"

"No," said the woman. "My name's Marigold."

Then she collapsed and passed out, and the wild crowd almost trampled her to death.

# Seventy-Six

# GOING HOME

* * *

It was late when Pete's tires rolled into Miss Warner's drive. The familiar farm welcomed him even though it was dark and he could see nothing but its outline against the sky. The little home was surrounded by buckshot stars, and the night seemed so quiet it was almost perfect.

He'd only been gone a few days, but those days had been long ones. Stringbean jumped out of the vehicle after him. He was careful to shut the truck door without making too much noise. Everyone would be asleep at this hour, and no lights were on in the house.

He walked through the yard, past the sleeping chickens roosting on the fence posts.

Pete stepped toward the barn and removed his hat when he looked at the place where he'd found Paul's fallen body. He bowed his head.

"You woulda been proud of me," said Pete in a quiet voice. "Least I hope you woulda. The dogs impressed that old man real good." He swallowed and closed his eyes. "I'm sorry, Paul. I'm just so sorry. I wish you coulda been there." He pinched the bridge of his nose.

He imagined the sound of Paul's voice. "Quit your sorryin'," he would've said to Pete with a stiff slap on the back.

Pete felt arms around him. He could only see a figure in the darkness. She wore a nightgown, and her hair was down. For a few minutes they held each other.

"You're home," she said.

"I can't live without you," he said.

# Seventy-Seven

# THE BIG HOUSE

\* \* \*

Marigold awoke on a cot. Her knees were drawn into her chest and her back hurt. When she opened her eyes, she was surrounded by brick walls and iron bars.

She was not alone in her cell. Beside her was the young man she'd met earlier. He sat with his back against the wall. Beneath her cot slept the old man she had touched. He was snoring.

The county courthouse had two cells in the building, which were actually one large cell divided by iron bars. Marigold focused her lazy eyes on the adjoining cell. The big man was in it, sleeping in his cot, one large leg hanging off his bed. His suit was torn, covered in dirt and blood.

She tried to remember what had happened, but she couldn't get past her tiredness. She was depleted. Her head hurt, her neck stiff from sleeping on an unforgiving cot that was hard enough to qualify as a medieval torture device.

The deputy in the jailhouse was listening to a small radio on a desk. He leaned backward in his chair with his hands behind his head, staring at the ceiling. The sound of singing was coming through the small speaker. *"Savior, like a shepherd lead us, much we need thy tender care . . ."*

Marigold got lost in the music. And so, it seemed, did the young man in her cell. The sound of the tinny voice was so honest it sounded like a child singing.

The young man was seated at the foot of her cot, listening with his eyes closed. When he felt her stir, he looked at her. The young man's face was bruised, and his lip was bloody. His two brilliant eyes seemed to grin at her before his face did.

"Morning," he said.

"Morning."

"You were out like a light."

"How long have I been asleep?"

"A long time. I was starting to worry."

She glanced at the sleeping old man beneath her cot. The man was in a fetal position wearing a half grin. "Your friend doesn't look too worried."

"Joseph," said the young man. "His name is Joseph. And no, ma'am, Joseph don't worry about much except food."

"But you worry?"

"You could say I do all the worrying for the outfit."

They listened to the radio again. It was preaching. A voice screaming so loud, the speaker sounded like it was going to crack. The deputy turned it up. And listened. He nodded from time to time and said, "Amen," in earnest.

"My name's Marigold," she said.

"I know," said the young man. "You told me last night."

"Oh."

"I'm Coot."

"Coot? That's your real name?"

"Short for Cooter."

"Is that a nickname for something?"

"Cooter-tastic."

She laughed.

The deputy turned the volume of the radio louder to drown out their conversation.

"You don't have to blow our eardrums," said Coot. "We got rights, you know."

Marigold and Coot listened to the radio show. The preaching filled the room, and they endured the guard's *amens, hallelujahs,* and moderate bouts of clapping. When the broadcast ended, an announcer's voice blared loud enough to blow the roof off the courthouse.

*"This week in Saraland, folks, come see America's preacher, J. Wilbur Chaplain, bringing God's Holy Word, Friday, Saturday, and all day Sunday. See the healings and the miracles and the salvations . . ."*

Marigold listened with great curiosity.

*"And may God's people pray that revival hits our land, folks, in our desperate hour of need . . ."*

Then the announcer began to pray. The deputy bowed his head, removed his hat, and folded his hands.

The deputy's prayer was interrupted by the sheriff walking through the front door of the courthouse. The officer was carrying a large basket draped with a red-and-white-checkered cloth. "Good grief, Dip," said the sheriff. "You're about to bust the glass in here with that radio. Turn that thing down."

The deputy rose to his feet, saluted, then clicked the radio off.

"You don't have to salute me, Dip," said the sheriff. "This ain't the military, and I'm your first cousin."

"Yessir," said the deputy.

As soon as the sheriff set down the basket, the deputy poked his hands into it and removed a biscuit. He nearly swallowed the thing whole. Then he ate two more.

"Dip," said the sheriff, "there ain't but five biscuits in the basket, you hog."

The deputy wiped his mouth and held out the mutilated remains of his biscuit.

He swallowed. "You want the rest, Sheriff?"

"No," said the sheriff. "Your spit's all over it now, and I don't wanna catch your stupid." He pressed the brim of his hat upward, then walked to the big man's cell. He kicked the bars with his boot. A clanging noise filled the jailhouse.

The big man didn't move. The sheriff kicked the cell door so hard it sounded like gunfire. "Get up, Mister Willard," said the sheriff. "Right now."

The big man stirred but wouldn't acknowledge the sheriff.

The sheriff jammed his boot against the iron bars again. This time he used his heel to make the noise. "Up and at 'em, Preacherman. Rise and shine and give God the glory."

The big man finally sat straight and rubbed his eyes. Marigold caught a glimpse of the man's battered cheeks. He was black and purple, and his nose was swollen. His face looked even worse than the young man's.

The sheriff leaned into the bars and said, "Welcome to our humble home, Preacher."

The big man rubbed his temples and moaned.

"If you woulda gone peacefully, you wouldn't be feeling so ugly this morning."

The big man only blinked his eyes.

"Looks like you're a very important fella, Mister Willard," the sheriff said. "Very, very important. More important than anyone in this room."

The sheriff waited for a response, but none came.

The sheriff went on. "So important, in fact, that the state police *insisted* they come down here and take you off our hands this afternoon. Said they got you on charges of fraud, theft, extortion, liquor running, blackmail, and . . ." The officer removed a folded piece of paper from his pocket. "Looks like you got a trail of debts following you all the way back to Rogers, Arkansas."

The big man let out a laugh. It was deep.

Coot leapt to his feet. He walked toward the bars dividing the two cells. He gripped the bars and said, "He's a wife-beater too, Sheriff. Make sure you tell the state police *that*."

"Domestic charges?" said the sheriff. "That true, Mister Willard? You beat up your women too?"

The big man stood and stepped toward Coot. "She was never my woman."

"That's right," said Coot. "Keep telling yourself that."

"She was a loose girl," the big man went on. "Got pregnant on purpose. Hussy wanted to be with a big-time preacher, that's all."

Coot made a serious attempt at breaking through the dividing bars. Coot hollered until his voice broke.

"That's enough, Mister Willard," said the sheriff. "I won't have you picking a fight in my jailhouse."

The big man leaned backward on his cot and folded his hands across his belly. He seemed unaffected by his circumstances.

Coot pressed his face against the bars and said, "You're the devil, you know that? The devil!"

Marigold touched the young man's shoulder. She felt his fury, and she felt where the hurt came from.

The sheriff passed three large catheads into the cell. Coot took them and gave one to Marigold. They tore into their food. The ham was thick, the biscuits were soft, and the butter was even softer.

After Marigold had enough food in her, she began to think more clearly. She touched her ripped sleeve and remembered the way the crowd had tried to tear her apart the night before. They had swarmed her. It was as though the mass of people had lost their minds. They all wanted something from her, and they didn't care how they got it.

"Why am I in here?" she asked the sheriff.

The sheriff was staring at his desk, writing. "You were out cold. Couldn't leave you there. Those people woulda killed you."

"Those people were going crazy," Coot added.

"I didn't do nothing wrong. You can't keep me in here."

The sheriff didn't look up from his desk. "No, I can't, but it ain't safe out there, I can tell you that much."

"You can't hold me in this cell like a crook," she said.

"I'm doing it for your own good."

"What's that supposed to mean?" said Marigold.

"It means you're safer in here," said the sheriff. "A lot safer than you'd be out there with the nutjobs."

"I wanna go home right now," she said.

"Can't do that, ma'am," said the sheriff, still writing. "Too dangerous."

"What do you mean you can't do it? I got rights, just like anyone else."

The officer set down his pencil. "Okay, you wanna go home? Fine. Go home. But half the folks in the county think you're the Virgin Mary, and the other half think you oughta be burned at the stake. If you like those odds, be my guest."

"What're you talking about?" she said.

"I'm talking about earlier this morning, when Roger Farland and his sons showed up at Cowikee's with shotguns, looking for you."

"Roger Farland?" she said. "Who's that?"

"He's a nut who thinks you're a witch. Wants to do his Christian duty and get rid of evil on the planet."

"A witch?" said Coot. "How could anyone think that?"

"These are hard times," said the sheriff. "People think they saw a man get raised from the dead. They don't know what to think."

"Sheriff," said Marigold, "I demand that you let me outta here this second."

"Fine," the sheriff said, opening a desk drawer and removing a ring of keys. "Suit yourself. Go back to your house of ill repute and see if I care." He opened her cell door. "But I can't do nothing for you when you leave here, just remember that. I can't keep you safe."

"Safe?" she said. "Roger Farland and his sons sound like they're crazy, but surely they don't think I'm really a witch. How could anyone think that?"

"I don't know, but they do, and they aren't the only ones."

"People know me around here," she said. "People know about me. They know I'm only tryin' to help."

"You scared a lotta people last night, sweetie," said the sheriff. "Nobody's ever seen anything like what you did. That man was dead."

"I didn't do anything."

"Well, you scared me," said the sheriff. "And you scared my deputies, and you scared a bunch of fellas with the newspaper. I've had to beat away three different reporters this morning. The phone downstairs is ringing off the hook with nuts who wanna either murder you or worship you. And one man in Grove Hill wants you to pray for his laying hens that have bronchitis."

He led her to the window. He pulled the shade up and tapped on the glass. She looked down at a crowd of people standing on the lawn of the courthouse. The onlookers were backed up into the main street. A few carried signs. One poster-board sign read The End Is Near.

"Where'd they come from?" asked Marigold.

The sheriff dropped the shade. "Most of 'em are in town for the revival over in Saraland next weekend. They got nearly eight hundred cars over in Chickasaw, people camping in tents, all here to see J. Wilbur Chaplain. We got nuts, vagrants, and migrant workers from all over the state. Supposed to be the biggest gathering of holy rollers in history."

The younger deputy said in a solemn voice, "Revival's coming to Alabama. Glory." He had wide eyes when he said it, and a serious face.

"Yeah, well, I hope you're wrong, Dip," said the sheriff. "I had enough revival to last a lifetime last night."

"It's coming, Sheriff," the deputy said again. "Whether you want it or not. These is end times, wrath poured out without mixture."

"Is that right?" said the sheriff.

"Yessir," said the deputy. "I'm praying for glory."

"You know what I'm praying for?" the sheriff said. "I'm praying that you go take inventory of the storage room like I told you to do and quit eating all my flippin' biscuits, dang it."

The scene behind the window made Marigold's breath catch in her throat. She couldn't find words. There were people everywhere, spilling over the sidewalks and onto the side streets. The crowd was made up of more people than she'd ever seen in her life.

"What am I gonna do?" she said.

"You're asking me?" said the sheriff. "Every flap in the county has come to see the woman who raised a man from the dead. I was hoping you knew."

"I don't," she said.

"Well then, I can tell you one thing. In the next few days, every tent chaser within five counties is gonna be trying to get a peek at you. And some of these people ain't working with a full deck. If you ask me, you're safe right here."

She believed him, even though she didn't want to. She wandered into her cell, sat on the cot, and buried her head in her hands. The pure emotion hit her without warning. It swelled within her, and it made her feel so alone.

The young man sat beside her. He held her tight. It was as though he sensed no boundary between them.

"You're gonna be okay," he said. "It's all gonna be okay."

"How do you know that?"

"Because I'm the Great Cooter-tastic."

# Seventy-Eight

# BEARER OF NEWS

☆ ☆ ☆

Miss Warner's small kitchen was lit by the single bulb hanging over the breakfast table. The wood planks in the room looked aged and splintery. A lot like Miss Warner could be if you caught her in the wrong mood. Once, long ago, she had thrown a dictionary at Paul's head during an argument. Not a metaphorical one, a real, unabridged dictionary.

Ruth watched Pete tell her and Vern the news. She watched him without really paying attention to his words. Pete's face was lit by the yellow light with deep shadows on it. He was handsome, yes. But he was more than that. He was the rest of her life.

She could tell Pete was using as much internal strength as he had in him. Ruth could tell it was hard for him by the way he kept swallowing.

He told Miss Warner that he loved Ruth. And beneath the hard glare of Miss Warner, his explanation seemed juvenile. She had that effect on people. He tried to use bigger words. But even so, no matter how he said it, it came out sounding juvenile.

Miss Warner's first words were, "You're practically *brother and sister*. What will people say? This is an abomination, a humiliating tragedy, and I won't have it, not in my house. I never expected this of you, Pete."

So far, so good.

Vern only looked into his lap when Pete delivered the news. And Ruth kept her mouth closed, just the way Pete had begged her to. It was difficult. Ruth had more spirit than anyone at the table. She would've let the old woman have it. But the last thing Pete said he wanted was for a brawl to erupt between two women whom Paul had cared for.

Finally Miss Warner stood and left the room. She left without giving her blessing. Then she shut the door to her bedroom. She didn't slam it, but she shut it hard enough to make the lightbulb above the table swing back and forth. Ruth knew Pete must feel like a fool. She knew he was embarrassed.

Vern rested his paw on Pete's shoulder. "She be alright, Pete. She be just fine. You leave her to me."

"She hates me," said Pete.

"Just needs time," said Vern. "She just missing Paul like we all is. She don't wanna miss you too." Vern looked down at the floor. He sniffed a few times. "Well, I's missing you two already. I miss you both a lot."

Ruth threw herself at the large man and held him. She smelled his sweat and tried to remember everything about him so she could always take his memory with her when they went to Mobile to start a new life.

Vern looked at her with shiny cheeks. His eyes were wet, but the tears that rolled down his cheeks were hard to see in the dim light.

"I'll miss you, Ruth."

"I love you, Vern," said Ruth.

Vern wrapped both large arms around them and held them so hard Ruth could hear her own ribs creak.

And it occurred to Ruth for the first time that Vern would be alone. A man who'd always lived his life with Paul and a litter of kids would be alone, living next to a woman who threw dictionaries at people sometimes.

"You could come with us," said Pete. "There's good work in Mobile."

"No, sir," said Vern. "She need me here. Besides, I's too old. I don't even know who's in the mirror no more." He laughed, and his brilliant white teeth showed. "I'm an old man, boy."

His smile turned into wet eyes. She'd known Vern to endure anything. He was the strongest human she'd ever known. She'd seen him get bit by a copperhead on the ankle. He was sick for two weeks, but never once did he moan or complain. And he recovered.

He walked out of the kitchen. The screen door slapped shut.

"I told you she wouldn't understand," said Ruth.

★

Ruth sat beside Pete in the truck. He drove, keeping his eyes aimed at the windshield. Neither of them said much on the ride. She knew what they were doing was impulsive and youthful and irrational and unsmart. But it felt right.

The duffel bags of clothes were the only things she'd brought with her. She didn't even bring her jewelry boxes. She felt it would be wrong somehow, since Miss Warner was the one who gave her all the jewelry. Stringbean rode in the back seat.

They crossed the county line, and Pete stopped at a local watering hole. It was a swinging-door saloon, right at the edge of the neighboring town. Ruth waited on the porch while Pete asked the men inside where the justice of the peace could be found. The liquored-up patrons were in good spirits. They met Pete with whoops and hollers and laughter.

"Justice of the peace?" one man shouted. "What fer?"

"Can't you figure it out, Byron?" said another. "This man's getting himself hitched."

"You mean he's enveloping?" said another.

"Ee-*loooo*-ping, you big dumb drunk."

"Is that true, son? Is you errloping?"

"Yessir," she heard Pete say. Men began singing, shouting. One man tried to rouse the barroom into a chorus of "For He's a Jolly Good Fellow," but it didn't take.

The men emerged on the porch where Ruth stood. They made a fuss over her. They removed their hats and introduced themselves one by one. They were old men. Wiry men with happy hearts and red faces.

"She's lovely, boy," said one man.

"She is just a sweetheart, ain't she?" said another.

Before the men let Ruth and Pete go, they sang a few more songs and dedicated several raised glasses to the couple's honor. Pete and Ruth swallowed a glass to their own honor. The men cheered when they did.

Then one man whooped, "We gonna have ourselves a wedding, boys!"

The man stumbled from the tavern into the main street and started parading down the road like he was leading a marching band. A few others followed him, singing, crooning.

Pete and Ruth climbed into the truck and followed the parade. Before they knew it, eight men had piled into the bed of their vehicle. A ninth rode on the roof of Pete's truck, singing "There's a Hole in my Bucket, Dear Liza." And when the truck hit a bump in the road, the man fell from the truck roof and hit the ground and nearly broke his leg.

Pete slammed the brakes and said, "These men have lost their minds, Ruth."

Ruth and Pete helped the old man into the bed of the truck. He kissed Ruth on the cheek, then kissed Pete on the forehead and said, "Happy birthday to you both. Happy birthday from the bottom of my heart."

They followed the marching men down the streets toward the justice of the peace. The fields and oak trees passed them in the darkness. Ruth was beginning to feel a smile work its way onto her face. She was used to being serious. But tonight was different.

The parade ended in front of a small white house, lit purple by the moon. One of the men knocked on the door and shouted at the top of his lungs, "Benton! We gotta hitching for you!"

A light flickered in the upstairs window.

The men cheered.

A slender older man wearing a cotton nightgown appeared at the door. He came onto his porch, seeming unsurprised by all the commotion. He calmed them down and said in a formal tone, "Unless you have a license, this is a waste of my time."

"Got one right here, Reverend," said Pete.

"I ain't a reverend, son. I'm an elected official. There's a big difference."

In only minutes, the justice of the peace was standing on the porch, surrounded by sweaty older men with hats in their hands, bowing their heads. The justice of the peace held a small book and recited a passage from Psalms. And one of the men in attendance sang a stirring rendition of "Shall We Gather at the River?" One man cried.

No sooner had the justice of the peace pronounced Pete and Ruth husband and wife than one of the witnesses fired a handgun into the air and screamed, "Yippeeeeee!"

The man who'd fallen off the truck roof marched onto the porch and said, "Can I be the first to kiss the bride? After all, I think you dadgum broke my leg."

Ruth let him kiss her cheek. The men began to holler and argue among themselves. They formed a single-file line to kiss her cheek. And with each kiss, each man handed her wads of sweaty cash from his pocket.

"What's this?" Ruth asked.

"A blessing for the happy couple," the men said.

★

Ruth and Pete spent the night in the bed of their truck, covered with a quilt. Stringbean slept between them. They slept with clothes on, holding each other close until they fell asleep. She kept Stringbean against her so tight that she couldn't feel her arms anymore. And when she fell asleep, she had strange dreams. She heard music, and she saw the woman from her dreams, the red-haired woman who seemed to haunt her sometimes.

When they awoke, it seemed that Ruth had never seen a sky as clear and bright and blue as the one above them. Pete lay still, sleeping with his head on her shoulder. She removed a slip of paper from her pocket and unfolded it.

The words "Lost baby . . ." The photo of an old man holding an infant. She didn't care what the clipping said. She wasn't lost anymore.

# Seventy-Nine

# SONGBIRD

✦ ✦ ✦

Coot felt strange. To see the big man in the cell beside his was like reliving his childhood all over again. Only this time it was being lived through the eyes of an adult. When he looked at E. P., boyhood feelings came back to him, but this time the feelings were different. He remembered the man's good moments from long ago. When he used to give Coot candy, then wink at him. He remembered the great pains the man had gone to to teach Coot to wink when he was four years old. It took Coot a week to learn how to do it right.

It's funny what a mind remembers.

Now he had a man's mind. And things weren't as clear-cut as they once had been. During childhood, he'd known who the heroes and villains were. As an adult, he wasn't sure who they were and who they weren't. And he wasn't sure which side he was on himself.

Joseph was sleeping, curled in a tight ball. Coot hadn't heard him cough or wheeze since Marigold had touched him. He didn't know how this could be.

Coot had gone most of his life feeling that the whole universe cared little for him.

A low voice from the cell beside him said,

"Cherokee, just outside Pittsburgh, Kansas."

The words shocked Coot. He didn't know what to say.

"We did a week of revival there," E. P. said. "When you were little." The big man didn't look at Coot. He only stared forward in his cell. He dabbed his forehead. The man had always been a professional when it came to sweating. "You came down with a fever. We thought you were dead."

"I don't remember that."

Nothing was said for a while. The old man seemed to be caught in his own private recollections. He only leaned back into his bed and let out a mighty sigh now and then.

"How old was I?" Coot finally asked.

"Six or seven. You were so sick, vomiting, crying, sick as a dog, and you got up on that stage, right there in front of God and Kansas, and you preached anyway. Forty-five minutes, white as a sheet, high fever and all. I'll never forget it. Long as I live."

The man laughed, then rolled over on his bed.

Coot wanted to let the man have it. He wanted to give the man every ugly word he had stored up from his years of living. But he also *didn't* want to. And he didn't want to more than he wanted to. "You ruined my life," he finally settled on saying. "You ruined me."

"Kid like you?" he said. "Nothing could ruin you."

Later that day, the state police arrived. Men in uniforms opened the big man's cell, and E. P. became a different man altogether. He became E. P. the joyful preacher. He was charming. He was clever. He was nice to the officers, and funny. And he even made a few of them smile.

Before he left the jailhouse, he turned to face Coot and he winked.

# Eighty

# YAWNING PARTNERS

*★ ★ ★*

It was late. The jailhouse was faintly alive with the sound of a young man's tenor voice making a gentle melody. Coot hummed something. It was familiar to Marigold's ears, but she couldn't place the tune.

She listened, lying on the cot with her eyes closed.

The humming stopped. "You awake, Marigold?" Coot asked her.

"I'm awake," she said.

"But your eyes are closed."

"I'm pretend sleeping."

"Pretend sleeping? Why?"

"Because I don't know what else to do."

She opened her eyes and saw the outline of Coot's tall frame standing near the window of their cell. He was looking out at the world. He was a serious young man, but his eyes were kind.

"You okay?" he said.

She sighed. "Oh, I don't know."

More silence.

"What about you?" she asked. "Are *you* okay?"

"Who, me? I'm great. What a marvelous day, what a delightful jailhouse."

She laughed. It felt good to laugh. "Now you're the one who's pretending. I just wanna go home."

"Home," he said.

She couldn't think of anything else to say. She wanted this man to like her. He seemed like a genuine person. But words were hard for her to find, and she was too busy wondering what would become of her.

She was ridden with irrational fears that would not leave her. She wondered what people thought of her. She wondered if they were right. And she wondered what this young man thought of her. He probably thought she was a freak after what he'd seen her do. She wasn't so sure she *wasn't* some kind of freak.

"You ever been to the Gulf of Mexico?" he said.

She rolled over on the cot to face him. "You mean the beach?" she said.

"Yeah."

"Sure. It's not far from here."

"Is it everything they say it is? You know how people exaggerate about stuff."

"It really is. It's breathtaking. You'd like it."

"It seems like every time I get close to it, it gets farther away from me."

"I know what you mean."

And in fact, she did know what he meant. Sometimes it felt like everything she had ever loved drifted from her before she got close to it. Sometimes she wondered if the universe was against her.

"I heard the water's bluish green," said Coot. "Like emeralds and such. Heard it looks like a fairy-tale drawing."

"Yeah, I guess so. But it's the sand that's really impressive. It's so white, it looks like snow."

"Really?"

"Yep. First time I went to the beach, I thought the dunes were made of sugar. The girls all told me it was made of sugar, and I believed them."

"I'd like to see that one day."

"You really should."

Coot wandered to her cot and sat beside her. She heard him breathe. They were shoulder to shoulder.

"Will you take me?" he said.

Marigold had no idea what was to become of her life. The whole world seemed uncertain and unsteady to her. She wasn't sure if she could commit to such fantasies, and she wasn't sure it would do anyone any good to pretend that she could. But something about kindness from another made her feel hopeful.

"Of course I will," she said.

"Promise?"

"Sure, why not."

More silence.

"Marigold, are you scared?"

She liked the way he said her name. There was a familiarity to his voice. It was as though he were already family. "Yes," she said. "I am."

"Yeah, I was too."

"Was?"

"Oh, I was scared when Joseph got shot, more scared than I ever been, and believe me, I've been pretty scared before. Once I was so scared, I didn't sleep for three days. But this was worse."

"What made you unscared?"

He turned toward her. She heard the cot springs squeak when he did. "You," he said. "You made me feel that way."

"Me?" she said. "I didn't do anything."

"I know. You didn't have to."

*Eighty-One*

# NEWSPAPERMEN

✦ ✦ ✦

When Coot awoke, Marigold's hand was resting on his own. He could feel warmth coming from it. He didn't want to move it. He wanted to hold it, wanted to place his hand atop hers and touch her soft skin.

He looked at her hand. And he remembered how red it had gotten when she'd touched Joseph earlier. It had looked red and raw. But here it was pale white and a little clammy. He had kept his left arm so still the circulation had been cut off and his limb had fallen asleep up to his elbow.

He let his eyes fall shut, but he was not asleep. He was lost in the rapture of hand holding. It was something teenagers experienced but he had never known.

The moment was short-lived. The sound of shoes startled him. When he opened his eyes, he saw shoes with hard heels making clicks on the jailhouse floor.

Coot sat up straight and saw four men in suits holding paper pastry boxes, paper bags, and tin thermoses.

"Thank God," said Joseph, who was already awake. He pinched out his cigarette and wedged the butt behind his ear. "The food committee finally arrives. I'm starving myself half to death."

But the men paid no attention to Joseph; they only whispered to each other. They set the pastry boxes down and scanned the cells with quick eyes.

"Over here," said Joseph. "Let's have that breakfast. I could eat an elephant, one leg at a time."

"That must be her," said one suit, pointing toward a sleeping Marigold.

"That must be the old man," said another suit.

"Better move quick," the suit said. "That sheriff's a real jerk when he gets mad."

"Hey," said Joseph. "Pass that food this'a way, son."

One suit walked toward Joseph and removed a notepad from his jacket pocket. "Are you the one?"

"The one?" said Joseph. "I'm *the one* who wants whatever's in that box."

"I'm with the *Herald Tribune*, sir. Mind if I ask you a few questions?"

"Huh?"

"Was it true that you were dead for nearly an hour, sir? How did that feel?"

"Hey, what is this?" Joseph said. "I've already answered these questions with the sheriff. Now I'm hungry enough to eat your foot, son, and I ain't talking without food."

But there was no food. The men were opening the pastry boxes and removing cameras with flashbulbs attached to the fronts.

"Hey!" said Joseph. "Where's my breakfast? I got rights, you know. I'm a paying customer."

But the suit kept asking Joseph questions. "I'm with the *Post*, sir. Was it a religious experience? Are you a religious man? Where are you from? What was the nature of your relationship with the woman who touched you? Who did you vote for in the last election?"

"I ain't telling you a thing," said Joseph. "Ain't talking to no newspaperman."

The other suits had zeroed in on Marigold. They cranked their cameras and lit up the cell with their flashbulbs. The bright light didn't stir her.

"Someone wake her up," said one suit. "Picture's no good if she's sleeping, dumbbell."

One of the suits flicked a smoldering cigarette butt at Marigold and spoke in a strange accent. "Hey, sweetie. Give us a smile, would ya? One little smile?"

But Marigold was sleeping too hard to be stirred.

"Hey!" Coot shouted. "Get outta here! Leave her alone!"

The men ignored him.

"Sir," the suit said to Joseph, licking the tip of his pencil. "Did you see any *beings*, or any *bright lights*, or hear any strange *sounds*?"

Coot reached his hands through the bars at the men. He made an attempt to choke any of the suits who came near him. But the suits leapt backward. One man laughed and said, "Whoa, this one's grumpy."

"Sheriff! Sheriff!" yelled Coot. "Get these men outta here!"

But the sheriff didn't appear.

Joseph followed Coot's lead. He turned from the men in suits and leapt onto his bed, grabbed the bars of his cell window, and hoisted himself up using his arm strength.

Coot marveled at this. Joseph's upper arms flexed, and his sinewy muscles showed through his old skin. Joseph looked like a man who'd lost five decades from his age. He pressed open the window and hollered, *"Sheriff! Get in here, Sheriff!"*

"Hurry," said one of the men. "That old man's gonna blow our cover."

"Charlie, I need a picture of her awake."

"She's sleeping too hard."

"Throw something at her, for crying out loud."

The man in the gray suit tossed wadded paper from the trash basket at her. But Marigold didn't move.

*"Sheriff!"* Joseph screamed out the window.

One man finally tossed a book through the bars. The book came crashing down onto Marigold's chest. Marigold rose from the bed.

"Shoot her!" said one man. "Take the shot!"

A chorus of flashbulbs lit up the cell. She shielded her eyes in the momentary lapse of blue light.

"Move your hand, honey," said one man, replacing a flashbulb. "Let New York see them pretty eyes."

"C'mon, doll," said another. "Smile for old Charlie?"

More flashbulbs.

Then came the onslaught of questions.

"Miss," said one suit. "Do you consider yourself a messenger from another realm? Are you here to deliver a message to people of this planet?"

"Are you a prostitute, ma'am?" another added. "And if so, how long have you been involved in such illegal activities?"

"Can you talk to the dead, miss?"

"Have you ever, or would you ever, or have you ever considered bringing small creatures back to life?"

"Do you consider yourself a humanitarian?"

"Are you in any way affiliated with the Communist Party?"

"Did you like the last Cary Grant picture?"

Coot removed his boot and flung it through the bars at the men. The heel of the boot hit one man square in the face. Coot couldn't remember ever feeling such satisfaction with himself.

But before Coot could work his other boot off, the door to the jailhouse opened and the sheriff walked in.

The sheriff's face was inflamed and his eyes were big. He stepped toward one man, removed the camera from his hands, opened the back compartment, and strung the guts out. Then he grabbed the man by the shoulders and shoved him out the open door. The other men scurried behind him, holding cameras high above their heads.

"Gimme those cameras!" shouted the sheriff, who darted after them.

Coot could hear everyone's footsteps reverberating in the hall, clomping down the staircase. Coot leapt onto his bed and looked out the window again. He saw the men in suits outrun the sheriff, leap into a car, and speed off, leaving the sheriff standing in the street holding his hat.

"Are you okay?" Coot said to Marigold. "Did they hurt you?"

"No," said Marigold.

"They're like wolves."

"They stink too," said Joseph. "Like cologne."

"I don't know how you could sleep through all that," said Coot.

"I wasn't," said Marigold. "I was only pretend sleeping."

## Eighty-Two

# CLIPPINGS

✴ ✴ ✴

When they entered Mobile, Ruth was too busy staring at the mansions that lined the streets to pay attention to the folded paper map in her hands. The iron railings and ornate houses were overwhelming. They drove across the cobblestones, and the vibration nearly rattled the old truck apart. Stringbean was about to have a nervous breakdown in the back seat from all the rattling.

Ruth pointed out the window. "Look at *that* house, that one's *so* pretty!"

Pete couldn't answer her; there were too many cars driving beside him, around him, and before him. There hadn't been this many cars the last time he visited. It was as though he were stuck in a deadly river of automobiles from which there was no escape. One vehicle honked its horn. He almost lost control of the wheel and his bladder at the same time.

"Look at that house!" Ruth yelled. "It's huge!"

They rolled across railroad tracks. The bumps taxed the axle of his truck. Stringbean was panting. Drool fell from her jowls. Pete knew Stringbean was just as nervous as he was.

"Look at this *city*," said Ruth, pointing out the back window. "It's lovely. It just goes on and on."

"I'm ready for it to quit," said Pete. "Why are there so many cars here? There weren't this many last time I was here."

"Beats me."

A delivery truck passed Pete at a high speed, the gust of wind blowing his hair backward and rattling the windshield. Pete almost made a mess in his pants.

"Do you think people actually *live* in those big houses?" asked Ruth.

Another truck passed. Pete gritted his teeth. "I don't know."

"Pete!" yelled Ruth. She pointed. "Stop!"

They were at the toll booth again. For the second time. This meant they'd been traveling in circles. Which was Ruth's fault. She was supposed to be reading a map, giving him directions, but she was too busy marveling at French architecture.

The man in the toll booth was eating his lunch. He held out his hand. "You again?" he said with a mouthful. "Two bits, kid."

Pete swallowed and looked at him. "Can't you just let us through? We're sorta lost."

"You wanna use the tunnel, it's two *dimes*. Now make it snappy, you're holding up traffic."

Pete reached into his pocket and removed some change. He handed it to the man and said, "This is highway robbery, you know that?"

"Yeah, I know," the man said, giving him change. Then he removed a piece of ham from his sandwich and gave it to Pete.

Pete looked at the pink chunk of ham. "What's this for?" he asked.

"It's for your dog, stupid," he said.

# Eighty-Three

# MUG SHOTS

★ ★ ★

The front page of the *Press-Register* showed Marigold's face, harshly lit with a bright flash. Her eyes were big and baggy, her hair a mess. The photo made her look like a drowning victim who might or might not have lice.

The headline read, "Man Raised from Dead."

The sheriff threw the newspaper on the desk and swore beneath his breath.

Marigold held her own copy. She was seated on the opposite side of the desk, sipping coffee.

Coot peeked through the blinds. "The crowd's been growing all day," he said. "Don't these people have lives?"

"We tried to break 'em up this morning," said the sheriff. "There were too many of them. It was like trying to catch a greased house cat."

This morning two bricks had been thrown through the jailhouse windows with notes attached. One of the bricks had a note that read, "Kill the witch." The people were getting dangerous. The sheriff had been getting so many calls that he had to keep his office phone off the hook.

The sheriff said, "The longer I keep her in this courthouse, the more things get outta control. And I simply don't have the manpower or the jail space to do anything about these people."

"There must be four hundred quacks out there," said Coot.

"What is it they want?" asked Marigold.

"They wanna see you *do* something," said Coot. "They wanna see a miracle."

"Who knows what they want," the sheriff said.

"They want to see a magic trick," said Coot. "Whether they think she's the devil or not, they wanna *see* something."

"How do you know?" said Marigold.

"Just a hunch," he said.

"Well, I don't care what they want to see," the sheriff said. "They ain't gonna see it here."

"Can you believe this?" said Joseph, who was lying on his cot, reading a paper. "Those hick reporters called me an *old* man." He lowered the paper. "Coot, do I look old to you?"

"I'm worried they're gonna try something tonight," said Coot. "If they don't get what they want."

"Try something?" said Marigold.

"I've got three of my men standing guard," said the sheriff. "But three men is all I got."

"The nerve of those journalist hicks," said Joseph. "Why, I ain't even in my eighties yet."

"You all have to get outta my jailhouse before someone gets hurt," said the sheriff.

"Leave?" said Joseph, lowering his paper. "But I like the food here."

"Where will we go?" said Marigold.

"Don't matter to me," the sheriff said. "But you can't stay here or these people are liable to go get pitchforks and torches."

A window shattered. A brick slid on the floor amid shards of broken glass. A paper note was tied around it.

The sheriff retrieved the brick. Without reading the note, he walked to the window and hurled it out. He shouted at the small clot of people, "Get off my lawn!" But his voice was lost in the sound of the crowd.

The sheriff turned to Coot. "Now, there ain't no charges pressed against you two. As far as I'm concerned, you were never here. I'm expelling you from the jailhouse."

"What?" said Coot. "You can't just throw us out. They'll kill us."

"We'll try to escort you somewhere safe," the sheriff said.

"Try?" said Coot. "Who, you and the three little bears? Those people down there are crazy. *Crazy* folks do *crazy* things. We can't leave this building—they might hurt her."

"I think I look pretty good for my age," said Joseph, who was facing the shaving mirror in his cell. "Pretty dang good."

The sheriff stepped toward Coot and pressed a finger into his chest. "You don't get the luxury of calling the shots. You know, I could have your neck stretched for trying to make off with that money, you and the old man. Two thieves like you."

The sheriff gripped Coot by the shoulders and held him. "You are trying my patience, son. Now, you're either with me or you're against me."

Another rock crashed through the window.

The sheriff hurled it back through the window toward the crowd and hollered, "Quit breaking my windows, you hicks!"

# Eighty-Four

# MOBILE BAY

\* \* \*

The motor inn was positioned on the wide Mobile Bay, which sprawled in each direction toward the horizon. The white clapboards were covered in a thin film of green, and the roof was rusted. The inn was filled with guests, but nobody stayed in their rooms. They all sat in the breezeway, smoking cigarettes, watching the bay water.

Something about the bay was otherworldly. It did something to Ruth. It made her think bigger thoughts than she normally thought. And that was saying something; her thoughts were already very big. She felt something here. Something familiar.

Stringbean sat on a leash beside Pete looking pitiful. Bean had never seen a leash in her life—and she didn't like it. Ruth didn't blame her. If she had been a dog, she would've hated leashes too. In some ways Ruth and Stringbean were alike. They were raised without mothers, in packs. They loved food, and they were born to be runners.

Stringbean loved to run more than any creature she'd ever seen. Even so, the animal sat beside Pete like a faithful companion, behaving, ready to do whatever Pete asked.

Ruth and Stringbean stared at the gray water. They were both still and quiet. The people in Ruth's life were almost doglike. And the dogs in her life were almost people-like.

This motor inn was the nicest place she'd ever been. Hands down. The room had green carpet, a small kitchenette with one burner, and a shower. A real shower.

Until the motor inn, Ruth had never taken a shower in her life, only baths in Miss Warner's claw-foot washtub. Since they'd arrived a few days ago, she had taken nine showers. She could not get over how exhilarating it was. It was a marvelous experience, maybe one of the best experiences she'd ever had in her life—except for the time she beat Daniel McGhee in a footrace at the county fair.

The room was small but nice. There were two single beds, a radio, and wallpaper that had little mermaids on it. Mermaids. It was heaven.

Ruth found a chair beside Pete and looked at the bay. "Beautiful, ain't it?" she said.

He looked at her like he was being recalled from a faraway place. "Yeah."

"Can you believe we're actually in *Mobile*?"

"Can you believe we're actually *married*?" he said.

She took his hand. "I can. I can believe it."

A smile made its way onto his face. "Married."

He looked at his lap. His face could go from being alive with joy to sullen in only a moment.

"What?" she asked.

"My mother," he said. "She always wanted to see the ocean. She woulda loved it here."

Ruth leaned against him. She smelled the salty bay water in the air and listened to the sound of it rush onto the shore. Water gathering onto itself, then dispersing. She felt hypnotized by this. It took her to a place in her mind that felt familiar.

For some reason it made her think of her own mother.

"I used to wonder what *my* mama was like."

"Your mama?" said Pete.

"Yeah, I wonder if she done things like I do them or looked like me."

"I'll bet she looked like you."

"I wonder if she ever thought about me."

"'Course she did. You know she loved you."

"How do you know?"

"Because who couldn't love *you*?"

"Then why'd she leave me? Who leaves their own baby?"

Pete gave no response.

Ruth closed her eyes. She smelled the languid air and took in the humid world. She thought of the dreams that were lodged in the back of her mind, untouched. Things she hadn't thought about in a long time. This water. It was as though she had seen it before. The thought started small, then grew like a weed inside her head.

Then an idea came to her.

She went inside and opened the cigar box full of her things. She emptied the contents, the sentimental knickknacks. The sticks of gum, the mood ring, the hard rock candy Vern gave her on her thirteenth birthday. She found the newspaper clipping. She traced her finger along the text.

## Lost baby rescued near Rabbit Creek, Mobile, Ala.

She wandered back outside to Pete and sat beside him. "I wanna go to Rabbit Creek," she said.

He read it and furrowed his brow. "What's this?"

"It was Paul's."

Pete read it a few times, then flipped it over. "How do we find Rabbit Creek?" he said. "We ain't never been here before."

She folded the clipping and placed it in her pocket. "You haven't, but I have."

# Eighty-Five

# MADNESS

**★ ★ ★**

There was a full moon that night. Marigold saw it and felt the beauty of it. It lit the night with an electric blue light. The crowd outside the courthouse had transformed the lawn into a camp. There were small campfires on the grass with people seated around them. There were tents with children asleep inside. There were vehicles parked in uneven rows on the grass, doors splayed open, with quilts hanging from the doors like awnings.

"This is madness," said the sheriff. "Who are these people?"

Marigold was dressed in a deputy's uniform. Her hair was tucked beneath an officer's cap, and she wore uncomfortable men's shoes that made her feet hurt.

The sheriff and Coot escorted Marigold to the squad car across the parking lot. Joseph followed them. Two deputies with rifles followed him. They weaved through the murmuring crowd, who all stood when the deputies passed.

Soon the whole crowd was on their feet, and it looked like they were going to swallow Marigold. She kept her head down, and Coot held her close.

"I'm scared," she whispered to Coot.

"Don't be," he said.

"Why?"

"I don't know. It just sounded like the right thing to say."

One deputy said, "I don't recognize any of these people. They ain't from our town."

"Reckon they're here for J. Wilbur," said the sheriff. "The whole world must follow him wherever he goes."

Marigold glanced at a license plate on one of the nearby vehicles. It was from Ohio. She saw another vehicle from Maryland. She didn't even know where Maryland was on a map.

Coot hooked his arm tightly around her. She leaned into him. They passed men who held shotguns, families with children who wore big eyes, and old men holding Bibles.

When they got close to the police car, they saw a man with a long black beard standing beside it, a rifle slung over his shoulder. The man's long hair was oiled against his head, and his clothes were tattered.

He spit when he saw the sheriff, then made a clicking noise with his mouth that sounded like he was calling a horse. Marigold saw five others emerge from behind the squad car so quietly, she almost missed them. Each man bearing a rifle.

The sheriff stepped forward and shouted, "I'm Sheriff Locklin, and you better let us through."

The man with the beard took two steps forward. He was joined by his allies, who all aimed their rifles at them.

The sheriff did not budge. "You're about to be very sorry if you don't step away from that vehicle, son."

The bearded man didn't move a facial muscle. He only stared at the deputies with slow eyes. Marigold noticed his eyes were so dark brown they looked black. She ducked her head.

The man said, "We want the harlot, Sheriff."

The sheriff withdrew his pistol. Black Beard and Company thumb-cocked their weapons almost in unison. The deputies behind Marigold also took aim with their guns and stood wide-legged and ready to kill something.

The man with the long beard shouted, "That woman is an abomination!"

"That's close enough!" the sheriff hollered. "If you move an inch closer, you're gonna have a big problem on your hands."

The bearded man wrinkled his nose. He peered over his rifle barrel and landed his eyes on Marigold. He gave a smirk when he locked eyes with her and swung his barrel toward her.

"That sure is a pretty deputy you got," said the man.

A loud blast.

Coot threw Marigold to the ground and draped himself on top of her. Joseph jumped atop Coot. And beneath the three-person dog pile, Marigold could feel her heart beating inside her throat. She was too scared to breathe.

The sheriff yelled at Coot, "Take her back inside!"

But Coot did not move, partly because Joseph had his knee dug into Coot's lower back.

"I said get her inside," yelled the sheriff. "Now!"

Coot and Joseph rushed her toward the courthouse, moving quickly through the people with wide eyes. She could hear the people mumble when they passed them.

When they reached the building, Coot beat on the door and said, "Let us in!"

The latch clicked. The door opened. Marigold, Joseph, and Coot rushed inside. Marigold collapsed in Coot's arms and began to cry so hard she almost vomited.

"This is turning out to be a great night," said Joseph.

# Eighty-Six

# HOW HIGH THE MOON

* ☆ *

The moon kept her awake. The light was too bright for sleeping. Ruth opened her eyes. She was lying in bed, staring at the ceiling. The motel room was filled with enough moonlight that she could make out the mermaid wallpaper. Pete was sound asleep beside her. She kissed his neck. He rolled onto his side.

She stood in the breezeway, watching the whitecaps on the bay. She could see them clearly in the glow of the moon. The long, dark flats of grass jutted outward into the water, disrupting the shallow waves, giving them something to crash against. The pelicans were all asleep. The wind from the bay tossed her hair in all directions. The taste of the salt air was in her mouth.

She missed Paul more than ever. Each day her loneliness seemed to get a little worse. It was as though her feelings were stored in different compartments within the same big box. She felt pure elation with Pete, to be here, to be married, and to have the modern miracle of a shower.

But standing here, alone, right now, in the cold night, against the wind, she could feel how alone she really was.

The older she got, the smaller she felt in this world. But Paul had always made her feel big. He made her feel as though the sun couldn't rise or set without her. And she'd somehow believed this for most of her life—for better or worse. But now that he was gone, now that she was in a world without him, she felt like she hardly mattered. The feelings of rejection came back. She was the child of a mother who didn't want her. A baby who had been left to die by the woman who was supposed to nurse her into life.

She started crying. She wondered about that woman and where she was. She wondered if the woman was having a marvelous life without her or if she was suffering. She cried, but not for too long. She had cried so much lately; she was weary of crying.

She watched the moon on the breast of the water. She sat on the bench beside her door and felt something beneath her.

She stood. It was a newspaper wrapped in twine. There was a picture of a woman on the front. And a headline: "Harlot Raises Man from the Dead."

She looked at it for a few moments. Then she tossed the newspaper aside.

She stared at the full moon until she fell asleep.

## Eighty-Seven

# FIRST TIMES

✳ ✳ ✳

Coot sat beside Marigold on the jail cell cot. They held hot tin mugs of coffee that burned their hands. The steam rising from the coffee gave Coot a fresh surge of energy.

The announcer on the radio read the news in a voice that sounded too urgent. He spoke about the price of corn, and the president sending troops to Korea. When the news announcer said that J. Wilbur Chaplain had arrived in Alabama, the deputy turned up the volume. The deputy's face lit up when he heard this. It was as though Santa Claus had just come into the room.

"J. Wilbur Chaplain," the static voice said, "is officially in Mobile, Alabama. His train arrived last night and was welcomed into the depot by the mayor and a loyal crowd of . . ."

When the news ended, the music on the radio began. Soft orchestras played ballads with enough rhythm to dance to. The sounds of muted horns and swelling violins seemed unfitting for a jailhouse somehow, but they dulled the harshness just the same.

It had been a long night. Coot hadn't slept at all. He'd sat beside Marigold in the darkness. She asked him to remain nearby. And it was the first time a woman had ever asked Coot to stay close. Ever. No woman acting of her own volition and free will had ever wanted Coot beside her for safety. This alone made Coot feel that his shoulders had become ten times broader, and his voice dropped four octaves too.

The deputies stood beside the entrances to the jailhouse, and the sheriff slept seated in a desk chair, mouth slung open. Joseph was snoring in the cell beside Coot and Marigold.

Marigold clutched Coot's hand in hers. There was something about this woman that made Coot believe in sincere things again. He didn't want to leave her; she was so easy to be near. She had an intensity to her. Looking into her eyes was like leaning forward to look over a cliff. They had a gravity in them.

"Is it true what they say about you?" he asked her. "Are you some kinda mystic?"

"No," she said. "I'm just me."

"What about your gift, though?"

"No gift. All I do is sorta touch someone and hope for the best."

"If that's all there was to it, everyone could do what you do."

"Well, maybe they can."

"And what, just hope for the best?"

She shrugged her shoulders and sipped coffee. "Maybe."

He glanced at her hand, which rested on his. "Is that what you're doing now?"

"That's all I ever do."

"And what else happens?"

"Not much."

"You mean you don't hear angels singing or saints playing harps and stuff?"

"No. Sometimes I don't feel anything."

"But sometimes you do?"

"Sometimes."

"What do you feel?"

"Oh, lots of things, I guess. Hard to give it a name, there's too much going on at once inside me."

"What did you feel when you touched Joseph?"

"Him?" She furrowed her brow. "Scared. That's what I felt. A lot of fear and terror all wrapped up into one big ball of . . . I don't know. Something."

Coot looked at Joseph. "You mean *he* was scared? Joseph don't never seem scared of anything."

"Either he was scared, or I was," she said.

"*Then* what happens, when you touch someone? What comes next?"

"Oh, I don't know. Nothing, really. Either they believe something is gonna happen and it does, or they don't and they walk away cussing me. But I don't *do* anything."

"Something happens if they believe?"

"Yeah, but not always what they think will happen."

"What do you mean?"

"Well, sometimes it's kinda like we're alone together, just me and that person, just for a moment in time. We're like old friends, meeting after being apart from each other for a lifetime. It's a kind of goodness. And sometimes that's all that happens."

Coot brushed a piece of hair from her face and tucked it behind her ear. He could feel the goodness she spoke of. He felt very forward for having touched her. He wasn't sure what had made him do it. But she didn't seem to mind.

"You make it all sound so simple," he said.

"Piece of cake," she said.

Coot squeezed her hand. "What do you feel right now?"

She looked at her hand and smiled. She set her mug on the floor and placed her other hand on top of his. She closed her eyes. A faint smile worked its way across her face. He could see the freckles that stretched from one side of her face to the other. Wonderful freckles.

"I feel like you are a friend," she said.

Coot was tired of being a friend to beautiful women. He wanted to be more than that. He wanted to be Gary dadgum Cooper for once in his life.

He leaned forward to kiss her. He felt unsure of doing this, it was so forward of him. But instinct took over. When his lips touched hers, he could feel how soft they were. He touched her face. And she returned the favor. When her hand touched him, it was so hot it was almost as though someone had set a skillet on his cheek.

He pulled away.

"What is it?" she said.

He looked at her hands. He touched them with his own hands and felt heat radiating from them.

"Your hands," he said. "How are you doing that with your hands?"

"I'm just hoping for the best," she said.

*Eighty-Eight*

# SWEET PETE

★ ★ ★

Pete had never felt so far from home. Not in all his life. He stood in a single-file line of men who waited on the docks outside the foreman's office. Each man, Pete noticed, had the same sorts of characteristics. They were all young, they all wore drab colors, and they all had hopeful looks on their faces. And Pete wondered if he had the same pathetic look on his face. He had been looking for a job for the last three days and found nothing.

The excitement of this city had been lost. He felt nothing except its cruelty.

He could tell that half the men in this work line were more qualified than he was, and older, probably with more experience.

The man ahead of him had scars on his face, as though he'd been burned. Pete could see hairless patches on his head showing beneath the man's cap. The man was friendly. They conversed. Pete tried very hard to look the man in the eye when they talked, not at his scars.

The man was self-conscious about them, Pete could tell. He touched them and said, "Yeah, I know these look pretty bad, but they look worse than they really are."

The man's burns were smooth and marbled with swatches of pink skin and ropy scars. They had contorted his eyelid so that when he blinked, it didn't close all the way.

"How'd it happen?" Pete asked.

The man sighed. "We were searching for explosives. The dogs started barking, we ran as fast as we could, but it was too late. Four guys got away in time, one man died, and I got burned."

"I'm sorry," said Pete.

"Don't be. It coulda been a lot worse for me. I might not be here."

"Yeah."

Pete had been applying at different places in town to no avail all morning. He'd been greeted by frowns and managers shaking their heads who said, "Sorry, son, I'd like to help you, but I can't."

There were too many people in this city. There was a frantic feeling in the air. There was more poverty here, and there were dangerous people who stood on street corners with bloodshot eyes. They watched people walk by, and Pete felt uneasy when their glares fell on him.

He'd made a mistake, coming here. He was a rural person who knew rural things. He knew dogs. He knew how to fix metal roofs and how to plant. He knew how to pick tobacco and how to shuck corn and how to fill a ten-foot sack with cotton. In the country, they had little, but at least they *had* it. Here, these people had nothing, and even *that* was about to be taken away from them.

The line inched closer to the main office. A man wearing a suit carried a clipboard and spoke to the men in the line. He scribbled things on his pad of paper after talking to each man.

Before the man got to Pete, he stepped out of line.

"Where're you going?" the man with the burns said.

"I'm going home," said Pete.

# Eighty-Nine

# MIRACLES OVER EASY

\* \* \*

The small café was filled with people. Young men wearing military uniforms accompanied by young women were sitting side by side in booths, leaning close. Old men sat on stools reading newspapers. A single waitress wearing a white apron bobbed and weaved through the narrow walkways between tables.

The quiet chatter of the morning bustle was coupled with the sound of crackling bacon on a flat stove. Dim lights hung over the bar where Ruth sat. She was positioned between men who wore denim, smoked morning cigarettes, and wore the lined faces of those who were poor.

They spoke among themselves in voices that were low-pitched and dry.

She ate her eggs and toast, and listened to them talk about their children and their wives using three and four words at a time. Men like them were not the kind to lay their feelings out in the open, but they did not hide them either.

"You going to the revival?" said one man.

"Hell no. You?"

"Don't know."

"Me neither," said another.

"Well, I sure as shoeshine don't *wanna* go, but my wife's threatening to divorce me if I don't."

"She's only trying to save your soul, Ben. Don't you need saving, Ben?"

All the men laughed.

"I don't need saving," Ben said. "I'm Catholic." He made the sign of the cross.

This drew more laughter from those nearby. Even those who were eavesdropping, like Ruth, laughed to themselves.

"Catholics don't *all* go to heaven," said one man. "My mother-in-law's Catholic and she's a flat-out Devil worshipper."

"Well, *this* Catholic's going," said Ben. "My daddy paid good money to get us in."

"It doesn't work that way, Ben."

"Maybe not for Baptists, but it does when you're Catholic."

Another man added, "I don't know about that, but I can say that after six years of Catholic school, if you're late to chapel, those nuns will slit your throat with a pencil sharpener."

"Yeah, well," said another man, "my wife's going to the J. Wilbur thing too. She's dragging all our young'uns. Tried to tell her it was a bunch'a hokum, but she's got her own ideas."

A young man leaned into the conversation. "J. Wilbur ain't all that bad. Actually, I think he's a good man."

The men slapped their knees when they heard this.

"That man's a phony if ever there was one," said Ben. "Mercy, I'm so glad to be Catholic."

"I like him," said the young man. "They say signs and wonders follow wherever he goes. I heard a man in Iowa sprouted a new leg at one of J. Wilbur's revivals."

"A new leg?" said Ben. "Where'd he end up putting it?"

Another man interjected, "Does that mean *you're* going to see him, Eddy? Tell us the truth, have you already bought your ticket to see J. Wilbur?"

"Don't need no ticket. Says on the radio that it's free."

An elderly man wiped his face and threw his napkin on the counter. "I swear. You idiots will believe *anything* these days. You're the reason the world's in such a mess."

"Yeah," said another older man. "What's happening to this world? I can't even read the papers no more, hogwash on every page. They claimed somebody raised somebody from the dead over in Washington County. Buncha horse flop."

Ben scoffed. "Newspapers will do anything to get a nickel."

"It's all bull. It's all bull."

"You can say that again."

"I just did."

"Hear, hear."

"I don't know if it's bull or not," said the young man. "My brother heard it was true, about the man being raised from the dead."

There was a long pause.

"Hand to God," said the young man. "My brother said the fella was dead as a roofing tack, then a bright light come outta the sky and . . . and . . ."

Another pause.

"And what?" said one old man. "And made him sprout a new leg?"

"No," said the young man. "My brother says the man sat right up and started doing all sortsa backflips and speaking in foreign tongues, and people was getting saved all over the place, and there was a brass band."

"Backflips? Brass band?"

"You're full of it!" said one man.

"That ain't what the paper said. They said it was a woman who did it, not a light from the sky. And I didn't read nothing about no backflips."

"A whore did it is what I heard."

"Get outta here."

"Yep, a whore raised the dead is what they's saying. Was right there in the paper."

"You're full of doo."

"I'm serious as can be. Read the paper."

"Well," said one man, tossing his money on the counter. "I don't read papers nohow. They'll print anything, even if it's horse flop."

Ruth watched them walk out of the restaurant. She saw them crawl into old vehicles and leave the parking lot. They reminded her of Paul and Vern and the people she missed.

When she paid for her meal at the cash register, the cashier was reading a newspaper. The photograph on the front page was of a man standing behind a pulpit. The man's face was lean, and his jaw was square. The picture showed him leaning over the pulpit toward an audience, shaking a fist at them.

"Who's that on the front page?" she asked the man who was holding the paper.

"Depends on who you ask," the man said. "Some folks think he's Jesus Christ."

"What about you?" she said. "What do you think?"

"Don't ask me. I was born Catholic."

# Ninety

# THE PERSUADER

\* \* \*

"This is a stupid idea," said Joseph, who was eating from a can of pork and beans.

"If you have a better one," said Coot, "I'm all ears."

Joseph sighed. "I don't see why we can't just leave town like the lucky crooks we are."

"No. I gotta do something."

Coot wheeled the truck into the train depot fast enough to kick up a cloud of dust. The place was almost vacant. Coot had expected to see a crowd of people, but there was nobody.

"Coot, this is grabbing at straws. You can't do nothing about a bunch of religious nuts on the courthouse steps. You're just one man."

"Those men wanted to kill her."

"But they didn't. See? God provides."

"She needs our help."

"Sometimes you just hafta know when to give up, kid. This is one of those times."

"Then give up," said Coot. "You wanna tuck tail? Fine. I'm not, not until she's safe."

J. Wilbur Chaplain's railcar was plain looking, dark green, with faded paint. Coot had expected something fancier. The car sat on the tracks, just behind a peanut field. It was so calm it made Coot feel jumpy.

"This place is empty," said Coot. "I wonder where everyone is."

"Beats me," said Joseph. "Probably on the courthouse steps, roasting weenies and reading the book of Revelation."

The windows of the railcar glowed orange in the night. The shades were drawn, but Coot could see the shadows of figures in the car, moving from side to side.

Coot watched a man open the back door to the caboose. The man lit a cigar. Coot saw the ember glow in the dark.

"You stay here if you want," said Coot. "I'm going to go . . . go do something."

"Go do *what*?" said Joseph with a mouthful of beans.

"I don't know," said Coot. "I'll improvise. If all else fails, I'll start crying."

"Crying? Have you lost your marbles? What kind of a man are you?"

"I ain't really gonna cry. I'm gonna fake cry."

"That's your big idea? You come out here to the middle of nowhere just to work up some phony tears? You're outta your mind."

"Well, what do you suggest?"

Joseph said nothing. He only shrugged and shoveled more food into his mouth.

"I can't believe you're eating at a time like this," said Coot. "I thought we agreed you would never eat beans again after the last time."

"So shoot me," said Joseph. "I've been hungry since I come back from the afterlife. All I can think about is food. They had us on government rations back in that hick jail. Thought I was gonna waste away."

Coot leaned his forehead against the window. He was deep in thought, with only the sound of an old man chewing with his mouth open and making little grunts of ecstasy.

Coot watched the man on the back porch of the caboose. The man tossed his cigar into the night, then walked back inside.

"How am I gonna do this?" said Coot. "Think."

Joseph smacked the glove box. He removed a pistol and tossed it into Coot's lap.

"What's this?" Coot said.

"What's it look like? Old Roscoe the Persuader. That's what it is."

"Are you nuts?"

"This ain't about me."

"I'm not walking in there with a gun."

"Suit yourself, but you don't have a chance any other way."

Coot placed the gun on the dashboard. "Don't be ridiculous, they'll shoot me."

"No, they won't, they're Christians."

"They'll shoot me twice."

"Where's your sporting blood, son?"

"You're nuts."

Joseph lifted the gun, spun the cylinder, then clicked it shut. "You pop in there holding Roscoe and say to that preacherman, 'Come with Daddy, sucker,' and he'll do it. Simple as that."

"Put that thing away before you hurt somebody. Haven't you had enough bullets to last one lifetime?"

"That's exactly how you'd wanna say it too, real forceful-like. 'Come with Daddy, sucker.' Pretty good, huh?"

Joseph was clearly impressed with himself.

"I'm only thinking of your girlfriend, Coot. That man ain't gonna give you a second look unless you got something worth looking at, like Roscoe."

"Gimme that gun," said Coot.

Joseph handed Coot the gun. "That's more like it."

Coot opened the cylinder and emptied the bullets into his hand. Then he rolled down his window and tossed them into the darkness.

"You dunce," said Joseph. "That's all the ammo I had."

He gave the gun back to Joseph. "No more guns."

Coot leapt out of the car. Joseph waited in the truck. Coot crept through the rail yard, rehearsing what he would say. Maybe Joseph was right. Maybe J. Wilbur Chaplain wouldn't hear a word he had to say. Maybe this was a wasted effort.

Coot climbed the steps onto the railcar and took a few breaths before he rapped on the glass panel of the door. He cupped his hand over his mouth and smelled his own breath.

He took a few steps back and waited.

A bald man opened the door and gave Coot a serious look. He stood in the doorway like a human tank. The neck on this man was nearly as big as Coot's upper thigh.

"Can I help you, son?" the man said.

Coot cleared his throat. "Um, yes . . . I am with the, um . . ."

The man raised his eyebrows. "Sorry, son. He don't receive visitors." The man placed a meaty hand on the knob and shut the door.

Coot pressed his boot between the door and the jamb. The door closed on his foot and he thought he might have felt a few bones break.

"I know," said Coot. "I know he doesn't want visitors, but . . . but this is an emergency."

"Emergency?" said the bald man.

"Life and death."

"Life and death? Write him a letter. You know how many people got life-and-death emergencies for J. Wilbur?" He pressed the door closed.

This time Coot wedged his torso through the door and said, "There's no time for letters. I need five minutes! Just five minutes! Please!"

The man placed his Virginia-ham-size hand on Coot's throat and shoved him from the doorway. He followed Coot outside and shut the door behind him. He gave Coot a smirk. "You're crazy, kid. Now get outta here before I teach you how to turn the other cheek."

He went back inside, then closed the door.

"Please," Coot shouted at the door. "Five minutes!" Coot slammed his fists against the door and beat out a steady rhythm. "Please!" Coot pretended to sob. "I'm begging you!"

The man opened the door again. He pressed Coot backward using his fist. He stared at Coot with a face that seemed more sympathetic than Coot had expected. The man drew in a long, annoyed breath.

"Wait right here," he said.

*Fake crying,* Coot thought. *Works every time.*

# Ninety-One

# J. WILBUR

* * *

The interior of J. Wilbur Chaplain's railcar was plain. There were no decorations, no intricate woodwork, and no chandeliers. There were only two beds, a kitchenette, and a fan in the corner, blowing.

Coot had only heard stories about him as a child. And he'd expected the man to be the poster boy for gracious living. But this man was traveling in a railcar that needed a fresh coat of paint and a few throw pillows. It was only a few notches above Coot's jail cell.

He stood before the man, remembering all the things he'd heard about him. He'd heard all the stories there were. This man, many claimed, had changed tent preaching forever. Until J. Wilbur's time, men had been preachers who begged sinners to come down the aisle using big words and high English. But J. Wilbur came into town and spoke common words, the people's language. Sometimes he even used words that made sailors gasp.

Or so the stories went.

Long ago, Blake told Coot that J. Wilbur once waved his hand over an auditorium and the whole place broke into spontaneous weeping for ninety-one minutes. People went crazy and started tearing their shirts and hiding beneath pews, praying for the wrath of God to spare them. And legend had it that J. Wilbur stood on a piano wearing only his underpants and preached for two hours.

But here, standing before the man, Coot couldn't help but doubt the facts within these stories. This man seemed quiet and reserved. He was nothing at all like the voice on the tinny radio speakers, and he didn't seem like a legend.

And all at once, Coot felt ashamed to be here.

"I read about this woman in the paper," said J. Wilbur. "The papers were not kind to her. They were using some coarse descriptions."

"So you've heard of her?" said Coot.

"Oh, you'd have to be hiding under a rock not to know about this woman they call the harlot."

J. Wilbur invited Coot to sit on the chair across from him while he ate a late supper. Coot told the man about what had happened. He told him everything, starting from the beginning, about how she brought Joseph back with just a touch.

Coot was surprised to see how kind J. Wilbur was. He did not seem like a man who would stand on a piano wearing only his underpants. He looked like anyone else. At times he was humorous, lighthearted. And he was calm. He was, in fact, one of the nicest men Coot had ever met. And this disappointed Coot. He wanted to hate this man for all he represented, for the world he came from. But there was nothing to hate.

Finally, when Coot had run out of words, J. Wilbur went to his cabinet and removed a can. He held it toward Coot. "Would you like some Ovaltine?"

J. Wilbur shook the can for effect.

"Ovaltine?" said Coot.

"Yessir," he said. "Ovaltine contains malt, milk, and eggs, fortified with necessary vitamins and minerals, and is America's food beverage assisting in maintaining and building up health and strength and energy and encouraging health-restorative sleep to keep your body and mind feeling strong and vigorous."

"Why not."

J. Wilbur opened the can, stabbed a spoon into it, then mixed the brownish powder with milk. "I never go anywhere without my Ovaltine. There's nothing like it." He fixed Coot a glass too.

Maybe he was the kind of man who preached for two hours in his underpants.

Finally J. Wilbur said, "You saw all this yourself, son? You *saw* her bring this man back to life?" When he said it, he gave Coot the first hint of a look that resembled a preacher's stare. Then he took a sip of Ovaltine and left a chocolate-colored milk mustache on his upper lip.

"I was holding him when it happened," said Coot.

"And what was it like?"

"Well, his body went from being stiff and hard and cold to being warm and moving. And now he's alive again, and he's a different man."

"Different? How?"

"Well, he used to have a problem with the bottle, and he hasn't taken a drink since it happened."

"Astounding," said J. Wilbur, killing his glass. "Absolutely astounding. Would you like some more Ovaltine?"

"No, I'm still working on it."

J. Wilbur fixed another glass. He approached Coot and started to say something, but removed his eyeglasses and placed the stem in his mouth, holding a far-off but dignified look on his face.

Coot wished he wore eyeglasses so he could do this.

"Son," said J. Wilbur. "You know, I've seen a lotta things in the heat of the moment. A lotta things. I once saw a man bark like a Labrador in Pittsburgh."

"I've seen people act crazy before," said Coot. "And I've seen bogus healings, more than I'd like to remember. This isn't that. This is the real thing."

J. Wilbur turned his glass of Ovaltine upside down and drained the whole thing in a few gulps. He wiped his mouth with his sleeve and said, "These are exciting times, ain't they, son?"

A spark filled the man's eye, and the roundness of his face faded, and his age momentarily disappeared.

"These are exciting times." He clapped once. "What'd you say your name was?"

Coot felt his thighs draw up into his bowels. He had gone the entire conversation without referring to E. P. And he didn't want to start now.

"My name?" said Coot. "It doesn't matter."

"Of course it matters. A young man comes to me speaking of the dead breathing anew, inheriting revitalized bodies. This young man has to have a name."

"My name is Coot."

J. Wilbur frowned. "Coot. What an interesting name. Is it a nickname?"

"Yessir. Short for Thurston Reginald McMillian the Third."

"Really?"

"No. It's just plain old Coot. I believe you knew my father." Coot paused. The words felt heavy coming out of his mouth. He'd never said those words before. Not like that. Not in his entire life had he ever used the word *father* in relation to E. P. In fact, he'd never called anyone Father, not even the Almighty.

"Who was your daddy?" said J. Wilbur, smiling.

Coot swallowed a sip of Ovaltine. It was too late to turn back now. "E. P. Willard, sir."

J. Wilbur let out a single laugh. He slapped his knee and leaned forward to look into Coot's face. He seemed to be studying Coot. "Why, I'll be dog!" the man said. "I thought you looked familiar. Why, you look just like him, boy. Eddie Willard, your father? *The* Eddie Willard?"

"The one and only."

"Well, how is your pa? Why, I haven't seen him in a coon's age, son."

"He's good. He's just been tied up lately."

"Oh, that's marvelous. I'm glad to hear it."

They were interrupted by a crash of glass. The door to the railcar was shattered by a rock that landed in the center of the railcar floor. Then a loud crash. Then the door flung open and slammed against the wall. In the doorway stood Joseph, bearing a pistol and flinty eyes that suggested he was not here to play patty-cake.

"Alright, Preacherman," Joseph said. "Come with Daddy, sucker."

# Ninety-Two

# JOY TO THE WORLD

Pete was lying in bed, watching the ceiling fan spin in lazy circles. He'd never actually seen a ceiling fan before staying in this motel. They were strange devices, but they worked so well. The gentle breeze fell upon him and did little to keep him cool, but it felt good nonetheless. This only led him to wonder what air-conditioning was like. He'd only ever seen one air conditioner in his life.

He'd heard if you breathed the air from an air conditioner too long, you would develop asthma or, in some extreme cases, go blind. He wasn't sure if it was true, but he was very careful when he went into places that had air-conditioning, and did his best to hold his breath.

Ruth was asleep beside him. Stringbean was lying on Ruth's feet, curled into a ball. He wanted more than anything to leave this town and go back home. He wanted to find a small house and start a small farm, maybe raise cotton or tobacco and, God willing, hunting dogs. But he knew that Ruth was feeling different things in this city, and he did not want to disappoint her. She was everything to him.

Ruth rolled onto her side. Pete could see her violet eyes boring into him. She was no longer asleep.

"What're you thinking?" she asked.

"I'm thinking that I love this ceiling fan."

"Maybe we can get one someday."

"Maybe."

She touched his face. She brought herself closer to him and spoke in a hushed voice. "I feel something here," she said. "I feel . . . I feel . . . I don't know."

"What?" he said.

"I feel like I should be here. Like there's something here."

He didn't want to tell her that he felt the exact opposite. He didn't want to ruin her excitement. She was a girl who had adventure in her, he knew this. He was a man who could stay in one place so long he developed moss on his backside.

"You like it here?" he said.

"No."

This confused him. He sat straight up in bed. "You don't?" he said, and Stringbean moaned. She did not like to be disturbed while in the throes of sleep.

"No," she said. "It's too big for me."

He felt elation. "You don't like it here?"

"No, but I feel something here."

"You feel what?"

"Something."

Ruth was hard to understand.

"I mean," she went on, "it's like I'm *supposed* to be here for something. Something big. It's a feeling in my stomach."

Pete nodded. "Well, it's hard to find work here." By "hard," he meant he had a better chance of becoming president of the United States than finding a job bagging groceries.

"I know. I know it is." She wrapped her arms around him. "I don't know what it is about this place, though. I don't know why I feel this way."

"Well, it's part of your history, I guess. I mean, you were born not far from here."

"Yeah, but it's deeper than that. You know how it is after Thanksgiving?"

"Thanksgiving?"

"Yeah, you know how everything feels when Christmas is on its way?"

"I don't follow you." Rarely did he ever.

"C'mon," she said. "You know how even though *nothing* is different about the world—the weather is sorta the same—it feels like a totally different place to live? Like there's something magic in the air?"

"Are we really having a conversation about the magic of Christmas right now?"

"No." She swatted his shoulder. "Listen to me, will you? I feel that same sorta happy feeling I get in December, but not in the same sorta way."

"Well," he said. "I'll be sure to pick up some garland on the way home tomorrow."

She laughed. "I mean it. I feel it, I really do. Don't you feel anything?"

"Do I feel anything?"

"Yeah, don't you feel something?"

He kissed her forehead. He wanted to tell her that he felt homesick. He wanted to admit that he missed home so bad he could taste it. He wanted to tell her that he felt alone in this godforsaken city, without a friend in the world except a spoiled bloodhound. He wanted her to know how bad he missed his bunk on Miss Warner's farm and waking up to train his dogs to follow trails.

He wanted to, but he couldn't. His life half belonged to her now. And her happiness half belonged to him. And even though he was dreaming of home, he would not tarnish her newfound happiness.

"I miss Vern," he said.

"Me too."

"And I miss Paul."

"Oh, so do I."

"I do not miss Miss Warner."

She started laughing. "Not even just a little bit?"

"Maybe a little."

"I know you miss home," she said in a serious voice. "I miss it too. But I'm glad to be here with you."

"I don't miss it that much," he lied.

She closed her eyes and fell asleep on his chest. She seemed to be wearing a gentle smile. He twirled a strand of her hair in his hand while watching the hypnotic ceiling fan above him.

"G'night," she whispered.

"Merry Christmas," he said.

# Ninety-Three

# RIDE WITH THE LORD

\* ★ \*

Coot, Joseph, and J. Wilbur Chaplain sat in the back seat together. They rode through the early light with the sunrise ahead of them. J. Wilbur wore a white linen suit with a high collar and brass cuff links. J. Wilbur was a man who had an endearing commonness to him. He seemed perpetually relaxed. Even after Joseph had threatened to gut him like a "godless trout"—Joseph's exact words—the man was easygoing.

Somehow Coot had managed to get the gun away from Joseph and convince the most famous man in America that they were not lunatics. Not entirely. And in only a few minutes, Chaplain had agreed to help them. They piled into the man's car and shot through the dark until the sun began to rise.

The morning scenery passed them at slow speeds. J. Wilbur Chaplain looked out the window. "You know, Coot, I used to be a professional ballplayer."

Coot was jolted from his thoughts. "A ballplayer?" he said. "You?"

J. Wilbur seemed almost surprised by Coot's response. "Didn't your father ever talk about me?"

Coot cringed at the usage of the word *father*.

"They called me Lulu the Lefty. I was a sidearm man." J. Wilbur showed his left hand to Coot. "I was one doozy of a left-handed pitcher. They offered me two thousand a year to play in Saint Louis, and I almost took it too."

J. Wilbur looked out the window. He was lighthearted and easy. Coot respected him for this alone. Coot himself was a passionate man who had a habit of worrying about everything.

"I went to this revival outside Atlanta," J. Wilbur went on. "In a big tent. I was only there because of a girl I liked. She wanted to go." J. Wilbur raised his eyebrows. "Oh, I thought she was as hot as an oven mitten. So I went."

Joseph had already fallen asleep beside Coot. He could feel Joseph's heavy breathing on his neck and smell his deadly mule breath. He adjusted Joseph's position so the old man's mouth would be aimed in the opposite direction.

"A girl?" said Coot.

"I'd never even set foot in a church before, if you can believe it."

"Really?"

"As I live and breathe," J. Wilbur said. "A girl will make you do strange things, son. Make you forget all about what you hold to be common sense."

"So I've heard."

"I'll never forget it. I saw this young man preaching on the stage, wearing all white. He was wild, theatrical. Before I knew it, I found myself walking down the aisle for salvation when the music played, almost against my will. That's how good he was."

Joseph adjusted himself against Coot. The old man released an aroma that filled the car and caused Coot to roll down the window.

"Anyway," said J. Wilbur. "When I got to the altar that night, long ago, I saw that this young preacher was about *my age*." He laughed. "I could hardly believe it. A man my age, making such a difference in the world, commanding an audience for the cause of goodness and charity and Christian kindness.

"The man prayed for me, and it did something to me. It changed me. He told me his name was E. P. Willard. Beautiful man. Beautiful man, your father."

The words stung Coot's ears.

"Are you *sure* it was him?" said Coot.

"We were friends for a few years after that. He taught me how to be who I was always meant to be."

J. Wilbur Chaplain closed his eyes. "I turned Saint Louis down. I was afraid I was doing the wrong thing. I'd never been so scared in all my life."

"And what happened?"

"I joined the revival troop for sixteen dollars a week. I changed my name. And that was the end of Lulu the Lefty."

"So J. Wilbur isn't your real name?"

"No, sorry to say it isn't. All the preachers back then were using initials instead of names."

"So what's your real name?"

"Herman Pickles."

The car neared the courthouse. Coot could see the crowds of people gathered like bees around a honeycomb. And he could see a change in J. Wilbur's persona immediately. The man went from being relaxed to assuming the personality E. P. had once used—only this was no act. It was the man he'd heard on the radio. A man who had inspired a country during times of war, pestilence, and famine. The man removed his eyeglasses and handed them to his driver.

"Bill," J. Wilbur said to the driver. "Pull right up onto the lawn of the courthouse. These people wanna revival, let's give 'em what they want."

The car leapt over the curb and jostled Coot and Joseph from side to side. Joseph was startled awake with a snort. He looked around and said, "What's going on?"

"We're here," said Coot.

"Already?"

"Yes."

"I musta fallen asleep. What'd I miss?"

Coot shushed him, then said, "I ain't never gonna let you eat another pinto bean in your life, old man."

The crowd parted and let the car through. The vehicle crept through the makeshift camp before the courthouse and ran over smoldering campfires and edges of tents. People pressed their faces against the windows. Coot could see children trying to get a better look at who was inside.

When the car came to a stop, there were people on all sides of the vehicle, standing in herds like cattle.

J. Wilbur straightened his collar and smoothed his hair. He leaned toward Coot. "I owe a lot to your daddy, son." He patted Coot's leg. "In fact, I owe your daddy my eternal salvation, you could say."

The dignified man bowed his head briefly.

Coot could see he was praying. Coot bowed his head too.

Then J. Wilbur Chaplain kicked open the door and stepped out. The man crawled onto the top of his car like a man half his age. His long legs were limber and his movements were quick. Coot was surprised to see the man move so fast. His shoes made banging noises on the automobile roof.

He shouted. He clapped his hands. He stomped his feet until he nearly bent the dome of the car. He removed his coat and rolled up the sleeves of his sweat-stained shirt. He unbuttoned his collar. Coot could see Marigold's face in the open window of the courthouse above. And he could still feel her kiss.

J. Wilbur Chaplain spoke of God and miracles and power and angels and healers. The veins in his head showed. Coot was unable to take his eyes from the man. And when J. Wilbur called sinners to repent, he waved his hand over the crowd and people nearly lost their minds. Elderly women fell backward; men started shouting and hollering. One woman claimed she'd been healed of gallstones. Another woman told news reporters that a goiter had gone down in size by three inches.

J. Wilbur Chaplain preached for ninety-one minutes. Fully clothed.

One newspaper headline read "Revival Hits Alabama."

# Ninety-Four

# THROUGH THE STATIC

\* \* \*

Ruth read the Friday morning edition of the newspaper in earnest. She was not normally a newspaper reader, but the image on the front page had caught her attention. It looked like hundreds of people, hands raised, surrounding a man standing atop a car.

She leaned against the counter of the kitchenette and waited for the dollop of grease to get soft in the skillet. She adjusted the knob on the stove so the flame swelled.

She felt like a grown-up, cooking and making breakfast. She felt even older when she gave the newspaper one swift shake to straighten it. She did it again, just because it made her feel so mature.

She studied the photo with great care.

She adjusted the hot skillet over the flame, then read about the most famous evangelist in America—a man she'd only ever known by name.

The paper said several hundred people had spontaneously had a revival as he preached a sermon while standing on the roof of a car.

She remembered Vern listening to this preacher on the truck radio every Wednesday night during her youth, sometimes seated in the truck cab by himself, staring through the windshield.

When she came to the part about the woman people called the harlot, she paused and felt a shiver run through her. She remembered overhearing people talk about this.

"Pete," she said. "Do you believe people can come back from the dead?"

Pete was wearing a white undershirt, shaving his face in the mirror. "What are you talking about?"

The grease in the skillet began to crackle.

"You know, like a miracle?" she said.

"I don't know," said Pete. "Why?"

The crackling sound of a skillet awakened the motel room and caused Stringbean to sit before Ruth's feet with a look of importance on her face.

Ruth ignored the hungry animal and kept reading the paper to herself.

Stringbean licked her jowls and positioned herself a few inches closer to the skillet. Her body was still. Her eyes were enormous. She touched her nose against Ruth's hand just to remind her that she was alive and hadn't eaten in over eight hours.

Ruth patted Stringbean's head without turning from the newspaper.

When the eggs were done frying, they sat at the small table. She loved this motel. She loved everything about it. She loved the mermaids on the wall. She loved the ceiling fan and the two-burner stove. The hot showers gave her life purpose. She felt something swell in her chest. She didn't know what this feeling was, but it was good.

Pete wasted no time digging into his food. But something about this felt wrong.

"Wait, Pete," she said.

He stopped eating. He wore a bewildered look. Grease slid down his chin. Stringbean also looked at her with a grave face.

"Ain't you gonna say grace?" she said.

"Grace? Over breakfast?"

"Don't you think we should start praying and saying grace, now that we're married?"

"Grace?"

She folded her hands.

Pete placed his fork on his plate and wiped his hands. He folded them together and cleared his throat. "What do I say?" he said.

"I don't know, just say something graceful. Pray that you can find a job today."

"Um, okay . . ." But he couldn't seem to find the words.

She interjected. "Thanks for everything . . . We just feel really happy about the way things are going lately. Keep up the good work."

She opened her eyes to see that Pete's eyes were still shut tightly.

"Pete?" she said. "You have anything you'd like to add?"

"God, it's me, Pete. Give my best to Mama, and Paul, and Louisville."

Silence followed. Only the sound of Stringbean's stomach gurgling could be heard.

Finally Pete said, "Are we supposed to say amen or something?"

"I don't think it really matters," said Ruth.

They unfolded their hands and started eating. And Ruth felt good inside, though she couldn't describe why. Maybe it was the words they'd said over their food that had done it to her. She looked at the newspaper, there on the table.

"Pete," she said. "I wanna go to a revival tonight."

"Do what?" he said.

"Revival."

"What's that?"

"I don't know, but I wanna go."

*Ninety-Five*

# GLORY

\* \* \*

The large sign by the road read Holy Ghost Revival in large red letters. The word *Revival* was written bigger than the other words and had dripped.

Cars were parking in the scalped field, forming a gulf of automobiles that blanketed the earth. The crowd was bigger than anything Coot had ever seen—and he'd seen giant audiences in his day. Once a crowd in Iola, Kansas, had been so big they had to tear down the tent because it wouldn't hold them. This was much bigger. Much, much bigger.

In the center of the ocean of automobiles was a large pine structure the size of a baseball stadium. It was a tent made of wood.

J. Wilbur had explained that this was only a temporary arena to house the revival and stand against the weather. It had been built especially for this weekend, and it would be torn down when the revival services were finished. The wood would be donated and reused by the needy, the large columns would be recycled into telephone poles, and the crossbeams would be used for public buildings. The building itself was a marvel. The tall support beams inside were towers, and the rafters were made from hewn logs that must've required a crane to lift them.

Coot bent his neck backward staring at it. He whistled.

The vehicles in the parking lot kept multiplying. Men in overalls and crumpled hats crawled out of them, accompanied by poor-looking families. Women holding children. Kids, skinny and quiet, dressed in faded clothes. And there were wealthy families too, dressed in light colors. Migrant workers riding in the backs of large trucks. Foreigners speaking in another language, with tan skin and dark hair. Entire church buses filled with men in suits.

Everyone found seats on long wood benches beneath the pine canopy. Hats in hands, heads held low, faces drawn in reverence.

Revival.

A woman played the piano. A brass band took the stage and joined the woman. People stood from their benches and sang. Their voices were so loud Coot could feel the vibrations in his ribs. Even from outside the building.

Marigold was seated on a bench beside him, behind the large building, just beneath an oak tree. He kissed her. She kissed him back. Coot could see she was trembling. Her eyes were staring at all the cars that stretched toward the horizon. He held her against him and took in the scent of her hair, like lavender.

She took his hand and held it. He was lost in the rapture of her. She was the kind of person he'd always wished he could be. He could tell it by the way she talked. There was sincerity in her that he did not have. A kind of heart that believed in more things than his did. When she leaned against him, it felt as though he had found salvation.

"I'm nervous," she said.

"Don't be," said Coot. He patted her knee.

"Thank you for being with me. Thank you for doing what you did."

"I'm not going anywhere."

This seemed to satisfy her. "I never wanted to be what I am," she said. "I never wanted any of this to happen. I don't feel like I belong here."

"You are the only one who does belong here."

He felt the familiar preshow jitters of his youth, and he felt the thrill of performance upon him. It was all coming back to him. And it made his heart sore.

"You know," he said, "for years I hated this."

"Hated what?" she said.

"This." He waved his hand at everything. "All my life, I hated every bit of this, and the cheats who were behind it."

"What do you mean?"

"I mean I grew up around these people, and there are a lot of dishonest men in this bunch, a lotta cheats, a lotta cutthroats and liars." He laughed softly and stared at his shoes. "But they ain't all like that."

She kissed him again. They'd been doing that a lot. And they both drew strength from those kisses.

"When you touched Joseph," he went on, "you did something to me too."

"I didn't do nothing," she said.

"You did. And I know what you're here for. You're here to do what you did to Joseph and what you done to me. You're here to revive people."

*Ninety-Six*

# RUTH SHALL SET YOU FREE

\* \* \*

The line of vehicles was a few miles long, stretching past the city limits. Ruth and Pete waited in a line of traffic until people began parking their vehicles in ditches and on hillsides, and some left them right in the center of the road. Pete parked in the ditch until his door was almost touching the earth and Ruth's door was high in the air. He crawled out Ruth's side and walked the dirt road where the other people were heading. Stringbean followed behind.

They reached the white sign that read Holy Ghost Revival, and Pete whistled when he saw the large wood structure in the distance.

"Have you ever seen so many cars in your life?" he said.

"No."

She didn't say anything else because she didn't know what to say. The truth was, it did seem rather bizarre. The people they passed on the road all seemed strange. The looks they gave her were not like the kinds of normal looks you get in daily life. It was as though everyone suspected something magnificent was going to happen.

When they neared the wood structure, she could hear the sounds of a tuba and other brass instruments, and a bass drum, and a snare, and singing. Lots of singing. There were so many voices she could swear she felt the earth moving. Stringbean looked almost frightened when she heard it. She stayed near Pete.

The closer Ruth got, the more her vision was blocked by other people. Ruth leapt up to get a better view over the sea of heads and hats. She jumped a few times but couldn't see where to go. The wood structure was surrounded by people like chickens gathered around a June bug.

"We're not gonna be able to get inside," Pete said. "There must be two thousand people here. We might as well turn around and leave."

She was not about to leave. She felt something in this place.

"You wait here," she said to Pete. "I just wanna see what I can see."

"Ruth!"

"Just wait here. I'll be back, I promise."

"Wait!" he said, chasing after her. But she had already left him in the dust.

Hordes of people surrounded the building on all sides. They were peeking into the gaps between the wood, and children were sitting on the shoulders of grown men. The crowd pulsated with brassy music. The closer she got, the louder the music became. People were standing outside singing along with the people inside, and it sounded like voices were either rising to heaven or coming from it. Ruth didn't know the words to the song, but the people around her did. She closed her eyes and let the sounds of voices swirl around her.

When the singing finished, there was applause from inside the wood building loud enough to blow the nearby trees out of the dirt. Then people outside the wood tent began to murmur among themselves. Eventually, one man standing in front of Ruth, who wore a white hat and a blue suit, turned to her and said, "The harlot's on the stage now."

The news spread throughout the crowd like wildfire. People spoke of the harlot with true wonder. Ruth could hear it in their voices.

The man beside Ruth was leaning on a crutch. "It's her!" he said. He started pushing his way through the crowd, leaning on the flimsy stick beneath him. He was a big man, dressed in overalls. He could hardly move on his game leg. He tried to weave through the tight-knit group of onlookers.

People were not gracious to him.

One man pushed the disabled man, who then fell onto his hind parts. And people ignored the fallen man writhing on the ground. Ruth rushed to him before he was trampled to death. She helped him to his feet, and she could hear him grunting in pain.

He leaned onto her for support and said, "Thank you."

"There're too many people here," she said. "We're never gonna get through."

He was panting from exhaustion, and he started to weep. It was as though this realization was finally beginning to land on him. She held him, this stranger. She could smell his sweat when he cried into her shoulder.

"Sshhh," she said.

"I gotta try," he said. "I just gotta."

She shook her head. "There's nothing we can do," she said. "I wanna get through as bad as you do."

"Please help me," he said. "Help me try."

Something came over her. A kind of determination. She couldn't explain where it came from.

Before she knew it, Ruth was nudging people from her path. The man was holding her for balance, doing his best to keep her pace. Ruth shoved people aside and offered *excuse-mes* when she passed them. They weaved through the clots of onlookers, saying, "Pardon us! Excuse us! Coming through!"

She was met with ugly stares from those who refused to let her by. But she worked through the maze of people a few inches at a time, using force when needed.

They finally stopped for rest. She was out of breath and her legs hurt from supporting the weight of the big man who held her.

"We're never gonna make it," she told the man. "This is pointless. We're no closer than when we started."

At first he couldn't answer, he was breathing so heavily. "Please," he whispered. "I come all the way from Greenville to see the lady healer."

"You really believe she can heal you?"

"If I can just touch her."

"And what? You think that will heal you?"

"If I can just touch her."

They worked their way toward the building. Ruth was unsure if she was getting closer to the entrance or farther away until she saw clumps of children seated next to the wood walls with noses pressed into the gaps between planks. Ruth wedged between the children, working herself near the entrance. The man lost his grip on her and fell straight on his face. She helped him off the dust and saw that his nose was bleeding.

"Are you okay?" she said.

"I'm fine," he said. "Keep moving. We're getting closer."

"You're bleeding."

"I'm fine."

She could hear people cuss them when they pushed past. She ignored them and kept moving. She clawed her way through a group of people until she finally neared the door. And she saw her. A woman. The woman stood only feet before her. She had brilliant red hair. And she was tall. And lovely.

Ruth found herself unable to move.

The woman looked at Ruth. She wanted to step forward, but her legs were stuck.

The man released Ruth's arm and hobbled to the woman with a labored gait. He limped so badly he could hardly remain upright. When he was finally before the woman, he doubled over to catch his breath.

The woman looked at the man and said, "What's your name, sir?"

He was too busy breathing.

The woman looked at Ruth. "Are you his daughter?"

"No, ma'am," said Ruth.

The woman knelt low. She touched the man's leg. "Is it this one?" she said. "Is this the one?"

He nodded. He cried.

The woman took a deep breath and rolled up his trousers, exposing a skinny leg, deformed and scarred.

The woman pressed both hands against the man's leg. His breathing slowed. Ruth expected to see something miraculous, but she saw nothing. His leg did not change. There were no lights from heaven. But his posture became strong, and he stood upright. He stood on his own feet. And he took a few steps with ease, as though he'd never had a problem in his life.

The woman moved her eyes back to Ruth. "You're a good friend," she said.

"No, ma'am, I don't know him."

"What's your name?" said the woman.

"Ruth."

"Ruth," the woman said. "You have such pretty hair, sweetheart." The woman reached her hand to touch the girl's hair.

Something happened. Something Ruth felt inside her temples. An unfamiliar feeling, and gentle. Not overwhelming, but soft. It worked its way across her head and through her eyes and down into her belly. It was a warm feeling. Like being dipped into a hot pond on a July afternoon.

The woman must've felt it too, because she looked at Ruth with large eyes and an open mouth. The woman pulled back from Ruth and placed a hand over her mouth.

And in that moment, the sounds of the congregation faded into nothing. The people around Ruth disappeared. All she could see was the woman's outline, and all she could feel was the woman's presence. It was unmistakable, the feeling inside her. It was a familiar feeling, located within the recesses of her person.

Ruth felt the dam inside her burst.

"Mama," she said.

# Ninety-Seven

# SEWN TOGETHER

✶ ✶ ✶

In her dream, Marigold was a child. She was lying on her back in the creek, her face aimed at the sky.

She was watching the clouds move upon themselves. They were slow, and the sky was powder blue. The groves of grass and monstrous pines loomed overhead, but she couldn't see them. Only sky.

It was always there, and bigger than everything that lives in the world.

She felt something in her hand. She turned to see a man lying beside her in the water. He was wearing a white linen suit that was ruined with creek mud. He was young. Handsome. And it occurred to her that he was holding her hand. This young man. This man in linen.

She turned her head to the other side. She saw a little girl, also lying beside her. The girl had a mane of copper that had turned dark with the flowing spring water. The girl stared at the sky with her eyes wide open.

The girl grinned and met Marigold's eyes. "Did you worry about me?" said the girl.

"I worried about you every second of every day," said Marigold.

Then Marigold was yanked from her dream and found herself in a bed in a dark room. The walls were covered with mermaid wallpaper. Her child, Maggie, was beside her. An adult woman.

Earlier that night they had talked and cried until they'd fallen asleep here. They had shed enough tears to make a creek of their own.

Marigold had tried to fit a hundred years into a few hours of conversation. And each word she offered had felt weak somehow. Pathetic, even. Her words had seemed like silly attempts to explain something that was big, universal, something that was larger than words. She tried to describe the depths of pain she'd felt and the heights of anguish. But none of her words did it justice. She feared Maggie would never know her the way she wanted her to.

What Marigold really wanted was to sew their hearts together with thread and needle so that Maggie knew everything, knew how scared she'd been, and how her entire life had been sadness without her daughter, and how she never stopped thinking about her, and how every ticking second on the clock was peppered with thoughts of Maggie. But hearts can't be sewn together. They will always be separated by flesh, bone, and distance. And weak words are all anyone can use.

Marigold crawled out of bed. She stepped over Coot, the young man who was married to her daughter, and the large dog who slept on the floor between them. The men were covered with flannel blankets, fast asleep on the floorboards. The dog was snoring.

Marigold walked outside beneath the night sky. From the breezeway of the motor inn, she could see Mobile Bay, calm as bathwater.

"Evening," said Joseph. "Going for a walk?"

"Yeah," she said. "You wanna come?"

"No thanks," he said. "But you be careful."

"I will."

She wandered toward the bay, down the craggy hill that led to a sandy shore. She touched her foot into the cold water. She stared up at the sky. She looked at the moon. It had been her friend for a long time. For most of her life it had represented the only friend she had. But now it was not needed.

All her life she'd wanted to be known. That's all anyone wanted, she thought, to be known. She wanted someone to worry about her. She wanted the gift of knowing that somebody concerned themselves with thoughts of her, the way she worried for others. Yes, that's what she'd always wanted. She wanted someone to lose sleep thinking about her. She wanted someone to care enough about her to feel the same worry she felt for Maggie.

But here on the sand beside the bay, she realized she had indeed always been known and worried about. She could feel it. From the sky. She could feel it from the earth.

"I don't understand," she said in a soft voice. "And I don't want to anymore. But I just wanna thank you. Thank you."

She hoped for something to happen when she said it. She hoped for the sound of a bird or the splash of a wave or a gust of wind. Anything would've been welcome. But that isn't the way life works.

She knelt on the sand. She folded her hands. She pressed them against her face. "Thank you," she said again.

She heard the sound of footsteps behind her.

She turned to see Coot standing at a distance.

"I was getting worried about you," he said.

# Ninety-Eight

# COLD HANDS

* * *

A healer. That's what people were calling her. They'd come from as far away as Atlanta to see her, to see the woman from the whorehouse. To have her pray for them. The crowd was even bigger than before. The wood structure wouldn't begin to hold them all.

News of the healings had spread far and wide. Newspapermen were in attendance. There were men cranking movie cameras, standing on tall ladders, perched on the edges of the field. The governor had shown up. There were sick people, and families, and children, and old people.

People gathered together and waited for the harlot to touch them. It was terrifying and inspiring and humbling.

And she touched them all.

But something was very different today. Marigold touched a woman who claimed she had a blind left eye, but Marigold felt nothing in her hands. She felt no heat, no jolt, no nothing. The woman cried and blinked her eyes, claimed she felt different, but Marigold knew nothing had happened. And even though the woman rejoiced, Marigold knew the woman still had a blind eye when she left.

A lady with rheumatism came to Marigold next. She touched the woman on the shoulders. The woman tried to stand upright. She smiled and cried beneath the pain. But Marigold knew nothing had changed inside the woman. Marigold felt no buzzing in her head, no vibration in her hands, no heat in her palms.

A man with bad hearing followed the lady. Marigold touched the man's ears. The man claimed he could hear out of his ear once again, but Marigold knew it wasn't true. There were no healings, no miracles. There were only people who wanted to be whole. People who wanted someone to understand them.

It was over. She knew she was not the woman she'd been the day before. She knew something in her had shifted. Something in the sky had shifted.

The sun set like it always did that night, and the stars came out to play. The large crowds of people left, one vehicle at a time. And after a few hours, the entire place was nothing but a peanut field again.

"What's wrong?" Coot finally asked.

She looked at his kind eyes and said, "For once in my life, nothing."

*Ninety-Nine*

# TEARING THINGS DOWN

## ✳ ✳ ✳

The world came alive with the insect sounds of early evening. The sky was smeared with the colors of sunset. And men labored beneath it, deconstructing the wood stadium. It had taken two days to tear down the structure.

Coot enjoyed the sweat and task of loading large planks of wood into a truck with Pete and Joseph too. Coot couldn't believe he was seeing the old man moving his limbs beneath the load of work, sweating. Joseph worked beside Coot, wearing a sweat-stained white T-shirt and work gloves on his hands. They hurled the wood planks like spears.

"How're you doing?" Coot asked Joseph.

"What do you mean, how am I doing? I got raised from the dead, that's how I'm doing. How are *you* doing is the better question."

"I'm doing fine."

"Well, I'm doing better than you."

Joseph lifted a large plank of wood and shot it toward the truck with the strength of a teenager. The old man's short-sleeved shirt revealed a skinny arm, loose-skinned but muscled.

One of the workmen whistled, then shouted, "Supper's here!"

Coot stood straight to see a chain of automobiles winding through the empty dirt prairie. One car following another. The cars stopped, and women wearing cotton dresses emerged from them. They were all carrying casserole tins and covered dishes and baskets.

"The food wagon," said Joseph. "Thank God, I was about to starve."

"What're you talking about?" said Coot. "You've done nothing but eat jerky and crackers all day."

Coot saw Marigold walking toward him. She carried a basket under one arm, her daughter walking close beside her beneath the other. Tailing them was a dog with very long ears and a big appetite. The two women had heads of hair that were the same shade in the setting sunlight. Like fire.

Marigold was watching Coot too. She stopped and their eyes locked on one another. Coot lifted his arm to wave at her. She waved back at him. She came near to him and wrapped her arms around his waist. He kissed her, and she kissed him back. He felt the closeness of her, and it was almost too much to bear. It was so rewarding it was almost dreamlike.

"I take that back," said Joseph. "You're doing better than I am."

# HOLLERING

✳ ✳ ✳

Rabbit Creek forked from the bay water and meandered through the thicket of cypress trees that poked from the water like little men, bearing the weight of their limbs. The longleaf pines looked purple in the distance. The live oaks were towering high, snaking their branches over the surface of the water.

There was a noise in the distance.

Marigold listened to Stringbean howl. The dog let out low, happy howls. She smiled at the dog. The animal's black-and-tan fur dripped with bay water that turned her hair into a curly mess. The animal had been swimming in the water all morning. Marigold never had so much fun, watching an animal play without holding back. She'd been tossing sticks for the dog to chase, and felt sorry that she'd gone almost an entire life without knowing the simple pleasures of a dog.

Ruth was beside her. Ruth hollered at the dog, and her voice cut through the air like a mother's voice.

"Get over here, Bean!" said Ruth, patting her thighs. "C'mon, girl!"

Her shouts bounced off the bay water and were met with the sound of a dog's paws clomping on the earth in a dead sprint. Marigold watched the animal gallop toward home, and it was stunning to see the muscles of the animal, flexed in the full sunlight.

The dog neared them and shook her coat. Water flung in all directions like a sideways thunderstorm.

She felt something stir inside her. How she felt when she watched the storms that used to flood the creek behind Cowikee's. The rains would fill the creek so high that the brown water would become level with the earth, and it was almost impossible to tell where the creek began and the earth ended. It always made her feel good to see so much rain falling at once. It made her grateful. It was a gift from the heavens to the earth. A simple gift. That's how she felt now. She felt like she'd been given a drink of water that filled her from the inside.

Earlier that day, Helen and the girls had come to visit. They had brought cold salads and baskets of blackberries and flowers. They'd spent the entire afternoon telling Ruth stories about Marigold's youth. They talked so much that Marigold was sure Ruth's head was going to split open. Before Helen left, with Abe's hand in hers, she held Marigold for so long that they almost forgot they were holding each other. No words were spoken because none were needed.

That evening Marigold went for a long walk with Ruth through the thick forest. She asked Ruth, "Would it be okay if I held your hand, sweetie?" And Ruth stretched out her hand. They touched. The girl's hand was warm, and Marigold's was not. They walked the shore of the bay until the no-see-ums and mosquitoes had destroyed their arms and legs. They picked a few wildflowers. And Marigold felt the warmth that was once in her hands move into her chest instead.

"Why did you name me Maggie?" Ruth asked.

Marigold told her the story and sang the lyrics of the song, and did her best not to cry. It was so odd to be singing it to this girl she knew but didn't know. She was not Ruth, not to Marigold. But then, she was not her Maggie either, but someone infinitely more beautiful and striking than Maggie could ever be. This was a woman. A woman who was her own person. Strong, brave, and kind.

Ruth pulled Marigold into herself. "You know, I always thought of you and wondered what you'd be like."

Marigold lost herself in their embrace. "I thought of you every second of every day."

They pressed themselves together and rested their foreheads against one another. Their red hair became mingled, and their hearts were as close as they'd ever been without being sewn together. Marigold could feel Maggie. And within the strange manner the universe works, she knew her Maggie had become the person she was intended to be.

"I'm sorry," said Marigold, for it was all she could think to say, and it was something she'd been wanting to say for a very long time. Anything else would have sounded wrong. Anything else would've been too much.

Ruth smiled. "Quit your sorryin'," she said.

# ACKNOWLEDGMENTS

*　⭐　*

This book never could have happened without my wife, Jamie, and my editor.
Thank you.

# DISCUSSION QUESTIONS

* * *

1.  Paul and Vern are migrant workers during the Depression and do what it takes to survive. Can you relate to their struggle? What words would you use to describe these two men and their enduring friendship?

2.  How would you describe Marigold's gifts, and what was the source of her power? How would you react if you met someone like her?

3.  Why is E. P. such a successful conman? What is he selling that people are buying? What are the people in his crowds desperate to hear?

4.  This novel is full of kind and generous moments. Did any particular scene touch you more than others? Did you see yourself or someone you know in any of the characters?

5.  What are the lessons that the adults teach the young in this novel? What sort of wisdom do the elders impart? And what, if anything, do the young teach the old?

6.  E. P. Willard is driven by greed as well as jealousy. How else would you describe this man, and what is the irony of his rivalry with J. Wilbur Chaplain?

7.  Discuss how this novel explores what it means to choose a family. Must people be related by blood to feel responsible for one another? How do people rise up amid hard circumstances to take care of their loved ones?

8.  Why do you think Marigold finds a home at Cowikee's? How does Coot wind up in Alabama?

9.  For much of the novel, people proclaim that either "revival is coming" or "the end is near." Do you think these sentiments were specific to the time and place, or have people always believed the world to be on the brink of destruction? Why or why not?

10. What is the significance of this novel's title—*Stars of Alabama*? Did you notice any references to the title while reading?

# A MEMOIR OF
# LEARNING TO BELIEVE
# YOU'RE GONNA BE OKAY

Now for the first time, "Sean of the South"
shares his unforgettable memoir of love,
loss, the friction of family memories, and the
unlikely hope that we're all gonna be okay.

 ZONDERVAN°

# ABOUT THE AUTHOR

*  *  *

Photo by Sean Murphy

Sean Dietrich is a columnist, podcaster, speaker, and novelist, known for his commentary on life in the American South. His work has appeared in *Southern Living*, the *Tallahassee Democrat*, *Good Grit*, *South Magazine*, *Yellowhammer News*, the *Bitter Southerner*, *Thom Magazine*, and the *Mobile Press-Register*, and he has authored ten books.

★

Visit Sean online at seandietrich.com
Instagram: seanofthesouth
Facebook: seanofthesouth
Twitter: @seanofthesouth1

Printed in the USA
CPSIA information can be obtained
at www.ICGtesting.com
JSHW032129300524
64068JS00008B/28

9 780785 231325